Coffee with Vodka

Lisa Shiroff

Coffee with Vodka

Lisa Shiroff

TASFIL
CONCIERGE PUBLISHING

ISBN ebook: 978-1-964014-64-7
ISBN paperback: 978-1-964014-65-4
ISBN hardcover: 978-1-964014-66-1

Library of Congress Control Number has been applied for.

Published by Tasfil Publishing, LLC
Voorhees, New Jersey

*To all the hens I'm blessed to have in my life:
The women I can count on
who never judge me,
who are always supportive of me,
and who are ever willing to laugh with
(or at) me.
I hope you know it's all mutual.*

Thursday, June 17

Dee

She was running out of time. Only a handful of people stood between Dee and the TSA agents. She couldn't put it off any longer. She swiped her thumb over the screen of her cell to wake it up, tapped the phone icon, and—

Thwap! Something hit her leg. *Thwap*! Turning around, she saw a little girl spinning in circles, slamming her with a fluffy toy dog on each rotation. *Thwap*!

Dee took a step a tiny step forward. Anything bigger, and the guy in front of her would think it was his lucky day. She pressed the green button to make the call. *Don't answer. Don't answer. Don't answer. Please, voice mail!*

"Hi, sweetheart!"

Shit! "Hi, Mom."

"What's up?"

"Me, almost. I'm at the airport."

"Tell me you're *not* going to your grandmother's funeral."

"Then I'd be lying to you." *Thwap!* She twisted back again, cleared her throat loud enough for the girl's mother to hear, and nodded toward the child. The woman rolled her eyes like Dee was the pain-in-the-ass but tugged the kid back a step.

"...and, honestly, Dee Dee, it's not the best idea you've ever had," Mom prattled through her headphones.

"Maybe. But I'm pretty sure I've had worse." The line shifted. Dee took a step. Freaking kid took two. "Anyway, I'm about to go through security, so—"

"Good! There's time to change your mind."

"Sorry, Mom, I have to go. I didn't realize how sick she was." Dee's eyes felt wet. "I should have been there before she…you know. I didn't get a chance to say goodbye." Her throat tightened. She sniffed. What was wrong with her? She wasn't going to cry, was she? The line shifted forward again. She needed to pull herself together. She also needed her ID.

In the slash pocket of her shoulder bag, she found a lone broken ink pen, no driver's license. What the hell? Didn't she just put it there? Sunglasses in the side pocket. Where was it?

"Did you hear me, Deirdre?"

"Um, what?" And now her nose was running.

"Why do you insist on spending time with those people?"

"You mean my family?"

"Toxic family are still toxic people. Everyone in Georgia is bad news for you. Especially Brett. I'll never forgive him for getting you arrested."

"We were arrested because Aunt Alma is an uptight shrew." She wiped her nose with the back of her hand. "Anyway, Mom—"

"Nothing good can come from this, Deirdre."

"What about closure? Paying respects to Granddad?" Only three groups were before her now. She tucked her cell under a bra strap and tore through her bag with both hands. "Those are good, right?"

"Sweetheart, phone your grandfather. Or send flowers. Frankly, a greeting card will do."

"Honestly? You know how much she means—meant to me. I owe it to her. I—"

"You don't owe her anything. Just because you're related to someone doesn't mean you have to go to their funeral."

"Oh my God! I can't have this conversation with you right now."

Another wipe of her nose. "I'm almost at the TSA security point check person thingy gate, whatever. And I can't find my fucking ID."

"Seriously?" The girl's mom broke through a snowballing buzz of anxiety.

"Huh? Sorry." As if the kid hadn't heard an F-bomb before. They were in Philly for Christ's sake! What did she expect? "What am I gonna do if I can't find it?"

"Maybe this is a sign you should stay home."

"I barely obey traffic signs, Mom." It'd been two years since Dee had seen Gram. Two! How could she let that happen? She fell to her knees and dumped her purse out on the filthy floor. Felt like an elephant was stepping on her back.

Holding up her unruly blond hair with one hand, she rummaged through the crap from her purse with the other. There were enough crumbled-up pieces of paper to throw a ticker tape parade, but no stupid ID. The elephant pressed harder. Her breath came in short. "Anyway, I'm just going for today."

"Oh?" Mom's voice changed. "That's not so bad, then."

The guy in front of her stepped up to an agent.

"Yeah." She stared into the mess, tried to take a full breath. Mom couldn't know she was struggling to hold it together. "So if you try to reach me later or something, and I don't answer, don't think I'm mad at you. Check the news. See if there was a plane crash."

"Mommy? Is our plane gonna crash?"

Dee looked up, found the little girl's scared brown eyes six inches from her blue ones. "Oh, shit. Honey, no! Nothing's gonna happen to your plane."

The child wailed.

"What's the matter with you?" The mother swooped her away.

"What happened? Is everything all right?" Mom wanted to know.

"Yeah. Just some kid's crying." But nothing was all right. And damn it! Static filled her ears. She needed to get control. "I gotta go, Mom. Love you!"

"Call me when you land!"

Dee shoved everything back into her purse and stood. Her lungs were so tight that it didn't feel like air could get in. A TSA agent waved her forward, seemingly from the end of a long, distorted tunnel. There was too much noise around her, too many things moving. She couldn't get her brain to make sense of it all. She needed to breathe.

"Excuse me!" the woman, holding her sobbing little girl, once more broke through the anxiety noise.

"Go!" Dee remembered where she was and waved the woman by. What was she doing? Looking for her ID. Where was it? She shoved her hand in the pocket of her slacks. Hit something hard. The license! Thank fucking Christ! Her breath was gasps. Another agent waved her forward. She stepped up to her.

"Can I see your ID, please?"

Her shaking fingers seemed to belong to another body as she watched them hand over the license. Her breath came in faster and even shorter. The static ramped to a roar in her ears and drowned out whatever the agent said. As the panic attack reached its climax, she saw only a glare of light reflecting off the plastic barrier above the security podium.

The world stopped for a nanosecond.

Dee felt the ID back in her hands, sensed it should be in her wallet. Finding that in her purse was almost impossible, getting the ID into a slot....

"Ma'am? You OK?" The agent's eyes bugged behind her wire-rimmed glasses.

"What? Yeah." The roar lowered to static.

"Can you step aside, please?"

Dee obeyed and moved through fog, away from a herd of moving arms and legs. The static faded to a buzz. Deep breaths brought the jumbled mess back together. Moving arms and legs became people. People passed by. An annoying sound morphed into semi-intelligible words coming from a loudspeaker. Someone in a uniform by a conveyor belt shouted orders to empty pockets and remove electronics from bags. The static buzz stopped. Dee breathed like a normal human again.

What the hell triggered that? Should have waited until she got to the gate before she made the call, waited until she had nothing else to focus on. Not that she could have expected a lost license and Mom to be so distracting. Well, maybe Mom.

Weird, though. Didn't seem like enough stress to cause a panic attack. But it was over. She just needed to focus on one thing at a time. And keep breathing.

Maybe stay away from little kids, too.

She joined the herd, dropped her purse and phone into a gray bin, then headed to that sci-fi-looking thing where they blast you with radiation to see the underwires in your bra. The agent on the other side held up her hand like a drama queen saying she didn't want to hear anymore. "Remove your shoes, please."

Right! Shoes! She ran back to the conveyor belt, kicked them off.

"Are you freaking kidding me?" In Dee's hands were two almost identical shoes. They were made by the same designer, in the same style, with twin worn spots on the toes—the only difference: one black, the other brown.

"Ha!" A man screening bags laughed. "Bet you got another pair like that at home."

"I can't wear these." Her aunts were going to have a field day with her at the funeral.

"Honey, you already wore them through the airport." The man grinned. "Put 'em in the tray. We gotta keep the line moving."

Genevieve

Lola's death was yet more proof that there was no God; no supreme being would ever have allowed social media to exist. Yet, like an unquestioning adherent, Genevieve scrolled through the comments expressing sympathy for her dead dog and clicked hearts on each one.

I'll miss her sweet face! ♥
I'm devastated. So sad! ♥
I'm crying with you. ♥
I know how you feel. I was such a wreck when my Teddy went over the rainbow bridge.

Rainbow bridge again? Really? She thought she'd misheard the vet when he'd said those words. How was she supposed to take a grown man, a professional, seriously when he spoke like that? Was dressed like that? Over fifty and a hair-bun! Rolled-up chinos showing off My Little Pony socks! He was a middle-aged, educated man. And Genevieve was obviously an adult. He should have respected her enough to tell her the truth: Lola was dead.

A sob escaped.

There was no rainbow bridge.

Another sob.

There was no—

"Mom?!" Livvy's voice pierced the walls.

Privacy. There was no privacy. Lola's eyes didn't meet hers when she glanced at the bathmat. Right. It was no longer the two of them against the world.

"Just a sec!" She flushed the toilet to maintain her charade. A deep breath later, she opened the bathroom door and almost plowed into Livvy standing on the other side.

"What were you doing in there?" Livvy asked.

"You have to ask?"

"You've been going to the bathroom, like, every five minutes lately."

"Oh, I have a UTI."

"Gross." Livvy wiped an invisible hair away from her face. "I don't need details."

Genevieve plastered on her friendliest smile. "What do you need, honey?"

"Look!" Livvy yanked the neck of her T-shirt over to the side. "Do you see this?" She pointed to the general area below her chin.

"Your collarbone?"

"Ugh! Look higher."

Squinting didn't help. "Your neck?"

"I don't have time for this right now, Mom. Look!" She wrenched her head to her shoulder.

Genevieve clamped a hand over her mouth and scanned her daughter's neck, admiring the dewy, youthful look she herself spent too much money on unsuccessfully trying to fake. "I need a hint, Liv."

"God! Don't go anywhere!" Livvy stormed out.

Genevieve sat on the bench at the end of her bed. Where did Livvy think she could go? Her only option was back to the bathroom, which wasn't necessarily a bad place to be lately. It had been well over a decade since she'd spent time alone in the bathroom. The past two days in there were sublime…when she wasn't thinking about Lola.

"Come look!" Livvy barked as she zoomed past, cell phone in hand.

Even though all the lights were on in the bathroom, Livvy shone her phone flashlight on her neck. "Now do you see it?"

"This?" Genevieve touched a scaly patch of skin running down from her daughter's ear.

"Yes!" Livvy shut off the flashlight and set her phone on the counter. "It itches like hell."

"Olivia! Do you have to swear like that?"

"I'm an adult!"

Genevieve didn't understand why being one month into legal adulthood justified using obscenities, but she let it go. Arguing with Livvy never ended well. "Looks like eczema. You used to get it when you were little."

"Why do I have it now?"

"I don't know, honey. You must be reacting to something." Probably to her. Livvy was most likely having a reaction to her mother. The girl had only bristled, sighed, rolled her eyes, and acted annoyed with her since she turned thirteen. Clearly, Genevieve's existence aggravated her. Though why it would take five years to show up as a rash, Genevieve hadn't a clue.

"Mom!"

Genevieve realized she'd been staring at Livvy's reflection in the mirror and shifted her eyes to Olivia-in-the-flesh. "Yes?"

"What are you going to do about it?"

"I'm sure a little anti-itch ointment would work."

"Will it make it go away by tomorrow?"

"What's happening tomorrow?"

"I'm going to the shore, remember?" Livvy did that thing with her eyebrows that assured Genevieve her daughter questioned her intellect. "Natalie's parents rented a house for graduation. I told you this."

"Yes, honey, you did." Genevieve tried to screw her eyebrows into a similar expression. "But I thought you weren't going until Monday."

"And miss the parties this weekend?"

"But Sunday is Father's Day."

"I know. I asked Dad. He said me being happy was the best gift I could give him."

"Oh…that was…nice." Genevieve felt the urge to straighten her spine.

"Yeah. So I'll be back next Friday to help with Aunt Brynn's wedding and celebrate Remy being alive and whatever."

So now Genevieve would have only one kid, Remy, to buffer her on Father's Day. That wasn't good. Remy wasn't exactly verbose. She might end up having to have a conversation with her husband. Oh no! What would they talk about?

"Do you have something?" Livvy leaned sideways over the sink, stretching her neck before the mirror.

Genevieve opened the medicine cabinet and shuffled the myriad bottles of ointments and creams, not sure if she knew what she was looking for. Everything just seemed so…hopeless. She'd spent her entire life taking care of people, and now, at just twice Livvy's age, she wasn't sure how much longer she could continue. She had to acknowledge to herself, because God knew no one else in the house would listen to her, that, although things had manifested materially better than she'd ever anticipated, being a wife and mother hadn't turned out to be all that fulfilling. In fact, it was rather draining, as if she was running out of something—what, she wasn't sure.

"Mom!"

Startled, Genevieve turned back to Livvy. "You have nothing in your bathroom?"

"If I did, I wouldn't be here." Somehow, Livvy's jaw didn't move when she spoke.

Genevieve faced her cabinet again. Not for the first time, she wanted to get into her car and drive away, just go however far a full tank of gas would get her. She could probably make it to the western edge of Pennsylvania. Maybe even to Ohio. She didn't know anyone there, but Ohio was in the Midwest. From what she understood, people were nicer there than in Jersey. Maybe she could settle among them, possibly get another dog—

"MOM!"

Dee

Last in, first out. Dee parked her rental at the end of a long line of cars flanking Granddad's driveway in LaGrange. Looming ahead of her was the enormous beige stucco mansion towering over the landscape. Its columns ran the full height of the façade, like sentries protecting an ancient fortress from outsiders who didn't know the secret code to enter.

Maybe that's why she always felt like she didn't belong here, felt like she was unwelcome by all but Gram and Brett. Maybe, if she knew what to say as she approached the front door, she'd be admitted as a welcomed family member.

Maybe.

Now, without Gram, it would be only Granddad's place. His *estate.* Would she come back? Probably not. Why would she? Damn! Why was she here now?

The trip seemed to make sense last night when she talked it over with Cooper. Granted, she'd been drinking. Cooper and Cabernet: probably not the best mix for making good choices. Because now that she thought about it, being here didn't make sense. How could she say goodbye to Gram, if Gram wasn't here anymore?

She hated when Mom was right, but she could have sent Granddad a card. What the hell was she supposed to say to him?

She googled *how to pay respects* on her phone, then clicked on link after useless link until, while reading a macabre article titled *10 Funeral Taboos You Wish You Never Knew* a text from Hayleigh came in:

Holy Wow! 100,000!

Dee called her.

"This is when you say, 'thank you, and yes, you deserve a raise.'" H's voice boomed through the phone's speaker.

"I didn't even know I was paying you."

"That's the point. You should be able to afford me now."

"Because...?"

"Because, thanks to me, you now have over 100,000 followers re-pinning every freaking thing you and Max post on Pinterest, all your live online classes are full for the next two months *with* waiting lists in case someone bails at the last minute, *plus*, we have a couple hundred local peeps here in South Jersey waiting for you to start offering in-person classes. And it's all because your kid sister's a freaking marketing genius."

"Holy shit!" There was too much of a disconnect between H's words and the eighteenth-century view outside Dee's windshield. "Holy...fucking...shit."

"So, am I getting paid?"

"Yes! Oh my God. Damn! I gotta do some math. Maybe I'll need to hire someone else to help. I mean, I don't know how to run a store. Why didn't anyone ever point that out to me before? Even if Max joins me, that's a shit-ton of people we need to handle for those classes. Who will work the store while we teach? Wait! When will I blow glass?" And now there would be things like payroll, paperwork, and more crap for her accountant to complain about when she forgot to do them. This was no longer a "wouldn't it be cool" thing to do one day. She was actually making a pivotal career change—bohemian artist to business owner. This shit was real.

"Breathe, Dee! You got me and Max. It's all good!"

"God, I hope so."

"It is. Let's celebrate at lunch."

"Sure...no, wait. I'm in Georgia."

"What?"

"I'm..." What was she doing? "I'm in La Grange. I came for my grandmother's funeral."

"Really? I didn't know you were going."

"Yeah, it was a last-minute decision."

"Well, I know this is gonna be tough on you, but I think you being there is the right thing."

"Wish Mom agreed."

"You were brave enough to tell her?"

"Brave or stupid. You pick."

"Ha! Glad she likes my dad's family."

"Kaz doesn't have any family."

"Good point."

>*Service gonna start soon*

The text was from Brett.

"I gotta go. Funeral's about to begin." Dee unbuckled her seatbelt. "Crud! I was supposed to call Mom when I landed."

"I'll tell her you made it."

"Thank you. And yes, you get paid. I have no idea how much, so don't ask yet." She clicked off, scrolled to the last text from Maxine, and typed.

>*Can't do this without you!*
>*Please say yes!*

As soon as she hit *send*, another message from Brett

>*Where u at?*

>*Driveway. Where u at?*

>*Sunporch. Drinkin without u*

She set the alarm on her phone to alert her when it was time to leave and grabbed her purse. No. That'd be too easy to lose. Finding it might make her late for her plane. Keys and phone fit in her pants pockets. Was there anything in the purse she'd need? She scrabbled through. Maybe tissues. Tissues would fit in her pockets, too...she'd look bulgy, but given the state of her shoes, that was the least of her worries. Her phone dinged with Max's reply.

Yasssss! I'm in! I'm in!
Telling Dane now.

Dane better not talk her out of it. Dee stared at the phone screen, wondering what to do next. *Oh, Brett on the sunporch.* She sighed. *One thing at a time. One thing at a time.*

With her purse locked in the rental, and phone, keys, and tissues in her pockets, she raced up the drive, walking as fast as she could in her not-quite-matching heels. Such a stupid contrast she probably made. Should have at least tried to tame the hair. Probably looked like a wild beast roaming around the perfectly clipped hedges. Maybe an aunt would order her capture and put her where she belonged.

Which wasn't here.

Inside, disapproving gazes from Granddad's ancestors looked down on her as she passed by their gilded frames hung in the central hall. Apparently, being greeted by Gram's ghost floating over the sisal rugs and wooden plank floor was too much to ask for. She was tempted to make a detour through the living and dining rooms so she could press a hand against one of the murals. Perhaps she'd feel Gram's pulse in the art she'd left behind.

But she didn't believe in ghosts and shit. What was up with all the sentimentality, anyway?

She slipped into the kitchen, nodded to a caterer as she nabbed an olive off a cocktail tray, and threw it too far into her mouth.

Choking, wheezing, she made it to the sunporch, where *Bam!* Brett nearly toppled her with a bear hug and a cloud of bourbon fumes.

"Dude!" Coughing, she pushed him away.

"You OK?"

"Olive." She pointed to her throat. "Went down wrong." Fully able to breathe, she pulled her cousin into another hug. "So glad you're here."

"Where else would I be? Biggest. Show. In town, babe. Here." Sharp enunciation. Brett was level-one drunk already. They'd invented the system when she was sixteen. They would sneak gin from Granddad's liquor cabinet and mix it with cherry Kool-Aid. If they stayed at level one, no one seemed to notice. Slurring betrayed level two. That's when they each hoped the other would hear it and get them both away from the adults. He handed her a full shot glass "It's. Been. Waiting. For you."

"Nice!" She held it up. "Here's to you and me making it through this shit show."

He clinked, they sucked down the bourbon.

"How you holding up?" she was able to ask despite the burn in her throat.

"Not. Sure. I am. You?" He reached for the bottle and measured out two more drinks.

"I don't think it really sank in yet. What are we gonna do without her?"

"Carry on. Fucked up. As. We are. Here." He handed her another shot. "Let's. Toast. Gram."

"To the woman who taught us we were artists." Dee raised her glass again.

"And that we. Have. Gifts. To give the world." He lifted his higher.

"And that we don't have to be normal." She clinked hers against his.

"Hell. She. Better. Be. Right."

Brett seemed to inhale his shot as Dee sipped hers. "Holy shit!" She noticed the table where he'd set up his makeshift bar. "Did you make this?"

"Yep. Granddad. Commissioned it."

"Really?"

"I made one for a couple. Gettin' married. Said he wanted one."

"I do too. It's freaking amazing!" Dee ran her hand along the dark wood. Was it walnut? The table was made of two boards: the outside edges were straight and smooth, the interior live-edge and separated, but filled with something blue and clear so it looked like a river passing through the table. "What did you use? Epoxy?"

"Resin, yeah. I'll...*hiccup*...make you one. If. You. Really want one." He took her shot glass and topped it off.

"I can't bud. That's it for me today."

He handed her a full glass back anyway. "Why. Aren't. You. Drinking with me?"

"I gotta leave right after the funeral. But seriously, make me two tables. One for my place, and the other I'll sell in my new store."

"OK. But. Why. Do. You. Have. To. Leave?" Brett ran a hand through his short, sandy-blond hair, making it stand up and curl back on top. He tugged on his tie, as if trying to loosen its grip on his neck. Dee couldn't remember ever seeing him in a suit before, and wondered if it was really his.

"I have business shit I gotta take care of tomorrow." She wanted to reach out and loosen the tie but had no idea how they worked. "Trust me, I know you need me here. I'm sorry."

Outside, Aunt Louise trotted toward the sunporch. "Your mom's coming." She tugged Brett's arm. "We should head out."

Her aunt pushed the door open. Dee hoped she had to pee and would pass by, but she stopped just inside. "Hello, Deirdre." As always, Aunt Louise's clam-white face reminded Dee of a mask, a really good one, like the kind they used in soap operas that the villain pulled off in a climactic moment. Realistic, but still fake. She was always emotionless, even when she smiled, as she did now, while approaching them on the other side of the table.

Though around the same age as Dee's mom, Aunt Louise looked much older. A full head of steel-gray hair cut in a blunt bob and reading glasses hanging from a black beaded chain gave her the appearance of a retired school librarian, which, as Dee remembered, is what Brett's mom was.

Dee tilted her head and did her best to improvise an angelic grin, wishing she had dimples she could point to. There were two versions of Aunt Louise. One was a sweet lady who was charmed by everyone around her, including Dee. The other was a Southern Belle who tolerated everyone with gentility, weaponized by passive aggression. Dee would have to play her out a minute before she'd know which one she got today. "How are you, Aunt Louise?"

"All right under the circumstances." Louise eyed her son. "Brett."

"Yesh, Mama."

Oh shit, slurring!

"They need help setting up more chairs," Aunt Louise told him. "Can you lend a hand?"

Brett saluted, reached for Dee's arm.

"I'd like a word with Deirdre, first." She pulled out a chair and sat at the amazing table.

Dee echoed her movements, sitting directly across from her while Brett left.

"Is that a pink streak in your hair?" Aunt Louise asked with such sweet curiosity that Dee knew she got the bitchy Southern Belle.

"Yeah. My sister did it."

"Your half-sister."

"My sister."

"Well, at least you're in black." Aunt Louise lifted her chin as if to study Dee from a slightly different perspective. "While I suppose coming here was the right thing to do, Deirdre, I really wish you hadn't."

While refreshing, the directness smacked. "Good thing I didn't ask for your approval."

"Deirdre, *you* of all people, know what I mean. This is nothing personal. Your presence here just makes everything…worse."

"That's not supposed to be personal? Wow. Go fuck yourself." Dee stood and stopped before turning around. If she left, Aunt Louise would win. That wasn't happening. She deserved to be here as much as everyone else.

"Let's pause so you can pull yourself together." Aunt Louise's voice was gratingly gentle.

"Pull myself together?" Dee pressed her hands against the table and leaned over it as she made eye contact with her aunt. "I have trouble pulling myself together on a good day. You know that. And today is not a good day." She almost kicked her leg up to show off the shoe she'd covered with a black marker while on the plane, but she was afraid she'd rip the seat of her pants. "Who the hell do you think you are to kick me out of here? I used to think you were one of the few people who had a little empathy down here."

"Deirdre, I am sympathetic to your condition. And I'm sorry if my comments came off as, well, as unwelcoming." Aunt Louise's mask slowly melted into what appeared to be a genuinely sad expression. "My concern…well, I need a favor."

That could be interesting. Dee returned to her chair.

Louise tilted her head, lowered her voice. "Mimi hadn't been gone twenty-four hours before the talk started."

"What talk?"

"The usual." Louise briefly closed her eyes. "Alma put together a prayer circle for you."

"Me?"

"She's going on about you being under Satan's influence and that we need to be prepared for what you might do when you're here."

"Damn. Should have shown up in red leather." Dee snorted. "I'd look so badass."

"What?"

"Isn't that mandatory dress code for Satan worshippers?"

"Can you please be serious?"

"Sometimes." Dee sat straighter in her seat to prove it. "It's hard at times like this. My shrink says my humor's a defense mechanism." Besides, thinking about all the times Aunt Alma tried to save Dee was just too funny. And Gram! How beautifully she played the diplomat—buffering Dee, while placating her Bible-thumping daughter.

But Aunt Louise had apparently moved on from Alma and was talking about her sister, Aunt Francie. "…Deirdre, I'm trying to tell you I'm not the enemy."

"Aunt Louise, I'm sorry. And I'm not being sarcastic here, honest, but I think I'm missing part of this conversation."

"Dee Dee, I love both my sisters-in-law. I will always appreciate how Alma and Francie still accept me as part of their family."

"Maybe that's 'cause you are?"

"You know what I mean."

No, Dee didn't know, but before she could say that, Aunt Louise continued.

"I don't feel right talking about them behind their backs. But, as soon as their mama died, they brought it all back up again. And I want you to know, I don't agree with them."

"Agree with what?"

"I'm sure Alma's sincere. But Francie's poisoning everyone against you because she thinks you only come around to secure a share of your grandfather's will."

"That's not true!" The bitches!

"Again, I don't agree. I'm sure the last thing you want anything to do with is your grandfather's business. Frankly, I don't even care if they're right. *I'm* not your enemy." She squinted as if against an interrogation light. "I just want them to stop talking. Your Granddad got them to shut up for today, but they've already gotten inside of Brett's head. He's all tore up about it. So that's what I'm trying to ask you. Please, stay away from my Brett."

Her Brett? Dee's head jerked back as if her aunt's words hit her like a slap. She always thought they shared Brett, with Gram. "He's hurting, Aunt Louise. We understand each other like no one else. We—"

"That's exactly what I mean, Deirdre." Were there tears in her eyes? "That's why you have to stay away from him. You do nothing but remind him of what happened."

Dee looked at her shot glass. Still almost full. That meant she'd only had one drink. "Can you start over? I'm confused."

"I'm saying, I understand the games Francie and Alma are playing." Aunt Louise slowed her speech. "But you and I are on the same page. I know who was really at fault. And I'm sorry, I really am, that things turned out the way they did. But that doesn't mean my Brett has to suffer."

Dee blinked her eyes a few times. Did she miss something else? She realized she was staring behind Louise at one of the giant elephant tusks standing on its flat end, framing an equally giant window. It was a leftover from the darker side of the antiques and artifacts business her grandfather had inherited from his father, who had inherited it from his. The tusk had been in that house for forever, as far as she knew, but suddenly it seemed so out of character to her that it somehow made the conversation even more confusing. "What the hell are you talking about?"

"Now that your grandmother is gone, there's no need to keep the secrets and pretend something else happened, girl." The mask was back, and the voice was annoyed. "We don't have to protect Mimi from the truth anymore; God bless her soul." Louise pushed her chair back from the table and stood. "But I will always protect Brett. So you don't need to come back anymore and pretend like, well, like it was all an accident no one could prevent." She started heading toward the door.

Dee tried to get the words to connect with meaning. "I'm still lost, Aunt Louise. What secrets? What—who was protecting Gram from what?"

Louise stopped mid-step and turned toward Dee, her face almost human. "You really don't know?"

"What?" Dee stood.

"I'm sorry, Dee Dee." The mask returned, smiling and frowning at the same time. "I don't know what I was saying. Probably just rattling foolishness. Mimi's death has me shaken up." She ran her hands over her stomach and smoothed out her black dress. "The service will start soon." She sped out of the sunporch, letting the screen door slam behind her without looking back to see if Dee was following.

Maxine

Relief. Maxine rested her backside against the kitchen sink and relished the relief as it washed the tension out of her body. No other decision had felt so good before. Yes, she was in. She was *in*.

Never again would she stand, ignored, at the front of an elementary classroom trying to teach a group of six-year-olds while they ate a snack, fell asleep, talked to someone next to them, or picked their noses. Never again would she tolerate being yelled at by some outraged mom for not understanding that her precious fifth grader was gifted in every area and chose not to do an assignment because he was artistically expressing himself and should receive an A. Never again—

"Where you at?" Dane entered the kitchen.

"What?"

"Your face. You were a million miles away." He nodded toward the phone in her hand as he pulled a glass from the cupboard.

"Something up?"

Max sat at the table. "Just texting Dee." How was she going to tell him?

"Hm." Dane's movements through the kitchen traced a methodical path. He handled lunch the way he handled breakfast, which was the way he handled everything in his life: without variation. She watched him, predicting each move before it happened. First, he filled a glass with water, then set out a placemat where he always sat at the table. His glass went into the upper-right-hand corner of the placemat before he got a small plate. He centered a napkin on the plate, topped it with a bowl, then, at the same spot on the counter every day, he ladled out two scoops of soup. Once covered with a paper towel, the bowel was placed in the microwave for two minutes and forty-seven seconds.

Maxine smiled at the precision of his movements, her opposite. He was so stable. She was secure in knowing who he was and how reliable he was. Despite all the negativity lately, that was still something he gave her—security, dependability, reliability—which told her they could get through everything together. Looking at him, he suddenly became filled with swirls of color; a house stood in his solar plexus. Yes. He embodied the feeling of home. She'd have to paint that.

"Dee send a joke?" His voice brought his actual features into focus—the chiseled cheeks, the tawny-brown skin, the full lips and close-cropped curly black hair, the horn-rimmed glasses: her intelligent, logical, linear-thinking Dane. "That's some smile."

"Actually, I was thinking about a painting I'm going to make."

"Cool." He nodded as he scooped a spoonful of soup into his mouth.

"So…" What were the right words? Were there any? Change was always difficult for Dane, at first. That master bath redo last fall stressed him enormously, but now he was glad they did it. She knew he'd get that way with this. But man! Getting over that hump would take some work. Especially with how rough things had been lately.

"So." He paused before taking another spoonful. "Are we seriously stuck going to your dad's place on Sunday?"

"Afraid so."

He smirked and continued eating.

"On the plus side, we'll be well fed that day between breakfast with your parents, lunch at his restaurant, then dinner with Lauren and Kaz."

"We have to do all three?"

"You could go to your parents alone—"

"Fine." A sip of water. "Like you said, at least we'll be well fed."

Why did the kitchen suddenly feel so empty with the two of them in it? She watched him eat, wanting desperately to say something. To bring some laughter into the room, some lightness, some warmth. She never used to have to work for those. They were always there. They always used to be there.

She couldn't wait, though. He'd return to his office soon, and then she'd have to screw up the courage to have this talk later.

"I've decided to go into business with Dee." The words felt like they escaped by accident.

"Good. I know you didn't want to teach at a camp again this summer. I'm glad you found something else. But I still don't understand how she even has a business."

"She has a business because she's an amazing artist, and Hayleigh knows how to market on social media to an extent that almost scares me. *And*, Dee's business exploded this past spring, in part, because of *my* contributions. That's why she asked me to partner with her." She watched his face. His chewing slowed; a crease formed between his brows. By the time he swallowed, she knew the words had sunk in.

"So, you don't mean just for the summer?" The lift in his tone on the last syllable felt mocking.

"Right. It's a permanent thing."

He stared at her.

After a full minute of silence, she continued. "I told you how she bought that building downtown to set up her own store and studio."

Dane remained mute.

"We'll be creating, renovating things, like we've been doing, making new pieces out of old. I'll sell my paintings, and Dee will sell her glasswork. We'll both continue taking commissions. The store will be a showplace for what we did and can do. And we'll continue teaching the online classes, but we'll do some in-person, on the premises, too."

"I see." He quickly finished his soup in silence. Equally silent, he stood, rinsed his plate, bowl, and glass the way he always did. Placed everything in the dishwasher in the same spots he always put them, and left the kitchen.

Maxine followed him to the spare bedroom upstairs that had become his office when his job went remote—another change that stressed him at first, but once he got used to it, he realized he much preferred it over going into the office.

"Are you OK with this?" she asked as he settled into his chair.

"Sounds like you already made up your mind, Max. Doesn't seem like it matters if I'm OK with it."

"I'd like to know that you support me."

"I'm not sure what you mean by 'support.'" He wiggled his mouse and turned to face one of his monitors.

"Our lives won't change much, Dane. I mean, yes, I'll work some weekends and evenings, but Dee and I will alternate, so it won't be every weekend and evening, which is better, right? I mean, look at how often I'd take parent calls or grade projects in the evenings and on weekends, on top of making things to sell. And as soon as we get set up and open, like all the stores downtown, we'll be closed on Mondays, which means—" She met his eyes when he looked up and realized nothing she said got through to him. She knew she could say, "Look, I love you, we'll get through this," and walk away. That's how they usually fought. He'd say his bit; she'd say hers. They'd do their separate things for a while, and the issue would eventually fade. But a career change, like baby decisions, wouldn't fade. They were going to have to figure out how to communicate about important things they disagreed on at some point. "Dane, why can't you tell me you're OK with this?"

"You can't just quit teaching to go work with Dee."

"I didn't ask for your *permission*. I asked why you can't *support* me in this…this opportunity to have my dream job."

"I can't support you quitting a stable career to partner with a woman who gets lost in an elevator."

"How can you say that? Dee is one of the most talented people I know. And she's smart as—"

"I'm not saying she's dumb. I'm sure she's smart, but only when she can pay attention long enough to finish a sentence."

"Who *are* you? When did you get so mean?" Never had he spoken about Dee like that before.

"Look." Dane pressed his fingertips together over his keyboard. She tried to find the swirling colors in him again, but all she got were crisscrossed steel beams. "When my wife tells me she's walking away from a secure job with great benefits to take a chance on...on what? A gift shop?"

"Are you kidding me?"

"An art store? Whatever. I'm worried, Max. We have a mortgage. And your *secure* job helps pay it."

"My *secure* job as an elementary art teacher barely pays for anything. The extra income that helped make the mortgage payments while we redid the bathroom came from *my* art, which I did *part*-time, that Dee sold on her website. *Your* job is secure. We can afford for me to—"

"So you think we just risk everything so you can go play 'business' with your BFF?"

"Play business?" Maybe working through problems was overrated. Max gave herself time to do some yoga breathing before continuing. "You do realize that Mama's custom clothing business is very successful, right?"

"Not the same thing, Max."

"And she started it with Dee's mom, her 'BFF,' when Dee and I were just six years old."

"Things are different for us. Your mother had a different lifestyle. And she was younger than you then. You're thirty-two. Now is when we get serious about our future, about baby-making. How are you going to take maternity leave when it's just you and Dee doing this, this thing?"

"There won't be a *need* for maternity leave." Tears stung Maxine's eyes. She told him she couldn't continue putting her body through any more fertility treatments. He knew she wanted to stop. Why did he ignore that?

"Baby." Dane closed his eyes. "I'm sorry. I...I just don't know why you're so willing to walk away from a good job with great benefits to...to do *what* exactly? Sell lampshades you rubber-stamped flowers on? You think that's a sustainable business plan?"

"Did you really just go there?"

"Go where?"

"Rubber-stamping lampshades? You think that's what I do?" Maxine reached over his desk and clamped his hands together. "I'm an *artist!* Remember me making you go to that gallery celebrating Black female artists? Didn't you recognize *my* name on any of the plaques? I *make art*." She released him with force.

"I know!" Dane's eyes were wide. "I saw your work. I was proud of you that night. I still am. But isn't 'making art' what you do all day in the school?"

"I teach little kids how to draw a horse by connecting circles. I bore them stupid, showing them how to mix blue paint with yellow to make green."

"And you get paid to do it."

"*But that's not art!* I've made more pieces over the past year than ever. And it sells! People love my work!"

"Of course they do! You make great stuff. That's not what I'm talking about." He returned his attention to his monitor and struck a couple of keys. Clearly, he was ready to be done with the argument.

"It's what *I'm* talking about. And you're not listening." Maxine clenched her fists at her sides.

He looked at her with just his eyes, didn't turn his head. "Explain. What are you talking about?"

"Yadira."

"What?"

"Yadira Pacheco. Remember her?"

Dane blinked a few times, then completely faced her. "That music teacher who had cancer?"

Maxine nodded. "We used to laugh together about how one day we'd both quit. She'd perform in some jazz lounge, and I'd have my own gallery shows."

Dane watched her for a few more heartbeats, then returned his freaking attention to his computer. Maxine saw only grayness in him now, greige to be exact, that sterile, lifeless gray-beige color everyone had painted on every wall in their houses for the last decade. She wanted to pick him up and shake the colors back into him. "Yadira died with her music inside her."

He remained quiet, eyes glued to his monitor.

"Did you hear me?" He continued to stare at his computer. "I'm not dying with my art inside me." She straightened, pulled her waist-length braids together behind her head, and waited him out.

Finally, he looked up and met her eyes. "Sounds like you made another decision without me, Max. Go make art."

Dee

Allies. Dee needed allies…and to stay away from Aunt Louise. She'd have to call Brett later, maybe tomorrow, hopefully he'd be sober enough by then to tell her what his mother was talking about. She crossed the back patio and took a path leading to the crowd by the lake. Felt like she was about to step into a swamp filled with snapping turtles. These people moved slowly, and she knew they had a vicious bite. She didn't want to set any of them off.

Scanning for faces with the potential to be friendly, not for the first time on that property, she realized there were far too many of the other kind. Louise huddled in a coven with some older women she didn't recognize. Various cousins and people whose names Dee never remembered cliqued into different groups. Brett set out chairs. If anyone else noticed his tiny stumbles or how he leaned over a little too far at times, no one let on. Then there was Granddad…no. She wasn't ready for him.

There had to be someone...where was Great Aunt Josie? Didn't she and her son, Evan, fly down earlier that week?

Oh hell. Somehow, Aunts Alma and Francie were both standing before her in designer black.

"I didn't imagine you'd have the audacity to show up today." Francie somehow had a brilliantly kind smile on her face. Unlike Louise, Francie was aging as well as Dee's mother, with smooth alabaster skin and blond hair pulled back in a low bun.

"Why wouldn't I?" Dee didn't try to smile back.

"It's fine that you did, Dee Dee." Aunt Alma fingered a cross at her neck. "In fact, it's right. How long do you intend to stay?"

"I'm leaving right after the service."

"Good." Aunt Francie's perfectly arched brows lifted. "We

don't have to worry about you making any trouble."

"Seems to me I'm never the one who starts it." Dee spotted Josie heading toward an easel holding a large photo of Gram. "If you'll excuse me—"

Francie grabbed her arm in a not-very-gentle way. "You won't be returning, then, right?" Instead of giving Dee a chance to retort, she gripped tighter. "Things are different now that Mama's dead. We don't have to protect her anymore. So after today, you can forget about this place, forget about all of us, and what you caused here. You go home, keep on pretending to be an artist, and leech off your mother." She let go of her so forcefully that Dee almost stumbled.

They walked away as Dee stabilized on her feet, too stunned to scare up a comeback. Granted, she'd never describe her aunts as welcoming, but this was above and beyond their usual bitchiness. And they didn't make any sense. Protect Gram from what? The secrets Aunt Louise assumed Dee knew? And what had Dee caused?

What the hell was going on? Sure, there were gaps in her memories, but usually, when people spoke to her, there were enough hints or clues for her to pick up or pieces to puzzle together, so that a clear picture forms. Not today. Today was like opening a bedroom door only to discover, on the other side, a playhouse stage. And she had no idea what the script was about.

At least they helped her make up her mind: she'd never come back. Brett could visit her.

She headed over to someone she knew would be on her side: Great Aunt Josie, who stood gazing at Gram's photo. On a pedestal next to it was a wooden box. Was that where Gram's ashes were? How weird it must have been for Josie to think that was all that was left of her sister. How weird to think that was all that was left of Gram: dust in a box. Like powdered charcoal, too sacred to draw with.

In slow motion, Dee approached her great aunt and touched her arm.

"Aunt Josie?" Her air cut off. She couldn't get any more words out. Josie embraced Dee with surprising strength coming from such a frail-looking body.

"I'm so sorry," Josie whispered.

"Me, too," Dee squeaked. She pulled out of the hug to get a tissue from her pocket. In the sunlight, her attempt to create two black shoes was laughable. One had a deep tone and was smooth—with a worn spot on the toe—the other, streaky. Maybe no one noticed. But as she blew her nose, she realized Josie was staring at her feet. "The light was out in my closet this morning." Dee lifted her formerly brown toe. "I didn't realize I put on mismatched shoes until I got to the airport. All I could find there to fix it was a Sharpie marker."

"Ah! Your grandmother turned off your light." Josie's face crinkled into a smile.

Dee understood and almost broke out in a laugh. Gram, the first to recognize artistic talent in Dee, had painted everything—the silk drapes in the house, the murals in every room, and several pairs of shoes. Dee's favorites were the pumps Gram had painted the willow tree across, half on each shoe—the same willow tree where her ashes would be tucked into a hollow that day. Dee decided to honor Gram by painting that tree on her shoes.

"Hello, Deirdre." Granddad's voice was soft, still gruff. His face unreadable, his presence, as always, commanding. Kind of like the columns gracing the front of his house.

Dee could touch him. She really could. She was a thirty-two-year-old grown-ass woman, after all, not a scared, confused little girl. She could...She could touch him.

She did. It was hard. Like using your hand to test whether a stove burner was hot, she reached out, touched his jacket sleeve.

He wrapped her in a hug. A real hug. Not the awkward, stiff attempts he usually made with her. This hug held emotion. Enough emotion to rip her apart. Gram was gone. Those weren't just words.

They were a thing. A forever thing. She sobbed into his lapel, probably smeared mascara on his jacket.

What the hell was wrong with her? She never broke down. She pulled herself together enough to step from his embrace, but no words came. She avoided looking in his eyes by searching for another tissue in her pockets.

"It's time," a man called. "Please be seated."

Granddad tapped her arm, then left to sit in the front row of chairs lined up beside the lake. Her aunts took the three chairs to his left. On Granddad's right were two empty seats, then Brett, and some other men. Dee saw Evan sit behind Granddad and took the chair next to him. Josie paused, looked like she was wondering where to sit. *Oh, maybe she wants to be next to her son.* Dee moved over a place and patted the seat between her and Evan. Josie smiled and took the chair.

It didn't take long for the talk to start.

"What's the matter with that girl?" Aunt Alma loudly whispered to Louise. "Too selfish to sit by her own grandfather and comfort him!"

She was supposed to sit by Granddad? Was Josie, too? Is that why there are two open chairs in the front row? For Gram's sister and granddaughter? *That's probably why Josie looked like she wasn't sure where to go. Shit!*

"I appreciate you staying by this old woman, Deirdre." Josie took her hand. "It means so much to me, having you on one side and my son on the other."

Damm it! Mom was right about *two* things: she shouldn't have come, *and* the people in her father's family were toxic. Every-freaking-one of them…except Gram and Brett. Maybe Granddad. The jury was still out on him because he seldom spoke.

Had they ever had a real conversation? After the accident that wiped out all the memories of the first five years of her life, Granddad and Gram would come up north every summer, stay with

Josie in Philadelphia, and pop over the river to visit Dee in New Jersey. Dee slowly got to know her brilliant and talented grandmother on those visits, while Granddad sat silently, and her mother anxiously hovered nearby. When she turned thirteen, Gram needed chemo and couldn't travel. She asked if Dee could visit her. Dee's mother almost called in the Coast Guard to prevent it, but somehow Gram prevailed, and Dee was sent to Georgia for two weeks.

That first summer was the greatest, and the worst. Gram had opened up levels of creativity and skill that Dee didn't realize she had. And Brett! Although a couple of years older than she, her cousin seemed hellbent on making sure she had the time of her life. But the others—she heard too many family members whispering about the wild children Gram coddled. That Brett who'd "never amount to much," and that "poor damaged Dee Dee." Then there was the direct nastiness toward her when no one else was around, followed up by hypocritical smiles over the dinner table. She was an evil girl. She was a no-talent gold digger. Apparently, even as a clueless teen!

But had she ever spoken to Granddad beyond saying *hello,* and *the flight was fine*?

She'd always been afraid of him, afraid to set his anger off, which she wasn't sure he deserved. Had he ever done anything to make her fear him like that? She walked on eggshells during that first visit, never relaxing, never able to sleep, constantly afraid of finding herself alone with an aunt or her grandfather.

When she returned home to Jersey that first year, Mom wigged out over how terrible she looked, how fragile she seemed. Mom was against her going back the following year. But she and Gram had remained in contact, and she wanted to go back for more art lessons, thinking it would be better with everyone else. But it wasn't. She skipped the year she was fifteen because of the whole breakdown thing she'd had. Mom's overprotectiveness was actually what Dee needed that summer. Then, when she came back at sixteen, she was stronger. Maybe that's what almost dying did to people. *Ha! Guess that phrase is true: what doesn't kill you makes you stronger.*

She'd returned nearly every year since—because of the love for Gram, because of how her art expanded exponentially with each trip, and starting that sixteenth year because of the fun-ass times with Brett. As she grew older, she developed a drive to symbolically say "up yours" with her presence to the rest of them with each visit. Did that include Granddad?

Dee was brought to the present by Josie—still holding her hand, rubbing a gentle thumb over a Sharpie stain from when the plane had turbulence. Josie's skin had a papery quality, as if it would tear easily. Dee wanted to cover it with a sealant, protect it for eternity.

The reverend's voice caught her attention, and she realized he'd been doing his thing, driveling on about eternity, God, grace, whatever. She sat up straighter in her chair and tried to focus on his words. But there was Brett, openly drinking from a flask, the willow tree swaying in a breeze she couldn't feel, and that wooden box on the pedestal.

On the other side of the lake was a small family cemetery, Granddad's ancestors. She wondered why Gram didn't want to be buried among them. Her father hadn't been either. His ashes had been scattered in the lake. *Wait. How did she know that?*

Who would have told her that? What would have prompted her to ask about it? Or did she ask? Was she even sure that's what happened to him?

An uncomfortable, bristly feeling rolled up Dee's spine. Why didn't she know for sure where her father's remains were? Could she have forgotten? Yes. But why didn't someone keep reminding her? Would that have been normal?

Dee felt Aunt Josie squeeze her hand and realized she'd stiffened in her chair.

"We know this life is not the final story," the reverend said in a voice that was suddenly loud. "And now, Mimi is in her next chapter. She has gone home, to heaven, where her sons welcomed her."

Meaning Dee's father. And Brett's. Were they waiting for Gram? Did people actually sit around in the hereafter and wait for people to die? Didn't seem like fun.

She looked at her cousin, who'd turned in his chair to face her at the same time. He cheered his flask to her, tipped his head back, and shook the remaining drops into his open mouth. He threw the empty flask to the ground and took off toward the house.

Dee stumbled down her row and ran after him, caught up to him in the kitchen at the set-up bar.

"Dude! You've had enough." She pulled him by the arm into the main hallway. "C'mon. Let's get you upstairs. Find you a bed somewhere."

"I wanna..." he fell against her, sending them both into a wall. Thank Christ they missed the table with the Ming vase collection. "I gotsa tell you shometing."

"Fine. Tell me." She pushed him upright, wrapped his arm over her shoulders, and began dragging him down the hall. *Like moving a fucking trash bag full of Jell-O.* "Granddad's gonna kill you."

"Nah. He's too fine, fined, refined for killin'." At the staircase, Brett heaved himself off her, tripped on the bottom step, and managed to turn around to sit. "Right? Part of Southern royalty since seventeen-fuckin'-eighty-two."

"Oh my god! You're wasted."

"Yep." His head bounced in a nod.

Dee looked up the stairs. There was no way in hell she could get him up there alone.

"Lishen, Dee." His head continued to bob. "There'sh a shecret."

"Everything OK in here?"

Yes! Evan! "Is the service over?" She asked him.

"Just wrapped up." Evan stood with his hands in the pockets of his slacks and stared at the slumped Brett. "People are paying their respects to your grandfather. They should be in soon."

"We have to get him upstairs. Get him in bed, propped up on pillows. Can you help me?"

"Think you can walk, buddy?" Apparently, Evan didn't spend much time with drunk people.

Brett lunged upright and fell into Dee again. She pushed against his Jell-O body and propped him against the wall.

"Ev- Effan. She goin' home now." His face crumbled, tears dripped down. "Tell Dee Dee shtay."

"What am I, a fucking dog?" *Please laugh. At least grin.* She'd settle for any sign that he was OK.

"You take care of her, Effffn. Gramma ain't here no more. Gotta protect Dee. Promish me."

"I'm not some needy pansy!" He knew she could handle her aunts. If he were sober, she'd rip into him. "Evan, you get one side, I'll get the other."

Brett pushed past them and wobbled down the hall into Granddad's study. Once more, Dee peeled off after him with Evan on her mismatched heels. Brett flailed his arms, keeping them away, until he threw himself into Granddad's giant brown leather chair. He slammed his feet up on the enormous, burled maple desk and crossed them at the ankles.

"Dee! You..." He let out a huge sigh. "You go on home, baby." His head fell back against the chair. "Maybe dat's better."

"Brett, I—"

"And, and, ask your mama 'bout who killed your daddy."

"What?"

Hands were on Dee's shoulders.

"It's all right, Deirdre." Granddad's voice was surprisingly kind. He rotated her around and gently prodded her back into the main hall. "Brett'll be all right." Granddad shut the door to the study. "Are you staying for dinner?"

She wanted to. She wanted to stay around until Brett sobered up and told her what he meant. Tell her what the secret was. Maybe tell her why her aunts were so fucking weird. Her father had died shortly before she was born. His death usually hung in the distance—on the other side of the lake—so far away that people couldn't, or wouldn't, talk to her about him. Since she had no memories of him, and it only upset everyone she loved when she asked about him, she'd learned not to press the matter much. But sometimes there was something she'd feel in the house, a presence she didn't know what to do with. Her art with Gram and wild carousing with Brett would distract her from it. With neither of those options handy, it was here now. With Gram nothing more than a box of ashes, and Brett a blathering idiot, it pressed in on her from all sides.

"Deirdre?" Granddad's hands were on her shoulders again.

There was an answer waiting for her to ask the right question. What was the question?

The alarm sounded on Dee's phone, startling her. "Oh, um. Yeah, Granddad." She pulled her cell out to silence it. A few wrinkled tissues fell to the ground. "I, actually, I can't stay. I have to go now."

Genevieve

Genevieve was quite pleased with herself. A beautiful salad of mixed spring greens and fresh strawberries chilled in the fridge. On the kitchen island, she had lined up five plates, each with an open burger bun. Below the plates was a cutting board with five neat piles of toppings.

Cross-referencing her notes, she double-checked that everyone would get what they wanted: Bun one had ketchup and corresponded with pile one: pickle slices. Bun two was slathered with Siracha and mayonnaise, and pile two had sauteed onions and avocado slices. Bun three: Dijon mustard. Pile three: tomato and bacon. Bun four: mayo with lettuce, tomato, and raw onion. Bun five was gluten-free and came with only lettuce.

Below the piles of toppings, she placed the preferred cheeses in order: American, Swiss, sharp cheddar, and provolone. Olivia's friend Jessica was staying for dinner, and not only was the poor girl gluten-free but also dairy-intolerant, so no cheese for her.

Genevieve lit both burners on the right side of her stainless steel, professional-grade range and set the griddle plate over them. While the plate warmed, she squished ground beef to form five patties, which she lined up on parchment paper next to the stove. Remy no longer liked his burgers well done and wanted his medium; Livvy wanted hers burnt, and everyone else medium-rare. She glanced at the clock. Right on schedule!

She set the timer and placed Livvy's burger on the griddle, salted and peppered it, then sprinkled on a bit of garlic powder.

"Oh, how pretty!" Jessica pointed to the neat rows of buns and toppings as she followed Olivia through the kitchen. "You should post that! It looks like art."

"Thank you, Jes. I actually wanted to be an artist at one time." Genevieve glanced at her timer. Two more minutes to go. "In fact, after Remy entered first grade, I attended college—"

She was alone in the kitchen again. The girls were on the back patio.

Maybe she should open that bottle of Merlot.

When the timer dinged, she placed Remy's patty on the griddle next to Livvy's. Another round of seasonings, then she reset the timer. After a little sip, she put out placemats. *Ding.* She flipped both burgers and placed the remaining three on the griddle. When it was time to flip those, she'd add the cheeses and call everyone to dinner exactly at six-thirty, as always. Perfect.

"Here." Remy materialized, holding a cell phone a few inches from her face.

"What's this?'

"Dad's phone. He said to give it to you."

"Where is he?" Genevieve wiped her hand on a towel and took the phone. "And who—"

"He's changing. One of his pilots is sick, so he has to fly someone to Chicago. I'm going with him. We're having a father-son weekend." Remy jogged away; the sneakers he was not supposed to wear in the house thumped on the hardwood floor as he headed toward the front and up the stairs.

"Oh, hello?" She put the phone to her ear.

"Hey, Gen!" her brother, Archie, laughed. "I should have called you to begin with, of course, *you'd* know the answer. Brynn sent me this long email about where I need to be next weekend. I was just planning on showing up for the big event, but now it looks like she's expecting more from her baby brother."

"Yeah, um, Arch—" Genevieve's timer went off. She flipped all the medium-rare burgers, but Livvy's still didn't look done enough. "Look—"

"So what's up with the dress code? I mean, what does 'casual chic' even mean for a man? Is that different from black tie?"

Since Olivia's burger needed more time, she couldn't cheese any of them. She moved her daughter's patty to the rear of the griddle and turned up the heat under it while turning it down on the front. Medium-rare was probably out of the question for anyone now.

"Um, so, yeah," Genevieve pinched the bridge of her nose and shut her eyes. What had their sister said about all that? She turned around to lean against the counter, trying to recall. "I think Brynn just wants everyone to look like they're someplace having fun, like a club, but you know, a club for people our age, in their thirties."

"So look nice enough to post photos. Smile big. Do what we

need to keep up the pretense that our sister isn't marrying a jerk. Right?"

"Archie! She's in love!"

"Don't know how that's possible. Ever spent time talking to the man?"

"Well, he does rather think highly of himself." Gen hated thinking she didn't like Brynn's fiancé. But Archie had a point: Todd made it hard to like him. She couldn't figure out what Brynn saw in him. "But we don't get to pick each other's spouses."

"Nor each other's noses. So do I have to wear a tie?"

"What's burning?" Olivia and Jessica appeared in the kitchen.

Genevieve turned around to discover a cloud of smoke rising from what used to be Livvy's burger—and what was everyone else's as well, because she apparently turned up both burners under the griddle plate.

"Oh, no! Arch! I have to go! I'm burning dinner."

She dropped the phone on the counter and flipped on the exhaust fan, but it was too late. The fire alarm, which, for years, she'd complained about being too sensitive for a kitchen, blared. Livvy and Jessica ran back outside. Genevieve dragged a chair under the alarm, picked up her notepad with the burger details, and climbed up on the chair to fan the smoke detector.

"What the hell is going on?" was yelled from the front of the house as soon as the alarm silenced.

He couldn't even check to see if she needed to be rescued from a burning building? He had to yell, and yell as if she'd done something wrong?

"Mom burned dinner!" Remy hollered as he thumped back into the kitchen.

Honestly? Genevieve's pulse pounded in her temples. Her throat tightened. She stared at Remy as he rummaged through the pantry. An already-handsome face topped his athletic frame: he had the same swarthy skin and dimples as his father, same chestnut hair and blue eyes. No wonder half the girls in his sophomore class at high school had a crush on him. But admiring her son did nothing to calm her. She wanted to hit something, throw something, until she climbed off the chair and realized the truth behind her anger.

Yes, she felt unappreciated, taken for granted, and put upon. But wasn't that her fault? Didn't that life coach on YouTube this morning talk about this while she ran on her elliptical machine? That we teach people how to treat us? She had trained her family to rely on the fact that she'd take care of everything so they could have a carefree life, and apparently, she'd forgotten to train them to say *thank you.*

"Looks like we'll need to order in." She pushed her chair back to where it belonged. "What would you like, Rem?"

"Ask Liv." Remy threw a protein bar into his backpack. "Dad said I should just grab a snack for now. We're gonna get pizza when we land."

"You're leaving *now*?" She fell into the chair.

"Yeah." He pecked her cheek with a kiss goodbye. "But don't worry. We'll be home Sunday night, so you can still take me to rugby camp on Monday." He grabbed his father's phone off the counter and was off, running back upstairs for whatever he'd forgotten.

Why would he think Genevieve would worry about him *not* making it to rugby camp? She'd be delighted, though she had to admit that taking him gave her something to do. Driving him to camp was in her schedule: drop him off every morning with a full belly and a backpack loaded with food and Gatorade, then pick him up again at five. In between, she'd listen for the phone call she couldn't help but feel was bound to come—the call letting her know his arm was broken, or nose bloodied, or worse. *Rugby! Could he have picked a more dangerous sport?*

She stood. "Livvy!" Where was she?

"So, like, me and Jess are gonna go out for dinner." Olivia was back into the house, picking a set of keys from a hook near the mudroom door.

"Oh, well..." Genevieve couldn't get her thoughts to form whatever it was she wanted to say.

"Want to join us?" Jessica asked.

Olivia's face contorted into a look that told Genevieve it would cause her unbearable pain if her mother went to dinner with her.

"Um, no, thank you." Genevieve tried to smile at Jessica. Felt like something was in her throat. "That's sweet of you, but I think I'm just going to drink my Merlot, order a pizza, and...and...browse Pinterest for the rest of the night." Happiness dared to flutter up from Genevieve's stomach as she realized she'd be alone all weekend. Even better: she wouldn't have to spend Father's Day with her husband. How lovely! Maybe those artists she followed posted new projects or had a new class she could take. Maybe she could spend the time creating something. Maybe she could lounge around in her pajamas and browse on Pinterest to her heart's desire. Maybe there'd be pins telling women how to find new families. Or at least how to get away with murdering their husbands.

Friday, June 18

Dee

Man, but she needed this sunshine! Sunshine, being out in the open, in the fresh air…yes, she needed it all. What a night. Took forever to get to sleep, and then such weird-ass dreams. Nightmares! Been a while since she'd had any that bad. Hopefully, it would be a lot longer until the next time.

Letting a to-go cup of coffee rest on the bench beside her, Dee tilted her head back, bundling her wild hair into a makeshift pillow. Maybe the sun would beat into her brain and burn out the ugly leftover energy. No need for ugly on a day like this. In a place like this. She was in the sunshine in front of her building—her building! Well, part of it was hers.

Over a century old, the whole building was a block-long, connected string of two-story units. Each housed a small shop or restaurant downstairs, and most, like Dee's, had the upper floor converted into an apartment. She now owned the end unit. She was on *her* bench in front of *her* building. She fucking owned something.

Her eyes drifted closed. She could fall asleep on her bench, right? Or was it her bench? Did it belong to the city?

She struggled to sit upright and sip some coffee. She'd need to ask Kaz about the bench. If it was hers, then she should do something with it—paint it. Would be cool to attach wings to the back. Ooo, maybe paint a flying carpet underneath. She leaned forward to check out the brick sidewalk—a leftover relic from colonial days when the township was established. Maybe Dee could stain the bricks; paint would need more upkeep to maintain, but it would be easier to change if she wanted. Of course, she couldn't do anything unless she owned the sidewalk. She'd need to ask Kaz about that, too.

"You all right?!"

She shot up, spilled her coffee.

"Jesus Christ, Kaz!" She hopped off the bench, half-empty cup in hand, one leg soaked.

"Sorry, kid!" He reached into a paper bag and pulled out a napkin. "Here. I brought donuts and coffee."

"Thank you." She sopped the coffee off her jeans.

"Good morning, by the way." Kaz kissed her cheek. "You hungover?"

"What? No. Why?"

"Thought you were about to fall off the bench."

"Oh." Dee stared through him, blinked a few times, trying to remember what was just happening. "I dunno what I was doing."

"Doesn't matter." He nodded toward her building. "Can we go in? I'd love you to show me the home of Altered States Gallery and Studio."

"Yes! Walk this way!"

"If only I had the grace."

The door was just a few steps from the bench, but Dee had to set him up with that goofy line. Yeah, it was corny. It was cheesy. It was the least original thing she could say, but it was *their* line. Only she and Kaz said it to each other, and somehow only during moments that meant something to her.

The first was when she was eight. She'd led him to get some ice cream on the boardwalk in Atlantic City. It was the day he asked her if he could marry her mother. She couldn't remember every time—

and there was a strong possibility she wouldn't remember this one—but she never forgot the first *walk this way*. And she relished every single one of them.

"This is so fucking, freaking, amazeballs!" Her voice echoed in the empty space. In the center of the front room, she turned toward him, threw out her arms. "I own my own shop, my own studio. How is that possible?"

"Money from a life insurance policy that's been growing interest, a generous gift from your mother, and the most awesome dad in the world who knows how to take advantage of a short sale."

"Thanks for downing my high."

"Anytime, kid, anytime." Kaz grinned and sat on the wide front window ledge. He placed the bakery bag beside him, pulled out two coffees, set one on the ledge, and took the lid off another. "Your mom and I are proud of you, you know." He blew on his coffee before sipping.

"Proud of what? Like you just said, I didn't earn this place." She finished the remainder of her cup and looked around to find a place to put it.

"There's plenty to be proud of." Kaz's eyes, so brown she couldn't make out the pupils, stared into her. "You've built quite the business on your own—"

"With Max and Hayleigh's help."

"You're a self-sufficient artist—"

"Whose mother still brings her food several days a week just in case I'm hungry—and I usually am."

"You've let the money from your father's insurance policy grow interest instead of blowing through it—"

"'Cause you and Mom gave me plenty to piss away."

"Kid, why are *you* downing *my* high?" He raised his salt-and-pepper brows and grinned again. "Why can't we be proud of you?"

"Just feels weird." Dee turned away from him, away from the conversation, and walked a circle through the empty room. Yeah, she could have burned through the money from her dad's policy before now, but somehow using it meant…well, it meant using something she only had because she lost her father.

Lost him. Like he was a sock or something.

His death flew home with her the day before and hovered nearby as she finished packing for the move. No wonder it was hard to sleep last night…and the nightmares! She wasn't used to thinking about him. Didn't know how to feel about him…yet she felt his presence late into the night. Thank God it faded with the sunshine.

"How are you going to set up in here?" Kaz startled her again.

She set her empty cup on the window ledge and watched him pull a jelly donut out of the bag. "This big front room will be filled with small pieces and jewelry. We'll put the checkout counter there." She pointed to the back left corner before walking through the first doorway. The downstairs was broken into three rooms—how had the Realtor called them? Enfilade! Enfilade style—one room after the other, connected by large open doorways in the center of the walls. It had once been a restaurant, with dining spaces in the first two rooms, the kitchen and restrooms squeezed in the back. She couldn't imagine it that way now. She could only envision the way she had it planned in her head, the way she described it to Kaz.

"Then this middle room will be split in two. On that side," she pointed toward the shared wall, "will be a consultation area for commissioning work and framing. On the other side we're gonna put the larger pieces—like the big furniture we've transformed—things that are hard to steal since apparently overhead cameras will be a bitch to get installed properly."

She headed to the back and raised her voice since he was still eating in the front window. "Then, back here is where the magic will happen." The best for last: the creating room. "We'll have worktables for classes and us to use. And I'll set up my glass-working area in the corner, by the sink. Need to hook up an exhaust fan to blow outside and get a film to cover the window and all that."

"Sounds perfect!" Kaz shouted.

It did sound perfect. And in her head, it looked perfect. A large window was on the back wall, next to it a door, then the sink area in the corner. The remaining wall held more windows and faced the side street. She could see herself there, with a flame blasting out of a torch, melting and pulling glass.

She opened the rear door. The stairs ended just beside it, they ran down across the back window, which was kind of stupid. But whatever. In front of her was a dead-looking strip of lawn and a garage.

Her dead lawn. *Her* garage. *Her* stairs running up to *her* apartment.

Back inside, the imagery of her studio filled her head.

This. She inhaled, twirled slowly in the open space, held on to the visions...this is what it would look like. This is what it felt like to have a dream come true. Proof you didn't need magical shoes or a satin ball gown. And certainly didn't need help from some prince. She floated back to Kaz in the front.

"When are you moving in upstairs?" He sipped his coffee.

"I have that Two Guys company lined up now. If we pass the inspection today—"

"You will."

"I'll text them to meet me at my apartment—my *old* apartment. The idea is to get me settled upstairs this weekend, then Max and I will start bringing in everything we have stored all over town for down here."

"So, I'll be able to get my car in the garage again?"

"Which explains why you and Mom were so willing to give a girl some cash." She accepted a paper cup full of black coffee and looked through the window behind Kaz. "Some dude's out there holding a clipboard, looking up at the roof."

"Must be the inspector. I think clipboards are part of their uniform." Kaz took the last bite of his jelly donut as if there was nothing to worry about.

"What could possibly be wrong with the roof?"

"Nothing."

"Then what's he looking at?"

"Probably checking out the gutters."

"Think something's wrong with the gutters?"

"Kid." He wiped the corners of his grinning mouth. "I can promise you he will find *nothing* wrong with *any*thing in this building that would prevent a Certificate of Occupancy today."

"Oh, so you know a guy..."

"Of course." Kaz always knew a guy. He was more connected than Kevin Bacon. Somehow, the top family attorney in South Jersey had ties with any- and everyone you could ever want to do business with—successfully do business with. Dee pulled her phone from her back pocket and texted the movers. She'd meet them at one o'clock, for sure. And maybe she'd be able to take a quick nap before they got there.

The inspector made short work of the inside. "There's an upstairs?" he asked Kaz.

"I know it looks like there should be a closet here," Dee opened a door just inside the front entry to show him the stairs. "But this will take you up to an apartment. There's a rear door up there that you can take for the stairs behind the building. I left the garage open if you need to go in there."

He nodded and headed up the front steps.

"A man of few words." She shut the door.

"Sometimes I prefer them over men who talk too much." Kaz stood and paced slowly with his hands in his pockets. "Speaking of which, I heard your cousin was quite the rambling mess yesterday."

"Brett?"

"Yeah."

"Who'd you hear that from?" Dee took his place in the window seat and peeked in the bag. Of course, he'd brought one of her favorite powder-sugar-coated cream-filled donuts.

"Evan." Kaz said the name while he walked around the empty room, eyeing up the air, as if this were a normal conversation.

Which it wasn't.

She took a bite of her donut, chewed slowly, then had a long sip of coffee. Josie and her grandmother were born and raised in Philly, just on the other side of the river. Gram had moved away, Dee thought it was after she'd met and married Granddad. That was all a little hazy as she'd never really thought to ask why who lived where. It never seemed to matter. Josie still lived in Philly, as did Evan. But Mom and Kaz had nothing to do with them—at least nothing that she was aware of. Josie and Evan were relics of Dee's, leftovers from her father's family.

It was only after Dee became an adult and finally moved out of the parental home in her mid-twenties that she ventured across the Ben Franklin Bridge to meet with Josie and Evan and his family— at the request of her grandmother. It was an awkward family meal, Josie's eighty-fifth birthday. But over the years, she'd visited several times and developed a connection with Josie and, to some extent, with Evan and his wife Hope, but not much with their sons, who were her age. She only told Mom about that first visit, and regretted it so much that she never brought them up to her again.

"I didn't realize you knew him." Dee tried to sound as casual as Kaz.

"I thought you knew I know everyone." He stopped walking and stared at where the ceiling met the wall. Dee wanted to hand him a clipboard, but none were handy.

"In South Jersey. Didn't realize your connections went into Philly." She sat up straight. "Yikes! Is he and Hope getting divorced?"

"Nah, he just wanted to chit-chat."

"About?" Dee wiped powdered sugar from her Ramones T-shirt, amazed once again she'd found such a treasure at a thrift shop.

"Just, you know, normal conversation."

Her head snapped back to look at Kaz as she remembered what they were talking about. Why wasn't he looking at her? Why would he and Evan have a "normal conversation" when they never spoke to each other? What the hell was a normal conversation, anyway?

"Is Aunt Josie OK? She did look kind of frail."

"Yeah, yeah." Kaz approached her, stopped, and looked over her head through the window. "So, he mentioned Brett had a few too many drinks."

"Yeah. He's hurting. Gram was his rock. Aside from me, she was the only one in the family who appreciated him."

"Maybe there's a reason for that." Kaz continued looking outside. Dee twisted around to see what was so interesting—looked like a typical summer day. People walked by on the sidewalk; cars slowly drove down Main Street.

"The reason is," she faced Kaz, "they're all a bunch of uptight, repressed assholes. You should see the table he created. Granddad actually commissioned it. I was surprised. I thought Gram was the only one who appreciated his work. The others all think he's—*we*—are wasting our time and everyone's money trying to be artists."

"Is that what you spoke about?" Kaz finally met her eyes.

"What do you mean?"

"You spoke to him about the table?"

"Why do I feel like I'm on a witness stand?" Dee laughed. "He waited for me on the porch because he didn't want to be outside, alone, with our shrew fucking aunts and that mother of his. Our other cousins are a bunch of kowtowing—

"Repressed assholes. Got it." Kaz grinned and nodded.

"Excuse me." The inspector made Dee jump in her seat. Kaz simply turned around to look at him standing near the back of the room. "I'm done. Everything looks good."

"Great! So she can move in today?" Kaz asked.

"She can." The inspector ripped a page from his clipboard. Dee stood to receive it, but he handed it to Kaz. Ordinarily, her hackles would have raised at that—ignoring the woman in the room who was actually in charge of the place—but that paper probably needed to be handled by Kaz as part of ensuring she got the Certificate of Occupancy today. "One thing: those back steps need some tread. If they get wet, someone could easily slip and fall. I suggest you get that taken care of right away."

"Will do." Dee almost saluted him but caught herself before smashing cream filling and powdered sugar into her forehead.

"I'm serious, kid. I'm so proud of you." Kaz folded the paper and slid it into a pocket after the man left. "Your mom and I both are."

"Thanks. But you know I wouldn't be here without you."

"We'll always have your back." He put an arm around her shoulder and pulled her into a sideways hug. "Just, please, call your mother and ask her to help you unpack and get settled."

"Her body will end up in the river, Kaz."

"You don't have to do it at the beginning. Maybe call her when you're almost done. Just save something, anything, for her to do, will ya? Let her feel needed."

"All right. But if she makes me crazy, I'll hose down those steps before shoving her out the back door."

"I'd expect nothing less." He gave her a final squeeze and let go. "And it might be a good idea if you stay away from your father's family for a while."

"I intend to." She finished her donut and wiped her hand on her jeans.

"Good. Give yourself a chance to grieve your grandmother without their interference."

"There's no 'their' there. Brett's the only one I'll probably ever talk to again."

"Yeah, well, he probably needs a chance to grieve her, too. Maybe give him some space to get over her death."

Brett wasn't getting over Gram's death anytime soon. Dee loved that woman with all her heart, but Brett idolized her and relied on her to keep him sane in that family. He needed Dee to help him get over Gram's death. Dee was all he had left. He was such a mess yesterday. Would he ever be OK again?

"Hey, Kaz." Dee wasn't sure about bringing this up, but Brett's comment still needled her. Was probably why she couldn't shake her father yesterday.

"Yeah?"

"So, like, Brett did say something kind of weird."

"What?" Kaz gathered the trash from the window ledge.

"That I should ask Mom about who killed my father. Any idea what that might mean?"

Briefly, so briefly that Dee wasn't sure what she saw, Kaz stopped moving. Then he half turned away from her and finished putting the cups and napkins into the bag with more attention to detail than she thought necessary. "Yeah. That is weird." He stood tall and faced her. "Probably just the alcohol talking bullshit. Evan said he was loaded. You should forget about it."

"Yeah." But she'd seen Brett drunk numerous times, and he'd never gotten that dark.

A puzzle piece was missing from the full picture. Kaz and Evan "chit-chatting"? She didn't think that had ever happened before in her life. Granted, they could have, and she never knew. But who called whom? And when?

"...so we'll see you Sunday?" Kaz seemed to be finishing a paragraph.

"What?" She struggled to get back into the moment.

"Sunday, Father's Day? The annual day when the females I love most gather around to make fun of me while I barbecue them dinner?"

"Of course!" She pulled her phone out of her back pocket and checked the calendar. "Yes, it's on my calendar, and there's a notification the night before to remind me to set my clock, so I don't sleep in."

"Perfect!" He kissed her cheek. "I love you, kid."

"Love you, too." Dee followed him out the door, patting her jeans pockets for her car key fob. A few minutes later, she found it in the center console of her car, parked nearby. Good thing it was a safe neighborhood.

She plugged her phone in to charge while she drove and realized she'd forgotten to ask Kaz whether she owned the bench. She started scrolling to his name to text him, but her eyes landed on Brett's name. Kaz was wrong. She shouldn't leave him alone. Couldn't. Her aunts' behavior, Brett's cryptic gibberish, and Evan calling Kaz were all too far out of normal. Something was going on.

And Brett seemed to be the only one she could count on to tell her.

Had someone killed her father? She was pretty sure she'd been told he died in a boating accident on Granddad's lake. Why would anyone lie to her about that?

She tapped on his name and typed.

Dude! Call me!

Saturday, June 19

Maxine

The front door was unlocked. Maxine entered, carrying three coffee cups in a cardboard drink holder, and roamed the entire empty downstairs of her future workspace. Where was Dee?

Maybe she unlocked the store door for Max, then went back to sleep. Should she go up?

Maxine couldn't remember knocking on any door where Dee ever lived. She simply walked in. But it wasn't quite eight o'clock in the morning, and she knew Dee had frequent early morning booty calls with a mystery man.

Could she have let him in and forgotten to re-lock the front door while they christened her new place together? That was absolutely possible. And that would absolutely be awkward if Max flung the bedroom door open and found them. It would be absolutely funny, too, and she'd finally learn who he was.

Maxine climbed the stairs, not quite on tiptoe, but almost. Dee hadn't been in a real relationship for probably close to a decade now. In fact, she had sworn off relationships because they never ended well. Yet, she'd been with this same man for a year. Always saying he was just there for sex with no strings attached. But how could they keep sleeping together for this long without developing feelings?

Not that feelings were anything to brag about these days. Since

Thursday, she and Dane had barely exchanged more than a sentence despite all the feelings she'd been experiencing. He was still processing, was all he'd said, and asked for the space to do so.

Of course, she understood and gave it to him. And once again, she told herself his hesitancy would blow over. He'd eventually be happy with her decision to leave the school. But despite repeatedly telling herself that, she couldn't believe it. This decision felt like another wedge between them. A big one.

Not that he would talk to her about it or anything.

At the top of the stairs, she entered directly into Dee's living room. A half-dozen or so large boxes, all open, were scattered about with contents strewn as if by random. She went around the long bar that separated the kitchen area and found a similar situation, with pots, pans, and cooking utensils dumped haphazardly everywhere. *Girlfriend is having a tough time.*

"Dee?" Maxine hollered.

Rumpling came from the room behind the kitchen. Soon, Dee appeared in a doorway with her mass of wild pink and blond hair piled in a messy wad on top of her head. She wore a much-too-large Linkin Park T-shirt with the sleeves ripped off over paint-splattered leggings. An electric-blue athletic bra brazenly exposed itself through the armholes. She was barefoot and, if Max didn't know better, appeared to be strung out from drugs and no sleep. If Max painted her at that moment, Dee would be a jumbled bundle of violet, blue, and white with misfired static charges of light surrounding her body.

"Look what I brought." Max held the cardboard drink holder like a waitress a serving tray. "Coffee from Jhansi's Java across the street." She set the tray on the bar.

"Oh my God!" Dee stumbled through the room, threw her arms around Max, and squeezed tight. "You're my soul mate!"

"Good to know. Is this place big enough for two?" Maxine meant the words to sound light, like a joke. But they must have landed differently.

"Are you OK?" Dee pulled back and looked her in the eyes.

"I'm fine. Just..." Just what? She puffed her cheeks and blew out a loud sigh. "Having a moment with Dane. I don't wanna talk about it. It may be nothing." She picked up a cup of coffee. "Here."

"Is he pissed you're quitting a job with benefits and security to risk your financial future stability by going into business with me?" Dee lifted the lid of her coffee cup and took a long sip. "I mean, he's the most sensible man on the planet. I could see that making him a little unsettled." Another very long drink.

"I would prefer pissed." Maxine sat on a barstool at the counter. "Instead, he just kind of...dropped it. He was all against it, then simply told me to 'go make art.' And didn't mention it again."

"Is that a bad thing?" Dee leaned against the backside of a hideous wingback chair neither had been able to figure out how to transform into something attractive, and downed the remaining coffee in her cup. Max could picture the electric sparks of Dee's body making the right connections, soothing the frenetic energy into a lava-lamp morphing of blue, red, purple, and violet.

"I don't know. I'm sure he doesn't like it, which...whatever. That's fine. I don't need his permission, you know?" She nodded toward the last cup in the holder. Dee returned to the kitchen to get it. "But I'd like to know he's OK with it. I'd like his blessing or something." She finally took a tentative sip of her coffee. "Anyway, I don't want to talk about it right now. It only makes me suspect he's angry when...I mean it's Dane. You know how he is. He's just processing it in his own way. He has his life so well organized and mapped out; it takes him time to deal with change." She glanced around to survey the damage Dee had inflicted on her new home. "So, how'd you do last night?"

"Well, considering it's me, and I was solo, I think I did OK. At first, I just started ripping open boxes to see what was inside. But then, it got really confusing. There was too much shit, and I couldn't figure out what to do with any of it. Like, I got really scattered. It was bad for a few minutes. So, be proud of me, I did that fucking breathing exercise and staved off a panic attack. When I calmed down, I realized I should go in order of what I'd need. At that moment, I needed to pee, which meant find toilet paper. So, I unpacked one box at a time in the bathroom first. Thank fucking Christ I packed toilet paper." She joined Maxine in the living area. "Then I got hungry, so I ordered a pizza from Vito's down the street. I walked over, picked it up, and stopped in the place next door to get a bottle of wine with a screw-top cap."

"That was clever thinking." Giggles bubbled up in Maxine. God, how she loved Dee. "You didn't have to worry about finding a glass or corkscrew."

"Exactly! Anyway, that's pretty much it. I did my bathroom last night and some of my bedroom. Granted, you could have done the entire apartment in the same amount of time, but you know, that was good for me. I actually went to bed happy as fuck, thinking *damn, I'm doing great.* But then..." Dee returned to the kitchen, opened the refrigerator. "This happened."

Nothing was inside the fridge. "What?"

"I have no food, which means no coffee. I kind of panicked, started ripping boxes and shit open again. I can't find any food. Which is OK. But I need my coffee, Max." As if to prove her point, Dee finished off her second cup. Maxine still had three-quarters of her first.

"I know you do, hon." Dee relied on a delicate, and probably unhealthy, balance of perpetual caffeination to keep her ADHD almost in check. Max knew Dee wasn't joking when she said "panicked"—she'd seen her friend have full-blown panic attacks when her mind just couldn't organize. Sometimes caffeine helped with the organization. But just a little too much, and it made things worse, which is often when Dee would pour a glass of wine, or just drink it from the bottle, regardless of the time of day, because she said it slowed her thoughts down. Maxine had been tempted to ask if she could help pack *and* unpack, but it had meant something to Dee to do as much as she could by herself.

"So, thank you!" Dee blew a kiss over the bar. "But, I'm done pretending I'm this I-can-do-it-all woman. At least for today."

"Well, it really shouldn't take long. We can run over to your old place and get whatever's left later today."

"Do you think we can go now?"

"I suppose. Why?"

"Apparently, Mom's having a breakdown because I'm not letting her help. Hayleigh's bringing her over this afternoon, when hopefully there's little left to do, so she won't need to stay long. If she sees I forgot food—"

"Gotcha. Let's go now." If Lauren saw Dee had no food in the cupboards, that would make *her* panic, and things could get ugly— though funny. Lauren was always good comedic fodder when she panicked over thinking her Dee Dee was having a hardship.

"What's with the grin? You picturing Mom showing up every morning with armfuls of unnecessary groceries?"

Max nodded. "Sneaking in while you're working to stock the fridge and pantry."

"Subscribing me to every meal delivery service possible so I'd get breakfast, lunch, dinner, and snacks dropped on my doorstep in a perpetual rotation."

"You'd be able to open your own food pantry for the homeless."

"C'mon, I'll drive." Dee looked around the kitchen, disappeared into what Maxine presumed was the bedroom, came out a few minutes later. "Huh…shit! I've no idea where my keys might be."

"I'll drive. But, what about shoes?"

"Oh yeah...I had some flipflops on last night when I went out..." she continued talking as she disappeared into the bedroom again. Maxine wandered around the space. The living room was very large and bright. Dee would be able to create in there with ease during the day. On the other side of the kitchen, a door opposite the one Dee had disappeared into led to a laundry room and some storage. A door at the end of it opened onto a landing and a set of stairs that ran down to the side street. She stepped out and could see Dee's car, where her keys probably were, parked in the driveway in front of the garage. If all went well, by this time next year, the detached garage would be converted into a hot shop for glass blowing, and Dee wouldn't have to rent time at another one. When they'd planned this scheme, Maxine had been amused and excited; returning to the kitchen, she realized that the amusement had been replaced by anxious hope. She needed this thing to work out.

"Have shoes, will travel!" Dee announced. She led the way down the front stairs into the shop.

"I guess this means we can't lock the front door, either." Maxine realized she should make sure she got the spare set of keys from Dee today, wherever they were.

"Oh...hell. Good thing the downstairs is obviously empty. There's nothing to steal. Shit! I spent the night with all the doors unlocked. God, my mother would have a fucking breakdown."

"We'll find them today—just act like it's no big deal if she's here when we do."

Inside Max's car, Dee held up her phone. "Do you mind if I charge this while we drive? I kind of can't find a charger, either."

Dee

Maxine was the best! Max was always the best. If Dee had asked Max to help her pack, she would have. But she hated being needy. All probably would have gone OK if the fucking neighbors from upstairs at the old place hadn't complained about her loud music as she was boxing everything up. What a bonus not having complaining neighbors would be—Kaz had nosed around and discovered the high-end hardware store next door used their upstairs only for storage. Though in all fairness, her old neighbors would probably find it a bonus if whoever replaced her didn't blast music whenever they needed to concentrate.

Her phone dinged with a text as Max pulled into the space in front of her new building when they returned.

Monday morning too soon?

Max must have read something on her face. "Is that booty call?" she gripped Dee's arm.

Dee wriggled free. No need for Max to read over her shoulder. "So, my place will be ready for his company by Monday morning, right?"

"I'm only answering that if you tell me his name."

Monday morning is perfect

"If I name him, then I have to keep him. Besides, it doesn't matter. It's not like he'll be showing up for Thanksgiving dinner."

"You've been sleeping with the guy for over a year. Why not have him come for turkey? Your mom would be delighted."

Dee reached for the door handle and heard a click. "Did you just lock me in?"

"Do you have feelings for him?"

"What?" But, oh! That was a good question. She liked him. She enjoyed his company. Were those feelings?

"Do you even talk?" Maxine's interrogation continued. "Or does he just show up at five in the morning, you bang like wild rabbits, and he leaves?"

"No. Sometimes he comes over at the end of his workday, too, for a 'coffee break.'" Dee smirked. Max showed no emotion. She was tough sometimes. "OK, so, yeah. We talk." She chewed her lip and thought about the situation. "We actually talk a lot."

"And?"

"And, what?"

"You talk and have sex?"

"I mean, yeah, and stuff."

"Stuff? Like what?"

Dee shrugged. Nothing immediately came to mind.

"Tell me about him," Maxine demanded.

"Like, what?"

"Name, age, how'd you meet, that kind of stuff."

"I'm not giving up the name. He's thirty-eight, just had a birthday a few months ago."

"How'd you meet?

"Kaz."

"Your dad introduced you to your booty call?"

"Not for that reason!" Dee giggled, glad to see Max's face relax into a smile. "He wanted to commission someone to paint his logo. Kaz referred him to me."

"What's the name of the company?"

"You're not that sly, you know."

"Can't blame a girl for trying."

"Yeah, well, here's a bone. The logo is based off his tattoo. It's a griffin. The tattoo is freaking awesome—huge, three-D kind of. The face looks out from his arm, and the wings and body morph around his chest and back."

"Sounds intense."

"It is. It's in honor of this guy, a friend of his, who was killed when they were in the military together. His friend kind of saved his life but died while doing it. So he honored him with the tattoo and wanted a mural of the griffin for his business."

"I see."

"So...well, Kaz had him connect with me to see if I wanted the gig. We met. The chemistry was almost instant. Neither of us wanted a relationship, but, well, a girl needs sex, you know."

"And apparently a guy does, too. But is that all there is?"

"Yes, why?"

"Dee, it's been over a year…There was something on your face. You seemed very happy to get a message from him."

"I like sex."

"Again, it's been over a year—"

"FUCK!" Mom waved at them through the front windshield. She held a plant in one hand. Did she bring a god-damned plant for Dee to kill?

"Hi, Lauren." Max, the ultimate wingwoman, was already stepping out of the car. "We just finished getting the last of Dee's food."

Dee stomped each step as she carried a box up the stairs. *Where the hell was Hayleigh?* She set the box down on a kitchen counter, pulled her cell from her back pocket, and texted her kid sister. Half-sister, to be exact. And if she kept this shit up, Dee wouldn't even claim the half part.

Mom's here!

*Wha? Shit! Sry! Told her I'd
get her at 3! Be there as fast
as I can*

"Where shall I put this, sweetheart?"

Dee fumbled her phone. Mom was like a cat—silently stalking in and out of rooms, scaring the shit out of people.

"Well…" Good god! Where the hell do you put plants?

"Does it need much light?" Max lifted the plant out of Mom's hands.

"Medium light and medium water." Mom followed Max around

the living room. "The man at the store said it would be hard to kill."

"I'm gifted at that." Dee hollered.

"I thought it would add some life to your new place." Mom beamed at her over the bar. "In case after work you come home and feel a little lonely, there would be something you could take care of and make you feel, well, better."

"I never feel lonely, Mom." Dee turned away to focus on her box. She half-hoped Mom didn't hear her. It would break Mom's heart not to feel needed, but at the same time, she wasn't needed.

"So!"

Jesus Christ! Dee jumped. Mom was beside her again in the kitchen.

"What can I do for you?"

"I think the most important thing in your apartment, Dee, is the whiteboard." Max seemed to have a plan. "Lauren, I just found a glass jar with nails and wall anchors in it. Will you help me hang the whiteboard, then you can organize all the art supplies under it."

"Yes!" Dee spun her mother around. "She's right. The whiteboard contains the contents of my mind."

"That *is* important. I'm on it!" Amused at the sight, Dee watched Mom get to work. Her glamor-girl, shoulder-length, cinnamon-brown hair with the big wave that somehow always made a perfect gentle zig-zag, swayed as if it weren't loaded with hairspray. She wore a pink satin wrap top with a big sash tied on the side—probably something of her own design that Max's mom, Mama Kat, patterned so she could make. At least she wore pants today, black slim-cut capris, not a skirt. It wasn't quite a manual-labor kind of outfit, but probably the closest Mom could get.

Dee returned outside to get another box of food. The art supplies should keep Mom busy all day, and she'd feel important because the whiteboard really did contain the contents of Dee's mind. The giant dry-erase board—the largest she could find—would take up most of a wall in her living room. It's where she left notes and drew images of things she wanted to remember. She lost her phone too frequently, and while there were a million notepads floating around her world, those came and went on a regular basis. The whiteboard, secured to the wall, was always there.

H arrived looking like she'd just rolled out of bed. She wore tropical-print pajama shorts and a tank top; her mass of turquoise curls, secured with a scrunchy, splayed out from the top of her head like a pompom, cheering them on as they unpacked. Soon, with the four of them and a head somewhat clear thanks to the gods of caffeine, Dee realized they were almost done; there really wasn't much to do. She didn't own a lot of shit—it was hard to keep track of a lot of shit, so she tried to collect the least amount possible in her life. The kitchen seemed to need the most attention, which was weird, because Dee didn't think she cooked that much.

"Dee Dee?" Mom was in the living room, holding her funeral shoes. "What happened?"

"Ha! Funny story." Dee went around the bar, pleased to see how nicely things had taken shape. H was chilling on the sofa. Max was organizing things on a bookshelf. Lots of flattened boxes leaned against the wall near the door to the laundry room. "The light bulb over my closet burned out in the old apartment. It literally popped when I turned it on last week. I was running late, and it was dark in there. I grabbed two different shoes and didn't notice until I took them off at the airport."

"The airport?" Mom's eyes bugged out. "You wore these to the funeral?"

"Yeah. I bought a Sharpie at a store in the terminal and tried to make the brown one look black." She ignored the snickers coming from H and Max.

"Well, I'll buy you replacement pairs. You can throw these away." Mom handed them to her.

Dee placed them on a chest set below the whiteboard. "Actually, I'm going to cover them with gesso and paint a scene on them. If it works, I'll take their partners and create some kind of class."

"Dee! That's a great idea!" Hayleigh jumped up. At the whiteboard, she used one of the dry-erase markers Mom had lined up on the ledge in ROYGBIV order to write *Shoe Art*. "Like, maybe..." She looked at Dee, mouth twisted to one side. "What?"

"I haven't really thought it through, yet. But maybe people could collage, glue on beads, or whatever. They could do it for a theme or something. Like, shoes can represent our life journeys, you know? Max! What do you think?"

"I think...a couple things." Max sat cross-legged on the floor like a graceful yoga goddess. "One, we all have those shoes we wore one time as a bridesmaid, or even a bride."

"Yes, one day, my sweet Dee, your prince will come, and your princess, too, Hayleigh," Mom alternated shining optimistic smiles at both her girls, who simultaneously rolled their eyes. "Your shoes will be beautiful!"

"And then we never wear them again." Max gave Mom an apologetic shrug. "That could be a fun after-the-honeymoon girls' night out, or even a year later when the bride and groom celebrate their anniversary: everyone could come paint their wedding shoes or collage them with memories of their friendship."

"I like it!" Hayleigh wrote *special occasions* on the whiteboard.

"Another idea," Max added, "isn't necessarily about a life journey, but maybe we could supply basic white sneakers or some kind of slip-on, and people could paint them with team colors and symbols to wear to games."

H wrote tailgating.

"What are you going to do with yours, Dee Dee?" Mom wanted to know.

Dee pointed to the shoes and tree she had drawn on the whiteboard. "I'm going to paint Gram's willow tree, half on each shoe. Then, I'm not sure how, but I wanna join them together. I'm thinking of maybe some glass flowers pouring out of the heels. I'm still not sure about that. The tree is definite, though. The willow tree by the lake is where they put Gram's ashes."

Mom's mouth formed a straight line. She turned around and shuffled the supplies that she'd already organized. "I'll still buy you replacement pairs."

"I can afford to buy my own shoes, Mom," Dee returned to the kitchen. *Shit!* She just started a battle.

"I know you can. I'm not buying them because you can't. I'm buying them because I want to." Mom's voice was a full octave higher than usual.

"Thank you, Mom. I appreciate it." *Let it go. Let it go. Let it go.*

"And if you don't like them, let me know. I'll return them." Even higher-pitched and a little shaky.

"I always like what you buy me, Mom." *Let's drop the subject, please.* Done with the food, Dee opened a final box labeled *kitchen.*

"Do you really think it's healthy to paint that on your shoes?" Mom screeched.

"I do."

"Why not something happy?" She literally squeaked.

"That is a happy scene, Mom."

"You JUST SAID HER ASHES ARE THERE!" When Dee peeled herself off the ceiling, she noticed Mom was in the kitchen, hands pressing against her temples.

Max and H had run in behind her.

"Mom, it's OK. I'm painting a tribute to a woman I love. I'll do the same for you one day, I'm sure."

"How do you know this isn't unhealthy grief?"

"I'll ask my shrink." Dee pulled out the wooden box that housed her kitchen knives.

"Oh, honey, put that down right now! You might hurt yourself!"

"Hayleigh!"

"Mom, let's go." H tried to pull Mom backward out of the kitchen. "I think Dee's about done."

"I'm sorry, Dee." Mom smoothed back her hair. "I am. I know you're not helpless or…or as fragile as, maybe sometimes I act like you are. You've just been through so much—"

"And I'm doing OK."

"You are, sweetheart. You're doing better than OK." Mom's smile looked as happy as a store mannequin's. "You know how I am. Every time you go South, I go on edge, not sure how you'll be when you come back. I can't stand how mean those people are down there."

"I know."

"Just look at what that Brett said! Kaz told me all about it. Why would he be so mean to suggest such a thing?"

"He was drinking heavily." *Interesting!* Kaz had blamed Brett's comment on the booze and told Dee to forget about it, yet he told Mom? "He was self-medicating to get through the day. I'm sure he doesn't even remember what he said."

"I should hope not." Mom tugged on her sash, fumbled with her neckline. "I never liked that boy."

Boy? Brett was older than Dee by a couple of years, but she let it drop. Mom breathed deeply and slowly, a little too worked up if you asked Dee. Granted, Mom was always over-protective, but this was a bit much, even for her.

Mom maintained her manufactured smile as she looked around the kitchen, then she returned to the living room. "Your place looks beautiful. But I think we should go furniture shopping. Maybe get you a new sofa, You've had that one since you moved out of our house, and Kaz and I had had it for years by then. And that chair! It's atrocious!" She approached the whiteboard, picked up a marker, and began writing. "It needs to go."

Dee remained standing before an open box, silent. She went with the booze line to appease Mom. But couldn't quite believe the bourbon was behind Brett's suggestion that her father had been murdered. She'd been drunk with Brett numerous times, and he'd never even hinted at such a thing. Now, Mom's voice was too… something—too tight, too forced.

"And that dinette table is much too small for the space," Mom continued. "Let's make a date to have lunch in Philly soon and check out the furniture stores. You'll have a much better selection there than here."

Mom replaced the marker's cap and deliberately set it on the ledge. Her shoulders, her whole upper body, seemed to fill with air then partially deflate before she turned toward Dee again. Her burgundy fingernails made a sharp contrast to her eggshell white skin as she scratched her neck.

"Sounds like fun," Dee placated. She needed to give herself time to make sense of Mom's behavior. "I was just thinking I needed new stuff." Something was off. And it seemed like it had to do with what Brett had said.

Once again, Dee wondered if maybe she hadn't been told the truth about her father's death. But what would be the point of that? Why would anyone lie?

To keep a secret.

Didn't her aunts talk about secrets?

Sunday, June 20

Genevieve

"That's Remy." Genevieve tapped *have a safe flight, love you* on her phone. "They're taking off soon. My weekend of solitude will end in about three hours."

"You'll be glad to see them." Brynn tied an apple-green ribbon around a burlap bag.

"I'll be glad to see Remy." Genevieve took the bag from her little sister and tossed it on the pile of others in a rustic wooden crate. "That's the last one. Wonderful! We finished all the wedding favors right on schedule."

"Of course! Because you're awesome!" Brynn stood to give her a hug.

Genevieve found no words to reply. Tears blurred her vision. She pulled away and tried to find something else to busy herself with.

"Are you OK?"

Of course, she was OK. She was always OK. But she was beginning to understand that OK was not the same as happy. She wiped her eyes and tried to organize the burlap bags. "Brynn..." The name felt thick. Was something stuck in her throat? Felt like a lump was there again.

"Yes?" her sister touched her arm.

The wine stopper and corkscrew sets inside the burlap bags were too bulky, they refused to allow Genevieve to make neat rows. She gave up, fell back into her chair, and deliberately swallowed. She should probably go see a doctor about that lump. It was the last thing she wanted to do, but there was an almost constant feeling of something in her throat. Sometimes it was barely there, but at others, like now, it felt like a golf ball was lodged in her esophagus.

"Gen, you're scaring me." Brynn's forehead creased. Genevieve wanted to smooth it, but she was too depleted. "Is something wrong with you?"

"Yes, no! I mean, physically, I'm fine." Maybe. Unless that lump means thyroid cancer.

"Then what is it?"

"I realized something after Lola died." She pressed her fingers to her throat and swallowed. "I couldn't quite figure it out at first, but, having this entire weekend alone in this big house with no one demanding anything of me, no one I felt obligated to take care of, well, it gave me a lot of time to think."

"About?" Brynn sat and handed Gen's wine glass to her.

"Look around." Genevieve circled her glass in the air. "Look how beautiful this house is. I drive a Mercedes. I own several expensive purses and wear designer shoes. My kids want for nothing. I even have a 'pool boy.'" She allowed herself a smirk. When Brynn was a teenager and Genevieve a much-too-young mother, they daydreamed about one day being wealthy housewives with pool boys. It never occurred to either of them that a fifty-something, overweight, scruffy man with an obnoxious barking laugh he often used over nothing funny would show up every week to check the chemicals. She took a tiny sip. Thank God the wine went down with ease. "I should be happy. I should be relishing every moment."

"But clearly you're not."

"I'm thirty-seven years old, Brynn. For as long as I can remember, I've been taking care of people I love. Correction. I've been taking care of people in my family, most of whom are people I love." The lump seemed to grow. "I'm running out of people now. Olivia is going to college this fall. Remy will have his license within a week."

"It's time you focused on you! I get it!" Brynn tapped her glass against Genevieve's.

"It is." She nodded. "And I think it also means it's time to get a divorce."

"What?" Brynn shot upright so fast she almost spilled her wine. "You can't."

"I can. Actually, I think I must."

"What? Why?"

"Because..." she thought she hated her husband, couldn't be said out loud. Gen needed a prop. "Let's go sit by the pool. Take our glasses. I'll meet you there in a sec."

In her office, Genevieve picked up her laptop. It felt too heavy. Or she felt too weak, she wasn't sure which, as she leaned against her desk and willed more tears away.

She didn't have time to have a breakdown. Brynn needed her. Her wedding was six days away. Gen could do six more days of smiles, of reassurances that all was well, that she was strong and confident, and...inhale...that she was fine. Yes, everything was fine. Some changes are needed, that's all. She could manage it. That's what she did best: she managed.

Her life had been a series of responsibilities that she'd managed ever since her mother showed her how to change Brynn's diaper when she was just six years old. So, when she watched a pink line form on a plastic stick Labor Day weekend of what was supposed to be a gap year before college, she knew what to do. She was prepared to step into the mother-manager role in lieu of going to college. She became a wife and mom, and she managed the care of Olivia. A few years later, she managed Remy, primarily by herself, while her handsome Air Force pilot, as she used to describe him to everyone, was off saving the world. Soon, she managed on her own while he became a private pilot, and then somehow even more on her own while he built his charter company. Equally, she'd taken care of their tiny base house, then their small first home, then, when he turned his one-man show into a successful business, their large suburban house.

She'd driven kids around, ensured school supplies, clothing, and personal care products were always stocked, and she'd done more laundry than what she felt a family of four could create. In between, she'd planned birthday parties, researched pediatricians, summer camps, dance lessons, and tutors, and was on every PTA and booster board that came her way. She kept the house clean, the dog walked, and everyone well fed. And managed it all with efficiency, grace, even, if you asked her.

She was a manager. And she could manage this last week until Brynn got married.

With that, she pulled herself upright and took the laptop out to the patio, where she settled into a lounge chair next to her baby sister.

"This is everyone's schedule." She was pleased by how calm, how confident her voice sounded. She hit a few strokes on the keyboard and tilted the monitor so both could see her spreadsheet. "It tells me who is where, who is home, and when. The yellow cells are when Chris and I are both home at the same time, and at least one of the kids are here. The red cells are when it's just the two of us."

"So..." Brynn studied the spreadsheet, "this week, you'll both be here alone Tuesday from five-thirty to seven?"

"Right, which means I have to figure out what to do with myself so I'm not in the same room with him. If you look in this tab," Genevieve avoided looking at her sister as she clicked to the next spreadsheet, "you'll see a list of errands or projects I can do. Your wedding has been very helpful, lately. So Tuesday, I'll run around getting items for the bathroom baskets. I'll leave at five and stay out until I need to pick Remy up from his coding club. I'll do a pulled pork in the crock pot that morning, and baked potatoes will be kept in the warming drawer, so dinner will be self-serve for everyone."

"This is..." Brynn tucked her straight, caramel-brown hair behind an ear. "I don't know what this is."

"This is how I live my life. In perpetual motion, so I'm never alone with my husband."

"But, but why?" Brynn took the laptop and moved her head closer to it.

"We can't stand to be around each other. At least I can't stand to be around him."

"Gen," Brynn clapped the laptop shut. "This is no way to, to, to—"

"To live. Right."

"So…you're going to…?"

"Get a divorce." It sounded so easy, so natural, so...right.

"You can't just give up on your marriage! What about counseling?"

"We're beyond that."

"How is that possible?

Genevieve leaned back in her chair and sipped her wine. "Brynn, I don't love him anymore. I'm not sure I ever did—we were so young when we got married, and we only did it because it was 'the right thing to do.' Yes, he kept his word and took care of the kids and me. But there's no love between us at all—I'm not sure if it ever was there to begin with. Instead, we argue about the stupidest stuff." Another sip, then Genevieve touched her sister's arm. "Like, since we've been together, dinner has been on the table by six-thirty on the dot every night."

"For as long as I can remember, dinner has been on the table by six-thirty on the dot every night."

"Those who don't cook, don't get to complain about the chef's schedule."

"As I've been told." Brynn took a long drink.

Genevieve paused. *Was it really too much to ask people to be aware of a schedule?* "Everyone knows all they have to do is tell me when they won't be eating at home, or if they'll be late."

"Again, I know the rules."

"So last week, Wednesday, I think, Livvy let me know she would be at a friend's. Remy was home. I didn't hear from Chris, so I made three servings of grouper almondine with garlic-mashed potatoes and roasted green beans."

"Wish you had invited me over."

"If I had then nothing would have gone to waste. Chris strolled in as Remy and I were finishing up. I'd put his dish in the warming drawer. He said, 'hello,' then headed upstairs to change. He came down dressed in shorts and a T-shirt and said he was going to work out. I mentioned his dinner in the drawer. He said he wasn't hungry and left. When he came home, it was close to nine-thirty! I told him I didn't appreciate him wasting my time and energy on his meal. He told me to quit cooking for him. Then I don't know what happened. Somehow, we started yelling at each other. He complained about me being judgmental and controlling and…" Genevieve finished her wine. "Well, it didn't really end. He said he had to make a call and disappeared into the guest room. We haven't spoken since. I hate living like this. And he must, too. I mean, think about this: my game of household Tetris has been going on for a couple of years. It started before the accident. After the accident, he moved into the guest room when I came home from the hospital with that awful cast that went all the way up to my hip. He never moved back in."

"What? Is this a…are you old enough for menopause? Is he having a midlife crisis?"

"We're both too young for that. As I said, this has been going on for a couple of years. I think the car accident and all those surgeries and stuff I needed just made it easier for both of us to not think about being a couple. He took over all the driving that Livvy couldn't do. I'd give him grocery lists, and he was almost always out of the house. But again, think about what I just told you. We are *never* in the same bed. Now, ask yourself, why is he OK with *that* situation?"

Brynn just stared at her.

"I think he's just as miserable as I am and doing everything *he* can to stay busy so he doesn't have to be around *me*." Genevieve took her computer back, closed it, and set it on the end of her lounge chair. "Before the accident, he started seeing a trainer three days a week before work, so he got up earlier, which meant he went to bed earlier. So, really, we haven't had 'bedroom time' for a long long time. And, since I've been mobile again, he's been taking on more clients than his pilots can serve, so he's been flying more."

"Do you..." Brynn turned her face to Genevieve. At thirty-three, she still somehow looked like a teenage tomboy: a smattering of freckles across her makeup-less face, almond eyes, shoulder-length limp, fine hair she never bothered to style. "I hate to ask this, but, do you, you know. Do you think there's another woman?"

"I don't know. But you know what?" Genevieve leaned back into her chair again. She found it interesting how relaxed she suddenly felt. As if finally acknowledging a truth out loud had been therapeutic. "If there is another woman, and that's why he hasn't wanted sex for...God! A long time! Then I guess I owe her a thank you."

"Gen!" Brynn stared at her, mouth wide open. "Jeesh. I don't know what to say."

"There's nothing anyone can say. But," Genevieve sat upright and turned to her sister again. "Actually, please let it drop for now. Let's get you married next weekend. I don't want to give anyone something else to talk about before your big day. You get married, then I'll talk to Chriss about a divorce while you're on your honeymoon." She finished her wine. Yes, that felt right.

Monday, June 21

Dee

That…was just…cruel.

Dee ripped open the bathroom door. Cooper, still naked, sitting on her bed, jerked his head up from his phone.

"You fucking ass-hat!" Like a wrestler in her robe poised on the ropes of a ring, she sprang through the air, landed on his head, and toppled them both onto the bed. They rolled, grappled. She managed to shimmy a knee between them, pried him off with enough force to fling him over, and climbed on top.

But he didn't play fair. He dug his fingers into her sides, tickling until she laughed so hard her resistance weakened. He lunged, they fell off the bed, landed on the floor with Dee on her back; Cooper straddled her and pinned her wrists down.

"How do you go from being in the shower to attacking me in bed?" He wanted to know.

"I wasn't *in* the shower. I had already gotten *out* and was listening to my jams, doing my hair and face shit, and guess what song came on?"

"'Sweet Caroline.'" His laughter shook her body. "I was singing along out here."

"When the hell did you do that?"

"Weeks ago! Remember when I videoed you with your phone?"

She puffed out a cheek, twisted her mouth as she tried to find the memory. "I think so."

"You had the torch going, huge flame, making a glass hummingbird."

"You were there?"

"Hayleigh was busy, and you needed someone to film you for your YouTube channel."

"Oh yeah, I remember now." He'd thought she looked so badass with the torch that they fucked on the studio floor.

"Well, you put the tool in my hands, honey. I just thought I'd expand your musical tastes a little."

"My musical taste is plenty broad."

"You're right. Who knew there were so many head-banging scream bands? I gave you a little balance."

"'Sweet Caroline'? You're lucky I'm weak with hunger, or I'd have kicked your ass by now."

"I do not doubt that." He kissed her forehead and rolled off. "So, how about I take you to breakfast?"

He made it into the bathroom and turned the water on in the shower, and she still couldn't come up with an answer. Breakfast?

They didn't *do* breakfast. She finished dressing, slipped several elastic hair bands onto her wrist for later, and put in earrings—five lined up the right ear, four lined up the left. A lopsided look gifted from Brett when she was seventeen. They'd graduated from gin and cherry Kool-Aid to rum and Diet Coke. She convinced him to pierce her ears, but apparently, they were too drunk to realize she didn't get an even number of holes. Thank God Gram was able to get the infection under control before Dee returned home.

Why hadn't he called? The text she'd sent on Friday said *read* under it. What the hell? Surely, he'd be sober by now. It's Monday morning, for Christ's sake.

She texted him again.

Hey! I need to hear from you.

She really needed to know about her father but couldn't make herself text that F word.

Cooper came out of the bathroom. The griffin's eyes seemed to glisten on his damp skin. "And?" He stepped into the briefs he'd worn when he arrived earlier that morning, then the jeans.

"And what?" Dee blinked at him.

"Breakfast?"

"Oh, I can't. Hayleigh's coming over soon. She's going to officially work for me—me and Max."

"Congratulations! Your first employee." He pulled his shirt over his head and finger-combed his wet hair. "How about lunch, then?"

"I don't get it." Dee led them out of the bedroom. "Where is this coming from?"

"Where is what coming from?"

"Breakfast, lunch..." She approached the whiteboard in the living room, picked up a marker, and quickly sketched a table on it in blue. "We don't eat out together." She wrote BRETT on the table.

"We haven't. But there's no reason we can't, is there?"

"Seriously?" She turned around to face him. "I think that sounds suspiciously like a string." That was the agreement: booty calls, safe sex, no strings attached.

"A string?" He grinned. "As in, we don't go on dates? We don't see each other outside the bedroom? Ha! Honey, I think we're beyond that."

"We are?"

"It's safe to say we're at least friends."

"Friends with benefits?"

"Well, I think more than that." He stood close enough to place both hands on her hips, and drilled his indigo eyes into hers. "Think about it, Dee, as much as you say you don't 'do' relationships, we're in one."

She tapped the end of the marker on his shoulder as his words sank in. "But—"

"Who was the first person you texted when you put a contract on this building?"

"You."

"Who did you talk to about whether you should go to your grandmother's funeral?"

"You."

"Who helped me calm down when I found out my accountant messed up, and I owed the IRS twenty grand?"

"Me."

"Who went with me and took care of me when I had a breakdown at Benny's grave?"

"Me."

"People having casual sex don't do those things for each other, babe." He smacked a kiss on her nose and released his grip on her hips. "People only interested in hooking up at odd hours of the day don't let each other have access to their phones like you did for that video. Face it, that kind of stuff is what people in relationships do."

Dee's heart kicked into a higher gear. He had a point. She had been so relieved when he arrived around five that morning and crawled into bed with her. Such a welcome, warm, and delicious way to recover from being awake for over an hour after another fucking nightmare. And what about all those "coffee breaks" when he actually brought coffee and pastries, and they'd just talk instead of hopping into bed? Or when he'd come by just to watch her work? What the hell? Those kind of sounded like relationship actions.

How could she let this happen?

"Holy shit."

"Is that a good 'holy shit' or a bad one?" He slipped his feet into his sneakers.

"Well. So, yeah, um, you might have a point. We might be in a, in a, you know, a, um…." She straightened her spine and stretched her neck from side to side, like a prizefighter getting pumped for a round. She needed to talk to her shrink about this. How could she do a relationship without fucking it all up? But Cooper still had a mess of his own to clean up. "What about…well…you?"

He sat on the sofa to tie his shoes. "I intend to take care of that this week—finish cleaning up that mess." He looked up at her. "So, once that's done, would you be willing to be seen with me in public?"

"Maybe." Static built up in her ears. Breathe in, two, three. Breathe out, two, three, four, five.

"I'd prefer a definite."

She turned back to the whiteboard. Breathe in, two, three. Breathe out, two, three, four, five. Once more, she read the quote Mom had written on Saturday:

Every woman is a rebel. And usually in wild revolt against herself. -Oscar Wilde

What was Mom trying to tell her?

And now, she was in a relationship! How could she let that happen? What was she going to do?

She picked up a red marker, wrote *Cooper,* and connected the tops and bottoms of the letters with arcing lines to indicate strings, then added *?*.

Maxine

"Are you sure?" Dr. Tan tilted her head to one side like a dog trying to understand what a distant siren was saying.

"Absolutely." Maxine nodded.

"And Dane is aware and in agreement?"

Maxine continued nodding. He was aware she'd made the decision a few months ago, but probably didn't know she was there, having the discussion with Dr. Tan at that moment, and he *certainly* wasn't in agreement. They'd barely spoken all weekend; otherwise, she would have asked him to come.

He had worked late Friday night, came downstairs to have a silent dinner with her, then zoned out in front of a baseball game on TV. After she helped Dee move on Saturday, they went through the motions of grocery shopping and another silent dinner. Sunday—Father's Day—he was uncomfortably quiet at the country club in northwest Philly, where his parents, as part of his mother's carefully crafted life, always had breakfast before his dad played a round of golf on Father's Day. Then he was awkwardly silent during lunch at the wild and messy barbecue restaurant her father owned in South Philly. Later, at Lauren's and Kaz's, she relaxed for the first time, and he retreated. She, Dee, and H regressed into their teenage selves, laughing and giggling on the round sofa by the fire pit, braiding and wrapping cords in Dee's hair. Mama and Lauren gossiped on the pool floats. And Dane almost hid on a chaise lounge in the shade, resisting Kaz's attempts to get him to try a cigar, saying he needed to recover from lunch.

He'd completely checked out and blamed it on lunch at her father's.

"I'm sure this decision isn't easy." Dr. Tan faded into a pixelated cloud as she tapped on her keyboard. "And there's still time. You're just thirty-two. Yes, the odds do get lower, but I know how much you and Dane want a child. He always seemed so supportive and eager. He's so looking forward to being a father. I just have to ask again: are you sure?"

Maxine shifted her gaze from the cloud to the "art" hung on the wall opposite her: a framed poster featuring an abstracted silhouette of a woman holding a baby, with "hope" in script beneath it. No father figure was in that picture. Why was Dr. Tan bringing Dane into this discussion? Did his opinion matter more than hers? It was her body that went through hell, had been going through hell for five years, to conceive a baby. She blinked against tears. "I just can't do it anymore."

"It's normal to feel frustrated. Perhaps it would help to speak to someone. I can recommend a social worker who specializes in talking to couples—"

"You're not listening to me." Maxine ripped a tissue from the box on the desk and wiped her eyes. Dr. Tan continued tapping on her computer. A printer came to life and began birthing a piece of paper. "Look at me."

Dr. Tan's face morphed out of the cloud and looked surprised.

"I've undergone five years of hormonal swings. I've swallowed thousands of pills. I've suffered daily shots. I've managed the stress from repeatedly bouncing between excited joy because I gained two pounds in a week to abject despair three days later when my period would start. Again, repeatedly. My digestion is shot. I'm constantly bloated. My energy is non-existent. On top of it all, we've spent thousands and thousands of dollars—"

"Oh, well, we have financial plans that—"

"*Listen to me!*" Maxine pounded the desk. "I—*me*, this human being sitting across from you, this *woman* you went to medical school for years to learn how to help and support. *Listen to me.* I. Can't. Do. This. Anymore. I'm done."

"And Mr. Booker feels the same way?"

Mr. Booker? Dr. Tan had always referred to them by their first names. *What the hell kind of move was that?*

"This is *my* body, not Mr. Booker's."

Dee

"Is Max coming?" Hayleigh covered the top of Dee's dinette table with an assortment of printed images and alphabet-covered papers.

"Maybe." Dee yawned and picked up an image—wide vertical stripes in pale pink, emerald green, black, and gold. "She had an appointment this morning. Not sure how long it will take."

"So, when can I start shit?"

"What shit are you starting?"

"Do I have to wait for you and Max to meet and agree on whatever before I do anything? I mean, is this a joint decision? Or is your word all I need?"

"Right! Business decisions. I don't think you need to wait for her." Dee's coffee pot beeped; her life force was ready. "She's doing all the day-to-day managing stuff—payroll, bill paying, hiring people, whatever. I'm doing what's left over, like whatever we're supposed to do today. Then we both make creative decisions, though I'm still not sure what that means."

"Cool. And you told her I want to be a W-9, not an employee, right?"

"What does that even mean?" Dee filled two cups.

"That I'm not an employee. You contract me to do marketing and stuff." H accepted her coffee and set it aside.

"So you won't be on the sales floor?" Dee sat across from her.

"Not at all. I have my own business to run. You're not my only marketing client, you know. Plus, I'm still teaching color guard at the high school. So I won't be around most weekends, anyway."

"Right." Dee picked up her phone and began to text Max.

H is

"You're a W-what?"

"I'm an independent contractor."

"I thought you said a letter or something." Dee finished the text.

"OK, so I told her you won't be on the floor. Now, what am I doing?"

"Branding colors!" H was too excited. "We should have done this months ago, but that's OK. I'll get us up to speed. We need branding colors and fonts, so that everything you do is in alignment and on brand."

"Alignment and on brand? This conversation is already making me want to choose contrasting colors, mix patterns, and cut out random letters from a magazine. I don't wanna be confined."

"You're not being confined. You're being a smart businesswoman by creating an image for Altered States Studio and Gallery that people will easily recognize and remember. You can do whatever you want with your work, but your logo and things like carpeting and shopping bags will all coordinate. And your awning, too." H pointed to the whiteboard where Dee had drawn her building with an awning. "Anything you use to decorate in the bathroom, whatever. Then in all your marketing materials, I'll use the same color scheme and fonts."

"Can I do red and black tartan plaid?"

"I suppose." H's forehead wrinkled. "But people might think you're a Christmas store. Not everyone knows you have a thing for dead punk rockers you're too young to have even heard of."

"Shit. How about—" Dee's phone dinged with a text. "Max says she knows and that she's already started looking for someone to work the floor. I guess I did tell her. Wait…" She read her phone. "So remind me before you go that there's a *help wanted* sign somewhere downstairs. She wants me to tape it to the front window if I can find tape."

"Cool. So, these are what I think…" H's voice morphed into a background noise. Dee had hoped Max's text was from Brett. Still no answer from the fuckwad. And that nightmare last night! It came back to her in a flash. The fear anyway. *What was in the freaking dream?* It was the second time she'd woken up in the middle of the night since she'd returned from the funeral, absolutely terrified. What was up with that? Such good timing from Coop. So nice to snuggle up with him. Yeah. Maybe they were in a relationship. How the fuck could she let that happen?

"Yo!" Hayleigh shouted.

Dee spilled her coffee down the front of her Joe Strummer T-shirt. "Shit!" She ripped it off and ran into the kitchen to rinse it in cold water.

"Sorry. But I just went through an entire presentation, and you were in La-La Land. Are you OK? You seem a little more scattered than normal."

"I dunno. Got a lot going on in my head right now." She wrung the T-shirt out over the sink, examined it for coffee stains. "I'll be back."

After she threw the shirt in the dryer and donned a plain black one, she found Hayleigh had poured another cup of coffee for her and was sitting at the table, with just three images on it. Each a series of colored stripes.

"Let's start over," she said. "Branding colors. First knee-jerk response, which set do you like the best?"

Dee chose the pink, green, black, and gold she'd originally picked up.

"Cool." Like a dealer at a blackjack table, H wiped the papers away and spread three new ones with font samples. "Now which?"

The middle one.

H looked at the back. "Of course, it's called Punk Posters. I'll find something that coordinates with it for things like the text in emails. You want me to create the logo, or should I send you the RGB codes and font info for you to create it?"

"You, please."

"That much on your plate?"

"I don't know what's on my plate, but that question felt overwhelming."

"Again, are you OK?"

"You asked already?"

H grinned. "Seriously, you're, like, beyond distracted."

Armed with her coffee mug, Dee ambled into the living room and stared at the colorful graffiti-like scribbles and images on her whiteboard. "I dunno. I think I'm just massively stressed. Been tougher than usual to focus."

"'Cause of all the changes? The new business? The move? Owning your own place? That all sounds stressful to me." H stood beside her.

"Maybe." Dee sipped. "And, H…well, I think I had a nightmare last night."

"Really? Like…I mean..."

"Yeah, like the old ones."

"Shit!" H gripped her arm.

"Yeah. But, it wasn't completely like the old ones. I mean, when I woke up, I knew it was just a bad dream. Like I wasn't confused or thought it was real. I have an appointment with my shrink tomorrow. I'll talk to her about it. Maybe the stress triggered it. But," she turned to face her kid sister. "Listen, this conversation doesn't leave my apartment."

"I don't know if I can promise that. I mean, if you think you might—"

"I'm not going to hurt myself. Like I said, I'm talking to Aisling tomorrow. Besides, it wasn't *that* bad. It was, like, a normal nightmare." She guessed. Dee had no idea what a normal nightmare was like. "It was just a bad dream. No biggie. But that's not what I'm talking about. Well, it's kind of what I'm talking about."

"I have no idea what you're talking about."

"Look, don't tell Mom or Kaz, but I think the nightmare was about my father, my birth father. Or maybe it was about Brett."

"Your cousin Mom hates?"

"Yeah. I'm worried about him. I think…Actually, I'm not sure what I think. My aunts were saying some pretty weird shit at Gram's funeral. And Brett, too. It all kind of got me thinking about my father."

"What about him?"

"Like, maybe there was something about his death that I don't know. I have nothing more than a feeling to base this on, but I think maybe his death wasn't an accident."

"You mean, like maybe he was killed?"

"Yeah, maybe." No, actually, that was *exactly* what she thought; she just didn't want to think it because if so, that meant…something. What, she wasn't sure. But that something seemed to involve Brett. "Anyway, if that's the case, then everyone has been lying to me for as long as I can remember."

"You mean everyone but me. 'Cause I don't know anything."

"Right. But Mom and Kaz seemed to know something."

"Well, you know the best way to get Mom talking, right?"

"Wine?"

"And a good mood. Nothing makes her happier than when we ask her to buy us stuff. You should let her take you shopping."

"Right. Just what I need. Another nightmare."

Genevieve

While not quite anticlimactic, the front of the building wasn't as awe-inspiring as Genevieve had allowed herself to expect. It looked identical to all the other storefronts on Main Street, only clearly it wasn't open for business. But it was definitely where the magic happened: a sign promising this was the future home of Altered States Studio and Gallery was taped to the glass front door.

She cupped her hands against the window and peered inside. Boxes, tables, pieces of furniture—oh! That étagère she'd seen on Pinterest stood center stage on the floor. The wooden supports and shelves were painted in a blend of peacock colors with gold leaf accents. It was even more magnificent in real life.

Was that drumming? Is there music playing inside? Was someone there? Should she go in and introduce herself, maybe ask when the live classes would start?

She stepped back to review her reflection in the glass. She'd just come from the salon, wasn't going to have a better hair day than this. Freshly colored chestnut roots. She was too young to be dealing with that right? Life just continued to be unfair.

Life is as fair as you make it. That's what that stupid life coach said on this morning's video. Could that really be right?

If it was, then it was time she leveled the score. She was due for a series of good days and happy encounters with kind people. Or at least an encounter with an artist she adored. She reached for the door, almost giggled. Like a schoolgirl standing in line for an autograph of a teen idol, Genevieve had butterflies in her stomach. She'd watched these artists so many times in their videos as they transformed damaged, outdated, tired, and worn items into functional works of art. "Altered," they'd call it. Should she tell them she'd attended a few of their online classes and amazed her friends on Facebook with the jewelry box she'd altered for Brynn? She'd done a second for Olivia but hadn't been brave enough to give it to her, yet.

The women who worked here were amazing, gifted, talented. They were unafraid of expressing themselves with color and texture, and that blond one, that Dee Dee, used quite the colorful language, too. Genevieve wanted to create like that, only without all the swearing.

She let go of the door. What was she doing? Was she seriously going to walk in and introduce herself to a couple of strangers—to people who were clearly out of her league talent-wise? And then what?

Her downcast eyes spotted a *Help Wanted* sign inside the door, on the floor, as if it had slid from the glass. Was that a sign from God? No, she didn't believe in God anymore. But it was a sign, nonetheless. Obviously, it had fallen. She should go in, pick it up, and place it back on the door.

She pulled the door open, but there was no tape on the sign, so it hadn't fallen. It looked brand new. Perhaps it had been dropped? She let the door shut behind her and took a minute to get used to whatever that music was. A man screamed over thrashing drums and what sounded to Genevieve like broken electric guitars. *Was he telling people to go get knives? Who would sing/scream in a song like that? Who would listen to that? Must be contractors working in the back.*

She almost set the sign down on a table, but there were too many beautiful things to see. They lured her further into the room. The étagère stood proud and broad—much larger than it had looked in the photos. There was also a tall lingerie chest, painted a very shiny black, with silver, copper, and gold leafing placed so that it looked as if the leafing was once liquid and thrown from a bucket: solid covering on the left side that appeared to splatter across to the right. Amazing!

An open box held an assortment of glass treasures—surely Dee Dee made those. Genevieve had been fascinated by the videos of her in action, spellbound as Dee Dee fearlessly manipulated molten glass with giant torches to create delicate-looking birds and flowers or blew through pipes extended into roaring fires only to create the most amazing works of art.

As if pulled by an unknown force into a magical world, she wandered into the next room, then the last, where she found someone. A woman stood facing the rear wall, head bouncing to the beat of whatever that music was. Apparently, she'd just finished painting a quote over a window: *Consistency is the last resort of the unimaginative. ~ Oscar Wilde*

Genevieve watched her place a paintbrush in a small bucket, then pull a phone from a back pocket of her paint-smeared jeans to photograph her handiwork. She was so skinny! And obviously braless in a tight, black tank top. Barefoot, she wore jeans a few sizes too big. They hung baggy and low on her hips; the bottoms rolled up to mid-calf, exposing bony ankles, one of which had several chains wrapped around it. Black hair bands surrounded a wrist, and possibly a few held up the messy knot of blond hair piled on her head. The hair assured Genevieve that this was, in fact, *the* Dee Dee Bremen. In the videos, the woman's long, wavy hair gave her a feral quality, as if she had just emerged into civilization after making do in the wilderness for years. Today, there were a few streaks of pink and a couple thin braids wrapped in cloth.

Dee Dee must have used the phone to shut off that noise because the room became silent.

"Hello," Genevieve said.

"Jesus Christ!" Dee Dee jumped, spun around, and dropped her phone. "You scared the fuck out of me."

"I'm..." What was she doing? She had no business here. Genevieve pressed a hand over that lump in her throat. "I'm so sorry. I didn't mean to sneak up on you. I guess you didn't hear me come in. That...the music was..."

"It's all right." Dee Dee picked up her phone. She looked at the screen and grinned. "New case is working. I've had this baby for a couple of months and haven't destroyed it yet. Might be a record for me." She slid the phone into a back pocket. "Can I help you?" She frowned—not in an unpleasant way—at Genevieve.

"Well, um..." What to say? She had no plan. Here she was meeting her artistic hero, and she was speechless? She swallowed against the lump and held up the *Help Wanted* sign. "Um—"

"Where did you find that? I've been looking all over for it." Dee

Dee took it from her.

"On the floor, just inside the door." Genevieve waved toward the front. "I was passing by and, well, I've been following Altered States on YouTube and Pinterest. I'm one of your biggest fans." Heat filled her face.

"You people are real?" Dee Dee's eyes grew large.

"I...I don't think I understand?" Genevieve realized this is how awkward felt. A strong desire to escape almost turned her around to leave, but an equal one wanted her to explain herself. But explain what?

"I'm still a little shocked by the number of 'followers' we have." Dee Dee crunched her fingers in quote marks. "It's hard to believe. But do know it's greatly appreciated!" She tugged on Genevieve's arm. "Let me show you what's going to happen where." She pulled her to stand in the center of the room. "Over there, we'll hold classes. I just painted that," she pointed to the Wilde quote, "because you wouldn't believe how many people send pictures of shit they made that look exactly like what we made. We wanna teach techniques and inspire ideas. We don't want fucking copycats, you know?"

"Of course." Genevieve nodded. She hadn't been copying anything when she made Brynn's box. She'd been a good student and only applied the techniques.

"Then, over there, I'll be doing glass work. Just fusing, lead shit, and lampworking—you know what that is?"

"With the torches?"

"Yeah." Dee Dee headed toward the back wall. She opened the door and pointed outside. Past the bottom of some stairs was a bit of dead grass and a garage. "At some point, we'll convert the garage to a hot shop to blow glass. Right now, it's just storage. Gonna have to do some structural crap in there or something. I really don't know what the hell the guy said. He spoke to my dad about it. And it's not like you can get contractors to return a fucking phone call these days." She shut the door and led Genevieve back toward the front, pointing out the plans for the future along the way. Near the entrance, Dee Dee's phone made a loud noise. "Shit." She tapped her screen. "I almost forgot. I gotta run. But I'm not the person to talk to, anyway. Maxine's handling the interviewing and hiring."

"Oh, um—"

"She'll be here tomorrow."

"OK, but—"

"I have no idea what to ask you at all. That's really her department. We've only spoken a little about the job. To be honest, we just realized last week that we'd need an extra hand around here. My sister H, I mean Hayleigh, does all the social media and marketing stuff, but she has no interest in working the floor, especially on weekends 'cause she teaches a high school color guard, and that monopolizes all her social time."

"I'm sure. But..." What was Dee Dee talking about?

"So, like, I know we're gonna need someone willing to be here on weekends and in the evenings. I mean, we'll be here, too. Hell, I'm living upstairs, so it's not like I'll ever be gone, really. But it'd be great if whoever we hire has some kind of artistic talent or knowledge. You said you've taken a few of our classes?" She continued to tap on her phone as she spoke.

Nights and weekends? Artistic talent or knowledge? Dee Dee thought she was here for a job!

And suddenly Genevieve knew: that was *exactly* what she wanted to do with herself. "Yes! I've taken several of them. Actually, I have an art degree."

"Great. If you have a portfolio, bring it." Dee Dee opened the front door for her. "Anytime tomorrow—no, not tomorrow. I'm texting Max now. She said Wednesday after nine-thirty. You cool with that?"

"I'll be here!" Genevieve nodded, smiling, genuinely smiling because this was the best thing that had happened to her since...since...well, maybe it was the best thing that had *ever* happened to her.

Outside, the sun seemed brighter, and the people on the sidewalk as she headed back to her car seemed happier. A portfolio? She had one. When Remy entered first grade, Genevieve finally went to college to get her art degree—at a community college, much to the continual embarrassment of her mother. Would a two-year degree be good enough? Her professors had all been impressed by her work, but it's not like they were world-renowned, in galleries, or had thousands of followers, or...

Tuesday, June 22

Dee

Outside, in a chair at the top of her backstairs, Dee begged the sun's morning rays to melt the tension out of her body. Breathe in two, three. Breathe out two, three, four, five.

That nightmare was the worst. Hadn't had one that bad since high school when they'd experimented with those fucking drugs that were supposed to help her focus. Her father was in the dream last night. Right? Maybe.

Or was it Brett? The little shit still hadn't called her back or returned the million texts she'd sent. She was almost worried enough to call Aunt Louise.

Almost.

Coffee was delicious. She placed her cup on a wine crate set on its end beside her chair. Breathe in two, three. The sound of cars on Main Street suggested it was already busy, but so far, no one was out where she could see anyone or they her from the side street. She had the privacy to collect her scattered thoughts as best she could and shake off the claustrophobic grip clinging to her.

She hoped Aisling could help with the nightmares.

Aisling had only been her shrink for a couple of months, but so far had been more useful than anyone she'd met with since she started seeing them as a kid. Dee must have told her about the other nightmares. How could she not tell her therapist that she'd tried to kill herself when nightmares had gotten too bad and too real? Maybe the previous shrinks had sent over their reports?

Aisling did know she was a crappy sleeper. She had spoken to Dee about meditation apps and stuff to help her improve her "sleep architecture," as she called it. Nothing really helped. Frequently, she'd wake up in the middle of the night, and, unable to go back to sleep, she'd head out to her glass studio, turn on all the lights, and blast some screaming music at the highest level possible. Then she'd fire up a torch or get the hot-box furnace going and set to work.

Interesting! She must have been woken by dreams. It just never clicked in that they were nightmares until now. She'd forget about them instantly when she woke. Aside from that crazy shit back in high school, the nightmares were never strong enough to bleed into her awake time. She'd just get up and head to the studio.

Some of her best glass pieces happened in the middle of the night when she'd create "something amazing, ethereally beautiful, out of the destructive force of fire," as one critic described her work at a gallery show. Without the studio ready, last night, from three to dawn, with only light bulbs blazing in her apartment and that French scream band Gojira drowning out any other possible noise, she painted her grandmother's willow tree across her shoes. She longed to set up a small torch and create some glass flowers to trail out of their heels. *What were those pink flowers Gram always had flowing out of pots? Boo-something...bougainvillea.* She'd need to find some photos...but she could do it. They'd be the first thing she'd create once she set up the lampworking station.

The glossy white paint on the landing and down the steps shone beautifully in the sun. *That was pretty freaking stupid.* The steps were so shiny, she could see how slippery they'd be when wet. *Who the fuck paints stairs with high-gloss paint?*

She reached for her phone to make a note about finding someone to fix that, but there was no phone on the wine crate.

Inside, she couldn't see for a minute or two while her eyes

adjusted to the electric lights, which seemed dim now. When she could see, she wrote STEPS on the whiteboard and couldn't help but giggle as she drew a falling stick figure. Brett's table was above it. Was it too early to call him?

She really didn't care.

Where the hell was her phone?

In the bathroom.

Back outside in the open sunshine with a freshened cup of coffee and her phone, she called her cousin.

He didn't answer, but he did text.

> *give me 5*

> *5 what? Days? Weeks?*
>
> *You fuck!*

It was more like seconds. When his name showed up on her phone, she answered before any sound went off.

"What the fuck is your problem?" she greeted him.

"Hell, Dee, where do you want me to start?"

"How about with why you haven't responded to my texts and calls?"

"Well, I—shit." He must have covered his phone because his voice was muffled as he spoke. "Sure. Sounds good." Then louder in the phone: "Granddad's making breakfast."

"He cooks?"

"Nah. He heats things up. Dottie James, the maid, 'member her?"

"Of course." No, she didn't.

"She cooks up a bunch of meals every couple of days. The man's got mad microwaving skills."

"Why are you there?"

"Yeah, I've been searching for the right wood for your table."

What? Oh, he can't talk. Shit. "Awesome. Anything I can do for you?"

"Nah, honey. I'm good."

"Oh no you're not." His voice was way too...well, it was the voice he used when he spoke to his mother. And he *never* called her honey.

"So, how many people you wanna fit at that table?"

"Jesus, Brett! I dunno. I guess four or five." If only they'd created more codes!

"Tables don't usually come with seating for five. You want a round one?"

"That would be perfect. I'm flummoxed."

"You're what?"

"Don't ask."

"OK, what color resin?"

"Ohhhhhhh...hmmmmm...green."

"And you want one for your store, too?"

"Yeah. Something big—like a family dining room table. Honestly, I don't intend on selling it. I'll have H make up some kind of brochure. Make it some other color. I don't care, but send me pics of Granddad's blue one."

"All right. I can do that."

"I'll take orders from people. They'll feel the table in the store and see the pics of what's possible."

"Sounds like a plan."

"We just made a legitimate adult business call. How fucking weird is that?"

"Seems about right for the times."

"I'm worried about you, bro."

"I'm doing enough of that about both of us, so you don't need to. I'll get back to you when I find the right wood."

Back inside, Dee topped off her coffee and approached her whiteboard. That was a perfectly useless conversation. Except she could erase the table she'd drawn. She also erased everything related to unpacking and organizing the apartment. She left the shoes but wiped away the tiny willow tree. In the new blank space, she drew a large puzzle piece, the kind that looked like four legs and a head with a flat bottom. In the center, she wrote *Father*. In one leg, she wrote *Evan Kaz* and put))) between their names to symbolize phone signals. In another leg, *Mom & Brett-boy*. Three female figures, like you'd find on a restroom door, and *shh* filled a third to represent her aunts and the idea of a secret.

She stepped back to sip her coffee. From this perspective, it didn't seem like she had much to work with. In fact, she wondered if maybe she was making up the connections. Like she was creating her own conspiracy theory. She erased *Father* from the center and replaced it with *conspiracy?*. Then, thinking about Brett's drunken *ask your mamma about who killed your daddy,* she wrote his name in the fourth leg, accompanied by a shot glass.

Maxine

"Are you all right?" Maxine ducked her head so she could look into look Dane's down-turned face as he zipped by her in the kitchen.

"Yeah. Why?" Instead of opening the cupboard for his usual coffee cup, he opened a different one and pulled out a travel mug.

"You're six minutes late coming into the kitchen." *And a travel mug?* "I worried you were sick or something."

"I'm fine." He filled his cup, ripped two stevia packs open, dumped them in the steaming coffee, then stared at the paper packets as if he didn't know what to do with them.

"Here." Maxine held out her hand. "Are you going somewhere?"

His arm stretched out of a brown boulder as he gave her the trash. "Yeah. I have an appointment."

"Dane, we really need to talk."

"I know." He screwed the lid on his cup, then finally, he looked her in the eye. "But not right now."

"When?"

"I need time, Max. I'm processing more than I can handle right now."

She nodded at the vision of him in stone.

He left without kissing her goodbye, without even saying goodbye. Really?

She wanted to be empathetic. She wanted to be understanding. But he was making that hard to do. Didn't it occur to him that she might be hurting, too? That she might be scared of a future without job security? Of growing old with him, knowing he resented her for giving up on having a baby?

No. He'd get over it all. He'd come back to her, return to his old self in time. He just would.

She hoped.

She filled her own travel mug and slipped her feet into a pair of loafers. The ones Dane teased her about—the "teacher vibe" shoes. Dee would be barefoot in the store, a pair of beat-up flip-flops somewhere nearby. And Max was as free as Dee now.

She ran upstairs for sandals. It was summer after all, and...she paused as she passed Dane's empty office. An appointment before nine o'clock in the morning?

His immaculate desk held no clues. A few papers were neatly lined up on its top: checklists. A software engineer didn't need much paper. She tried to bring his computer to life. The required password was not her name or their anniversary. She didn't risk a third try—fearing some kind of alert would lock the machine, and he'd know she was snooping.

She swiveled back and forth in his chair. Had he mentioned

something, anything? No. Had Dr. Tan reached out to him after she'd left the day before? Where would he have gone?

Oh! She pulled an app up on her phone—the one they'd installed on their cells a few years earlier, when someone had hit her car. She wound up in the emergency room, and her phone was left behind. This app was meant for parents to know where their children were but had a crash-detection feature to alert others of an accident if the driver was unable to. She had never used it and doubted if Dane had. But it was simple. She tapped it to life and immediately saw that Dane was driving west...heading toward Philly.

Did he have a job interview? No, he'd worn khakis and a casual shirt. And it wouldn't be a work meeting—otherwise, he'd have taken a laptop. Maxine lost track of time as she followed his dot across the Ben Franklin Bridge, then traced the exit for Fifth Street. The dot swung around under the bridge and headed south. Soon, it stopped. The app didn't tell Maxine what business he was at, but she was pretty sure it was a large hotel by the river. What the hell?

She texted Dee.

> *You OK if I'm a little late?*

I'm rockin it! No worries.

Max wound up in her teacher-vibe loafers, driving her car the same route Dane's dot took. Around twenty minutes later, her dot aligned with his on the map: Dane was at the Hilton.

She didn't see his car—most likely, he'd given it to a valet, and it was hidden in the garage. She handed her car over and entered the hotel through the giant sliding glass doors.

Now, what? What good reason would he have for being at a hotel?

If there was some kind of in-person event, surely they'd have a sign in the lobby telling people where to go, right?

None were evident.

Enough people were at check-in that she decided to wander over to the other side of the lobby, toward the windows facing the river, toward a nautical-themed casual restaurant. Toward Dane, sitting at a table with a woman she didn't recognize.

Her lungs collapsed.

She watched them from behind a large planter. The woman was her age and slender like Maxine. Her sepia skin seemed to glow in the sunlight coming through the window. She wore a cream-colored tank dress, the neckline just low enough to expose a little cleavage. Neither of them had a computer. They both had plates in front of them—clearly, they'd been eating together.

He came here for breakfast…with a woman.

"Can I help you?" An older man wearing a hotel-branded name badge was next to her. The badge read *Morris*. His eyes looked kind.

"I, um..." She peeked back around the plant. Dane and the woman stood. He briefly took her hand and held it. The touch didn't last long, but there was something intimate about it, or at least very familiar. She was not a stranger. Maxine pressed her hands together, as if in prayer, and brought them to her lips. She watched as they turned in her direction, outlined in high-contrast definition, the background abstracted, blurry.

"Don't look at them." Morris seemed to know what she was thinking. He placed both hands on her shoulders and shielded her view of her husband walking through the hotel lobby, inches away from another woman. After a few minutes, he let go of her. "You'll be all right." His eyes met hers. "And if it means anything, they didn't kiss good-bye."

Maxine appreciated his kindness, but one thing he couldn't prevent her from seeing was the woman's shoes. She wore what Mama would call hooker heels.

Dee

For probably the fiftieth time since Saturday, Dee read the quote Mom had written on her whiteboard: *Every woman is a rebel. And usually in wild revolt against herself. -Oscar Wilde*

And for probably the fiftieth time since Saturday, she almost erased it. But she couldn't. Mom was trying to tell her something. What was it?

Mom always resorted to Wilde when she couldn't find the words for herself. Dee couldn't remember reading the phrase before but was certain she had. Mom's adoration of the dead white poet was obsessive. According to her, no one understood the need for beauty and elegance like Wilde did. She had insisted on adding him to the homeschooling curriculum that barely provided Dee with enough education to pass the GED exam. Mom never paid much attention to any of the math or science aspects of Dee's education, but she'd said more than once that her daughters' lives would be incomplete without an intimate knowledge of Wilde's work.

Which meant Dee's life should be close to complete.

So this is what complete looked like: exhausted, haunted by nightmares she couldn't remember, regularly accused of being a poster child for ADHD, and frequently lost in time and space without even knowing it. *That couldn't be what Wilde had ever intended, could it?*

She pulled a drawer labeled "beads" out of the supply chest and placed it on the floor between the coffee table and the sofa. On the table went a tube of E6000 glue, a bowl of soapy water, a bowl of plain water, a roll of paper towels, and a container of toothpicks. She set the painted shoes on a strip of wax paper in the center and settled on the floor with her back to the sofa and, shit! She forgot to pour fresh coffee.

Her cell dinged while she was in the kitchen. Her phone wasn't in her back pocket. It wasn't by the coffee pot. Not on the dinette table, not in the dish by the door. Oh! On the supply chest.

The text was from her therapist; the Zoom was open. That's right. She'd forgotten to set up her laptop for the Zoom while she played with the shoes. There was no room on the coffee table, now, though...Another ding, from Aisling.

Are you joining me?

Y. Getting ready

She'd need to use her phone for the video, which meant taking a few minutes to rearrange. That stupid-ass plant made a good place to prop the cell at face height on the table. Maybe she'd remember to water it and keep it alive if she remembered to use it like that for her weekly calls with her shrink.

If.

With coffee within arm's reach and everything needed to alter the shoes around her, she logged into Zoom and repositioned the phone in the plant.

"Are you in your new place?" Aisling asked as soon as she let Dee into the video meeting.

"Yep." She squirted a puddle of glue on the wax paper. "Completely unpacked *and* organized."

"That's great!" Dee reminded herself that Aisling's kindergarten-teacher voice was unintentional. "Did you do it all yourself?"

"Ha! Hayleigh, Maxine, and Mom were all here on Saturday."

"I'm sure your mother loved helping you."

"With great enthusiasm." A few inches away from the glue, she tapped out piles of tiny glass beads from different tubes.

"When do you start with the store?"

"Start what with the store?" She jabbed a toothpick into the hole of a chartreuse bead, dabbed the side of the bead in the glue, then placed it on the shoe.

"Unpacking, organizing, setting up."

"It's started, a little. Max has had some appointments, so it's pretty much been me doing that little. We're giving ourselves a couple of weeks, so we don't get too stressed." More beads to highlight the shape of the willow branches.

"And how are you handling this so far? How's it hitting you?"

"Mildly anxiety-provoking."

"Yes?"

"It's tough controlling how many things I'm exposed to at once."

"Go on."

"Just gotta handle literally one thing at a time, or I have to fight off a panic attack." Dee held the shoe upside down with one hand, her fingers inside, rotating it as she planted beads. "It makes for a slow process, but I'm able to handle seeing a bunch of stuff in one box if I intentionally focus on removing just one piece at a time. Can't pull out more than that to put them on a table or something, then figure out what to do. Can't have more than one box open within eyesight. Otherwise, I can't seem to follow through on what I'm doing, and the scatteredness, as you know, stresses the hell out of me."

"Right. Too many focal points will do that. It's good you're recognizing when you have too many."

"Yeah." Dee bit her lip. They'd had this same conversation before. Granted, Aisling was the one to help her discover the trigger. But why is she paying this woman to confirm she's doing OK today? Next thing she's going to tell her is that if Dee could find something to mindlessly focus on—like gluing beads into a picture—that she'd be able to have a conversation without getting distracted.

"Competing distractions, your old nemeses," Aisling chirped.

"Just one of my old nemeses."

"I can hear in your voice, this is not what you want to talk about today, so I'm not going to ask about coping strategies. Is there something else you'd like to discuss?"

"Yes." Dee placed a few more beads, turned the shoe on its side, and set it down to let gravity help keep the beads in place while she continued gluing on more. "Um…how do I begin?"

"What's pulling on you the most?"

"Nightmares."

"Can I have more than one word?"

"Been having super intense nightmares."

"OK. Well, moving is one of the most stressful things a person can do. You just lost your grandmother. It wouldn't be a stretch to think you're having nightmares because of stress related to all of that."

"Maybe. But that doesn't feel right."

"No? Tell me more."

"Well, you know how you're always telling me I need to get in touch with my feelings and all that bullshit?"

A short laugh came from Aisling. "I never tell you what to do. But I do encourage you to explore your feelings. Why?"

"Well, I get the feeling the nightmares are because of my father."

"Your biological father?"

"Yeah."

"Ah, very good. I've been waiting for this opening. From the notes I have, one of the few things your previous therapists agreed on is that you are reluctant to discuss him."

"I'm not reluctant. There's nothing to discuss."

"Dee Dee." Aisling's pause lasted long enough for Dee to look at her on the phone. "Your father died in an accident just days before you were born. Your mother must have been grappling with grief while learning to deal with a newborn as a single mom. Your early childhood must have been fraught with stress, especially any time you asked your mother about your father. Young children are curious, you know. There should be plenty for you to unpack about those experiences."

Somehow Aisling held her gaze in the phone while Dee chewed on her words. "Maybe. If I actually remembered anything about my childhood, maybe you'd have a point." She returned her focus to the beads. She had several wispy willow branches in process. "But all that was knocked offline. How can I unpack what I don't remember?"

"Fair question. But why would you have dreams, nightmares, about him, then? If—"

"I didn't say 'about.' I think I said 'because' of him."

"Can you explain?"

"I kind of thought about him at the funeral. Not really him, but about what I'd been told of his death. And then, well, my cousin was totally drunk and kind of suggested my dad was killed, which would mean he didn't die by accident like I was told."

"Do you know what he meant?"

"No. I had to leave."

"Do you think there's any merit to it?"

"I honestly don't know. He was shitfaced."

"Have you asked your mother?"

"Aisling, for what I'm paying you, you shouldn't be asking stupid questions like that."

"It's not a stupid question, Dee. You have every right to know what happened to your father. Why won't you talk to her about him?"

She needed more glue, maybe some taupe or gray beads for the trunk. "We just don't discuss him."

"I know you don't remember anything before you were five, but as an elementary-school child, didn't you see other children with two parents and ask your mom why you didn't have a father? Weren't you ever curious?"

She tapped out more beads in different colors. "So, yeah. I remember a few times when I was really young. Like at the beginning of my recovery, or whatever they called it after the accident, when I was being re-taught how to speak and use language and all that. I asked her to tell me about him a couple of times. She would just say 'he loved you so much,' and would look so sad…I dunno. I didn't push for details."

"Ah," Aisling appeared to think Dee made sense. "It would be perfectly natural under such circumstances for you to internalize the subject of your father as taboo, something that would upset your mother, so you grew up thinking you couldn't ask about him."

"Sounds plausible. And then Kaz came into the picture a few years later, and suddenly I had a dad in the flesh, and didn't really think about the one who wasn't there."

"What about your grandparents? Did they ever speak of him?"

The first gray beads she tried were the wrong color. She had to scrape them off before the glue dried.

"Dee?"

"I'm thinking. You know, those early days, the first year or so after the accident, are really hazy to me. I just…at first, my grandparents were strangers in the living room who'd come visit me. Granddad all silent. Gram gushing over how much I grew, how pretty I was. She'd ask me what I liked to do, and when she realized it was drawing, all the questions were about favorite colors, subjects, whatever."

"She was trying to get to know you and connect with you."

"Yeah. Then, like when I visited them…Oh yeah. Ugh." A memory came so clear for Dee, it felt like a punch in the stomach. "I remember the first time I visited them, I asked Gram about my dad. She got all quiet, and then she just cried and cried. She had to go lie down."

"She reinforced he was off limits to talk about."

"My Gram wouldn't be that mean."

"Did you ever bring him up to her again?"

"No. Didn't seem worth it." Yes, that was the perfect color—a taupe.

"And now, that we're having this discussion about not being able to talk about him, how are you feeling?"

A whole line of taupe beads formed the edge of the tree trunk. "I'm kind of nauseous." Dee's voice came out quieter than she'd intended. "But not as in bad-fish nauseous. As in…you know, I felt this way when I looked at the amount in the trust fund from his insurance policy. The money I used to buy the building. It was like, weird. Like it shouldn't be there. Like I shouldn't be getting that much money because he's dead."

"Sounds like you feel guilty."

"Yeah. But I did nothing wrong."

"Dee, you survived a very terrible accident that could have killed you when you were five years old. Your father didn't survive his accident. Survivor's guilt wouldn't be out of the realm of possibility here."

Alma and Francie rammed into her thoughts. They'd always acted like Dee never belonged with the family. Like it wasn't fair that she was around when their brothers weren't. As if…the nausea pushed up through her chest, cutting off her breath. Static built up in her ears. "Holy shit!" she gasped. "What the fuck, Aisling? Feelings suck!"

"Inhale, Dee, one, two—"

"Is this really necessary?"

Genevieve

Was Chanel over the top? Genevieve held the suit jacket out at arm's length. It said chic, yet not formal. Only it was black. She'd never been on a job interview before but was fairly certain she was supposed to wear a blue suit. And she needed to do what she was supposed to do to compensate for what she hadn't been doing all along: working. Didn't years of being a PTA officer or organizing booster club bake sales count for anything?

She almost texted Brynn or one of her friends for advice, but she was afraid to tell anyone what she was doing. If she didn't get the job, then not only would that be embarrassing, but she'd be barraged with too many questions about *why* she'd want one in the first place. If she *did* get it, however, no one would care why she wanted one. They'd be excited to hear all about it. She'd probably even be called a *boss babe* on social media.

She returned the Chanel to the closet and pulled out a pair of Emporio Armani jeans with palazzo legs. Maybe that would be the right call. Topping it with a boho-style shirt? That would scream unique individual, right?

She'd be dressed like all the women coming in to shop.

She pulled on the jeans anyway. Twisting around to get a backside view was the wrong thing to do. Could that be any more depressing? Why did she look like she was wearing some old lady's clothes? Had her rear end always looked so wide and flat? Granted, she'd sat on it for a year, but that wasn't her fault. A broken femur will do that to anybody. She'd been on the elliptical every day since the doctor gave her the go-ahead. Why do things fall apart so quickly, only to take so long to get back together?

She used to be skinny. Not as skinny as Dee Dee. But thin.

Dee Dee would look amazing in these pants. She was so skinny. Like a drug addict. Scattered, like a drug addict, too. Walking around barefoot in jeans that were too big, wearing that paint-splattered tank top. Maybe she was an addict. The art world was full of them, wasn't it? Genevieve would have to look for track marks on her arm the next day. She'd need to Google what track marks looked like first, of course.

Could she work with someone like that?

Or maybe she was being judgmental. She returned the jeans to the closet and pulled out a pair of linen slacks. How many times had her husband accused her of being judgmental? Harsh, Chris had once called her. Why could he never understand that wasn't her intention? All she wanted was for life to be smooth for her kids—and him.

The linen slacks draped in a lovely way, but would they be too wrinkled by the time she arrived at her interview? Would Maxine know that was just the nature of linen and not that Genevieve was a slob? Max always looked so elegant in those videos. Usually in leggings with a long, flowy tunic. Such a polar opposite of Dee Dee.

No. Not the linen. But the blue Tahari suit! Yes! That could be perfect. She pulled a blue silk flutter-sleeved shell over her head. *What was that noise? Did someone open a garage door? No one is supposed to be home!*

Through the window, she caught the rear end of Chris's SUV as it slid into the garage. Hopefully, he'll stay downstairs. She stepped into the slim-cut trousers. Oh. That was a nice fit. She pulled on the jacket and adjusted it around her shoulders.

"Hey! Sorry! I...uh...I didn't know you'd be in here." Chris frowned at her, then looked down at his workout clothes. Had he started going to the gym in the afternoon, too? "Am I supposed to be somewhere tonight?" He met her eyes.

"No." Genevieve turned to the mirror and smoothed the front of her jacket. Was this the right look? Would he just go away? Why was he standing there like that?

"Cool. I got confused when I saw you in that suit. I didn't know if maybe someone died or something." He shuffled around in his dresser.

"Someone died?" Genevieve's nails dug into her palms as she watched his reflection behind hers. Lola died, but...really? "Do I look like I'm going to a funeral?"

In the mirror, he shut a drawer and visibly inhaled and exhaled before he turned around. "Sorry, Gen. That's not what I meant."

"Oh, well." She swallowed and faced him. "So, how do I look?"

"What do you mean?"

"I mean, how do I look in this suit?" How stupid could he possibly be?

"Um, presentable?" He pulled a hoodie over his head. "So, don't worry about me for dinner. Me and some guys are meeting up for pickleball and..." He poked his head through the neck and looked at her like he didn't recognize who was standing in front of him. "What?"

"Presentable?" The shrillness in her voice surprised Genevieve. It was so hard to keep her heels on the ground. Her body wanted to pounce. "What is wrong with you?"

His head fell back. "Look, Gen., I don't know what you want from me, OK? What do you want me to tell you?"

"Not that I look presentable!"

"So, what do you want me to say?"

That was a good question. She took her time to think about it, forced the air into her lungs, and leaned back on her heels. OK, good. Getting calmer. "You know, I don't want you to say anything."

"You probably shouldn't ever play poker."

"Excuse me?"

"I can see it on your face. There's some rule I'm not following. Some role I'm forgetting to play. Tell me what it is so I can apologize, and we can go on pretending all is perfect in our world."

"Are you kidding me? You're making *me* out to be the bad guy here?" That lump filled her throat. And her eyes...She wasn't going to cry, was she? Not in front of him!

"I didn't say that, Gen."

"You just insinuated that I'm...I don't know." She swallowed against the lump. "That I'm some kind of a tyrant here, forcing people to behave in ways they don't want to."

"All I'm saying is I can't read your fucking mind."

"Will you stop saying 'fuck' in the house? The children are saying it."

"I'm sure the 'children' are hearing it everywhere." He threw a hand up in the air. Why was he exasperated? Why was she going to cry? "You look fine. Is that good enough?"

Genevieve could feel her shoulders rise and fall with each breath. She once loved that man in front of her, well, she once got along well enough with him to conceive two children. Now, all she wanted was to be free of him. Not have to be around him anymore and..."I want..." This was her chance. She could tell him she wanted a divorce.

But Brynn's wedding was four days away. He would need to be there, with her on his arm. "I want…"

He waited, eyebrows raised.

"I want us to be nice to each other. Remember when we were friendly?"

His head twitched, as if she'd tapped him on his nose with an invisible finger. "It's been a long time."

"Think we could do that again?"

"It goes both ways, right?"

She could accuse him of insinuating, but this was an opportunity to lead by example. "Absolutely. Thank you for letting me know you won't be home for dinner this evening."

He nodded, headed toward the door, stopped at the threshold, and turned around. "Gen, right now's not the time, I'm rushing and…whatever. But, I think we need to talk about um, stuff."

"Stuff."

He nodded. "Our marriage."

"I agree." Her body felt light, as if something were pulling her up from above. "But give me this week. Brynn's wedding is Saturday. We have to be…I think it would be nice for Brynn…" How to explain she doesn't want an impending divorce to be a distraction from Brynn's wedding without having a discussion about wanting a divorce?

"You have a lot on your plate. And the family needs to be together to support her. I get it."

So he wasn't completely oblivious. "Right."

"Oh! Is that why you're in a suit? Is that for the rehearsal dinner?" He grinned. "And yeah, presentable wasn't a kind word."

A smiling face! She hadn't seen him smile at her in, well, too long. "No. Actually, I have a job interview and I—"

"A job interview?" He came back into the room, almost got too close. "What is that about?"

"My sanity." Genevieve stepped away from him. "I think my sanity needs me to get out of this house a little."

"Oh." His phone dinged. "Uh..." He fished it from the pocket of his sweatpants. Something new came over him. He changed, relaxed. In fact, his whole body seemed to shift into a more comfortable position without even moving. His eyes shone when he returned them to hers. "You look great. Good luck."

Wednesday, June 23

Dee

Cooper was already there, sitting at a cafe table outside a tiny restaurant a couple of blocks away from her store. He actually stood up as Dee approached the table, like a fucking gentleman.

"Look at you!" Dee let him kiss her cheek. "Who knew you had manners?"

He spread his arms out wide. "You doubted I was the kind of man your mom would approve of?"

She sat and took her time answering. Yeah, Mom would approve—she'd approve of any man in Dee's life if she thought he'd protect her from the world. Cooper clearly looked capable of that— tall, broad, stacked. And so fucking good looking. *All he'd have to do is wink an eye, smile into his dimples, and run a hand through his dark, wavy hair, and Mom would be smitten. No, no she wouldn't. Christ!* She was the smitten one.

"I think Kaz could help win her over." She looked around for a menu. "As long as she never learns you were the one who broke his nose."

"Basketball can be a tough sport. Kaz forgave me. He knew it was unintentional." Cooper settled into his chair. "There are no menus if that's what you're looking for."

"How am I supposed to know what I want?"

He pointed to a little sign on the table with a QR code. "This is how they do it here. I guess you haven't been out and about to support your local community, yet."

"Just the pizza place for dinner and the coffee shop across the street for breakfast. I'm the new favorite at the café. I think I may have secured the owner's firstborn's college tuition." Dee scanned the code with her phone and up popped the cafe's menu. "This is bullshit, by the way. This place is taking advantage of us. Saving two fucking cents a table by not having menus while making ordering inconvenient."

"Are you always this pleasant at breakfast, or are you crabby just this morning?" Cooper eyed her over his coffee cup.

"I need coffee, and I'm sorry. I guess I'm a little crabby. I haven't been sleeping well. Actually, that's a lie." She smiled at the waitress who came with a carafe of divine fuel, filled her cup, and left.

"What's a lie?"

"What?"

"You said you hadn't been sleeping well, then added 'that's a lie.'"

"Oh." Dee sipped her electricity. What the hell was she saying? "Oh! It's a lie that I haven't been sleeping well." Another sip. "The truth is, I'm not sleeping."

"At all?"

"I got, like an hour this morning around sunrise. Maybe about an hour and a half when I crashed last night. Though I did take a nap yesterday afternoon—right after I texted you. Didn't wake up until you texted back saying we could meet here."

"Why?"

"I guess you like the food?" She grinned at him. He grinned back, and that thing happened again. Like on Monday, for just a quick second, there was that…that thing…that knowing…It was like she knew him, *really* knew him, had always known him, and he belonged there, near her. *Oh, holy hell! Max was right!* She did have feelings for him. How could she let that happen? She looked at the menu on her phone again.

"Well, yeah. I like the food." He reached across the table and placed a hand on her arm. "Are you OK?"

She never really was, was she?

But wasn't she used to being borderline-OK all the time?

Why couldn't she handle it now?

Because relationships were the kind of thing she fucked up.

Unable to talk, she swallowed and shook her head.

"Is it me?" His hand slid down her arm to hold hers. "Is it this? Am I putting too much pressure on you?"

She shook her head harder, but maybe it was him. Still, she gripped his fingers. He didn't say any more. Just waited while she got control of her breath.

"I don't know what's going on, exactly. I mean, maybe it's us. This is new, you know."

"I know. I thought breakfast could be a way to ease into things. You want me to back off?"

He should. No strings would keep things so much cleaner. "No. I seriously want to be with you. And it's not you. I mean, there's, well, there's just shit going on."

"What kind of shit?"

"I think my grandmother's death kind of triggered some nightmares."

"Losing her?"

"No." How could she explain something to him that she didn't really understand herself? "Look, you know how I got this brain thing, right? Like it's hard to focus and remember and all that shit?"

"From an accident when you were a kid, right?"

"I don't really have all the details 'cause I was so young and just don't remember. In fact, I can't remember anything before the accident, but—"

"You guys ready to place an order?" The waitress's voice made

Dee jump in her seat.

She'd completely forgotten what she wanted, so she let Cooper order while she glanced at the menu on her phone again before telling the waitress avocado toast with a side of bacon and a glass of orange juice. How the hell could she forget that? It was her favorite breakfast.

"So," he encouraged her as soon as they were alone.

"So what?"

"Brain thing, the accident when you were little..."

"Right. So, like I was five. My mom and me were in Georgia visiting my dad's family. He grew up there but met my mom in Philly. My grandmother, the one who just died, was from Philly, so I guess…I don't know what I guess…things are kind of messy in my head about why he was here. Anyway, he met Mom when she was a fashion student, and that was that. They married, conceived me, and he died right before I was born."

"That must have been tough on your mom."

"Yeah..." What a selfish shit Dee was! Why hadn't she ever thought about how hard things must have been for Mom?

"So, brain thing, your parents…" Cooper prodded.

"Yeah, so, like, I guess my mom and my grandparents—my father's parents—used to get along well, and when I was really young, Mom and me would go down to LaGrange and visit every now and then."

"And down there is where the accident happened?" He massaged her hand with his.

"Yeah." God! But it was comfortable being with him. So comfortable, she felt like she could tell him everything. If only she knew everything. "There was a fire in some building on my Granddad's property. I was in it and…" and she wasn't alone. She knew that. *Now* she knew that. Had she always known that? Where was Brett? Her mother?

Both Cooper's hands were clasping hers. "Dee?"

"Sorry." She squeezed her eyes shut, trying to force a memory. It didn't work. "I don't really know what happened. I know there was a fire because people, my mom, told me about it. From what I understand, the building collapsed when I was in it, and someone pulled me to safety." Brett! It was Brett. No. It wasn't. He would have been seven. How could he? She blinked a few times. "I guess something hit my head pretty hard, so hard, it kind of erased everything in my life up until that fire."

"Everything?" He leaned his head toward her. "You have amnesia?"

"Sounds like a bad movie, I know." She nodded. "I woke up in a hospital one day. There were all these people around me—my mom, Gram, doctors, nurses. But I had no idea who they were. I didn't understand what was going on. Like my brain was a computer that had been wiped clean. I had to relearn language, how to talk, how not to walk into walls, who the people around me were, even my mom."

"Seriously?"

"Totally fucked up, right? There's this chunk of my life that's just gone. My Mom wigged out over it, which I guess makes sense. As soon as the hospital let me out, she whisked me up here, to her home turf. Here's where I became me through years of homeschooling and therapy. She hasn't really spoken to my father's family since. I'm not sure over what, but she had this massive argument with them after the accident. She hated that I would visit my grandmother, but I think she liked *her* enough to have some compassion for her. My grandfather, aunts, and whoever, though. Man! Don't get her started on them!"

"She holds a grudge, huh?"

"You have no idea."

Cooper loosened his grip, she relaxed, too. They both sipped coffee.

"I sound even more fucked up then you thought, huh?" She was almost too afraid to ask him.

"Not at all, babe. You sound like a miracle." His eyes crinkled with his smile. "Like you were supposed to be in this world."

"Don't get all woo woo on me and shit." She leaned back and took a longer sip.

"Ha! So, did something happen at the funeral?"

"What do you mean?"

"You were telling me about the nightmares, then brought up the accident. I was trying to make a connection."

Hell, what was she trying to explain?

"Do you think the nightmares are related to the accident?" Cooper was a trooper! Just kept trying. "Think something from the funeral triggered them?"

"Yes! I was telling you about the accident so you'd know why I haven't a clue about some things." She took one of the black bands from her wrist, wadded her hair up on the top of her head, and secured it in place. "So I went to the funeral and had a massive nightmare later that night. The second one came a couple days later, on Sunday night."

"Is that why you were so wound up when I got there Monday morning?"

Dee nodded, reached for his hand again. "Maybe. Father's Day was the day before."

"What do you mean?"

"I mean, I've never really thought about my father much. But ever since Gram's funeral, well, some shit's been going down that makes me think maybe his death wasn't an accident. It's kind of nagging me. I wanna know what happened to him. That was all I could think about on Father's Day. Well, I mean, all I could think about is that I have no real idea about how he died."

The waitress set two glasses of orange juice on the table. "Food will be out in a sec."

"Why don't you think he died in an accident?"

"My cousin Brett got massively drunk at the funeral and kind of said, well, he kind of hinted that someone killed him."

Cooper stopped sipping his juice and visibly swallowed. "Think that's a possibility?"

"Anything's a possibility. Hell, him being abducted by aliens is a possibility, because you know what?"

"What?"

"No one would ever talk to me about him."

"Really?"

"Really. And there's more."

"Tell me."

God, but he had a sexy-ass grin.

"At the funeral, one of my aunts told me we didn't need to keep the secrets anymore, and she acted like I should know what she was talking about."

"You didn't?"

"Hell no. Then my other aunts…I don't even know how to explain them. They were just worse than normal."

"I'm not on their side, but, they just lost their mother, right? Grief makes you act…well, grief fucks you up." He dropped his eyes and stared at the table. "I know all about that."

"I'm sorry." Was she always so selfish that she never thought about how others felt? Benny's death nearly destroyed Cooper. Shouldn't she be more sensitive and maybe not talk about this with him?

He met her eyes. "Nothing for you to be sorry about, babe. You got some shit you need to figure out. And sleep's important." His smile let her know he didn't think she was selfish at all. In fact, it seemed to say he felt like he knew her, really really knew her, had always known her.

Oh no. This wasn't just a relationship. This was a feelings thing.

How was she *not* going to fuck this up?

Maxine

Wow. Just wow. Of all the boxes to open, she had to choose one full of lamps and lampshades that she'd decorated. As if the universe was mocking her. In fact, the first one she pulled from the box had a rubberstamped pattern around the border—granted, she'd added gold leafing accents and textured mediums to it, but still…

Max returned the lamp to the box and opened another. Clocks. She pulled one out: a former rowing oar, the numbers and hands on the paddle. It'd been twenty-seven hours and thirty-two minutes, now thirty-three minutes, since she let Morris, that kind man at the hotel, lead her to a table and give her coffee. A little longer than that since she witnessed Dane in a secret meeting with a woman wearing hooker shoes. And almost an hour before then, she and Dane had had a conversation—the one where he didn't say good-bye. The one where—

"Hey, Max," Dee entered the back room. "That woman who came in the other day is here. And you know what? I totally forgot to get her name again. Sorry."

"It's all right." Maxine stretched her neck from side to side. She was tight. "I'll find out soon enough."

"You want me to tell her to come back or something? You don't have to be superwoman here. You can go home and tell that shit of a husband to look you in the eye and explain himself. Or, actually. No. Stay here and interview her. I'll grab a torch, the biggest fucking metal tool I have, and—"

"I love you, Dee." Maxine almost felt guilty over how easy it was to picture Dee "taking care" of Dane. "Thank you for the support. But I want to be here. And I don't want a hospital bill on my hands after you mess him up. Where is she?"

"I put her in the consult area. If you ask me, she's a bit overdressed for the part."

"Yeah?"

"Looks like she should be at the club with my mom, letting other people wait on them while they complain about their manicures. I dunno. I got a totally different vibe from her the other day."

"Dressing for success, maybe?"

"I think the price of her suit is more than she's gonna make here in a month—unless we're really paying well. Which, seriously, I don't even know how much we're paying her. Did we have that conversation?"

"It's a good thing you trust me. We did have it. I'll resend the file—"

"Oh, wait. That spreadsheet thing?"

"Yeah."

"I got it. Don't resend. That'd just make two things for me to ignore."

Dee was right. The woman sitting at the consultation table didn't look the part of a sales clerk or studio instructor. She must not have known how dirty the job could get. But who knows? Maybe she borrowed the suit.

"Hello, I'm Maxine."

"Of course! I'm Genevieve." The woman extended her hand. Max saw a navy-blue prototype of a woman, with sharp black lines detailing her shape, as if she were a dot-to-dot picture a preschooler tried to color. "Thank you so much for taking the time to speak with me. I brought a, um, well, a resume." She pulled a manila folder from a Coach tote bag, a large and authentic-looking Coach tote bag. "Admittedly, my work experience—my traditional work experience is rather thin."

At a glance, the resume—on actual parchment paper—was barely a resume. It was a list of volunteer positions, clearly chosen around children's activities: PTA offices, booster club committee chairs, and fundraisers for sport, dance, and cheer teams. Nothing about teaching anyone anything. But if the woman could handle obnoxious parents, maybe she had skills Maxine could use.

"You have an art degree?"

Genevieve sat a little straighter in her chair and raised her eyebrows. She looked so terrified, Max felt anxious. "Yes, granted it's from a community school. I—"

"Nothing wrong with community school."

"Thank you." Her face softened. "I've been following *Altered States* since you and Ms. Bremen were the *Dee Dee and Max Show* on YouTube. I, um," she reached to the floor and picked up a paper bag by its handle. "I made a couple of jewelry boxes from your 'Vintage Jewels' episode. This is one of them."

She set the jewelry box on the table between them. *Yes! Finally, a student who got the hint to do something original.* She had combined their techniques with her own style and, Maxine picked up the box to look inside, she had a great eye for balance, detail, and proportion. She could work...if she could handle the day-to-day responsibilities.

"This is really good!" Dee needs to see it, but when Genevieve leaned forward, Maxine glimpsed the lining of her jacket. Definitely high-end. Definitely something Lauren would wear to a casual lunch if she wasn't wearing something she and Mama created. Did people borrow a suit like that? "So, tell me, Genevieve, what made you decide you'd like to work here?"

"Well," with her hands clasped on her lap, and spine boarding-school straight, Genevieve gave what sounded like a rehearsed speech. "As mentioned, I've been following the *Dee Dee and Max Show* and the Altered States Pinterest and website postings. I've subscribed to your newsletter and taken some of your classes. When I realized you were opening a real-life, brick-and-mortar store so close to my home, I just *had* to apply for a job here."

"Just had to?" It was hard to follow the woman's motivation.

Max didn't want to invest in hiring someone only to have her quit the first time she scratched a nail.

"Yes! This isn't the kind of art I did in school. But it's the kind of art I want to do. I want to be part of your...your scene."

"Right. So, did you receive your AA? I don't see the date listed."

"It's been, um, quite some time. But I, I did." Genevieve almost frowned, but seemed to catch herself and opened her eyes wide. "And, as you can tell, I'm still eager to learn new techniques."

Max checked out the wedding ring on Genevieve's finger as she fiddled with her necklace.

"Could you give me a second?" She stood. "I just want to talk to Dee Dee privately."

"Of course." Genevieve nodded.

She found Dee outside the front of the store, her hands cupping her face pressed up against the glass.

"I need your intuition." Max let the door shut behind her.

"I have intuition?"

"I don't know what to do with the woman. I want to hire her, but I think for the wrong reasons. I mean, she's clearly creative, but she has no retail experience."

"Neither do we."

"Right. But she does have experience working on PTAs and booster clubs."

"And that translates to?"

"Handling dramatic, difficult people."

"Right. The people I don't wanna be around."

"But she could be one of them, judging by that suit."

"Yeah."

"Which is why I'm questioning myself. I want to hire her to deal with the people we don't want to deal with, but...she might be one of those."

"So...now what? Go back to the well?" Dee slid her hands into the pockets of her baggy jeans, making them drop even lower on her hips. "Do we even have a well?"

"We have no other applicants who seem any more qualified. We're behind already on getting this place unpacked because I've been focused on me—"

"Because we've a shit ton to do, and we're fucking humans. What's the worst that can happen? She gives us a couple days' help unpacking and quits?"

"OK. Come with me. Let's do this together."

In the consultation room, Genevieve was putting her jewelry box in the bag she'd brought it in. "I'm sorry I've apparently wasted your time." Was she about to cry?

"Did I miss something?" Dee asked.

Genevieve slid her resume back into her tote bag. "I know I'm not qualified. At least not on paper." She stood and sniffed.

"You didn't waste anybody's time." Maxine kept hold of Dee, hoping her grip would keep the snide or sarcastic comments inside her partner's head. "You totally misunderstood."

"What's there not to understand?" Genevieve's reddened eyes searched Max's then Dee's. "I don't belong here."

"Yeah, you have a point." Dee shrugged. "Look at this place. Look at us. Look at you. You look like you're on your way to the Junior League in Philly for a luncheon. I probably look homeless. And Max looks like she's grocery shopping at Whole Foods."

"Damn!" Maxine released Dee, giving her shoulder a gentle shove. "I was going for the Stop N Shop look."

Dee giggled, wandered over to the other side of the consult table, and sat on a stool. Genevieve almost smiled.

Max returned to her stool and gestured to Genevieve to sit. "Do you seriously want to get calluses, inhale wood splinters and glue fumes, only to be yelled at by some of South Jersey's worst during the holiday crush?"

The trace of Genevieve's smile disappeared. "Glue fumes don't sound so bad." She slumped, let her bag drop to the floor. "Maybe they'll knock me out."

"Genevieve." Max reached over and touched her arm. Yeah, there was something about this woman that was different from the façade she put on. "Why are you really here?"

Genevieve looked at each one separately again, sighed, placed both elbows on the table, and interlaced her fingers under her chin. "I just spent the past year recovering from breaking my femur. My driving leg femur. During that time, I had to rely on my family. I had three surgeries, there were complications...in short, it took a long time to heal."

"I'm sure." Max rubbed her thigh. She thought the femur was the strongest bone in the body.

"I was pretty much chair-ridden with nothing to do but think and get lost in Pinterest, in what you were doing, really. You sparked something in me. Meanwhile, I realized I kind of hate my family. I can't stand being around them. My husband and I were barely together as a couple before it happened." She sniffed, her eyes reddened. "I can't...see, I had this dog. Lola. I didn't realize how much she softened everything for me. But, she died, and...well..." she heaved a breath, searched through her purse for a tissue. "Well, it's nice that I can go to the bathroom alone. But without her, without that source of unconditional love...I think I hit a breaking point. The day I walked in here and found that help wanted sign..." She wiped tears from her face, "Earlier that morning, I seriously contemplated putting vodka in my breakfast coffee."

"Coffee with vodka?" Dee slammed a hand on the consultation table. "Is that good?"

Genevieve's mouth hung open a second before she responded. "I, I don't know. I just *considered* doing it. I realized that was a bad sign. I realized I needed to get out of that house before I hurt someone."

"I totally understand." Maxine nodded.

"Truth be told," Genevieve wiped her face again. "Aside from decorating my home and your classes, I haven't done anything creative for years. But I'm aching to make something beautiful again."

"I see."

"I have no other skills."

Dee burst out laughing. She fell off the stool and leaned against the table, laughing until she coughed.

"What's so funny?" Max braced herself for one of Dee's private jokes no one else understood.

"Max! This is fate!" Dee wiped tears from her eyes. "She's emotionally unstable, creative, and her family makes her nuts."

"You're right!" Max laughed with her. "She'll fit right in with us."

Thursday, June 24

Dee

Bam! She snapped her head up. "Ow! Fuck!" A wrenching pain shot from her shoulder up the side of her neck. She needed to find a different safe place for her mornings. The chair on her outdoor landing sucked as a bed.

"Good morning to you, too!" Hayleigh beeped her car locked.

"Sorry. Good morning. Your startled me when you slammed your car door shut I wrenched my neck."

"Am I too early? Aaack!"

"Oh shit!" Dee ran down the steps to where H had fallen. "You all right?"

"Yeah. Wow. Those stairs are slippery." She let Dee help her up.

"I gotta get someone to take care of that." Dee gripped H's chin and held her head still, so she could look for signs of a concussion in her eyes. "Did you bump your bean?"

"No. But I think I bruised my shin."

"C'mon up." Dee let go of her. "Let's put some ice on you."

In the kitchen, Dee sat H in one chair at her dinette and propped her foot on the other. "Jeesh, I'm sorry." She placed a Ziploc bag full of ice on the growing bruise.

"Nothing to be sorry about. It's not your fault."

"It kinda is. I've known about those steps since I moved in.

They're even on my whiteboard." She pointed into the living room. "I just don't know who to call."

"Get Marco."

"Mom's handyman? You have his contact info?"

H shook her head. "I live in an apartment where people take care of that shit for me."

Dee reached for her phone in her back pocket. Found it a minute later in her bathroom. "Why do I want this?" She held it up.

"Text Mom. Get Marco's info. Fix stairs."

"Right." Dee tapped in the message. At her whiteboard, she added a note under the stairs with a falling stick figure to follow up with Mom if she didn't get back to her soon.

"What's the puzzle piece?" H nodded toward the board.

"Oh, so like..." Dee scratched her head.

"A conspiracy?"

"Yeah. Maybe. I can't put it all together. But I seriously do think someone killed my father."

"Did you talk to Mom?"

"Wow. You must have hit your head, hard."

"Again, put a bottle of wine in her hand and go shopping. Maybe not in that order." H hobbled into the living room, holding the ice on her shin, and sat down. "You do need new furniture. This sofa sucks. Call Mom. Tell her to buy you a new sofa. She'll come clean about everything."

"I can't let her do that. I'll end up with some antique from colonial times that will cost so much I'll be terrified to sit on it. You know how messy I am."

"But you'll get your answers. And if you go shopping with her, you'll get answers and the sofa you want."

Answers would be good. If they'd make the nightmares go away so she could sleep, it might be worth asking Mom. But shopping with her? "You coming?"

"Aren't we spending Saturday together? Invite her to join us."

"Saturday?" Dee scrolled to her calendar. Yeah. *Shopping with H* was entered on Saturday. Her sister had convinced her she needed something that didn't have the I-just-got-out-of-bed look for working in the store. Dee wasn't exactly excited. In part, because she hated shopping in malls and department stores. But also, although she adored her baby sister, sometimes she wanted to knock her over the head. Hayleigh was one of her most favorite people on the planet. She would kill for her. But H sometimes made her more scattered than she already was. She was always so bubbly, so social. She had conversations with strangers as easily as other people scratched a mosquito bite. Everyone instantly became a close friend of hers—she was interested in them, and they in her. Every freaking one of them. It was almost intolerable for Dee—having to bounce her attention from the myriad compliments and bits of small talk H continually dished out to total strangers when they tried to do something like walk through the cosmetics department. Could she handle that *and* Mom at the same time?

"Call her." Hayleigh rearranged the ice on her shin. "Invite her to come with us. She'll buy everything. That will make her giddy, loosen her up. Then you'll question her and catch her off guard at dinner."

"And you will be there the whole time? You'll buffer me from her, so I don't shove her into traffic by accident when she tries to hold my hand in public?"

"I always got your back, right?" H giggled. "I'll hold her hand for you."

"You should have been born in Switzerland."

"It's too cold there."

Dee sat sideways on the other end of the lumpy sofa and scrolled to "Her" in the contacts on her phone.

Don't answer. Don't answer. Please, voice mail!

"Hi, sweetheart!

Shit! "Hi, Mom." She tried to shoot poison darts through her eyes at her kid sister.

"I was just about to send you Marco's information."

"Cool. But—"

"Are you doing some kind of home improvement already?"

"No. Um…" Deep inhale, two, three. "H and I are going into Philly on Saturday to do a little shopping for career clothes and—"

"Of course, I'd love to go!"

"Great." She strained to keep back a sigh.

"I'll put together a nice itinerary for us," Mom continued.

"Um, good." Hayleigh better be freaking right. "Just please include Dick Blick's Art Supplies and—"

"Shoe stores! Of course!"

"Well, that, and—"

"Furniture! Oh! This is so exciting!"

"Yeah, um, but can we just look at furniture?"

"What do you mean?"

"Let's just browse. You can get an idea of what I like, then you can handle the rest for me."

That sound Mom makes when she does an inhale shriek ripped into Dee's eardrum. "Are you giving me carte blanche to decorate your whole apartment?"

"NO!" Dee threw a couch pillow at Hayleigh. "I'm giving you carte blanche to pick out living room furniture only after you see what I like."

"What about that dinette?"

"Br—an artist friend is making me a unique piece. You can get chairs for it."

"How will I know they will go with whatever he makes?"

"I've seen a sample. It'll go with everything I like."

"I'm not sure. But, whatever! We can always replace the chairs." Mom's voice perked back up. "I'm so excited about this! A project for my Dee Dee! Thank you!"

"Oh, thank H. She's the one who reminded me."

"I will. And I'll pull some strings to make sure there's a table at Rouge set aside for us so we can eat dinner there without a wait. They've done something extraordinary for their outside dining. Have you seen it yet?"

Dee made eye contact with Hayleigh, pointed a finger at her head, and pulled an imaginary trigger.

Mom prattled on. "...they're calling it a 'streetery,' as it's outside on the sidewalk and goes into the street. It's just gorgeous! We'll make a whole day of it! Me and my girls!"

"A whole day!" She tried to find another pillow to throw. "Looking forward to it, Mom." Dee clicked off the call. H burst out laughing. "I will get even with you, you know."

"I'm sure." Hayleigh looked at the giant man's watch she wore. "But until then, let's get downstairs. We're late."

"For what?"

"We have a strategy meeting, then you guys are getting trained on your system."

"Really?" Dee looked at her phone, scrolled to her calendar. "Shit! I set the appointment but forgot to make an alarm for it."

"Good thing you got me in your corner."

"I'm still not so sure about that."

Genevieve

Genevieve was having second thoughts, more like ninth or tenth thoughts. She wasn't sure about anything related to this job idea anymore. Granted, it was only her first day, but still...It'd be totally different if Maxine was the only one in charge. In fact, Genevieve had a bit of a girl crush on Maxine. She was so elegant, so poised, so smart, and yes, so talented. The woman exuded confidence and capability. She was everything Genevieve wanted to be.

But that Dee Dee!

Genevieve couldn't believe it when Dee Dee burst into the store with her younger sister, late for their meeting. Was she late all the time? Must be. Maxine didn't seem surprised by it. They were supposed to be strategizing, planning their first in-store, in-person class. It was a big deal, if you asked Genevieve. And probably a big deal for Maxine, too. But Dee and her sister sat at the table giggling and trading private jokes like it was a slumber party. Hayleigh even stood behind Dee at one point and braided a feather she'd found into her sister's hair. How is that any way to run a business?

Thank God they decided to do a dry run for the first class. And they liked Genevieve's idea when she suggested she could get her sister and a few of her girlfriends—people who wouldn't mind if there were a few snags to work through—to attend.

"Great," Maxine shut her laptop. "So Genevieve, let us know if next Thursday evening will work for your friends. We'll supply wine and some finger foods, and of course, all they'll need supply-wise."

"This is so exciting." Genevieve meant it as she glanced over at Dee Dee. Maybe she'd be more professional when the shop was open, and they had customers. This job really could be something special. If Dee could just pull herself together.

"All right, I'm out of here for a few." Hayleigh stood up. "I'm meeting up with another client for a bit, but I'll be back for the POS training."

"POS?" Genevieve had no idea what the term meant and, frankly, was relieved when Dee said the letters in unison with her.

"Point of sale system." Hayleigh walked away from them as if she made sense. At the sales counter, she picked up something that looked like an iPad. "This is what you'll be using to ring up your customers in the store. The system will tie into the inventory so that if someone is shopping online, they won't buy something that was just sold in the store. A rep will be here later today to train us on all the deets."

"Oh, interesting." Genevieve accepted the iPad thing from her and looked at the blank screen. Hayleigh certainly seemed to know what she was talking about. But who taught her how to dress? She wore flared yellow capri pants, a white bowling shirt with a blue stripe running down the left side, and a pair of black, patent-leather platform Oxford shoes. She had a red-and-white flowered headscarf holding back her turquoise hair, a string of tattooed symbols running up her arm, several earrings, and a nose ring. How on Earth did the woman manage to get clients to take her seriously? Maybe they only communicated online. Face-to-face meetings must be surprising.

"How long before the POS training?" Maxine frowned at her phone.

"About two hours." Hayleigh kissed Dee on the cheek, then blew a kiss to Maxine and Genevieve. "Bye!"

"You OK, Max?" Dee pulled her apparently uncombed (except for the braid with the feather) hair up on her head and wound one of the bands that was on her wrist around the messy pile.

"No. But I don't want to get into it now." Maxine stared into Dee's eyes, her mouth in a hard line. Genevieve couldn't tell if she was angry or sad. Probably angry at Dee Dee. "Will you be all right if I run out for a few?"

"Of course." Dee waved her hand in the air like she had everything under control.

"Great." Maxine was already walking toward the back door. "I'll be back in time for the training."

Which left Genevieve alone with Dee Dee. A week ago, Genevieve would have been thrilled. But that was before she realized what a mess her artist heroine seemed to be. She swallowed against that stupid lump in her throat and formed a smile. "So, what should we do?"

Dee placed both hands on her hips and blew a raspberry with her lips as she glanced around the store. "Well, yesterday, Max and I were pretty busy." She went toward the front windows. *Oh my! She was barefoot! Barefoot!* "Looks like Max was setting stuff out up front here, kind of arranging it so it makes sense and looks good." She spun around. "I was hanging the framing samples on the wall. Why don't I finish that? You good with the front?"

"Of course." Genevieve gave a curt nod and moved toward the center of the front room, where there were a few open boxes and some still sealed. She began with one of the open ones and removed an absolutely adorable wind chime made from a wine bottle. The bottom had been cut off, and dangling from inside were the cutest glass fish on beaded wires. Most likely, Dee Dee had made it, at least made the fish. She set it on a shelf with the chimes dangling over the ledge. The next one out had a series of glass silly birds. So playful! What great gifts!

"Hello?" A very well-dressed woman entered the store.

"Oh, hello!" Genevieve was nervous about handling a customer when she had no training, but what on Earth could Dee Dee do with this woman? Besides, they weren't even open yet. "Can I help you?"

"I'm looking for Dee." The woman was wearing an extremely expensive pair of sunglasses that she swept up onto her head with a hand that sported the largest solitaire diamond ring Genevieve had ever seen. She almost shielded her eyes to protect them from the light refracting through it. *Uh oh. This woman couldn't meet Dee Dee.*

"I think she's in the back. I'm Genevieve. Can I help you?"

"Oh, I'm just dropping off a little something." She walked past Genevieve as if she owned the place. "Deirdre!" she hollered.

"Mom?" Dee yelled and ran into the front. "What the hell are you doing here?"

Genevieve clamped a hand to her chest. This beautiful, elegant woman was Dee Dee's *mother?* And Dee spoke to her like *that?*

Granted, she didn't sound nasty, just surprised. Still, why swear?

"Just stopping by, sweetheart. Kaz's secretary made us a *vat* of ice cream." She held up a plastic bag. "Just a *vat!* And I was like, 'who could eat so much?' *We* certainly can't, but you know Kaz would if I let him. So I divvied it up for you and Hayleigh. I thought she'd be here, too."

"Thanks." Dee accepted the plastic bag as she leaned in to let her mother kiss her cheek. "You just missed her. But she'll be back later. I'll give it to her."

"Wonderful!" Dee's mother reached into her purse, pulled out a tissue, and wiped her hands. "You might want to get that in a freezer as soon as possible. Homemade ice cream melts quickly."

"Oh, sure." Dee held the bag out at arm's length. "I'll, um, I'll pop it in the fridge upstairs."

"While you're up there, do you think you could measure how much wall space you have between the floor and the front windowsills? The ones facing Main Street? And maybe how wide the windows are? There's a gorgeous French chaise coming up for auction at Material Culture that would be perfect for your place."

"Yeah, um..." Dee glanced left and right, as if she were looking for something.

"I believe you have some rulers in your supplies under the whiteboard," her mother said.

"Right!" Dee perked up. "I'll be back in a few. Take a look around the store." Dee Dee left through a door near the front entrance.

"I'm so sorry, I didn't realize you were Dee Dee's mother." Genevieve held out her hand. How was that possible? And the poor woman! She knew right away that Dee was hunting for a ruler. So sad to see your grown child so, so, so needy. "I'm Genevieve."

"Lauren," she shook her hand. "Will you be working in the store?"

"Yes." Though if Genevieve were to be honest, she wasn't sure for how much longer.

"Lovely." Lauren roamed the front room. "I'm glad Dee and Maxine will have a little help. God knows I'd love to be here for them, but, well...do you have children?"

"Yes. A daughter who's eighteen and a son about to turn seventeen."

"Wow, that's close!"

"Yes, well…" ahem. That lump!

"And you certainly don't look old enough for teenagers!"

"I was a young mom." Genevieve waited for that judgmental shadow she'd seen on many women's faces when they realized she'd had a daughter at nineteen. It didn't matter that she had a private school education, that her family was one of Philadelphia's oldest, that she belonged—.

"Good for you for getting it done and over with! I was well over thirty when I had Hayleigh, and let me tell you, I certainly didn't have the energy to be the mom I wanted to be."

Genevieve released her clenched hands. *What a unique perspective!* She liked this woman. And how interesting…she spoke to people as if she'd known them forever, the way Dee Dee spoke to people. So casual and at home in herself.

"Anyway," Lauren continued, "you have a daughter, you'll understand. Dee Dee would interpret my presence as a sign that I think she needs help, and somehow that would breed contempt."

"Ha!" The laugh that escaped Genevieve surprised her. "I thought I was the only one whose daughter misconstrued everything."

"Heavens no!" Lauren waved her hand, again, the way Dee tended to.

"Well, I'm impressed that Dee will let you pick out furniture. I'm terrified to even suggest something as simple as socks to my daughter."

"You said she's eighteen?" Lauren picked up a blown-glass

olive oil or vinegar dispenser and rotated it.

"Yes. Her birthday was at the beginning of the month."

"Oh, she's perfectly normal. She'll hate you until she's about twenty-four. Then she'll become human again and appreciate you. But, she'll never admit she needs you for anything."

"So there's hope for me?"

"There's always hope!" Lauren glanced over the jewelry set out in acrylic holders on the étagère. "Hayleigh actually became human before she hit twenty. Which was a good thing, otherwise, my liver may not have survived. I think I doubled my wine intake for a while with her. Between her diabetes and the emotional distress she felt from being gay, whoo! She was tough. But look at her now. Just twenty-two and thriving with a marketing business she started as her senior project in college."

"She does seem to know her stuff."

"Yes," Lauren continued about the store picking up and looking at things. "Though, granted, she did get a lot of therapy. I'm sure that helped her mature quickly. That and the impact on all of us from dealing with Dee's condition."

"Condition?" Compared to Lauren, Genevieve might have things easy. She set another wind chime on the shelf and turned around to face the woman. "Is she sick?"

"She didn't tell you?" Lauren met her eyes, briefly covered her mouth. "Then I probably shouldn't either, but...Moms never quit worrying, right?"

"Right."

"So, mother to mother, can I confide in you?"

"Of course." Genevieve nodded.

"When Dee was very little, she was in an accident that damaged part of her brain. The result is an assortment of symptoms they lump under 'executive dysfunction.' I'm sure you've noticed some. She has attentional problems, short-term memory issues, and God knows she's organizationally challenged. When she's stressed, it all gets much worse, and she'll have panic attacks. I'm so worried that—"

"Thanks again, Mom." Dee burst through the door. "I've always liked Mrs. D'Angelo's ice cream."

"Who doesn't?" Lauren clapped her hands together. "Did you measure?"

"Yeah." Dee handed her a torn piece of paper. "I sketched the area."

"Wonderful! And the store looks amazing. When can I tell my friends to come in and shop?"

"I think we'll be completely set up next week, that weekend is Independence Day, right? H said we could have a soft opening, whatever the hell that is, the week after. Or maybe the next week?" Dee pulled her phone out of her pocket and looked at it. "I'm not really sure right now. But, I think we have an official opening on Saturday, July 10. By then, whatever kinks need to be worked out will be worked out, so we'll have a kink-free grand opening. H isn't inviting any of her friends for that."

"Why not, dear?"

"It was a joke, Mom. Never mind."

"Very good." Lauren pulled her into a hug. "I'm so looking forward to shopping with you on Saturday!" She turned to Genevieve and pulled her into a hug, too. "So, I can count on you to watch her like a mother?" she whispered.

"Of course."

Friday, June 25

Dee

"Good morning, Dee Dee!" Jhansi greeted her with a smile so bright, Dee could almost see her reflection in her teeth. "Two very large, black coffees and a croissant for my favorite customer."

"You are the best, Jhansi. You must come to my store when we open next week." Dee handed her the postcard H had made her promise to give to everyone she saw. "I mean in two weeks." Or whenever, because she forgot, again, to ask H for clarity.

"I will! Do you have more? I'll put them on the counter. I must help keep you in business."

"Of course! How else will I keep *you* in business?" Dee grinned and handed her the whole stack. She almost felt human. She'd slept fitfully, but at least she'd slept the night before. Perhaps the nightmares really were just from the stress of the move and losing Gram. Maybe it was more than she'd given it credit for. Maybe her imagination just got the best of her about her father. Maybe—her phone dinged. Brett!

You OK?

Am I ever?

She hit send, then immediately added to it.

Yeah. OK. You?

It was so good to hear from him. Maybe they'd finally freaking talk. Maybe she'd finally freaking figure out what's going on. And maybe she'll finally freaking sleep unfitfully again.

She found a table outside on the sidewalk and set down her tray with her coffee and croissant, settled in, then changed to a chair facing the opposite way because she still hadn't found her sunglasses. What was taking Brett so long to type a stupid response? Why didn't he call her? She bit her croissant, wiped the crumbs from her t-shirt, and chewed. Waited until she couldn't take it any longer.

She hit the call button for Brett. He didn't answer. What the hell?

Why were men so mind-fucking weird? It was Friday morning. She should be in the shower with Cooper dozing in her bed right about now. But he had to fly down to DC for a client. That's fine. But shouldn't he have asked her what she was doing? Did he just want to have breakfast with her now and nothing more? Was sex before breakfast now out of the question? What the hell was wrong with that man?

She scrolled to the last text he'd sent and typed

WTF is wrong with you?

Laughter erupted. What the fuck was wrong with her? She replaced the message.

doesn't feel like friday

He responded with a half-selfie; the left side of the shot featured a man in a suit, sprawled out in an airplane seat, asleep with his head flopped to the side, mouth wide open.

Wish I was with my favorite
friday morning company

Evan's name and number lit up her phone. A nauseous pit in her stomach told her not to answer. She did anyway.

"Good morning?" she hoped.

"Hey there." His voice sounded tired. As if that two-word

greeting took as much energy as wrestling a grizzly to the ground. "Did I catch you at a bad time?"

"No. Just eating breakfast. What's up?" *And why did you talk to Kaz?*

"Well, Mom turns ninety-five tomorrow."

"Holy shit! Really?" She put her phone on speaker so she could talk to him as she clicked on her calendar to text a reminder to call Josie. There was already a reminder. She returned the call to non-speaker.

"We're having a luncheon for her on Sunday."

"Nice."

"And she'd like you to come."

"You bet. What time and where?"

"It'll be at her place, around noon."

Back on speaker, she entered the details into her calendar, then created a reminder for it a couple of hours before noon.

"Um, Dee?"

"Yeah? I'm here." She took the phone off speaker, held it to her head.

"Mom's…not doing so good."

"What does that mean?"

"That means…" she heard his breath shake. "We started hospice today."

"Hospice? As in…"

"As in…that. She doesn't have much time left."

"But…" Dee stared through the traffic going up and down Main Street. Josie had just held her hand. Rubbed the Sharpie stain on her thumb. Hugged her. "But she's not sick."

"She's had a heart condition for a long time…the doctor said…she'd been battling some kind of walking pneumonia," she heard Evan say. "I didn't know. She never mentioned anything to me about it. Her doctor had told her not to travel, specifically not to go anywhere people gathered, he was afraid she'd pick something else up."

"She had to go say goodbye to Gram, I get it."

"Well, anyway, like I said, she would like to see you."

"I'd like to see her, too."

She clicked out of the call and stared at the screen of her phone. Josie...was she losing Josie now, too? Granted, she wasn't as close to her as she was to Gram, but somehow Dee had it in her head that Gram wasn't completely gone, in part, because she still had Gram's sister. A text lit up her phone.

I think we need to talk

*I thought we already did!
Isn't that why we had
breakfast?*

After she sent it, she noticed that the talk message had come from Brett, not Cooper. She typed more to Brett.

*Sry! That was to the wrong
person. And yes, we do need
to talk!*

Once more, she sat back in her chair and waited for both men to reach out to her.

Instead, Maxine called.

Maxine

Maxine rolled down the passenger window to yell through it. "Is the front door locked?" The last thing she needed was someone to look in the window of the store, see all the beautiful merchandise, enter, and notice no one was working.

"I just triple-checked it before coming out the back." Dee got in and buckled her seat belt. "Do I get to know why you need me to come with you? And where we are going?"

"In case I need help burying the body, and I don't really know yet." Maxine watched Dane's dot on her phone. He was just a couple of blocks from their house, heading north.

"Whose body?"

"Dane's. Here." She handed her phone to Dee. "Watch that blue dot. Figure out where he's going."

"Um...shit, Max. I can't tell where it is...oh, actually, it's on Cuthbert heading toward Route 70."

Max put her car in reverse and watched an SUV pass by in the back-camera monitor.

"Why are we axing Dane? Oh, no. You didn't catch him with hooker-shoes, did you?"

Dee was probably looking at her, but if Maxine allowed eye contact, she'd probably cry. "Let me catch you up." She backed into the side street. "So, that same app has a notification you can set that will tell you if someone leaves a specific place. And yesterday, wouldn't you know it? The notification went off when I was at the store at the end of our meeting. He'd left the house, *during working hours*, which he *never* does. So, I wanted to know where he went."

"Is that why you left?"

"Yep." She banked a hard right on Main Street. "I found him at the bank. Couldn't tell what he was doing. He didn't know I saw him, but when I looked online later, I saw he got out a couple hundred dollars in cash."

"Interesting. Are you stalking him to see where he's spending the money?"

"I'm not stalking." She turned onto Cuthbert. Not seeing his car, she stomped on the gas and began weaving around the slower traffic on the two-lane road. "Well, maybe I am. Damn!" She hit the brakes when she saw a gray Volvo just two cars ahead. "Is that him?"

"I think so." Dee leaned forward in her seat.

"Look at the dot. Is my dot close to his dot?"

"Which dot's your dot?"

"Are the two dots close to each other?"

"Oh, yeah. Yeah. That's him." Dee set the phone in the console. "But what happened yesterday? Why are we doing this?"

"He's having an affair."

"No, he isn't."

"Yes, he is."

"Dane can't be having an affair. That's not the kind of thing Dane would do."

"That's what I thought. But he is."

"So, yeah, hooker-shoes is hard to explain. But, it's freaking Dane! He would have had to plan this out years ago. Beta-tested it somehow. Tracked what worked and what didn't in a spreadsheet using some AI shit to help him—"

"Please don't make me want to love him right now." Maxine's vision blurred from tears.

"Dane is as loyal to you as I am."

"I hope you're more loyal. I couldn't take being betrayed by both of you." The sobs erupted in her throat. She almost pulled over to the side of the road to cry it out, but she saw him head west on 70. *He must be going into Philly again. To see that bitch in the heels?* She wiped her face with one hand, sat straighter in her seat as she headed west, too, maintaining a decent distance between them. "He's barely said a word to me since he left Tuesday morning to sit with that ho."

"But didn't you say he needed time to process you quitting your job?"

"He's never had to leave home to process things before." She lost sight of him and sped up. "Nor find company to help him."

"Well...so you followed him to the bank yesterday, then what?"

146

Dee picked up the phone. "He's at the bridge."

"He's probably going to the hotel for a late-morning tryst." Max gripped the steering wheel harder. "After the bank, he went to a lab."

"A what?"

"A lab. Like where you get blood work done."

"Do you think she works there?"

"Oh! I hadn't thought of that..." Maxine let the idea sit with her for a few minutes. "Maybe, I mean, it's not one that's on our insurance, so he wasn't going there on doctor's orders."

"How long was he there? Did he have a bandage on or anything last night?"

Maxine thought back to the night before. "He was wearing a long-sleeved shirt. I remember that. He rolled the sleeves up when he helped me with the dishes."

"A long-sleeved shirt in summer? It was hot as shit yesterday. I think he got blood work done."

Maxine nodded. "Maybe." But *yes*, was what she was thinking. She slowed to keep pace with the traffic. "What kind of blood work? And why?" Please Dee! Max needed a good reason.

They rode in silence a full minute, then she felt Dee's hand, lightly this time, on her arm. "Is it....I mean, I hate like hell asking this, but, like, is it possible he thinks he has an STD?"

Maxine's breath came in and out short, her nose ran. "That's what I thought. That's exactly what I thought! Damnit!" She banged her hand on the steering wheel. "Can you believe him?" Tears ran down her cheeks.

"That shit!" Dee pounced to face forward. "What the hell? Max! I'm so sorry!"

"You have nothing to be sorry for. His ass, though..." Maxine sniffed. What about his ass? What was she going to do? She stopped at a light. "If we lose him before we get to the bridge, find him on my phone again."

"OK, but hey, Max. I still can't believe it. This is Dane. There has to be another reason. Something else must be going on."

"For example?" Max found a used tissue in the console and wiped her nose.

"Is it possible he's interviewing for a new job or a promotion or something? Maybe he needed a drug test for it."

The light changed to green. His car was nowhere. "Find him." Max ordered. Though her tone wasn't as harsh as she intended. Her breath came easier. "You know, I did wonder at some point if it was a job interview."

"Yeah. So I've never had a real job, I don't know how interviews actually happen, but he works for a big company. Didn't they fly him out to Chicago to interview for this one? Maybe this time the interviewer came here."

"Maybe. And, some tech companies are really casual. He might not be expected to wear a suit for an interview."

"He's off the bridge, taking that loop that swings under it."

"And he didn't kiss the woman with those stupid stiletto shoes." Max tried to remember the scene in detail. "But he did take her hand."

"And hold it?"

"Maybe it was just a shake, and I misinterpreted?"

"Think about it, Max, it's Dane. His life is so well-scripted; when could he ever have done anything with someone?"

"I don't know." She slowed as she went through the autopay toll booth.

"And do you ever spend any time apart? I mean...he would have been seeing her only during business hours, right?"

Maxine chewed over what Dee had said. She hadn't even thought of how much time they spent together. In fact, they were always together, except for when they worked. "You're making some sense."

"That should scare the fuck out of you." Dee snorted.

"What do I do now?"

"Do you want to try to find him in the hotel?"

"I don't know."

"If you storm the place and find him, then what?"

"If I confront him, and it *is* a job interview..."

"That could ruin things for him."

"So it looks like I have to wait for him to tell me what's going on?" Which could explain why he's having such a hard time. He's trying to process her changing careers and her changing her mind about having a baby, while possibly getting a new job for himself. Poor Dane. She owed him some grace. "OK. Let's get back to the store. Genevieve should be showing up soon, anyway. It'd be good if we were there before her. I didn't think this through."

Dee

Finally! It'd been a couple of weeks since Dee did any glasswork. Felt like a couple of years. But the lampworking space was finally set up. She was good to go. Well, not really. She was being irresponsible, firing up a blow torch with nothing on the window in case someone looked in. But she needed to do this. So she used the little torch. It wouldn't be as bad.

She checked the front door to be sure the store was locked, though she was certain she'd done that already, maybe even a few times since Max and Genevieve had left. Shut off all the lights except the one in the back, where she was in the glass studio area. Flicked on the exhaust fan. Connected her phone to the Bluetooth speaker and chose a montage of nineties grunge music that she set at high volume.

Pictures of bougainvillea were spread on a side table. She looked at her stash of lower-quality glass rods to use as practice. None was the right pink. In fact, that was going to be a tough get in any quality. Pink glass is always hard to find. But that's all right. She'd experiment on whatever colors she had, then, when she finally figured out how to make the flower, she'd source the right color of rod.

She fired up the little torch, then, with tungsten-tipped tweezers at the ready to stretch and form the shape, she pulled on her safety goggles and held a rod in the flame. As it started melting, a call came through her speaker. Seriously? Who calls her on a Friday night?

Who calls her, ever?

Probably Mom, wanting to make sure Dee remembered to breathe.

She tipped the rod into a container of water, turned off the torch, and picked up the phone.

Gram.

What the fuck?

Oh, Gram's house. Granddad.

What the holy fuck?

She let it ring long enough that her phone silenced, went dark. Didn't realize she was holding her breath as she waited for a voicemail notification until she had to suck in some air.

No voicemail came.

The only time Granddad had ever called her was to tell her Gram had died.

God, but it was tempting to ignore this call. If she could ignore it forever, then maybe she'd never have to hear whatever horrible thing he was going to tell her. Never experience that pain.

But it could be about Brett.

Her phone remained dark in her hand. She was going to have to call him back.

Shit.

She needed reinforcements.

Upstairs, she filled a rocks glass with ice, then poured vodka a quarter of the way up. Halfway up. That would save her from having to make a second drink. One semi-brown lime remained in the fridge. She cut it in half, squeezed it into the glass, then added the emptied half shell.

Where would it be safe to talk to him?

With every light on in her apartment, she chose the lumpy sofa, sitting sideways at one end, feet tucked close to her rear, and rested the phone on the back cushion. With her glass perched on a knee, clenched safe in a fist, she tapped on the number to return Granddad's call.

Once more, she didn't realize she was holding her breath until he answered.

"Hope I didn't cause you any worry," was how he answered. "I probably should have left a message."

Yeah, he should have. "Is everything all right?" *Please. Please be OK. Please, Brett, be OK.*

"Sometimes I'm not sure if anything ever is. But we're all living life like we always do down here."

"Cool. Good." What the hell did that mean? "Um..."

The silence lasted long enough for a sip of vodka.

"What about you?" he broke it.

"What about me?"

"Are you all right?" Wow? Was he checking on her? In his smooth and rich Southern drawl? *Wonder if the man knew he could have sung country music with that voice?* She felt herself smile, even relax a little at her private joke. *Maybe Granddad missed his calling. He could have been a crooner.* She realized he was waiting for an answer. "I guess so. I mean, you know, for me."

"Good, good."

It was the longest conversation she'd ever had with the man. He had always seemed distant to her, or uncomfortable, or...something. And now that Gram's death was forcing them to communicate, it was clear they were both in need of practice. The puzzle piece seemed to hang in the air between them. She should ask him about her father. "So, um, Granddad...do you think Brett will be OK?" *Why did that come out?*

She thought she heard ice clink in a glass. Granddad must be taking a little solace in some bourbon. She sipped her vodka so he wouldn't have to drink alone.

"Lord, I hope so, Deirdre."

"Is there anything I can do? I mean, I know Aunt Louise thinks the best thing for him would be to never hear from me again."

"Well, that woman was never an arbiter of good judgment." More ice in glass. Was granddad drunk? "Brett just has some demons he needs to slay."

Yep. Drunk.

"And," he continued. "I think he needs some time to grieve Mimi a bit 'fore he can do it. Maybe she can even help him. I don't know how all that works."

"I don't even know what you mean."

"Heheheh." His low laugh surprised her. He had a sense of humor? "So I invited him to move in with me for a while. He set up some tools in your grandmother's studio."

Good. That meant Brett was going to be all right. Gram's studio will still produce art. He'll heal in there.

"Said he was making a couple of tables for you. Is that right?"

"Yeah. Like the one on your sunporch."

"Nice. Does your mother know?"

Dee snorted.

"Didn't think so."

Dee opened her mouth to make a joke, but Granddad kind of ruined things.

"You don't need to worry about him, now. I'll watch over Brett."

Watch over?

"You take care of yourself, Deirdre."

The line went dead.

Dee took another sip, stared at the puzzle piece on the whiteboard. Her face was wet. She wiped it with the back of her hand. She should be there with Brett. Or he should be here with her.

At least he could make art. With Gram's spirit guiding him. If spirits did those kinds of things.

She swirled the ice around in her glass. It would be nice to have Cooper there with her. Would his family thing be over by now? Didn't he say he could come by late in the evening if it ended early enough? Was it over? Is it late, yet? What did he fucking mean?

Genevieve

Genevieve's cheeks hurt. She had politely smiled through the rehearsal. Politely smiled over the stupid small talk at dinner. Then more polite smiling, because Todd had insisted they all have a drink at the bar before everyone went their own way for the night. His last drink as a single man! *How could he say that? As if getting married to Brynn was a prison sentence where he'd never drink again. And how could Archie cheer him on like that?* Granted, her baby brother, ever the perennial bachelor, didn't understand what it meant to be in a committed relationship. But shouldn't his loyalties be with his sister? Instead, he was there partying it up with Todd, like he liked him. Though that was interesting. She never realized before, but that's how Archie had always behaved at her family events. He and Chris would "chill" together in front of some game on TV while she and Brynn cooked, and the kids did whatever they did.

What would happen going forward? If she and Chris split up,

which she really thought they needed to do, what would holidays look like? Would Archie now chill with Todd?

She rubbed her cheeks, as she stared out the front window of Chris's SUV. How was it possible that the ride home was more uncomfortable than the ride to the rehearsal. Such a silent ride. The ride to the rehearsal was awkwardly silent, but at least there had been music playing on the radio. There was nothing now, just uncomfortable silence. Uncomfortable silence as she worried about Brynn. What was Chris thinking?

He drove with his right hand on the steering wheel, his body leaning away from her. Seemed he was as uncomfortable around her as she him.

"I'm concerned about Brynn." Genevieve dared to break the silence when he stopped at a red light.

"What?" Her voice seemed to startle him. "Why?"

"I don't think she loves him. She looked, well, disappointed all evening. I think she's settling."

He remained quiet until the light turned green. "Well, it's her choice."

"I know." But no one should settle. Settle is what Genevieve and Chris had done. And where did it get them?

At the next light, he picked up his phone, glanced at it, and threw it back in the console.

"I guess we set a precedent." Genevieve wasn't sure if she was ready for this conversation, but the words flowed out anyway. She must have been very tired.

"Meaning?" He didn't look at her. Kept staring straight ahead. Not risking the occasional glance. She could be anybody in the car with him.

"Can you remember the last time either of us said 'I love you' to each other and meant it?"

He shifted in his seat some, seemed to try to move closer to the door, and cleared his throat.

"Granted, ours wasn't exactly a love match to begin with, but…Chris, do you realize we haven't said a word to each other all night? Forget about proclamations of love. We don't even talk to each other. Not a word on the way to the rehearsal, at the rehearsal, and we wouldn't be talking now if I hadn't brought this up."

"Yeah, we uh…yeah."

Well, he never was one for eloquence. "What did you see in me?"

"What?"

Surely his vocabulary wasn't that small! "When we first met? That summer we met. Remember? I was staying in my uncle's shore house; you were on leave." It was the most freedom Genevieve had ever had. Her mother was in Europe with her latest admirer. Brynn and Archie were at a sleep-away summer camp. Uncle Fritz seemed to realize she needed a break and had invited her to spend the summer with his family at the shore. She saw a handsome airman at a beach party, and he'd seemed quite taken by her. "What attracted you to me?"

He drove quietly, but she wasn't letting him get by with that. She knew what *she* had done back then: it was the only time in her life when an attractive man expressed interest in her, *and* she wasn't burdened by taking care of her siblings while her mother "entertained." She had leaned into that interest. "Chris? Please, I really want to know. What did you see in me?"

She caught him briefly look her way in the passing light of an oncoming car. "You were, well, vibrant, you know?" He cleared his throat. "You were all set on becoming, on being an artist. You were full of life…fun."

"I was alive."

Again, Mr. Silent was at the wheel.

Genevieve had been accepted to Bard College, into their fine arts program. But she was so torn—how could she leave Brynn and Archie? They still needed her, especially Brynn. She was going into her freshman year of high school. She couldn't let her suffer the angst of that year with their mother at home. And who would feed Archie? Bard was OK with her taking a gap year, so that summer she was free to be, well, free.

She didn't quite know how to do that. But there was that handsome airman who just wanted a summer fling.

"I'll never forget how terrified you looked." Though she knew she was equally terrified. What would her mother say?

"What do you mean?"

"When I showed up at Ft. Dix to tell you I was pregnant. You looked absolutely terrified. You were about to be shipped out to the Middle East and could handle that somehow. Your mission didn't scare you as much as the concept of being a dad did."

"I had plenty of training for my mission. None for being a dad. You know my father certainly wasn't a role model."

"Neither one of us was fit to be parents."

"Not true. You were overly qualified."

Interesting. He seemed to know her, know something about her. What did she know about him? He was a sports fanatic. He flew planes…What was his favorite color? Song? Food?

They were home. He hit an overhead button to open a garage door.

She had only a few more seconds to tell him she wanted a divorce, but it seemed so hard to get the words to form in her mouth. Maybe she just needed to try to know him a little more. Maybe their distance was her fault?

His phone lit up in the console with a text. He parked, looked at it.

"Shit. I have to go back out to the hanger. Joey needs me."

"Joey?"

"No one for you to worry about." So dismissive. They'd almost had a connection, and he, well, he just dismissed her. She put her hand on the door handle.

"Chris?"

"I need to go."

"I'm sure you do. And I need a divorce."

He met her eyes, held them for a heartbeat, and nodded. "That's what I wanted to talk to you about earlier in the week."

"Good. Well." She didn't have to force her smile. "Maybe that's something we can finally agree on. Hopefully, we can speak civilly to each other at some point this week to talk about how to proceed."

Saturday, June 26

Dee

Dee remembered learning about the wine windows in Florence. How a couple of centuries ago, those brilliant Italians invented a curbside drink pick-up of sorts. They put little windows in the walls of buildings. The windows had wooden doors. You'd knock on a door, someone would open it, you'd give them some money, and they'd supply a glass of vino.

Philadelphia needed to bring those back for shopping days. Between Mom's inane prattling about whatever happened to be going through her brain at the moment, and H's over-the-top extroverted personality that insisted she interact with every human being in the vicinity, Dee's head was about to explode. She'd begun the adventure with her caffeine gauge pointed at *full*, but it wasn't working well enough. She needed wine. Or maybe she should try Genevieve's trick: put a little vodka in her coffee.

Of course, if she'd been able to sleep the night before, maybe she would have been more human, and the perpetual distractions and spirited energy of two people she was pretty sure she loved would have been manageable.

But sleep was too scary last night. The nightmares woke her around two-thirty, and she spent the rest of the night/morning downstairs working with the torch, trying to perfect those damn bougainvillea flowers, accompanied by a medley of Linkin Park and

Soundgarden.

She supposed that if there were a personality test to determine whether you were part vampire, she might score more on the vampire side. Up all night listening to dead singers, and now the blinding sunshine hurt, and those fucking happy goofballs walking along beside her clearly were not of the same species as she, right? *Were vampires considered a different species?*

They stopped at a crosswalk. There were still a few hours before Rouge would save them with food and wine. God, how her head hurt. She hoped she could hang on. She rubbed her eyes with the heels of her hands, saw the puzzle piece she'd drawn on her wrist, and remembered her true goal of this suffering. "Hey, Mom."

"Yes, sweetheart?"

H gave an energetic wave to someone in a car at the red light.

"Is that a friend, dear?" Mom reached for her girls' hands as they stepped off the curb at the crosswalk. H clenched it; Dee batted it away.

"No idea who it is." H chirped.

"Why did you wave to a stranger?" Dee pinched her forehead.

"I accidentally made eye contact with him. It would have been awkward not to acknowledge him."

"It would have been normal." But her sister was anything but normal. Ordinarily, Dee appreciated that. This afternoon, though—

"Oh. My. God! You look amazing! You go, girl!" Hayleigh told a little old lady wearing a leopard-print jogging suit with pink sneakers.

"Thank you, sweetheart!" The woman blew a kiss as she walked past.

"What did you need, Dee Dee?" Mom was apparently talking to her.

"I'm sorry, Mom. Too many people here for me to concentrate."

"That's OK, dear."

"What did you say?"

"I said that's OK."

"No, I mean..." Oh, good god! She was going to lose her fucking mind. "What did you say when you asked me—"

"Oh! I thought you wanted to ask *me* something. Maybe about the sage green?"

"Sage green?"

"I was saying I think that sage green color would look lovely in your apartment. You have such great lighting, it will look so warm in there. Would you be OK if I had Marco come in and give it a fresh coat of paint?"

"In sage green?"

"Yes." Mom tapped on her phone when they stopped at the next corner. "I just texted Marco. We'll see when he's available. Now, if we go with sage green on the walls—"

"Oooh! You could get an emerald green velvet sofa." Hayleigh reached for Mom's hand as they walked across the next street. "Or maybe brown leather. Oh! You're adorable!" She dropped to the sidewalk to rub her face against the snout of an uninterested hound.

"You're sitting where homeless people piss!" Dee pulled her sister to her feet.

"It's the sidewalk."

"Same fucking thing."

By the time they arrived at Rouge's streetery for dinner, an "acceptable" brown leather sofa had been found, but Mom was sure there was a better one out there. Two Eames-style black chairs, a giant white furry ottoman, and several cocktail tables were considered, "probably right," but Mom still needed to research alternatives. H had three new pairs of Oxford-style shoes; both pairs of Dee's dress shoes were replaced; and Mom bought a new Coach bag (because she didn't have one in that color). Dee had several new pairs of jeans that fit her according to Mom, and an assortment of billowy, flowered tops she knew she'd never wear. Plus, there were all the art supplies Dee ordered to be sent to her apartment on Mom's dime, even though Dee had tried to explain to her that not only could she afford them, but that they would be a business expense.

"How many?" The hostess looked annoyed.

"Three." Mom told her.

"It'll be, like, two hours."

"Oh, I don't think so." Mom paused to give her a closed-lip smile. "Please let Ayla know Lauren Bremen is here."

"Of course!" The hostess's face changed expression to a let-me-impress-you smile. "I'll be right back."

"You look adorable," Hayleigh told a little girl waiting in line behind us.

"I'm going to vomit." Dee pulled her hair back and held it behind her head.

"Are you sick, dear?" Mom placed both her hands on Dee's cheeks. "Do you think you're dehydrated?"

"No." Dee gripped her mother's hands, pulled them off her face. Deep breath. "I'm just a little scattered with all the distractions. But look, I've been trying to tell you, um, that table that my artist friend is making?"

"Yes?"

"Look." Dee fished her phone out of her purse and showed her a few images Brett had sent of Grandad's table.

"Oh, I've never seen anything like that! Amazing! Now I'm definitely thinking we go with a pink suede sofa, and you need green velvet chairs for that table! Who is the artist?"

"Brett."

Mom's face held the smile in place, but somehow the emotion left it. The light even dimmed in her eyes. Dee could see her swallow.

"Brett? Your...cousin?"

"Yes! Can you believe how talented he is?"

"Um, well, yes." Mom turned her back to Dee.

What the holy fuck? "I don't get it, Mom." Dee, rather roughly, gripped her mother's arm and turned her back around. "What do you have against him? He's been nothing but good to me."

"He's been nothing but a troublemaker for you, Deirdre. He got you arrested—"

"We were with a group of his friends at a bonfire near Granddad's lake. There was a guy with an acoustic guitar. I swear to god, it wasn't Brett who was the problem. It was Aunt—"

"Deirdre, I just don't like any of those people."

"I'm freaking aware."

"Hello, Lauren!" Presumably, the magic-making Ayla, said. "Of course, we can seat you right away. How many?"

"Three, thank you," Mom turned away from Dee. As if they were done talking. Seriously?

"Mom!"

"Deirdre?" Mom faced her again, eyes open wide, expressionless.

"This way, please." Ayla didn't seem to care that she was interrupting a family discussion.

"I need you to tell me the truth." Dee walked close behind Mom.

"About?"

"About my father."

Mom stopped at a table and waited while Ayla pulled a chair out for her. She sat before answering and visibly took a deep breath.

"What would you like to know, sweetheart?" Her gentle smile disarmed Dee.

She wanted to know whether her father had been killed. But Mom wouldn't smile like that if he had been, would she? She had taken a minute, probably to gather herself, to get prepared for whatever Dee was going to ask her. Like she knew she'd be sad, the way she was when Dee was a child, and Dee asked about him. This was so wrong.

"Dee?"

She couldn't torture Mom. "Did he like his family?"

"He loved your grandmother."

If her husband had been killed, Mom would have been sad *and* angry, right? And wouldn't she seek justice? Dee had never seen her very angry. She'd only seen her…Holy shit! This woman loved her so much, she'd stop the world from spinning if it would save Dee from getting a hangnail. What the hell was she doing interrogating her? Dee realized Ayla was still waiting for her to sit. She did, across from Mom. H took the seat next to her.

"Oh my god, I love your manicure!" Hayleigh held Ayla's hands and ogled the tie-dye effect on her nails. H was back at it again.

"Please shove a steak knife in my temple," Dee told Ayla.

"Deirdre Hildlegarde!" Mom almost yelled. "Don't you ever joke like that again."

"Don't you ever say my middle name in public again!"

"Can we have a bottle of wine right now?" H asked Ayla. "Any kind will do. Whatever is closest to you."

"It's so warm." Mom waved her hand in front of her face. "How about a dry rosé?"

And just like that, things were back to normal.

It was such a waste of time. Despite the free art supplies, shoes, and furniture. It was such a waste. Dee was tilting at a windmill here, whatever the hell that phrase meant. She'd created a mystery around her father's death instead of facing the stressors in her life that were probably causing the nightmares.

Like the store. No, that wasn't so stressful, yet.

And the move was smooth.

God, could Cooper really be the cause?

Maybe she should call him, confess…something.

She poured a glass of wine, turned on all the lights just in case she got scared, and picked up her phone.

Oh! Shit! What the hell's up with all those text messages? Seemed like everyone important was trying to connect with her that day. Dee had shut off the notifications when Mom and H were at their peak of, well, of being themselves. She'd reached a saturation point, and the texts were the only thing she could control. So she shut them off. And now…from Brett were photos of wood he was using to make her tables. Evan sent a reminder about Josie's luncheon the next day.

From Cooper:

> *I was hoping for a sexy shoe*
> *pic*

She replied with a shot of her feet in mismatched slippers: one white bunny missing an ear and the other a rainbow unicorn with a burn mark.

Yeah, she needed to have a full-on conversation with him about him, about her, about them. She needed to make sure he knew what he was in for. But what was up with Max?

One, two, three...eleven texts:

> *Dane is gone. Just gone. He*
> *turned off the app!*

> *He's still gone—left this*
> *morning at 10*

> *He's still gone! Like GONE!*

> *Clothes are here. Computer*
> *is gone.*

> *What does this mean? Where*
> *are you?!!!!!!!*

What am I supposed to do?

Where the hell are you??!

WTF? I just called his dad.
He hasn't heard from him.

Where the fuck are you? I
was just at the store!?

He's still gone. I don't
understand.

Where are you? I can't find
him! I can't find you!

Dee hit *call.*

"I can't talk right now." Maxine's voice was low.

"I'm so sorry! I was in Philly with Mom and H. I couldn't think—wait. What do you mean you can't talk?"

"He *just* came in. I'll fill you in tomorrow."

Maxine

"Hey."

Hey? *That's* how he greets her? Like he hadn't been gone for— Maxine looked at her phone's screen—almost twelve hours? She opened her mouth, wanted to rip into him, to yell at him, maybe even beat her hands against his chest, but her mother's voice sounded in her head—*play it cool, girl. Play it cool*—as she found herself in the exact situation she swore she would never be in: her man strutting in the door like that was usual, even though he'd been missing for a while.

Just like the day her father walked into the home she shared with her mother and grandmother, wanting, finally, to be her Daddy. She was thirteen years old, had done just fine without a "Daddy" since he'd walked out when she was three.

She had wanted to launch into her father. Verbally attack him, shred him to nothing, but Mama reigned her in. Mama spoke levelly to him, with integrity to herself, and made it clear she wanted nothing to do with him.

Maxine did the same.

He kept coming back, though, trying. He and Mama never got back together, but Max developed a relationship with him. Then he left again, a few years later. That became his pattern: here for a couple of years, gone for a couple. Right now, he was back. Max had gone through the motions of pretending to be an interested daughter, but she never felt close to him the way she did with Mama.

Was that what would happen here if she played it cool with Dane? No sense of comfortable, unconditional love? But he'd be physically around most of the time?

Would she have a better result if she went off on him?

"Were you about to call me?" He nodded at her phone.

"No." She dropped it on the coffee table. "Was talking to Dee. She..." he didn't need anymore. It didn't matter. Dee wasn't there for her today because she just wasn't able to be. She'd come running over now if Max gave her the word. Maxine knew that. Two weeks ago, she would have thought Dane would do the same. Dee and Dae: her supportive double Ds. "I did call you a few times today. Left messages. Didn't you get them?"

"Yeah." He took another step into the living room and threw his keys toward the tray. They missed. He picked them up and put them where they belonged. Because that's what he did: he puts things where they belong. Dane was about order, about routine. What...

"Where the hell have you been?" *Play it cool, girl.* She lengthened her neck and breathed deeply.

"Um, well." Dane looked tired, very tired. Like too tired to make eye contact with her. He dropped to the sofa and sat with his elbows on his knees, head hanging low.

Oh God, how easy it would be to reach out to him, touch him, promise they could get through this together. Whatever it was. But she stayed in the armchair. She had no idea what they were going through. She couldn't make any promises. She could only wait for him to talk.

It took an eternity. He turned to cold, gray granite in the chair.

"This is big, Max." The granite moved; he lifted his head and morphed into her Dane, met her eyes. "So big. And all I can think about is what happens if I lose you?"

"Why would you lose me?" She had made an oath to love him through better or worse. Yes, Dee had tried to make her put in amendments that Maxine had found laughable at the time. Dee really was the smarter one. No one ever gave her credit for it, but Max always knew.

"I really messed up, Max." He rolled his head back, blew air at the ceiling before looking her way again. "Where do I begin?"

"People always say the beginning is a good place." Maxine clasped her hands in her lap.

"In that case, this begins about eight years ago."

She did the calculations. "When we were in grad school?"

"Just finished. Graduated."

He proposed to her on the day of graduation. The happiest day of her life. "What happened?"

"You went away."

"What?"

"You…" He stared at his fingertips pressed together, almost in prayer. "You went on that cruise."

"Oh. Yeah."

"I never told you how angry that made me."

"What?"

"I'd just proposed to you, and you left."

"I went on a trip that was a gift to me. That had been organized several months before. Why would that make you angry?" Lauren and Kaz included her and Mama on their family vacation that year to commemorate her grad school graduation: a cruise through the Greek islands.

"I didn't think it was right."

"That I went?"

"Yes."

"Because?"

"Because..." he still wouldn't look at her. She wanted to rip his head upright.

"Because?"

"Look, I'm not proud of this." Finally, he met her eyes. "I didn't realize how truly close you and your mom are to them. Or maybe I was jealous and immature. Huh." His head bounced as he smirked. "Maybe it's all of that. But I kind of interpreted you going with them as being willing to let them bribe you."

Max felt her head jerk back, as if escaping a punch. "Bribe me to do what?"

"I, honestly, babe, I didn't get it at the time, and maybe I still don't, but I thought they were kind of paying you to be Dee's friend. And I couldn't understand why you'd let a rich, white family do that. It bothered me a lot. I thought you had more integrity than—"

"Paid me to be Dee's friend?" Maxine stood. To hell with playing it cool. "I don't even know how to answer that! Mama and Lauren go way back—"

"I thought your mother was her seamstress or something—"

"They have a business together!" She had explained that to him when they were dating. Lauren grew less active with the business as the years went by, but she was still a vibrant, creative partner to

Mama and always would be.

"I didn't see it as that. I don't know exactly how I saw it. I guess I interpreted things wrong. It seemed to me your mom was at Lauren's beck and call—"

"How *dare* you?" Max wanted to throw something at him and storm away from him at the same time. He'd been harboring this resentment for how long? "Dee Dee is like a sister to me! Hayleigh, too! Lauren and Kaz would do anything in the world for my mother and me, and the feeling is mutual. We are family, but for the lack of blood. Who the hell do you think you are—"

"Look, I get it now. I do!" He stood, grabbed her arms, which she just realized she was flailing around in anger. Not at all playing it cool. "I do. Back then, I didn't. I know, there's a genuine relationship now. I just didn't see it at the time."

Max shook free of him. "Why are you telling me this now?"

"Because it kind of explains what I did."

She stepped back from him, took a few deep breaths. "What did you do?"

"I was at a party. Someone's grad party. Sulking. Looking at the pics of your trip that you'd posted. And...um." His voice shook. Max realized he had tears in his eyes. "There was a girl there, a woman. We'd been in a couple of engineering classes together."

Max had an overwhelming urge to run away, but she stayed, frozen in place, while her stomach churned. She wished she could see him as that gray, cold stone again—emotionless, unmoving. Because the vivid image of him before her with pain and fear in his eyes was gut-wrenching. "And." Her voice had trouble making it through her throat.

"And, her boyfriend had just broken up with her. She didn't understand why. Felt rejected."

Max felt her head shaking back and forth. *No.*

"We drank. A lot."

She shook her head faster.

"Yeah, we, um, slept together."

"We were engaged!"

"I know." He reached toward her. She slammed his hand away. "She got pregnant. Max..." his eyes seemed to plead with her, "I have a son."

Sunday, June 27

Dee

What the fuck was that?

Dee's wide-open eyes only saw darkness. Was that an explosion? There *was* a boom, right?

Where the hell was she?

She threw off whatever was on her and...wait...that was a blanket. She was in a bed. Her bed? Slowly, she moved her hand across the sheet beneath her, to the edge of the mattress, and knew she was in her bed. She just knew it.

"Jesus Christ!" She reached over and found a lamp—felt like the one she'd made from an antique brass hookah—and pulled the chain to turn it on. Yes, that was her hookah lamp. Yes, she was in her bed. Soaked with sweat, chilled now from the air conditioner.

Was there really an explosion? She'd been dreaming again...or maybe not?

Phone showed 3:43 a.m.

She took a quick shower, much quicker than she'd wanted because she couldn't shake the fear and feeling that she wasn't alone in her apartment. She needed to be in bright light, where she could see everything around her. She knew she needed it. But she didn't know why she needed it.

She left the light on in the bathroom, then went through her apartment, turning on all the lights and opening all the doors to the closets and cupboards to be sure no one was hiding. After double-checking that the doors were locked, she stared at her whiteboard for ideas on what to do. There were a number of partially finished pieces lined up on a few shelves. The shoes still needed work, but she wasn't feeling it. Instead, she chose the glass cones she'd blown before moving. Cones of various heights and widths, colorless glass. On the whiteboard were notes about wire wrapping them, sculpting bases with thicker wire so they'd stand up as vases. She could do that. Maybe even bead the thin wires before twisting them into thick, strong ropes...

Soon a 1980s playlist exploded around her. Scream, Government Issue, Minor Threat, and others vibrated in the air, drowning all thoughts as she slid beads onto wires. Threading, twisting, wrapping, she created a form to fit a glass cone, a form in almost violent oranges, yellows, and reds. Thicker wire with larger beads came together in a coiled rope to make a base. She did another. Then a third...Eventually, the sun shone bright enough through her front windows that she was confident it was day. She was safe.

Her phone read 5:57 a.m.

Sitting on the floor of her apartment, surrounded by the beaded forms, all the color of blazing fires, she knew whatever was going on with her in the nightmares had nothing to do with the move. Nothing to do with Cooper.

Gram's death didn't feel right, either.

Maybe her father, but that didn't seem possible because they were definitely about the fire. That's what kept coming back to her.

The fire she barely escaped. Brett had saved her then, right? Didn't he pull her out? Why did she think that? Had someone told her?

Who would have?

She couldn't remember the last time anyone spoke to her about the accident. Or was it an accident? Holy shit! Was the fire on purpose? Arson? Who started it? Why would someone start a fire with people inside a building unless they wanted them dead? Or was it accidentally caused? Like by…by a kid playing with matches?

Fuuuuuck.

Had she set something on fire? Brett would know.

But what did any of this have to do with her father's death?

She dragged herself to a stand and approached the whiteboard. Yes, this was about the fire that messed up her brain. Would she be able to ask Mom about that? Ask Brett? Granddad?

She picked up an orange marker, sketched flames coming out of the puzzle piece's legs.

Genevieve

Genevieve survived.

What an interesting way to look at it.

She wondered how Brynn was doing. She should be landing in St. Lucia soon. Hopefully, she'd enjoy her very short honeymoon. Who goes away for just a couple of days for their honeymoon? Todd! That was his idea. He couldn't be gone from the office too long. How important did he think he was?

She hoped Brynn was finally relaxed, now. Or at least feeling more comfortable than she obviously was at her wedding last night. She'd tried to joke with Genevieve and the bridesmaids about almost getting cold feet. But Genevieve saw right through the pretended silliness. She had practically raised her siblings. A bipolar mother and an absentee father had set Genevieve up to be the primary caregiver at a very early age. She knew Brynn and Archie better than they knew themselves, and she was appalled to realize, way too late to do anything about it, that Brynn was settling.

How had Genevieve missed it? Granted, the engagement happened the day before her car accident. A broken femur, shredded blood vessels, three surgeries, and weeks of painful physical therapy can be a bit distracting.

Still, she'd failed her sister.

Entering the kitchen with her arms laden with freshly delivered pizza boxes, she couldn't understand how she just kept failing everybody. All she ever did was try to do what was right.

Today was Remy's seventeenth birthday. Next Saturday, he'd have a raucous good time—the typical pool party. That was one of the nice things about summer babies: it made birthday parties easier to plan. But this afternoon, despite the delicious aromas of the oregano, pepperoni, and whatever they put in their sauce down at Luigi's, approaching her family with those goods felt more like bringing them a sacrificial lamb.

She'd failed them, too. Obviously. No one was happy.

Livvy looked as annoyed as possible. Remy was there because, well, he was told to be, and that was obvious. They were eating a birthday lunch because his latest girlfriend had arranged for a gathering of his friends at her house later. Archie's chair was empty because he was on the phone out by the pool. And…*Good Lord! What a great father figure! Distracted. Looking at his phone at the dinner table! There had been a family rule for years—no phones at the dinner table. Since when did the rule not apply to him?*

In horror, she set the boxes down on the island and realized they would have to tell the children before they told anybody else that they were getting a divorce. She should have thought of that sooner. *What if he already told the guys who work for him? Or his trainer? Or those idiots on his new pickleball team? Or whoever else he runs and sweats with?* Granted, she had never been part of that world, nor had the kids, so the odds of anyone there gossiping and their kids hearing of it were slim. But still, they needed to discuss how to broach the divorce with the children.

But not right now. It was Remy's birthday. Hopefully, Chris hadn't said anything to anyone. She inhaled as deeply as possible.

"Ta da!" She turned around with Remy's favorite pizza in an open box in one hand: extra cheese, extra pepperoni, banana peppers. "It looks beautiful, doesn't it?"

"Hmm," came from Livvy.

"Yeah." Remy.

A nod from the end of the table.

Why was she serving these...these...Dee would call them assholes. Maybe she had a point. Genevieve opened all the boxes, pulled plates from the cupboard, and then set the paper napkin holder in the center of the table.

"Help yourselves," she called over her shoulder before choosing a bottle of pinot noir. Sure, it was just twelve-thirty, but it was a special occasion.

Pizza was on all the plates. Mouths were taking bites and chewing. She'd pull out the birthday cake and candles in a few minutes. But it would be lovely if there were some kind of lively discussion. This must be awful for Remy. "So, are you excited to have Dad take you for your driver's test tomorrow, Rem?"

"Yeah." More chewing.

She looked at Chris. Was he excited that his youngest offspring would be getting a driver's license? He continued to eat, occasionally glancing at his phone.

"And what's on the docket for you tomorrow, Livvy?"

"Um, like, something has to happen with my car."

"What does that mean?"

"It means it's time for an oil change." Look at that! He was paying attention. "But I want them to do a good look-over, check her brakes, and all that."

He was good about those kinds of things. Genevieve appreciated that.

"So it's a car day for me," Chris continued. "I'll follow Livvy over to drop hers off at the mechanic, then we'll have breakfast at a diner, and spend the morning doing whatever she wants to do. I'll take Remy for his license test in the afternoon. If he gets it, we're buying that Jeep, right Rem?"

"Right!" Remy's eyes lit up.

A Jeep? Was that safe? And what Jeep? It sounded like they'd been speaking about a particular car. Something they spoke about when Genevieve wasn't around. And he and Livvy would eat breakfast together? He acted like he had a relationship with his kids. The audacity!

"Well…isn't that wonderful?" Genevieve took the smallest bite of her pizza. That lump thing appeared again. She needed to bite the bullet and call her doctor.

More chewing, drinking, silence.

Thankfully, Archie's call finally ended. He'd liven the group. "Sorry to do this, but I gotta run." He kissed Genevieve on the cheek before turning to Remy. "I know your mom thinks gift cards are impersonal, Rem. But I remember turning seventeen. Cash is king, right, my man?"

"You got it, Uncle Arch! Thanks again." They fist bumped.

Archie slapped Chris on the shoulder. "Tuesday, right?"

"Meet you out there." Chris didn't bother to get up to see his brother-in-law out. But then again, Geneveive couldn't make herself stand to do it, either. It was unsettling, to say the least, that she realized she hoped Chris would get her brother in the divorce. Had Archie always been so…so…obnoxious? Why did it feel as if she didn't know anyone she was related to anymore? She needed to get control of things. "Livvy, we've been so busy with Aunt Brynn's wedding, I didn't ask. Did you have fun at the shore?" Judging by the pics she'd posted on social media, her daughter had spent the week wearing little and holding her face and breasts very close to young males.

"Yeah. It was great."

More chewing, drinking, silence.

"Well, I had a great week, too," Genevieve tried. "I'm enjoying my new job quite a bit."

"You got a job?" Livvy asked. Remy seemed to be asking the same thing at the same time, just in different words.

"Yes! Where did you think I've been spending my time?"

"I hadn't noticed you were gone." Remy's eyebrows made squiggle lines.

"Well, to be fair, Rem, I was only there a couple of days last week, and it was when you were at rugby camp."

"Ah." He nodded.

More chewing, drinking, silence.

Weren't they even curious about what she was doing? Rage pumped up from her core like a fountain blasting water four stories tall. "Don't you people even care?"

"About what?" Livvy looked so genuinely clueless, Genevieve couldn't answer her right away.

She wanted to say *about me, about my decision to get out of this house, about my need to have something to do where I was appreciated.* But she knew those words would hurt her daughter's feelings. So, she had a choice: hurt herself and smile like nothing was wrong, or… "I'm more than just someone who cooks and cleans and makes sure your precious little lives go according to plan." The words came out with the force of a dam bursting. "I'm doing something for me, that is important to me, and none of you give a damn!" Genevieve stood, grabbed her wine glass, and left the kitchen.

"Jesus!" she heard Livvy say. "She's such a drama queen! Everything is always about her. Have you noticed? She just ruined

Remy's birthday."

"I'm getting a Jeep. My birthday's not ruined."

Dee

OK, so this wasn't what Dee was expecting. Josie sat upright in an armchair, a normal wingback, wearing a beautifully old-fashioned flower-print dress. Maybe Dee misunderstood what "hospice" meant.

"Oh my, look at your hair!" Josie held Dee's shoulders as she gazed at the mane of wavy blond and faded pink hair that Dee had actually tried to tame that morning. "Like an exotic wild animal."

Was that a compliment? But then Josie pulled her into a hug that lasted so long, Dee was glad she'd showered and worn deodorant. And she decided the comment *was* a compliment.

"Please, sit near me." Josie pointed toward the end of the sofa closest to her.

Dee sat, happy she'd listened to Hayleigh. She'd called her little sister to apologize for being so intolerant the day before. Of course, H forgave her.

"You need to use your voice for good, not just evil." H had laughed. "Tell me when I'm making it hard for you to think. It won't hurt my feelings, you know. I understand."

"I appreciate it. If I ever remember that in the moment, I'll ask. But right now, I have another question. What am I supposed to wear to a ninety-fifth birthday luncheon?"

"Since when did you make long-term plans?"

Dee remained quiet while H cackled.

"So you didn't think that was funny. A luncheon, huh?"

Hayleigh cleared her throat. "Did they actually use that word?"

"Yes."

"Oh, Jeesh. I dunno. I guess you have to look nice."

"How nice?"

"Maybe ask Mom."

"I can't, she'll ask me where I'm going."

"Where are you going?"

"My great aunt Josie's birthday party."

"Shit. Yeah. Mom can't know. Did you try Mama Kat?"

"Do you seriously think she and Mom keep secrets from each other?"

"Right. Oh! I know! The only time we say 'luncheon' is for Mother's Day when we don't do brunch. Wear what you would for Mother's Day."

So she showed up at Josie's place wearing a lilac pantsuit Mama Kat had made for her three years earlier that she'd worn for yet another Mother's Day at the club. She had to take a wet washcloth to wipe the dust off the shoulders, but she was right in line with Josie's lemon-yellow flowered dress and Evan's wife Hope's pink blouse and white slacks. Evan was in khakis and a polo, his standard uniform. His sons and their wives also looked like they were heading to a club for a buffet lunch.

"The flowers are lovely." Josie nodded to the bouquet Dee had picked up at the supermarket. "But you are my gift today."

"If only I had known." Dee accepted a cup of coffee from Hope, who immediately returned to the kitchen, leaving them alone. "I'd have worn a ribbon on my head."

Josie's laugh sounded like it needed a nap. "You're so clever. Oh, how you're so much like your father."

"Mom, can I get anything for you?"

Thank God for Evan! Dee never would have expected a mention of her father to suck the wind out of her like that. She'd gone for years with him being a blip in the background of her mind to being a presence that just wouldn't go away once it felt invited by a mention. Yeah, like at the funeral, now there was a presence in the room. But it wasn't just hovering in the air waiting to be noticed. It wanted to be felt.

Dee had never believed in ghosts, but she was pretty sure if they were real, they didn't travel. So why was her father's presence here, now, in Josie's townhome in Philly?

"Is that all right with you, Deirdre?" Josie's voice was half-breath.

"I'm sorry. I guess I wasn't following." She noticed both Josie and Evan were staring at her. "Is what all right with me?"

"Mom's tired." Evan explained. "We're thinking we should just eat here in the living room, then call it a day."

"Whatever Aunt Josie needs is fine with me."

Within minutes, Josie's family and Dee were crowded in the living room, eating a cardboard-tasting lunch. Except Aunt Josie said she didn't have much of an appetite and wanted nothing. Maybe she knew how bad the food was.

Dee and Hope sat on the sofa, their plates set on the coffee table. Evan was in a side chair. Their sons and their wives or whatever dragged chairs from the dining room into the living room and ate from plates on their laps. It was a horrifically quiet and uncomfortable meal.

Each bite Dee took was like swallowing a wet wad of papier-mâché. Conversation was so stilted, it was almost comical.

Josie livened up at the prospect of cake and managed to eat a little of it when dessert was passed around—birthday cake, no candles.

Then eventually, the inevitable happened: lunch ended. Hope took Dee's plate, as she would a child's, and headed toward the kitchen. Evan took Josie's and did the same. Their adult kids seemed to vanish. Dee was left alone with her dying great aunt.

"Dear," Josie's breath came in pieces, a little inhale here, a little exhale there. "Thank...you."

"Stop saying 'thank you'!" She reached over to take Josie's hand. "You keep making me think I forgot about something I did."

"Ha..ha..." her tired laugh seemed to require even more effort. "Your father...he was funny...too...very funny. Did you know that?"

"Um, no. I just learned he was clever a little while ago." Why was it necessary for her to bring him up again?

Click. Light streamed in through the crack in the door.

The memory didn't flood in. It suddenly appeared in her mind. Very clear. Stark. Someone had opened the door of...what room was she in? Why was it dark?

"There..." Josie pulled Dee's attention back to the present moment. "Evan?"

"I'm here, Mom." He appeared beside her chair so quickly, Dee wondered if he'd been hovering within earshot in the dining room.

"There..." Josie's whole body seemed to inhale with her breath, "is a box...on my bed." She leaned back in her chair. "Please...give it to Deirdre." She rested her head in the nook of the chair back, eyes half closed.

"Are you OK, Aunt Josie?" Dee placed a hand on her knee, feeling stupid for asking. Clearly, the woman wasn't OK.

"I need...rest. That's...the beauty...of my...condition..." Josie went still for so long, Dee stood up to call for Evan. But then she started talking again. "I get to nap as..." long inhale "much as I want."

"Cool." Dee's head bobbed up and down in an uncontrolled nod. What the fuck? Where was Evan? How long did it take for him to find a stupid box? Josie needed more than a nap! Whatever it was, someone needed to give it to her. NOW.

"This one, Mom?" Evan returned to the room holding a cardboard box. Covered in a floral pattern, it had a solid red lift-off lid.

Josie stirred in her chair, looked at the box in his hands, and nodded. She retreated back into the corner of her chair.

"I think she's had enough." Hope came from the kitchen. Oh. Perhaps Dee should have helped in there. "Thank you, Dee, for coming. It really meant a lot to her."

"Why are you already talking in past tense?" What the fuck was their problem? Josie was tired. She wasn't dead. Yet.

"So, um," Evan thrust the box into her hands. "I guess this is for you. I've no idea what's inside."

Dee's stomach suggested he was lying, that he knew exactly what was inside. Why else would it have taken him so long to get it? He probably opened it and rifled through. She tucked the box under her arm. "Let her know I said 'goodbye,' and I, um..." she what? Josie looked so peaceful in her chair. "I hope to see her soon." She glanced around her for a jacket, then remembered it was summer. "So, um..."

"I'll see you out." Was Evan a little too eager?

She followed him to the front of Josie's townhouse. Reaching to take the door from him, she saw the phone image with K and E on either side that she'd drawn on her wrist. As soon as she stepped outside, she turned to face him. "So, um, Ev. I was surprised to hear you and Kaz spoke."

"What?" He lost control of his face, as if she'd hit him in the balls when he was expecting to be served an ice cream cone.

"Yeah, he'd mentioned you two spoke after Gram's funeral."

"He did?" Evan's Adam's apple bobbed.

"I had no idea you even had each other in your contacts."

"Well." Evan glanced over her shoulder, toward the street. "We're family. Shouldn't we?"

Dee twisted to see behind her. No one was there. "Ever call him before?"

"Yeah, I mean, not often." He took a tiny step back.

"Really?" If someone had asked her what a guilty face looked like, she'd have drawn a picture of his at that moment.

"Maybe." Evan nodded very quickly, stepped back. "So, I think Mom needs me. Thanks again for coming, Dee." He shut the door.

Maxine

"You sure you want sweet-and-sour chicken?" Mama did that thing with her mouth that made her look like she stepped in fresh dog pooh; her look that said *you're making a bad decision.*

"I'm sure." Maxine tapped to place the order on her phone.

"Last time you had it, you got sick."

"Which means I should be fine this time."

"Nothing wrong with eating something with less sugar," Mama muttered the words as she took the phone.

"What are you getting?" Maxine hated to admit that her mother was right. She'd gotten sick from the sweet-and-sour chicken last time. But she had such a strong craving, she just couldn't pass it up. It was all she could think about all day.

"Buddha's delight. Steamed vegetables and noodles." Mama tapped the phone, then handed it back to Max. "I'll put on some green tea."

Max had hoped for wine. "Delivery should be about forty-five minutes." She paid for the order on her phone.

"Fine. Now, why are you buying me dinner?" Mama filled her kettle from the reverse-osmosis water tap in her kitchen.

"Well..." Max leaned back in the rattan kitchen chair. She closed her eyes and repeated the explanation she'd rehearsed on the way over. She had hoped that by making it a rote exercise, explaining would hurt a little less. "Dane cheated on me when we were in Greece after we graduated Penn. He just found out he has a seven-year-old son from that…that incident. I'm having a tough time talking to him about it. I think I need some space to deal with whatever it is I'm feeling right now. Can I stay here for the night?"

Mama hummed as she gathered the tiny porcelain tea cups she'd purchased on a trip to Japan with Lauren the year they both turned forty. She placed loose-leaf tea in a strainer in the matching teapot, then, when it seemed as if there was nothing left for her to do, she turned around and looked at Max. Her fingertips were pressed together, hands forming an upside-down triangle over her stomach. "I never liked that man."

Max could only laugh. "Does that mean you'll be OK with me staying tonight? I could sleep in the guest room at home, but…"

"I think he should be the one to leave, but I'm fine with you being here for as long as you need or want to."

The kettle whistled. Mama poured the water into the porcelain pot.

"Thank you. He doesn't understand why I can't get past it. We can't even talk about it because he keeps expecting me to…to…"

"Take care of his feelings when you need to take care of your own."

"Exactly." Of course, Mama understood.

"The only problem is that your old room is in the process of being transformed. I told you I was bringing in another sewist, right?"

"Yes." Great. So, there was no place for her to sleep? Maybe she could stay with Lauren and Kaz.

"She's going to work in what I used to use as a storage room. So everything that was in there has been emptied into your old room. Your bed is covered with boxes."

They still had about half an hour before the food was to arrive, so Max took her tea upstairs to see what kind of work was ahead of her.

Mama wasn't lying. She had a thriving business making custom dresses and suits for women throughout South Jersey and Philadelphia. Lauren contributed design strategies and helped Mama brainstorm ideas, then Mama did the actual work of bringing those ideas to life. They'd been partners for almost three decades now, and it appeared that everything Mama had collected during that time was in Max's old room. Her bed was covered with boxes; bolts of fabric leaned against each other like drunken soldiers two to three deep along the walls. Plastic bins full of thread, buttons, rhinestones, and more were piled on top of each other. Then there were the file cabinets that Max knew held the custom patterns Mama and Lauren had drawn before they found a computer program to do it. There was so much in the room that if she removed everything from the bed, there'd be no floor space for her to walk to it.

"What is this?" Max picked at the tape from a box that didn't look sewing-related.

"Memorabilia. I set it aside to see what you wanted me to do with it." Mama ripped open a different one. "Looks like your old dolls in this one."

"Are you kidding me? Get rid of them!"

"No sentimental value?"

"None." The only thing Max ever hoarded was something she thought she could use in art.

"What about these old board games?" Mama peeked in another box.

"Those could be useful. Dee and I make some really fun jewelry and stuff out of old game pieces." She opened a plastic box. "Baby clothes?"

Mama replaced the lid. "I kept some of the special things you wore just in case…"

Mama's voice trailed off.

Max turned around, went downstairs. She didn't have her old room anymore. She didn't have hope for being a mother anymore. She had no idea what she had for a marriage.

At least there was sweet-and-sour chicken on the way.

Dee

What a strange-ass day. Dee still had trouble shaking whatever happened to her at Josie's, and now Cooper was in her apartment, on a Sunday evening, eating take-out cheesesteaks like they were a normal freaking couple. Normal! The word was mildly anxiety-provoking.

"You all right?" He wiped his mouth with a napkin.

"I never know how to answer that question." Dee swigged her beer. It was considerate of him to bring the food and drink. She had only Mrs. D's ice cream in her fridge, which was what she'd planned on having for dinner, until he texted. "Why?"

"You look a little spacey."

"Oh, um, yeah, I guess I'm…" She waved her hand through the air. "I don't know what I am."

"Is it the nightmares? Are they still happening?"

She nodded.

"Still no idea what triggered them?"

"I'm beginning to think it was the fire."

"The one that caused the…" He pointed to his head.

"Yeah, the brain damage. But I'm not sure. I wanna talk to my shrink about it. Last week, we were thinking it was stress-related or maybe because I'm not dealing with emotions." Was that what Aisling had said?

"She knows you don't go for that touchy-feely business, huh?"

She clinked her beer to his. They both sipped.

"Yeah, so about touchy-feely," she swirled her bottle around the tabletop. "This is kind of weird, huh?"

"It's awkward, but a good awkward. Or is it a bad awkward for you? Again, am I pressuring you too much?"

"No. I mean, yes, dinner is good. Weird, but good, and I don't feel like you're pressuring me. I..." *Click.* What was that? Something just flit through her head. Like what happened at Josie's. Was that a memory from her nightmare? Felt like it.

"You what?" He took her hand over the table.

He wasn't pressuring her, but something was. And if the nightmares were beginning to bleed into her awake hours, perhaps she should warn him. "So, like...let's go back to the nightmares. They really aren't new. I mean, there's been times before when I had them."

"Yeah?"

"Yeah. And they don't just scare the fuck out of me, and I wake up, get a glass of water, and then I'm fine. I wake up and, like, I'm still scared, and I gotta get outside, out of my apartment and do something until daybreak. Or just go outside. I've been going out on my little balcony at the back of my place, and after a while, I feel safe again. And..."

They got this bad once before. And when it happened the last time, things got so bad, she had what they called a psychotic break. She wound up in a psych ward. But did he need to know that?

"And?" The way he asked sounded like he really wanted to know everything. Like he actually freaking cared. But when he decided she was too much, what was that gonna be like? Or, when they got so close, and she wigged out, how would he handle it? Maybe she should start with that, and if he was still around later, she'd talk about the other nightmares.

"So, let's go back to the fire, first. You probably get why my mom is so hyper-protective of me. Ever since that happened, she's tried to control my life so that I never have what she would think is a bad day or that I never experience anything remotely uncomfortable or unpleasant."

"I could see that. I mean, I'm sure that's probably a normal parental reaction if someone should almost lose a kid."

"I have to keep reminding myself of that because she totally fucking goes overboard sometimes. Makes me crazy. I mean, that's why she homeschooled me and not Hayleigh. That's why she still insists on buying me clothes, brings me food, makes deposits into my bank account on a regular basis because she's afraid I'll accidentally run out of money. If she had things her way, I'd still be living with her and Kaz and never leave her sight."

"Again, I get it. If I'd almost lost you in a bad accident, I might be a little overprotective, too."

"And that's part of *our* problem."

"What's part of *our* problem?"

"You."

"So, I am putting too much pressure on you for a real relationship?" He leaned back in his chair.

"You're not putting anything on me right now."

He scratched the back of his head, lifted his beer off the table. "Just tell me, are you OK with us doing this?" He motioned between them. "You know, dinner? Or do you think this is causing the nightmares?"

"I am. I mean, I am OK with it, and no. I don't think it has anything to do with the nightmares…" She inhaled long and deep. He seemed to know she needed a minute to collect herself, and quietly sipped his beer. "OK, there are a couple of things. First, one of my old therapists, before I met you, had convinced me to take a hiatus from men."

"And then you met me."

"It had been about a year or so later, but yes."

"I ended your hiatus?"

"I'd convinced myself it was OK to be with you because it was just sex."

"With no strings attached."

"Exactly."

"And now, we're connecting strings."

"You're so smart."

"Not smart enough to understand why that's a bad thing."

She took a bite of her cheesesteak and chewed, letting her brain marinate in the meaning she wanted to convey, looking for the right words. "OK, honestly. I don't know if I can trust you."

"Look, you are the only one—"

"Not that way. Strangely enough, I trust you to be faithful."

"Then?"

Apparently, those weren't the right words. A sip of beer. A nibble of a French fry. Christ, the man was patient.

"Look. I used to...I had a tendency to let things progress too quickly with men in the past. I didn't give them a chance to really know what tolerating this brain is truly like."

"Tolerating?"

"Eventually, one of two things would happen. They'd decide they just can't take any more of my scatteredness, forgetfulness, and whatever, think I'm too damaged to deal with, and dump me."

"Never."

"Or, they'd turn into something like a male version of my mother and want to control my world to the point where I'd feel suffocated."

"Dee—"

"I honestly believe you have feelings for me and would probably go the second way. And I don't want to be responsible for you turning into a controlling prick."

"Dee—"

"Then the third way my relationships would end is...I don't even know how to say it except, I'd kind of lose my shit on them."

"And that means what?"

"I dunno." She felt her breath coming in shorter. Shit. Slow down. Slow down. "So, like, have you noticed that I don't have any real friends?"

He shook his head.

"Yeah. So, there's Max. And I know a bunch of arty people that I've met at shows or shared studio space with or something. Most of them are as fucked up as I am. But, like, real friends? There's just Max and my sister. When my mom realized that my social skills absolutely sucked when I was a teen, she put me in a public high school because I begged her to send me where Max went. That was completely disastrous, and on multiple levels." She dipped a fry in ketchup. Her breathing was good. She was handling this. "So I'm not really good with relationships. In the end, I don't know what I do, but I fuck things up with people who get close to me. I get scared. Really scared. Then I get fucking weird."

"For example?"

"I don't even know how to explain it. Different therapists have said different things. Like maybe abandonment issues similar to how some adopted children feel due to my dad's death. Or maybe imposter syndrome, like deep down I don't feel worthy of being loved by a man." That made it hard to breathe. She hoped she'd remember to tell Aisling about that body response. "Regardless, something unconscious kicks in, and I take control of the situation and end things when people get close. I do it before they can do it to me, so, like, I don't have to, you know, like, be hurt." Yeah, hard to breathe.

"I know all about abandonment issues."

"Really?"

It was her turn to be patient while he rearranged some meat on his sandwich before taking a bite. He chewed thoroughly and swallowed before continuing. "Yeah. When my mom decided she couldn't take my dad beating on her anymore…she just left." A sip of beer. "I was seven. She left me with him." Another sip. "Left me to be his punching bag."

"Oh, I get it now. This is why the no-strings-attached thing was cool with you, too."

A lopsided grin lit up his face. "We seemed perfect for each other."

"But now you want more?" She pointed a French fry at him.

He nodded, took the fry out of her hand, and ate it. She watched him chew, swallow, then meet her eyes again. "What about you?"

Tension left her body. "I wanna give us a chance. I really do. I wanna, like, date, and spend time together doing things, not just fucking, but you know, whatever people do in relationships."

His cell buzzed. He leaned back in his chair to pull it out of his pocket. "Like have dinner together."

"Yes."

"Do I get to stay the night?"

He still didn't think she was a lunatic. How was this possible? "I suppose I could let that happen."

He read his cell. "Shit! Ed's calling out. Damn it! I have to go in."

"You'll have to spend some other night." Wow, she was talking like this was all good, like she was OK. And yeah, that's how she felt. Still, the whole thing was mildly anxiety-provoking. It might take a while to get used to this.

"Or, I could come back later." He glanced up from texting. "I know you're feeling vulnerable with the nightmares and all."

"Are you out of your fucking mind?" Dee stood, wrapped up the remains of her sandwich with so much force she probably ruined the possibility of leftovers for breakfast.

"Is this an example of what you meant by 'wigging out'?" His eyes were wide under his frown.

"No. This is sane and rational anger." She threw her sandwich mush into the refrigerator. "I just told you the last god-damned thing I wanted was for you to turn into an over-protective—"

"I get it!" He stood, grinning. "I'm sorry. I wasn't insinuating anything. You didn't have a good night last night. Are you gonna have a good night tonight?"

"I don't know." She didn't know if she'd ever have a good night again. "But that doesn't mean you get to make assumptions that I'm some kind of weak-ass punk who can't handle life."

"I'm not making any assumptions!" Cooper cleaned up his side of the table. The shit was actually laughing. "I promise, I'm not turning into your mother."

"I'll be fine."

"Good. So, can I come by tomorrow before breakfast?

"Like you always do on Monday mornings, not because you're checking in with me, right?"

"Yes."

"Absolutely. That's cool. That doesn't have to change."

Monday, June 28

Dee

"You look like hell," Max announced as if she thought Dee needed to know.

"Yeah? Well, so do you." But Dee wasn't really sure about that. It was hard to get a clear view of Max with her cheek pressing against the dinette table so hard, it squashed one eye into blurred vision.

"And I feel like hell." Max plopped into the other chair. "You?"

"You have no idea, Max."

"Wanna tell me?"

Max deserved at least an attempt to be human. Dee pushed herself upright, but very slowly. Stabbing pains jabbed her temples in rhythm with her heartbeat while a constant burning band squeezed all around her head. She should have let Cooper stay over. Maybe if he had, she would have fallen asleep easily. Then, when she woke up, scared, he'd be there to help her get back to sleep. But she wasn't that weak. She wasn't going to risk him turning into her mother. "I've got a wicked headache."

"Did you do anything to deserve it?"

"Well, I kind of had to drink myself to sleep last night. But it didn't last long."

"What didn't last long?"

"The sleep. I think my headache is a combination of hangover and sleep deprivation. I can't go on much longer like this, Max. I gotta figure out how to sleep a whole night. Just one night. It's hard to function."

Max glanced around the kitchen. "It's looking that way."

"I need to make some coffee."

"You probably need some water."

Dee stood, but that weird gray fuzziness that happens before passing out clouded her eyes. She slammed back into the chair, placed her head between her knees. This wasn't just hungover. This was worse. Her vision cleared. She leaned back in the chair. Maybe she was dying. She could feel her heart beating everywhere in her body. And God, but she was tired. She wished she could lie down in a dark room and sleep, but she wasn't going anywhere dark for a while. She was going to have to tough it out. Or maybe sleep in the sun, out on that dead patch of grass.

"Dee?" Max's hand was on her knee; she squatted in front of her. "What's happening?"

"I'll be fine." Long inhale. Her stomach roiled. Please, no puking. No puking. "Just stood up too fast."

"The post office is faster than you right now. Do you need a doctor?"

"No. Just food."

"When did you eat last?" Max started moving about the kitchen, presumably on the hunt for food.

"I think, um…Oh, last night. I had a cheesesteak."

"So you're just hungover?"

"And sleep deprived."

"And probably dehydrated."

Max poured her some water. "You know, I was sick as a dog this morning, too. Thought it was from bad sweet-and-sour chicken last night. Do you think we have a stomach bug?"

"I'd love that explanation to be right." Dee rested her elbows on the table, supported her chin with her hands. "Fuck. When are we supposed to be in the store?"

"About a half hour ago. That's why I came looking for you." Max handed her a glass.

"Christ! I'm sorry, Max." She slugged back the water. How long had she been out? She remembered getting Cooper's text that morning—double-checking that he could come by. That must have been around five. But she'd been awake for hours by then, making glass flowers, and had a pounding headache already, so she said to try her later. Was she already in the kitchen then? Must have been. She must have fallen back asleep there. Right, she'd finished off a bottle of wine to help the sleep come the second time. "This isn't how I planned things to go with this store thing."

"It's all good. I wasn't around much last week. If you need time to sleep or whatever this week, that'll balance things out. We're partners, right?"

"Yeah." She accepted more water from Max, but she needed coffee. "So, um, tomorrow on my call with Aisling, I'm going to ask her for drugs."

"For?"

"Sleeping."

Max's face froze.

"I know." Dee caught herself before nodding. No need to move her head more than necessary right now. "But there has to be something new on the market since the last time I tried them. I need to sleep, Max."

"It's that bad?"

Dee just scared Max by mentioning medication. She didn't need to worry her even more by telling her about the nightmares. This insomnia had to be a temporary thing. Maybe, if she could sleep a little, she could think straight—well, straight for her, anyway—and if she did that, then maybe she could get to the bottom of whatever was bothering her and causing the nightmares. Maybe then…then…something. She wasn't sure what. But sleep seemed to be required to kickstart the process. "Yeah. It's that bad. I can't get more than an hour or so at a time. And it's kind of killing me here."

Max stood and began making coffee, silent.

"So why do you look like hell? Bad sweet-and-sour?" Maybe a change of subject would do them both good.

"That and I spent the night on a sofa at Mama's house."

"Why?"

"She's moving things around. My bed was covered with boxes."

"But why not at home? Did you and Dane…?"

"I like this Mexican bean." Max measured out some coffee. "You order it online, right?"

"Yeah. On subscription. But you and Dane?" The water seemed to have washed some of the hair from her tongue.

"Well, good thing you're sitting down."

"Should I grip hold of the table?"

"I don't think you have the strength." Max filled the carafe with fresh water.

"For Christ's sake, Max. What is it?"

"Dane's a father."

The words came out sounding the way Max would say the wind is blowing. Like there was nothing ridiculous, painful, or insane about it. Dee was pretty sure she'd misunderstood. "Um, this is gonna sound crazy, but I thought you just said Dane's a father."

"It *is* crazy, and yes, that's what I said." Max continued to focus on making coffee.

"Like with a human baby?"

"Would there be any other kind?" Maxine finally turned around. Dee was happy to see a grin on her face.

"I mean, people call their dogs and cats their children." Dee shrugged. "I was just trying to make this make sense."

"There is no sense in it."

"Holy shit, Max!" Dee scraped her hands over her oily face. "Was he taking a paternity test at that lab?"

Turns out he was. Max vomited out all the shitty details of her life with that fuckwad of a husband of hers while Dee drank her coffee.

"He has a seven-year-old son?" Dee finally felt strong enough to stand up to get another cup of God's juice. "A fucking son?"

"Yes, a fucking son."

"And who is this...this hussy who shows up out of the blue?"

"Hussy?" Maxine laughed. "Oh God, I love you, Dee! Who says 'hussy' anymore?"

"I guess I do."

"I don't really know who she is. But now you're up to date. We should probably get down to the store. It's not fair to leave Genevieve alone so much. We barely even know her." Max rinsed out her cup.

"OK. Let me change clothes and wash my face and stuff. I'll be quick."

Genevieve

"Oh, Dee!" Genevieve called as soon as Dee entered from her apartment. Good Lord, the woman looked like she'd just emerged into civilization after living in the wilds of a dense forest for the past decade. Her messy hair was half up in a knot and the other half in a tousled spray down her back. She wore a black-and-yellow flannel button-down top, as if it were fall, and black leggings. On top of it, she was barefoot, of course.

But none of that mattered at the moment. Genevieve needed a buffer. She grabbed her arm. "Max is in the garage. A giant hutch just came in. Looks like it will be fun to alter. But before you go back to see it, let me introduce you to a couple of people. My husband and daughter popped by to check out the store. Come meet them." Genevieve tugged Dee's arm to slide her into the shield position between herself and her family. On the one hand, she was delighted Livvy had shown some interest, but on the other, it was clear she had dragged her father in. He kept looking around like he was afraid of breaking something, completely out of his element. Genevieve wanted them to leave as soon as possible so she could keep her sanctuary sacred to her alone. "Olivia, Chris, let me introduce you to the amazing and talented Dee Dee Bremen!"

"Cooper?"

What? He knew her already? Of course! He'd spent their entire marriage flying about the globe, meeting amazing people, while Genevieve stayed home, raised their kids, and made the annual family trek to Disney that no one enjoyed. She swallowed against the lump in her throat, forced a smile. "How do you know Chris?" she asked Dee, because she had no interest in speaking to *him* any more than necessary.

"Uh..." Dee seemed unable to connect thoughts. The poor thing.

"Must be a military buddy. They all call him Cooper." Genevieve gently prodded, trying to gently encourage Dee's brain to make a connection. This must be what her mother meant. "Was it at an event of some kind?"

"No. Um. I met Dee through her dad, Kaz Bremen." Chris smiled, though his eyes looked…well, haunted somehow. Like he was scared. Granted, Dee was a bit rough today, but who was he to judge? "He's um, Kaz, is on my basketball team. And, and everyone calls me Cooper, but you, Gen."

"Oh, lovely." Yes, the basketball team, the gym, and recently, pickleball ball even though Genevieve thought he was still too young to be on a pickleball team. All were distractions that kept Chris spending time away from his family. Just like his perpetual need to take on more and more work. Like last night! Why is it that his guys continue to have problems, so he has to be at the hangar so much? Ridiculous!

The awkward silence bothered her only because of the look of terror that was on Dee's face. Poor thing, obviously, she was confused. She probably couldn't remember why she knew him. Must be a frightful way to live. Genevieve fought for something to say to save her.

"I've yet to meet your father, Dee Dee." What else could she say? "I hope he comes in soon. What does he do for a living?"

"Oh God." Dee blinked several times. "My, um, Kaz, um. He's an attorney. I did this mural thing at his office." Her mouth hung open, brow creased. She was obviously trying hard to make things clear; Genevieve wanted to pat her on the back and tell her everything would be OK.

"Yeah." Chris took a step backward, as if he wanted to escape. "That's how we met. I was in Kaz's office one day and complimented the mural on his wall. He told me his daughter was the artist and took commission work. So I commissioned her to paint the griffin on my building. Um, Liv, we should get going."

Dee shook her head, but not in a way that suggested disagreement. Genevieve knew Dee had finally realized how she'd met Chris. She just needed to hear the word "griffin." That hideous thing he had tattooed. He must have shown it to her so she could paint it. It probably traumatized her.

"Well," Genevieve pressed her fingers against that spot on her throat. "I've never been to the office, so I guess there's one masterpiece Dee Dee made that I haven't seen."

And she was glad she'd never been there. What a classless Chris-thing to do! Have someone so creative paint that horrific...thing on his building! It was bad enough he'd put it on his body where only people who knew him well could see it. That griffin tattoo was the first sign of bad things to come for her. But what was wrong with Dee? She still didn't seem right. She continued to stare at Chris as if he were pointing a gun at her: fear and confusion emanated from her. And why was he in such a hurry to get Liv out? How rude! Granted, this wasn't his scene, but still, he could pretend to be impressed. Though Genevieve wanted to shove him out of the store and protect Dee from whatever he had conjured in her muddled head. "Are you OK?"

"Um, yeah. I mean..." Dee tugged on a lock of hair, twisting it into such a tight rope that Genevieve worried she'd pull it out. "I...umm...can you excuse me?" And with that, Dee stepped backward. She turned and bumped into a mannequin wrapped in a hand-loomed cape that Maxine's mother had made and knocked it off its stand. She set it back, patted its head, and took off running out through the back of the store.

"She's…interesting." Livvy's eyes were wide.

"Don't be cruel, Livvy." Could her family be any worse? "There's an old saying about how there's just a thin line between genius and madness. I think Dee Dee balances on that line."

"Who's being cruel now?" Chris's eyes drilled into her.

Who did he think he was talking to? After how rude he just was to Dee? Genevieve had to turn away and pretend to look for something on a shelf. She'd stuffed every single mean thing she'd ever wanted to say so far deep into her body that someone would have to pry it out of her after she was dead. He should know better than to accuse her of ever being intentionally mean. If he knew her, then he'd know better. Which, of course, was the problem. "Dee has a rare kind of mental disability. Something must have set her off kilter. I'm sure she'll be OK."

She faced her soon-to-be-ex-husband and daughter again, forced her familial smile. "Thank you so much for coming by. Livvy, you should check out the jewelry. I'm sure you'll find something you love. If you do, set it aside, and I'll buy it for you. Meanwhile, I need to get back to work."

Dee

Dee bounded out the back door and found Maxine locking the garage.

"Holy Jesus fuck, Max!" She jumped into Max's path. "It's Gen with a G."

"I think you forgot a sentence."

"You're gonna fucking kill me." Dee's breath came in spurts.

"Should I find out why first, or just go ahead and put us both out of our miseries?"

"Her name is Gen with a G."

"What?"

"Gen with a G.

"Dee, you're hurting me."

"What?"

"Let go of me."

Dee realized she had a death-grip on Maxine's shoulders. It was all she could do not to shake her.

"I'm so sorry, Max!" How the fuck was any of this possible? She paced in a small circle while she caught her breath. "OK. Are you ready?"

"Oh, man, Dee Dee." Max sat on a glossy white step, rested her elbows on her knees. "If you have to ask, then that kind of tells me the answer is 'no.' But go ahead."

She looked so tired, so burdened. Dee hated herself for what she was about to say. "So, um, booty call—"

"You don't have to tell me."

"Oh yes I do."

"Why?"

"I call him Cooper, because that's how Kaz introduced him." She waited, hoping Max would connect some dots that maybe were pretty far apart with a few obstacles between them.

"Cooper? That's Genevieve's last name." There was one connection.

"I guess so. I never knew it."

Max's eyebrows lifted higher than Dee had ever seen them. "Wait a minute." She must have been making more connections.

"So, like, Kaz introduced him as a client," Dee continued.

"Oh, no."

"Yeah, as a client wanting a divorce."

"Oh, hell no!" Max shook her head. All dots were connected, and Max didn't seem to like the picture.

"I'm sorry, Max!" Dee wanted to hug her again.

"You never connected the names?"

"I never knew hers!" Dee threw her hands out in the air, something Mom tended to do when she was exasperated, and quickly put them on her waist. "When he'd talk about his family, he called his wife 'Gen.' I thought it was short for Jennifer."

"Shit! Dee!" Max popped up on her feet, walked to the edge of the sidewalk, and turned around. "How is this possible?"

"I have no fucking clue! I mean, it's a small town, but…I dunno, Max."

Max opened her mouth and paused for what was probably just a second or two, but felt like a decade to Dee. Thank God, she started laughing. "Only you, Dee. Only you could create such a shit-show."

"Are you saying that with affection?" Dee took one of her hands in both of hers.

"Of course."

"Thank God!" Dee pulled Max into a hug. "Thank you."

"Please don't mess this up," Max whispered. "I need this to work out. I need this store, this business to work, Dee."

"I know. I need it to work, too." She released her grip and

scratched the back of her head. "But, what the hell do I do?"

"There you are!" Genevieve threw open the back door of the store. "Come see how I set up the front! I think it looks beautiful! I can't thank you enough for letting me join you. You've re-opened my creativity."

Fuck!

Tuesday, June 29

Maxine

If Max didn't know any better, she'd think she was hungover. She lay on the red upholstered sofa in her mother's workroom and stared at the ceiling. Granted, she hadn't slept much the night before, but she felt more exhausted than she deserved, and she was so nauseous. It'd been more than a day since the sweet-and-sour chicken. Did she have a stomach bug?

She sat up, slowly, placed her feet on the hardwood floor, and waited for the room to stop spinning. Food poisoning or not, she'd made the right decision to stay here again. How was it possible that Dane could take the whole week off?

Dane never took time off from work without months of preplanning. He didn't even take an afternoon off to help her and Dee move into the store.

Yet somehow, magically, Dane, who didn't handle change, who planned every moment of his life in advance, was taking a whole freaking week off to get to know his son.

Tears blurred her vision. She wasn't sure if she was more hurt than angry. Or if equally both.

Her cell buzzed with a call. Dane.

"Yes?" She wasn't sure why she answered, other than she was so nauseous listening to the phone buzz seemed like a worse idea.

"Hey."

Hey again. She waited him out.

"Just wanted to, you know, check on you." His voice was soft, caring.

That was nice. Good start.

"You all right?" he continued.

"Honestly, Dane, no. But I don't want to have the same conversation we had yesterday."

"I miss you."

Well, that was a different conversation. She leaned back on the sofa. Three mannequins kept her company. Two were nude, but the third had a giant, ballooning black satin quinceañera gown fitted to it. Looked like Mama was almost finished attaching red embroidered flowers to the bodice. The bottom was bordered with similar flowers. Some young lady was going to look beautiful in it, would feel like a princess, and would probably hope to impress a number of young men. If only Max could go and tell her what it was really like to marry your prince charming.

"I guess you don't miss me." Dane's voice was quiet.

"I'm sorry, Dane. I really am. I, I do miss you." No, she didn't. "Actually, I miss who I thought you were." God, she felt awful. She just wanted to lie back down.

"I don't know what that means, Max."

She slid into a semi-reclined state and closed her eyes. "Dane, I used to be able to predict every move you would make, almost everything you would say. There was something comforting and safe about thinking I knew you that well."

"You do, baby. You know—"

"Please let me finish." She paused. He remained quiet. "I had no idea you ever thought anything so terrible about me and my relationship with Dee and her family."

"You have to admit it's not normal."

"It's perfectly normal. Mama and Lauren are best friends—two single mothers bonding over shared circumstances and a love of design. They helped each other rebuild their lives."

"I get it now, Max."

"But even if you didn't get it back then, how could you think so poorly of me?" Trying to lie on her back seemed to make things worse. She stood, slowly, and inched over to the big bay window that looked down into the backyard. Her playset was long gone. In its place was Mama's Zen garden, complete with a grounding chair, a fat hote Buddha, and a small meditation pond. Max ached to feel the serenity Mama seemed to feel all the time, the serenity she felt because she kept her cool while she spoke her mind. Max needed to channel her vibe now. "Dane, you harbored a really awful opinion of me, you thought terrible things about Dee's family, and I never knew. Don't you remember me wanting Kaz *and* my father to walk me down the aisle? That's how much that man means to me. They're my *family*." Tears stung her eyes. She cleared her throat and took a deep breath in through her nose. *Keep it cool.* "And you thought I was using him."

"Max—"

"You kept all that bottled up, just like how you never told me you cheated on me. You—"

"I didn't want to hurt you, Max."

"And it never occurred to you that it might be possible I'd find out? And if so, that the longer you put it off, the worse I would feel?"

She heard him breathing on the other end. "Honestly, Max, I don't know what I was thinking."

She turned away from the window, too quickly. Her stomach lurched. She needed Pepto.

"So, what happens now, Max?"

That was a good question. "I don't know. I don't feel well right now. I need time to process things. It's my turn for *you* to give me the space to process things. OK?"

"OK. I get that, just—"

She wasn't sure if she was going to belch or vomit.

"Dane—"

"Real quick, Max. I'm going to pick up Jamaal at the hotel now. What…what do you think I should do with him?"

She clicked off the call and ran to the bathroom.

Her empty stomach had nothing to give despite the heaving.

The cold, pink-tiled floor chilled her bones as she rested, sitting with her back against the tub. She didn't want to leave. But, if she stayed at Mama's today, that would mean Dee and Genevieve would be alone together...was Dee in a place to handle that?

Was Dee in a place to handle anything right now? She was about to ask for sleeping meds!

Max remembered all too well visiting Dee after she came home from the hospital. They were both newly fifteen, and there was Dee, her best friend, her sister, but for lack of common DNA, curled up in a ball in the corner of that giant suede sectional sofa Lauren and Kaz had in their den. She looked so scared, so confused.

"You know how in TV commercials they say some drugs might cause suicidal thoughts?" That's how Lauren had tried to explain what happened to Dee back then. Lauren, too, had looked scared and confused. Max didn't know what she was talking about. She had never really paid attention to TV commercials. But she wanted to reassure Lauren, so she nodded. All she understood from the conversation that happened afterward was that the medications they'd given Dee had broken her mind a little more, and it hurt her so bad, she'd tried to make the pain go away by swallowing a whole bottle of pills.

Thank God Hayleigh found her so soon.

Who was going to keep that close eye on her now?

How could things get so freaking messy?

How could Dane be such an ass?

"Maxine?" Mama's voice carried up the stairs. "I made breakfast, honey. Come on down."

The thought of breakfast made her heave again.

Dee

Pick up. Pick up. Pick up. Please, Mom, pick up the god-damned phone.

Voice mail.

Her grip on her cell was so tight it hurt her hand. How was it possible that her mother didn't pick up right away? The one fucking time she actually needed her!

Her lungs felt so stiff and tight. She couldn't inhale. Static built up in her ears. She needed to breathe. Inhale, two, three. Close eyes, exhale two, three, four, five. Inhale, two, three, four…

The static eased. And the air came in clear again. Panic attack, averted. But where the hell was Mom? Should she call Kaz?

She continued to sit cross-legged on the floor between the coffee table and sofa, breathing deeply. The plant that had just been her phone holder for the Zoom therapy appointment drooped. Maybe it needed water.

Mom still hadn't called back by the time she returned with a glass of water.

"Here you go, drama queen." Dee poured water into the soil. How was she to know if it was enough? Another thing to Google.

At the whiteboard, she drew an unhappy plant as a reminder. Her breathing was completely back to normal, the electricity that had flickered through her veins when she ended her appointment with Aisling had waned. She was going to be OK. Just keep breathing. Focus on one thing at a time. She needed to get to the store soon. But it sure as hell would be great if Mom called before she got down there. The last thing she wanted was to have

Genevieve hovering over her, listening as Dee held a conversation with Mom about the time she tried to commit suicide.

She had to admit Genevieve had done some pretty cool shit in the store. She obviously had an eye for color, balance, and design. But Dee assumed her daughter had to be dragged into the store. Why would she want to see her mother? Genevieve must be overbearing at home. Yes, actually, Gen with a G *was* overbearing at home. Cooper had mentioned that, didn't he?

Cooper!

He'd texted and called so many times the night before, she'd shut her phone off.

But she couldn't block him.

Dee closed her eyes to bat back a sadness creeping up from her belly. Felt the same as when Granddad had called and told her Gram died. Jesus! Was she grieving Cooper? Did she really have to break up with him? BREAKUP? It *was* a relationship. But why the hell did he come into the store? Why had he blindsided her? Was he trying to hurt her? Oh God! She was actually attached to him! She let herself get attached to someone, but the Velcro didn't line up properly.

She felt herself rocking back and forth, her breath coming in shorter.

"Fuck!" Eyes wide open, fists clenched at her sides, she tried to get control of her breath again. How could she let herself get so freaking attached to him?

Where the hell was her phone? A text from H helped her find it.

U ready for consults?

Yeah. Where the hell is mom?

Cool. I got some people
wanna custom stained glass

door. And I dunno.

*K. What you do you mean
you don't know?!*

*I mean I don't know. You call
her?*

*Of course I ducking called
her!*

FUCKING called her!

Fucking auto-correct!

Are you OK?

No!!!!!!!!!!!!!!

Hayleigh's face filled the screen as an incoming call.
"What's wrong?"
"I'm not fucking sleeping." Tears! What the hell? Why were there tears coming out of her face? Why was she shaking?
"Worse than normal?"
"Way the hell worse than normal." Dee tried to pace in circles around her living room. The orange beaded forms were still scattered about the floor. A blanket and a couple of pillows tripped her up. She brought Cooper into this mess? But she'd always been a mess. He knew that! God! Why did he come in the store?

That fucking buzzing sound started up in her ears. She couldn't have a panic attack with H on the phone. She couldn't let anyone know she was that close to breaking down. She straddled over an empty box that she wasn't sure where it was from, stopped moving, and managed to modulate her voice so she sounded as calm and sane as she ever was. "I just had a Zoom with Aisling." Long, slow inhale. "She thinks maybe I should try some sleep medication."

Long, slow exhale.

"Oh shit! Really? Does she know your history with meds?"

"Yeah. I mean, she knows only what I could tell her. And, honestly, I don't have all the facts. Like a whole cocktail was prescribed to me back then, and I can't remember what it all was. She needs to know so that she can try to do something totally different."

"Are you OK with that?"

She couldn't get a full inhale in. Suddenly, her knees couldn't quite support her; she crumpled to the floor. Tears poured down. "Fuck, H. I don't know what I'm OK with." She wiped her face with her T-shirt. "I mean, the last thing I want is to have a repeat of what happened before. But I'm not fucking sleeping. And I'm so goddamned tired."

"Are you crying?"

"Don't fucking tell Mom!"

"Dee—"

"I just need some sleep. And, like, I'm self-medicating now to the point where I'm beginning to worry."

"What do you mean?"

"My recycling bin looks like I'm hosting ragers every night. I kind of have to black out in order to fall asleep. But then..." She fell back onto the floor and stared up at the ceiling.

"But then?"

"The nightmares. Man, H. They're starting to get to me again. They're almost as bad as...wait. Mom's calling."

"OK. I'm on my way to the store."

"Get coffee!" She clicked over.

"Hi, sweetheart! I'm so sorry you didn't get me. Would you believe I dropped my phone between the seat and the center console of my car?"

"I would believe it, Mom." Dee sat upright and cleared the mucus clogging her throat. She wanted to sound clear on all levels—

clear-headed, clear-throated. Make Mom think she was fine. "Happens to me all the freaking time."

"Well, what matters is we find them, and I did."

"Right." Once again, she tried to maintain a steady breath. She should have taken Max and Mama Kat up on their offers to do yoga with them.

"What's up, sweetheart?"

"Um, so, don't freak out, but...I need to know what all those prescriptions were back when I, um, you know. When I was a teen."

Cars drove up and down Main Street in front of her building. The noise came up as gentle swishes through her closed windows. A dog yapped from somewhere, probably the neighborhood behind her. The air conditioner hummed. Mom remained silent.

"Mom?" Dee felt strong enough to stand again. At the window, she watched the tiny downtown street, cars politely driving twenty-five miles an hour, then stopping and honky like impatient assholes at people trying to parallel park. "Mom? Hello?"

"I..." Mom coughed. "I'm here, honey. I, I think I misunderstood you. What did you ask me?"

"You didn't misunderstand me, Mom."

"Sweetheart, I did everything in my power to put that era behind me. I never should have let you go to a public high school. I certainly never should have let that psychiatrist prescribe—"

"Mom! I'm not asking to re-visit any of that shit." The cutest fucking dog ever was taking a dump across the street, right in the gutter, as if it knew where it should go. Its human scrolled on a phone, not paying any attention to how damned smart her dog was.

"Dee?"

"What?"

"I wanted to know why you were asking."

"Oh." Dee spun away from the window and returned to her whiteboard. "Aisling, my therapist, thinks..." Above the shoe, she drew bougainvillea flowers, trying to remember what they looked like from the printouts. "She thinks, maybe, well, that, you know, um..." The flowers looked like pink rabbit shit. She erased them. A sigh escaped. "So, look. I haven't been able to sleep since..." since she got back from Gram's. Mom would freak about that and immediately blame it on *those people*. "I haven't been able to sleep for a while. I guess the stress of moving, the a new business—"

"It's a lot to handle."

"Right, well, I seem to only be able to handle it when I'm awake. I've been having some really horrific nightmares lately—"

"Come home." The words hit through the phone like pistol shots. "I'll take care of you."

"I don't need anyone to take care of me. I just need to get a decent night's sleep. Aisling wants to prescribe something, but since the only time I've taken any kind of prescription I fucking wigged out and tried to off myself, she wanted to know what those meds were. She wants to make sure whatever she gives me now won't have the same effect."

"I should hope not!"

Dee searched for a blank space on the whiteboard. "So, what were they?"

She had to make some room for a new thought. Everything related to the move could go except for the image of the stick figure falling on the steps. She also erased the Wilde quote.

"I can't quite remember." Mom took her time answering.

Really? Dee pressed the eraser hard against the board, held it there as she processed what her mother had just admitted. Dee had had a psychotic break and tried to commit suicide because she couldn't tell the difference between nightmares and real life due to a god-damn drug, and Mom couldn't remember what the fuck it was called?

"Seriously?" Dee knew her voice had enough attitude that Mom would notice, but at least she refrained from calling her names. "I mean—"

"As I said, I tried to block that out of my mind. I can't stand the thought that I almost lost my...my little girl—"

Fuck, Mom was crying. Dee waited it out. She knew this was tough on Mom, and really it was all Dee's fault. She had begged to go to a normal school. The school had begged for medication to control Dee's ADHD. The pressure from being a weirdo arty kid in a public school, the meds…that was tough enough for Mom. She didn't want her to hurt any more, but she really needed to sleep.

She scanned the board for anything else she could get rid of. "Cooper" with the strings needed to go. But suddenly, it was pretty damned difficult to use the eraser.

"Mom. I just need the name of the meds." And now she was crying, too. Again! Dammit!

"I know. I will have to, to look for the records. How soon?"

"Now would be great."

"Oh, um..."

Max texted in.

U ok?

"Look, Mom. I gotta get to the store. Can you just call Aisling and tell her what it was?"

"I guess so. Send me her information. Oh, but will she listen to me? What about that HIPAA thing? I couldn't even get information about Hayleigh's root canal, even though I paid the bill."

"I have no clue. But I'll text Aisling that she can talk to you about the meds." But only the meds. 'Cause Mom didn't need to know about anything else.

"Please do that, let me know, send me her contact info, and I'll call her."

Dee remained in place before the whiteboard as she texted Aisling. Then, before heading downstairs, she pulled several markers out of the bin. Above the puzzle piece, she drew a black blob to symbolize the weight she felt on top of her right before waking up every night—morning, whenever. To the left of it, she drew Gram's willow tree. To the right, she wrote *Brett*. Neither the tree nor Brett was ever in her nightmares. But she knew Brett was there the night of the fire. He saved her, pulled her out of it, right? Did someone tell her that? Or did she remember it? Maybe she just *knew* it. That's what Brett had always done. He was always there to save her.

Save her from what, though? What else besides the fire? Or was it just the fire? What really happened that night?

And why did it feel like her father, a man she'd never met, was there, in the room with her?

Genevieve

The door leading up to Dee's apartment opened. If Genevieve hadn't recognized the hair, she would have assumed some junkie had broken into the store. Thank God there were no customers! What would people think of her? Red-and-black plaid pajama pants—flannel again in the middle of summer—and a black sports bra under a threadbare concert t-shirt. Barefoot, again. Would she wear furry animal-shaped slippers in the winter?

If that weren't bad enough, her eyes were swollen and bloodshot. And those bags! Had she been crying? She looked like she'd been punched. Maybe she was malnourished. It wouldn't surprise Genevieve to learn Dee forgot to eat. But she seriously looked like a junkie! What were they going to do with her?

"Good morning, Dee Dee," Genevieve tried to sound soft, encouraging as she approached her. "Are you feeling OK?"

Dee frowned, blinked her eyes a few times. She reminded

Genevieve of when her children were babies, and they'd wake up from a nap, blinking at the world as if they weren't sure where they were.

"Um, actually, I feel fine, Genevieve." She pulled her wild hair on top of her head and secured it in place with a few of the dozens of black bands she always had around a wrist. "Why'd you ask?"

"You look..." Genevieve wished she had something in her hands. She squeezed them together in front of her. "Well, tired, I guess."

"Oh, yeah. I'm not sleeping much these days."

"Well, Maxine was just saying we're ahead of schedule for setting the store up. Maybe having a few days off to rest before our soft opening happens will be just what the doctor ordered."

"Actually, the doctor ordered a prescription, but a couple days to sleep wouldn't be bad." She rolled her shoulders. "What uh...what's happening down here?"

"Well, there are workmen in the back putting something on the windows—"

"The window sheets!" Dee's face brightened.

"Yes." Genevieve remembered how pretty Dee had looked in the videos. She had cleaned herself up and dressed appropriately for them. Of course, she'll make herself presentable for customers. She pressed her fingers against her throat and swallowed. The lump was barely noticeable. "I think that's what they said. Maxine spoke to them."

"That's so freaking awesome." Dee patted her pants as if looking for something. Found her phone in her bra top. "H is bringing shit from Jhansi's. Want something?"

"Oh, I'm fine, thank you." Genevieve rounded the checkout counter to finish setting up a display of papier-mâché animals on the wall. "But what are window sheets?"

"It's like a film for the windows. Sodium flares from the torch can damage people's eyes. That's why I wear glasses. The sheets will protect anybody outside who might look in when I'm doing flamework."

"That's so exciting! You're going to do that in the store?" Genevieve spun back around to look at Dee, and was surprised, once again, by what a mess her artistic hero was. "I can't wait to watch."

"You should learn." Dee placed her phone on the counter.

"You would teach me?"

Dee's eyes grew wide. Was she excited about the idea of having a mentee?

"Um, yeah. If, you know, you really want to learn." She paused while she turned a full circle. "So, like, what should I be doing here. Any idea?"

"Oh, Maxine wanted to finish the classroom area today and rearrange the seating for consultations in the framing room."

"Cool." Dee bounced her head in a slow nod as she headed toward the back. "Where is Max, anyway?"

"She ran out for some Pepto. Her stomach was off." Genevieve returned her attention to the display behind the check-out counter. What would these women do without her? Here she was, a brand-new employee literally watching the store while Dee overslept, and Max could barely stand because she was so sick. Not that Genevieve needed the money, but she was beginning to assume she wasn't being paid enough.

"Hidey ho, bitches!"

What on earth? Genevieve spotted Hayleigh strutting in through the front door.

"Hey, Gen! Where's Dee?"

"She's, um..."

"Framing!" Dee hollered. "You pick up my coffee?"

"Of course. Your addiction is my command!"

Genevieve watched in something close to horror as the two sisters hugged in greeting. How was it possible that Lauren was their mother? She was so put together, so classy, so very much how

Genevieve herself wanted to be. And yet that Hayleigh with her magenta hair—wasn't it turquoise the other day? And *what* was she wearing? A long, flowered sun dress, red patent-leather platform oxfords, and a man's herringbone suit jacket. Would her Olivia ever dress like either of them?

Her Olivia lived in joggers and tank tops in the summer, joggers and hoodies in the winter. Except in the photos she posted on social media. Genevieve was going to have to talk to that girl about the dangers of showing cleavage like that. Surely it was an accident, but it wasn't the first time she'd left little to the imagination on social media.

"You look like hell." Hayleigh handed a cup of coffee to Dee Dee.

"You look like you lost a bet." Dee ripped the lid from her cup. "Did you steal that jacket from Kaz?"

"He gave it to me." Hayleigh stepped back and opened her arms wide to show off that hideous outfit. "It's an Armani. Mama Kat altered it to fit me. Isn't it gorgeous?"

"Yeah. I'll give you that." Dee cheered her with her cup and took a long sip.

"Hey, Gen."

"Yes, Hayleigh?" Did she really just call her *Gen?*

"I had a meeting with another client this morning and snagged Dee a stained-glass commission. Lemme show you guys how to enter that in the system."

"Oh, wonderful!" Genevieve found herself genuinely smiling at the thought of watching Dee Dee, in person, create a custom stained-glass piece. Though who was Hayleigh to call her "Gen"? Only close friends and family did that. *This could be such a dream job. If only these women were more professional.*

Hayleigh showed them how to enter the job details into the computer, including how to upload the image from her phone to the customer's order. Dee was to take the image, their logo, and create a stained-glass version of it.

"Easy peasy." Dee videoed Hayleigh with her phone. Genevieve quietly took detailed notes on a steno pad. Did Dee mean the system was easy or that the stained glass would be easy? The woman was so confusing. But Hayleigh certainly knew what she was doing, and she obviously had very successful clients for her marketing services. It must make Lauren crazy seeing her dress the way she does.

Or was that just the way artistic people were? How did she dress back when she was young and free? Right. She was never free. Would things have been different if she had never had children, gotten married? Would she have her own business where she'd show up looking like she just rolled out of bed while...

"'Preciate it." Dee put her phone back inside her sports bra.

"No prob. Always happy to support the cause." Hayleigh pulled out rose-colored gold-rimmed aviator glasses from her jacket pocket and put them on. Genevieve was certain she'd never dress like her, nor Dee. Creative, yes, but, well, presentable, too.

"Are you OK, Gen?" Hayleigh tipped the glasses down to look at her over the top. "You look a little off all of a sudden."

She shook her head, shook that word *presentable* out of it. "I'm fine. Just thinking about what you just showed me."

"Well, if you ever have any questions, I'm just a text away. Do you have my contact info?"

"I don't think so."

"What's your number? I'll text it to you." She pulled out her phone.

Genevieve recited her phone number, battling off an unsettling, unsteady feeling, as if she had a touch of vertigo.

"Do you need to sit down?" Hayleigh had a hand on her arm.

"I'm fine."

"No, you're not." Dee dragged a stool out from the consult area. "Sit."

What was going on? She was the one who had it all together.

Well, not quite *all* together. Her marriage had fallen apart, she had failed her sister, her son had a horrible birthday, and, frankly, Olivia dressed like a slut every time she left the house. Her grip on what she thought the world was supposed to be was slipping, and now she didn't feel sure about anything anymore. Just look at these two "women"—one looked like she lived in a homeless shelter, and yet she owned a business and was a thriving artist. The other looked like she stole clothes as she ran through a thrift store and was beyond brilliant with computers and marketing. She, too, had a thriving business.

And here Genevieve was at their mercy, always properly dressed—even presentably dressed—and...and what?

What was the point?

"Drink this." Dee shoved a plastic bottle of water into her hand. "Do you have blood sugar problems or something?"

"What?" Genevieve realized she was blinking like Dee.

"I'm a diabetic." Hayleigh pulled back her jacket and pointed to a white plastic thing stuck to her arm. "My insulin pump. You're really pale. I guess you look like me when my blood sugar drops. Are you shaking?"

"I'm..." Genevieve held one hand out. There was a tremor.

"Here. Eat these." Hayleigh pulled a bag of jellybeans from a jacket pocket. "I never leave home without them."

"Um, thank you." Genevieve popped a few of them in her mouth.

Within a few minutes, the world seemed right again.

"You know, I didn't eat breakfast this morning," Genevieve remembered. "Maybe my blood sugar did drop."

"Not good!" Hayleigh continued to stare at her. Concern, maybe even compassion, shone through her face. Dee, too, looked troubled. These girls actually cared about her! When was the last time Olivia, or Remy for that matter, or Chris had such empathy?

"Thank you." Suddenly, an overwhelming desire to bond with

these wild creatures filled Genevieve's heart. Bonding with people who accepted her! This is what she'd wanted when she came for this job. "Thank you for your help, and thank you, Dee Dee, for this job. I'm so looking forward to watching you do stained glass."

"Maybe Dee should teach you? We could video that and put it on her channel. Hey! Could you do a stained-glass class, Dee?"

"Yeah, we'd um, mentioned that—mentioned me teaching Genevieve something." Dee didn't seem as excited as Hayleigh and Genevieve. "I probably could. Stained glass would, like, need to be a series. I'd have to think it out. Plan it."

"Speaking of classes." Hayleigh slapped her sister's arm. Dee punched her back, gently. Somewhat. "Let's talk about Thursday's class. We should beta all the touch points of the process."

"And in English?" Thank God Dee asked, so Genevieve didn't have to.

"Sign-up went great. Thanks, Gen, for getting everyone to try it. But, I'd like to roll out the confirmation, which should include parking info, and I dunno what else. I mean, will they need to wear protective goggles? I see you in them sometimes, Dee."

"Not for this one."

"OK."

"But maybe don't wear big or loose sleeves." Dee found her coffee cup again. If she were an addict, Genevieve was sure it was to caffeine. "That could get messy."

"Cool. I'll include that in the confirmation email. Then when they get here, should they check in, come in the back door..."

Hayleigh rattled off all sorts of "touch points" while Dee did her best to answer while doing that slow bobbing thing with her head. That must be what she did to bide time while her brain tried to make sense of whatever was coming to it. How terrible! The poor thing. Dee needed her as much as she needed Dee.

"So, we're set," Hayleigh eventually said. "You have a lesson plan of sorts, I could see?"

Dee

Dee didn't recognize the number that sent the text at first. Until she read it. *Oh, the pharmacy. Aisling and Mom must have connected.* Her prescription was ready.

Wow. So, this was a definite option. She'd expected to be relieved, to have that pointy anxious feeling ease up in her chest. But it was taking its time. Meanwhile, it was almost five o'clock. She'd managed to get all the frame samples attached to the wall in a pleasing way and could justify leaving. Max and Genevieve would be leaving soon, too, anyway.

Then she remembered she couldn't drive anywhere. She'd lost her key fob again. The last time she had it was Sunday, coming back from Josie's place. Later that night, she remembered she'd put that box in the back seat and forgotten about it. But she couldn't get it because she somehow remembered to lock her car before losing the fob.

She found Maxine on a step ladder hanging a clock made from an old Ouija board planchette. "You feeling better, Max?" Dee sat on the consultation table.

"Yeah. I don't know what's going on with me. But it must be passing. I feel great now." Max climbed down and faced her.

"Awesome."

"You all right?"

"Not really."

"Wanna elaborate?"

"So, like, Aisling called in a prescription for me."

Max stood still, watching her with eyebrows raised.

"To help me, you know, sleep."

She nodded, slowly. "Does your mom know?"

"Yeah. Um, I had her talk to Aisling to kind of compare notes, so we don't have a repeat experience."

"All righty!" Genevieve came into the room, startling Dee to the point of falling off the table. "The front area is complete!" She looked way too happy. "So I guess tomorrow we can finish up this room and then the back?"

"I think that's the plan." Maxine smiled at her. Dee struggled to respond. She really wanted to hate the woman, but it was so hard. As annoying and mom-like as she was, there was something sad, almost pitiable, about her. Dee wanted to inspire her to adopt a little attitude, look a little less repressed. She knew that didn't come from Cooper. Whatever had shaped Genevieve had happened when she was a child. What had he seen in her to begin with?

"Very good, so I'll get on that first thing tomorrow morning." Genevieve and Max had apparently been talking. "Good night, my lovelies!"

Dee waited until she heard the chime at the front door that signaled Genevieve had left the building. "Did she really fucking say 'lovelies'?"

Max nodded, giggling. "How are you, really?"

"Maybe borderline OK, probably brokenhearted. And I think I'm more in danger of accidentally harming myself by falling asleep as I walk up or down stairs than if I take the medication. Your turn."

"I stayed at Mama's again last night. Dane's taking a week off from work to get to know his son."

"What the fuck? Dane never takes time off from work without planning months in advance!"

"Yeah."

"Wait! I don't understand. Are you at Mama Kat's because Dane's spending time with his kid?"

"No. I just don't want to be around him right now."

"Gotcha. I don't wanna be around him either." Fucking ass-hat.

Max pulled another clock from a box: a Wedgewood blue china plate with white bas-relief images around the edge and white hands. Mom would love that. Max held the clock against the wall in a few different places until she decided she'd found the right spot: just above a clock made from the lid of the wine crate Dee used as a side table on her tiny porch. "Making things worse, he's also acting surprisingly selfish. I don't want to be around him."

"Are you fucking serious? After what he pulled?"

"Right." Max set the Wedgewood plate clock down to pound a hook into the wall. "I feel like I have no idea who he really is anymore. Even worse, I am craving an emotional response from him right now, and it's not coming. And I don't think he even gets that. He gets that I need time to process things, but…I don't want only the rational, problem-solving Dane right now. I want, I *need* something from him I don't think he can give me."

"Oh man, Max." Dee scribbled on a Post-it note: *don't sell til Mom sees. Does she want it?* She stuck the note on the back of the clock before handing it to Max. "I'm so sorry. I wish I knew what to say."

"So that's why I'm at Mama's, on the couch in her workroom, getting a sore back." Max slid the clock onto the wall and then faced Dee. "Since I'm homeless right now, what about you? Do you want me to stay the night with you, in case...?"

At first, Dee couldn't figure out what the "in case" was in reference to, so it took a second for her to respond. "Oh! No. Not tonight. I don't think I'm going to take the meds tonight. I figure tonight I'll stay up Googling the potential side effects."

"And yet you wonder why we worry about you."

"Seems to me I got it all under control." She nodded. "But, um, could I ask you a favor?"

"Of course."

"I can't find my key fob—."

Maxine's shoulders shook with her laughter.

Maxine

Positive, again.

"Maxine?" Mama yelled from downstairs. "I'm aging down here!"

"I know. Just another minute!" Max stared at the stick, unable to accept the truth.

Could she get two false positives? Was that possible?

Maybe she should get another box of tests. One from a different drugstore. Maybe the one where she took Dee had a bad batch?

While Dee had stood in line to get her medication, Max couldn't help but wonder: *could* she be pregnant? She'd been nauseous for the past couple of mornings, and it would always clear up as the day went on. Today was the worst. And her periods hadn't been regular for years...Could it be possible?

She'd slid over to the back wall where the pregnancy tests were, on the pretense she needed a few things for her stay at Mama's, then bought a box of two at the checkout counter near the front of the store before Dee had finished with the pharmacist in the back. The first showed positive, but she'd told herself it probably wasn't accurate.

Now she had two positives. They sat side by side on the pale pink sink in her childhood bathroom.

Two positives: she was pregnant.

Yet she was undecided whether she wanted to continue her marriage.

"Maxine!" Her mother burst through the door.

"Don't tell Lauren!" Max couldn't believe that was her first thought.

"I'm going to be a grandmother!" Mama's hands clamped on her cheeks. The joy on her face as she gazed at the test sticks was unbearable. "What do you mean, I can't tell Lauren? We've been waiting for this for so long!"

Finally, Mama looked at Max. The joy melted into empathy and compassion. Clearly, she saw what Max was thinking. "Listen, me getting pregnant with you wasn't good timing, either." Mama sat on the edge of the tub. "But you wound up being the best thing that ever happened to me. It'll be all right."

Max wanted to believe her. "How do I make it be all right?"

"You don't make be all right, girl. You just let it."

"But what do I do right now?"

"I think you should call that husband of yours and make him come over here and talk."

"And say what?"

"What do you want?"

"For him *not* to be a father to another kid. For—"

"What do you want that you can control?"

That was a good question. Max didn't have an answer. She'd given up on the idea of having a child, had resigned herself to that life. Now she's pregnant, and Dane's got a son from another woman.

"I'll tell you what I want right now that I can control," Mama interrupted the silence. "I want to sit in a comfortable chair. Meet me in my design room."

Her design room was downstairs, in what was originally an office space. She kept the messy work of sewing out of sight—upstairs in the extra bedrooms. Her design room was always neat and tidy, with a computer station, one mannequin, and a bulletin board covered with images, fabric swatches, trim samples, and other ephemera. It also housed two very comfortable armchairs, where Mama said she'd sit and relax, and let her designs "come" to her.

"Last time we tried to speak," Max settled in one of the chairs, "was this morning. He called under the guise of checking on me, but really wanted advice on what to do with the boy."

Mama raised her eyebrows.

"Then he sent me a text today when I was working. I didn't look at it until I was waiting on that last test. He asked how I can let my father come in and out of my life and always welcome him back, even though Daddy inevitably hurts my feelings, but I can't let him back in after this one mistake."

"What did you tell him?"

"I haven't responded." Max shook her head. "Honestly, Mama, I don't know why I forgive Daddy over and over, and I can't forgive Dane this once."

"Oh, that's easy." Mama reached out for her hand. "Because you don't expect any better from your father. You have higher expectations of Dane."

Mama was right. "But that makes it sound like forgiveness is on me. That I have to let Dane off the hook and lower my expectations of him if—"

"Not at all, Max. That's not what I'm saying at all."

"Then what?" Max held tight to Mama's hand.

"Do you want this child?"

She no longer had a steady job with good benefits. She no longer had the marriage she thought was rock solid. Perhaps it was irrational, but yes, that was one thing she knew for sure. She still wanted to be a mother. She could only nod, though, because she knew it was dangerous to count even this one egg before it hatched.

"Then, the way I see it, these are your options. You can forgive him, go back to him, and try to figure out how to make a family that includes the boy at some frequency *and* a baby. Or, you can forgive him, leave him, and figure out how you and your baby will have a relationship with him in the future. Or, you can resent him and let that poison you from having any kind of happy life going forward because any relationship you have with him will be strained and stressed."

"So, I have to forgive him."

"If you want to live in peace."

"Any advice on how to do that?"

Mama's face shone with a smile. "The track I took with your father was to focus only on what I appreciated about him. Which was one thing: you. You have more with Dane: you've had a good six years together in marriage; he supported you in your career change—"

"No, he didn't."

"Well, you'll need to figure out what you appreciate about him then and focus on that. That will eventually replace the resentment."

"But that doesn't tell me whether I want to stay with him."

"It will. Just give yourself time." Mama squeezed Max's hand. "I'm not trying to pressure you, but…when can I tell Lauren?"

Wednesday, June 30

Dee

Dreamy yet heavy, thunderous music from Deftones vibrated Dee's body. She pulsed to the beat as the singer's voice ranged from hypnotizing, otherworldly crooning to hardcore screaming. He guided her as she pulled the molten glass, bringing it to points or melting it down to bulbous forms again. She was one with the sound. It controlled her, directed her movements as she wielded a glass rod and used gravity and metal tools to turn it into recognizable shapes in the blaze of a torch. No thoughts, just instinct in sync with the music.

Unaware of time and space, she filled the kiln with thin twigs covered by tiny flowers, the petals triangular: blooming bougainvillea stems she'd melt together later in a form that would cascade out of the shoes.

There was no more room in the second kiln. She had to stop. She cut off the gas and oxygen supplies to the torch, took off her safety glasses, and felt the grooves they'd left in her face. *Damn. Must have been at it a long time.*

She hit pause on her phone. In the quiet still of the studio, she shut her eyes and let the music's energy drain from her body.

The time read 5:07 when she opened her eyes again. The sun should be rising. She could probably go to sleep now. With all the curtains open, the lights on, with only a blanket over her in the center of her wide-open living room.

Holy shit! Someone was watching her.

Or was it her imagination?

No. There was definitely a silhouette of a man standing on the other side of the window. With just a hint of sun coming in behind him, and the window film preventing any studio light from revealing his features, he was a shadow facing her, arms loose at his sides.

Or maybe he wasn't standing there. *Maybe this wasn't real.*

She'd been awake for about twenty-four hours, probably longer if she stopped to do the math.

Maybe she was sleeping.

Maybe this was a dream.

Maybe this was the dark blob in the dream. The heavy weight that pinned her down.

Was blob a man? Had some*one* pinned her down? Not some*thing*?

He raised a hand, waved it back and forth.

What to do? What to do?

Is he fucking real?

Was she awake?

She touched the tip of the tungsten tweezers to her forearm. FUCK! That burnt! That was stupid as shit. But it meant she was awake.

Was she hallucinating? Did she feel things when she hallucinated last time?

She realized her chest was popping up and down with her breath. That buzzing sound filled her ears.

Think Dee! What to do?

Frozen. She was frozen in place.

Jesus Christ. It's like a stupid horror movie.

"Breathe Dee!" she wanted to shout, but it came out a whisper. That buzzing grew louder.

Breathe. She needed to breathe. In, one, two, three, four,

five. Out, one, two. In, one, two, three, four, FUCK! He's walking to the back of the building.

What the hell? What was she supposed to do? Work brain! Work!

Call the police!
She grabbed her phone. He opened the back door of the studio. She dropped the phone. Grabbed a metal paddle and swung it at his head. He ducked, shoved his shoulder into her stomach, and lifted her up off the ground. The paddle landed hard on his ass, pounced out of her hand.

"What the fuck, DEE?" Cooper shouted. He set her down but kept a tight hold on her arms. "I figured you'd be upset, but violent?"

His voice seemed to blow through her head. Her whole body shook, breath came in gasping. "I...I didn't know...it was you...I thought..."

He loosened his grip. She collapsed against him and let him hold her until she could breathe without trying, until the buzzing in her ears faded. "There's a film on the window. You looked like a shadow."

"I'm so sorry." His hand smoothed over her head, down her back. "I...It's Wednesday morning...I had to see you. I haven't missed a Wednesday morning with you in—"

"Don't go there." She stepped out of his embrace, though not quite strong enough to feel confident she could stand. She slumped on a stool.

Cooper lifted a hand, palm pointed up, and opened his mouth. Silence for a full minute. Yeah, he couldn't think of what to say, either.

"You have to leave." It came out as a whisper. And why he needed to leave, she couldn't understand. She didn't want him to go.

"Why can't we talk through this Dee?"

"Talk through what?"

"Us."

"Is there an 'us?' How can there be an us?" She picked her phone up from the floor. Whew, still no cracks.

"I don't understand why there can't be an us." Cooper touched her arm.

His energy traveled all the way to her womb. That was dangerous. Who knew she had a responsive womb? She needed physical distance from him. He can't touch her anymore. She slid her phone into her back pocket, stepped around him, and went outside through the back door.

"How long?" She sat on a glossy step, forcing him to remain standing, out of reach. "How long have you known Genevieve worked here, with me?"

"Monday, when Liv called her. She wanted to see where her mother worked." He put his hands in his jeans pockets, leaned back on his heels.

"And you thought you'd just pop in like that? You couldn't warn me or something?"

"My daughter and I just dropped off her car to get repaired. She got in mine, saying she'd texted Gen and wanted to see the store. How was I to get out of it? I couldn't come up with an excuse not to. I'd promised to take her wherever she wanted to go that day. She was in the passenger seat, so I couldn't text you to give you a heads up. I was panicking all the way over here, Dee. The last thing I wanted to do was blindside you."

Well, that was good to hear. He wasn't intentionally being an asshole.

"But you know what *I* don't get?" He placed a hand on his chest.

"What?"

"Why didn't you say something to *me*?" He stared into her. "I mean, I'm kind of pissed, Dee, that you never told me."

"Told you what?"

"Something like 'I hired a Gen Cooper, any relation? She's got two kids with the same names as yours.' "

"Don't get all pissy-sarcastic with me." Dee stood up again. The step made her taller than him. "First, we call her Genevieve. I always thought your wife's name was Jennifer. And second, I never knew her last name. Max handled all that."

"Oh."

"Yeah, oh. And she would only say 'my daughter' or 'my son.'"

He nodded, grinned. "So…can we have breakfast today?"

"There is no breakfast today."

"What?"

"You have to leave."

"Why?" He spread his arms out.

Dee was so tired, she wanted nothing but to lean into him, let him wrap those arms around her, and hold her as she fell asleep.

"I've been up all night, Cooper. I don't have the strength to do this." She fell back to sit on the step again.

"There's nothing for you to do, baby." He stepped closer, squatted in front of her, placed a hand on her knee. "Yes, this is awkward, but we can still be together."

"How? There are so many things wrong with this situation."

"What do you mean?"

"Max will kill me if I fuck up our business by losing Genevieve."

"Is she that important to your store?"

That was an interesting question. Was she? Could they manage it without her? "I honestly don't know. But—"

"Dee, you know my marriage has been over for a long time. If it weren't for the accident, she would have applied to work here as a divorced woman. Kaz has paperwork drawn up to finish the process. As soon as she reviews it, it'll be done. Gen wants a divorce, too."

Dee let her fingers caress his on her knee. "She's said nothing about that."

"I can't explain her, Dee. Maybe she's waiting to tell other people after we tell the kids."

"And when is that supposed to happen?"

"I don't know. We don't really talk. But I promise, I'll get it done by the weekend."

"And then what? We openly see each other? You meet me at work, take me out to lunch while she minds the store? Do you seriously think that could work?"

He nodded.

It did sound doable. But she was so fucking tired, could she trust her judgment? "I really need to sleep." She brushed his hand off her knee. "I can't think straight right now. Give me time to figure out how to do that."

Genevieve

"Did I miss anything?" Maxine asked, coming in from the back.

"H just showed us how to steal people's identity from their credit card purchases." Dee's wit was surprisingly quick.

"Damn. I always miss the good stuff."

"We just reviewed what needs to happen tomorrow night." Hayleigh found a paper clip and flicked it at her sister. "Gen has five friends coming. Do we want more? I'm sure Mom and a few of her peeps could join us."

"I'm sure the class would be canceled if that were the case." Dee flicked the paper clip back.

"I could ask a few more people." Genevieve knew dozens of people from all her school-related activities. Yet, she just realized she wasn't sure if she wanted to bring them here, in what had become her sacred space. The kids still didn't know about the impending divorce. And every female she knew fawned over Chris like he was a good catch. She would have to taint this special store by being defensively quiet and pretending to be her happy old self, who had always pretended to be a happy wife and mom. She can't do that here. She wasn't sure who she was yet, but she knew who she was no longer.

"No, I think five is enough." Hayleigh tucked her phone back in her jacket pocket and pulled out her rose-colored glasses. "Just be sure they're nice! We can't have people slamming us online because something went wrong during our first live class."

"Oh, they won't be judgmental about the systems not working, but they may raise their eyebrows over Dee's swearing." She laughed, but Dee's face didn't seem to be amused.

"My fucking swearing? If your friends are such judgmental harpies, then they don't have to come. I'd rather deal with my mother's pansy-ass whiners."

"Dee! I was just joking." Genevieve's face burned. "I've, honestly, never heard a woman swear as much as you. It takes some getting used to."

"Do you realize what the hell you just said?" Dee's eyes drilled into Genevieve so hard, she took a step back.

"I'm not sure."

"You said you've never heard a 'woman' swear so much." The gentle bob of her head was replaced with sideways jerks in sync with her words. "And that's partly why I say whatever the fuck I want to say in whatever the fuck way I want to."

"I don't understand." Genevieve's back was pressed against a display of handmade greeting cards. Dee obviously was still not sleeping well. Had barely stayed awake as Hayleigh reviewed how to give the class participants a discount if they wanted to buy something afterward. Was this anger simply because she was exhausted?

"Swearing has been under the domain of men for centuries. Women always had to speak like a lady, but a man could swear like a cunt whenever he felt like it. Who the hell thinks that makes any sense? Swearing is yet another place where *we* take ownership of how *we* get to express ourselves."

"Oh my. I see your point." Genevieve put her hand over her heart. "I can't believe I never noticed before, but I, well, I had to take care of my baby brother and sister when I was a teen, and I still tend to mother them. I frequently get on my sister for her potty-mouth, but I don't think I've ever said anything to Archie." Dee was much more astute than Genevieve had given her credit for.

"Right, because a lady is too weak and feeble to use strong language." Thank God, Dee Dee smiled, granted it was more of a smirk. But she wasn't mad at her. "Don't get me wrong here. This isn't a feminist thing. It's a human one. Nothing in language should be under anyone else's domain. Language is where we all express our personal power."

"But..." That foul mouth is…but was it really foul? Who had the power to say so? Genevieve realized the hand she'd placed over her heart was gripping her top in a tight fist. Where was her power? She couldn't even ask what she was thinking about!

"But what?" Dee maintained eye contact.

"But, don't you worry about what other people think of you?"

"I can barely keep track of my own thoughts. I can't worry about anyone else's." Dee pointed to her temple and laughed. Her body held no tension. She wasn't angry anymore. The emotion came and went. She was just raw Dee Dee Bremen. She was always raw Dee Dee Bremen. "And seriously, if someone's offended, they can shop elsewhere. I'm sure I won't be wherever they land. And if I am, I'd probably be offended by their behavior. So, we should all just stay on our own turf."

"I guess I get your point." But whose turf did Genevieve want to be on? The harpies' or Dee's?

Dee

Was that the police? A firetruck?

She had to get up, get out of this...this...oh, tangle of sheets. The lumpy couch cushions from her make-shift bed shifted apart, and her butt landed between them on the hard living room floor.

There was no siren.

Had she dreamed that? Was she asleep?

Evening light glowed through the front windows, highlighting everything around her in a golden halo. She must have been asleep.

Outside, cars swished down Main Street like normal.

There was no fire.

Why did she think there was?

Dreaming.

But she almost felt OK. Maybe this is what she needed to do—get a couple hours of sleep before sunset, then a couple after sunrise; always in the middle of an open space with the blinds up so the sun could shine in. Then, she could create at night and work in the store during the day.

Feel like a zombie all the time. And would the headache ever go away?

Time was 6:27 p.m. She probably had a couple of hours or so yet before sunset. Judging by the empty takeout containers decorating her apartment, it'd been a while since she'd ordered pizza. She could do that: walk over, pick up a couple bottles of wine on the way back, and be in her place with all the doors locked and lights on before it got completely dark.

Her phone was about dead. She plugged it in by her bed, shuffled through the shit on the coffee table until she found her laptop. The battery said 7 percent. Enough to order pizza online.

After she placed the order, the puzzle piece on the whiteboard seemed to tell her she could try a Google search. An avenue she'd never gone down before. She could now, there was 5 percent of juice left in her machine. But there was also the possibility she'd forget about her dinner.

She grabbed a marker, wrote PIZZA on the back of her hand, then Googled her grandfather's name and *fire.*

Nothing.

She tried his name and LaGrange, Georgia. A few things, but nothing helpful. A few minutes later, armed with a year's subscription to an online newspaper archive service, she found an old headline from a press in La Grange, *Tragic Explosion at Stoker Estate.*

According to her computer's calculator app, the article was published twenty-seven years earlier. She'd been five. This was it! She clicked on the link, and her computer died.

No more battery. Shit! Where was her cord? Where was anything? Her apartment was a mess!

PIZZA in giant letters on her hand reminded her about dinner. She found her flipflops, scribbled "newspaper tragedy!" on her whiteboard, and headed out.

Brett answered on the second ring. She was chewing.

"Fuck." Came out as a gargle.

"You all right, Dee Dee?"

She swallowed, took a sip of wine, and realized if anyone were watching her, they'd liken her to a spider: She was sitting on the floor in the corner of her living room with an unobstructed view of any door someone could enter. When she'd returned from getting dinner, she realized she'd left the back door unlocked. She had wanted to check out her bedroom and bath to see if anyone was hiding in there, but was too scared. She felt too foolish to call someone local to keep her company. She knew it was ridiculous. No one was in her apartment. Probably…

"Dee?"

"Yeah. I'm all right. I wasn't expecting you to answer so soon. Was in the middle of chewing my dinner. How's it going? You still at Granddad's?"

"Yeah. I'm bunked in the guestroom you used to stay in. Just came downstairs from being out on your old balcony."

That meant he'd been looking over the back grounds, where he could see the willow tree where Gram's ashes were supposed to be lodged and the lake behind it.

Connected to a lifeline, Dee stood, picked up the box of pizza, and set it on the coffee table. With Brett's voice in the air and wine glass in one hand, on footsteps like cotton, she headed toward her bedroom. "Did you climb up the trellis to get in?" Hoped her voice sounded light, fun. How many times had they tested the strength of that trellis, entering the house in the middle of the night?

"Walking in the door isn't as fun, but it's still a good view." Sounded like he took a sip of something.

"How long you gonna be there?" She flipped the overhead light on in her bedroom, ducked. What the hell? What was she ducking from? How would that help anything?

"Not sure. Maybe permanently. Frankly, I think the old man likes my company."

She crept to the side of her bed and set the wine glass on the nightstand, wishing she believed in prayer. "Wait a minute." Even though she didn't need the extra light, she pulled the chain on the hookah lamp. "What old man are you talking about? *Our* granddad?" Slowly, gently, she squatted to look under the bed.

Shoes, loose socks, dirty underwear, and a few hair ties. Otherwise, dust.

"Heh, heh. *Our* grandad."

"*Our* granddad likes having you around?" She didn't think he liked having anyone around. "Are you cooking for him? Doing the laundry?" Good, no one was behind the shower curtain. She left the light on in the bathroom, then, feeling somewhat brave, she checked the bedroom closet. She left the light on in her closet and continued searching all the nooks and crannies of her apartment to make sure she was alone. All the while Brett described what he'd been doing with Granddad—breaking a new horse, going to antique car shows, watching black-and-white westerns on television.

"You're almost making him sound human." She checked the deadbolt on the back door again. Was she developing OCD on top of all the other shit wrong with her?

"Ain't that somethin'?" Brett laughed, and she knew he'd be OK. And finally, now that every light in her apartment was on and all doors were open, even the cupboards in the kitchen, she knew she was alone. She should be OK. She still felt spooked, like something or someone was watching her. But she knew she could handle anything now, knowing it wouldn't be real. Would be just her imagination. Probably from sleep deprivation and the nightmares.

Maybe she could take the pills tonight, as soon as she hung up from Brett. Maybe.

"So, you're all right now." She refilled her wine glass. "I mean, at the funeral, you were…" *Suggesting someone killed my father.* Why couldn't she go there?

Brett was quiet so long that his voice startled her when it came through her phone. "Yeah. I didn't handle Gram's death very well."

"Dude, listen." She looked around for a place to sit. The chairs at the kitchen table had partially empty bags on them from the bizarre crap she'd bought at the drug store to eat. The table was covered with just shit. The sofa was torn apart from her attempt to make the floor more comfortable to sleep on. All that was left was that ugly, crappy wingback that was beyond rigid. Mom was right: she needed new furniture. She dropped to a cushion on the floor, sitting with her wine on the coffee table within easy reach. "I'm so sorry. I feel like I let you down. I should have figured out a way to stay longer."

"Dee, no. Look—"

"Maybe if I'd been down there with you, I—"

"If you'd been down here, well, I mean things may have been different but...shit." Sounded like he took another drink, she sipped with him and waited. "God, I'm just really fucked up right now," he said. "I'm not sure what's right, wrong. I don't know what to do."

"Do about what?" The lights reflected off the windows. It was completely dark outside, technically night, probably. She tried to swallow against a growing pressure coming up from her stomach. He wasn't OK. Something was terribly wrong. And that thing, that presence she thought she'd felt before, that presence that might be her father, it hung there between them.

She heard ice rattling. "I think. I need. A little more. Bourbon. Right now." Brett had obviously had more than one before she called him.

"I'm uh…" She drained her glass. "I'll refill my wine."

"Your voice don't. Sound. So. Good."

"I'm OK. Just sometimes, the dark gets too dark. I don't know why." Before refilling her glass, she took another quick look in her bedroom. Her breath tightened. "Tonight seems to be one of those nights."

"I'm. Triggering. you." Brett hiccupped. "I shouldn't have called."

"I called you, you shit!" She managed to cough out a fake laugh. "I needed to hear from you. I needed to know you're all right." And she needed him to keep talking until she could make the buzzing in her ears quiet, get the heart palpitations that were suddenly so fucking strong she thought she could hear them, to settle down.

"Keep talking to me. I need you to talk to me right now. Please!" She couldn't keep sitting in the middle of the floor like that, with nothing against her back.

"So, um, what about?"

"Anything. Something." She knew she was being a needy pain in the ass right now, and he was probably too drunk to be of any good to either of them, but what else could she do?

She sat in the middle of her cushionless sofa, feet curled up under her, hunched in a ball. The view of her living room looked far away, down a tunnel, or maybe from a different dimension. The buzzing in her ears was so loud, she knew she was in danger of her eyes clouding over, of passing out. She had to force her vision to work. The whiteboard across from her was light-years away. The images, scribbles, incomprehensible to her now, except for the giant 3 3 3 always at the top.

The rule of three. Name three things you see. "Whiteboard."

"What?"

"Cushions."

"Dee?"

"Table."

"What?"

"Just working through a panic attack here." Inhale, two, three; exhale, two, three, four, five, six. Inhale. Name three things you hear.

"What do I do?"

"Brett."

"Yeah?"

"Brett, again."

"I'm so fucking confused."

"Brett, three times." Inhale, two, three; exhale, two, three, four, five, six. Heartbeat calmed. "OK, see..." move three body parts. "There's this rule of three." She wiggled the toes of her right foot. "It's what you do to stem a panic attack." She clenched and unclenched her left hand. "You name three things you see, then three you hear." She slowly shook her head back and forth. "Then you move three parts of your body. On top of breathing long, slow breaths." The well-lit apartment came closer to her. Inhale, two, three; exhale, two, three, four, five. The buzzing in her ears lessened. Yes, she felt like she was in the room now.

"Did I…make that happen?" Brett's voice was soft, like a scared little boy.

"No. I'm just, I'm just super stressed right now. Got more going on than I can handle. You know how everything that's wrong with my head gets even more wrong when I'm stressed?"

"I shouldn't've answered the phone."

"That would have made things worse! I needed to hear from you. I need to know you're OK."

"I'm work'n on it." Ice clinked in a glass. "Granddad's heading in. I should go."

"OK, but first, Brett—"

"Yeah?"

"You, um, at the funeral, you said something about—"

"Dee, don't pay no attention—"

"Brett, you said, you hinted that maybe someone killed my father. Is that true?"

Silence. She heard ice land in a glass. The clink of what sounded like a bottle against another. "Honey, must have just been the ramblings of a drunken man. I wouldn't pay it no mind." He cleared his throat. "Hey Granddad. Poured. You. A drink for the movie."

Dee clicked off without saying goodbye.

Brett took way too long to answer. And he'd called her 'honey' again. She managed to stand, stared at the blackboard, the puzzle piece. Oh! That headline. What did it say? Right. She wrote, *Tragic Explosion.*

The black blob seemed bigger. What was it?

Or who was it?

Was it someone? Was that who made the explosion happen?

And tragic? What made it tragic? Would losing a building and brain damage to a little girl be enough to call something tragic?

Why was thinking of all this making her scared of the dark?

How long was this going to last? How long was she going to be afraid? Would it all just get more intense, like it did when she was a teen, until she couldn't take it anymore?

Back then, she had just started taking the meds that were supposed to help her brain regulate. They only made things worse.

Maybe she shouldn't take anything this time. Maybe she just needed to muddle through. Maybe she'd get used to being afraid.

Wait a minute! She hadn't even taken a pill and was already heading down that slope toward not knowing what was real. So maybe it *wasn't* the meds that had messed with her head. Besides, people faced their demons all the time on mushrooms and shit. Why hadn't she thought of that before? She could do it on the prescribed meds. She wasn't a teen anymore. She was older now. Who knows if she was any wiser, but hell, she was a kid last time, and the monsters were a surprise.

She was one step ahead of them this time. She knew they were coming. And she was more secure with herself.

She'd face those fuckers and figure out what they were all about, and then maybe, just maybe, she'd have enough answers that she could erase part of her whiteboard.

Maxine

Max shut off her car but remained sitting in it in her garage, rehearsing what she would tell Dane. She was pregnant. Not far along. And she had an appointment with her OB on Friday. Would he like to come?

Then she'd gather a couple more days' worth of clothes and return to Mama's.

She was still angry, still hurt. But she felt he deserved to know he may be a dad of two. She refused to allow herself to celebrate the pregnancy. Not yet. It was too early. Dane's rational mind will help her stay on an even keel.

She released the seatbelt and got out of the car. She knew what she wanted: his help staying level. His help staying cool. *Ha! There were too many things wrong with this situation.*

"Aaa! You startled me." In the mudroom, Max clamped her hand to her chest.

"Sorry. I saw your headlights, heard the garage door." Dane enveloped her in his arms. "I'm so glad you're home, Max."

Was this the emotion she'd ached for? She leaned into him, pressed her face to his chest. This is where she belonged, where she truly wanted to be. Wasn't it?

She moved her arms up, wrapped them around his neck.

"Oh, Max, baby." He squeezed her tight, then leaned back to look in her face. "Thank you for coming home. I need you right now."

"You...what?" *He* needed *her*?

"Jamaal is here."

"Who?"

"My...my son."

"Here?" She hadn't counted on that. It was close to ten at night! Was he sleeping over in *their* house? She didn't know this kid, this person who was a result of Dane cheating on her. And now this...this proof of his transgression is just...just lounging in her, her *family* room? Max couldn't bring up the pregnancy under these conditions. She pulled out of his grip.

"I need you to help me tonight. I have no idea what to do or say with the kid."

"You didn't really just say that to me, did you?"

He reached for her hand.

"You...I can't believe you!" She stepped away from him. "Who *are* you?" Actually, he was who he always was: logical Dane. He realized he had a weakness being around the child, and he knew that she had experience in that world. He was true to form.

Max just didn't want anything to do with that form right now, on this subject.

"Maybe you should call his mother." She stepped around him and entered the kitchen. "I only came for a change of clothes."

"Max." He followed her to their bedroom. "I'm sorry! I really am. I realize that was pretty...I guess insensitive."

She opened a large suitcase on their bed and stopped to look at him. "You just guess?"

"No. I was searching for the right word...I *know* it was insensitive..." He crumbled into the armchair in the corner, wiped a hand over his head.

She waited for something more to come from him, but he didn't seem capable of more. Wasn't that interesting? If they were at a party where he didn't want to be—at Kaz and Lauren's, or a gathering with other teachers from her school—she'd sense that he didn't seem capable of saying anything, so she'd take the mantle and speak for him, carry the conversation by including him in it, drawing him out so he'd be more comfortable. She'd always assumed that's just the way he was—he needed to warm up to a room with other people.

But it was just the two of them now.

And apparently, eight years ago he had no trouble warming up to some chick he barely knew. In fact, they got so warm, they created a kid he now can't relate to.

That was Dane's problem.

She turned her back to him, opened a dresser drawer of leggings and emptied it into her suitcase.

"Max?"

"Dane." She threw a couple pairs of socks into the suitcase, placed her hands on her hips. "I'm not in a place to help you here. You're an adult with a child downstairs who needs *you*."

"And I need you."

"That's just one of the problems here, Dane." She resumed packing. "I don't want to be in your life because you need me. I want to be there because you *want* me to be."

"I do, Max!"

"And," she crossed in front of him to open her closet, "I want to trust you to be honest with me. To trust you respect me."

"Max. I have been completely faithful to you since that stupid day."

"No you haven't." Somehow, she continued to play it cool. Her voice was level, yet it took everything she had not to throw the hangers, the shoes, and whatever else she could find in the closet at him. Instead, she returned to the bed to fold blouses into the suitcase. "Being faithful, to me, means being honest and not keeping secrets. You never—" Such a spike of anger ran up her spine she had to look at him. "You never told me about that incident. We were *engaged*! You kept that secret—"

"To be honest, babe, and...and at, at the risk of sounding like a complete ass, Max...I never thought of my, of what, of the thing with Shawna as a secret. It was just something I did that let me know I was making the right decision by being with you."

As his words sunk in, he became a shadow figure in the chair. A murky light filled his chest and stomach, barely bright enough to expose an empty bird cage in the center.

She blinked away the image, stared at the man, the human, she'd admired because he was so clear about things—there was always a right way and a wrong way with Dane, there were always logical steps, rules to follow that created order, a promise of safety, of security...or so she had assumed.

"That's interesting." She shut the suitcase. "Really interesting that cheating on me helped you realize you were doing the right thing by marrying me—me, someone who, apparently, made decisions you didn't respect, someone you suspected was OK taking bribes from rich white people. Seriously, Dane, I'm surprised you didn't hide the silver in the house from me."

Thursday, July 1

Dee

She had to shut that fucking alarm off. Where is her phone? The sound sucked the nerves out of her head, making a searing, squeezing, pulling pain in her skull. Holy mother of hell! This headache!

Finally! She felt her phone on the coffee table. Quieted it. *What time? Seven thirty. Thursday, right? Yeah, Thursday.*

The glowing times listing the alarms she'd already set for the day stabbed the back of her eyes. The first was 8:55 a.m. to remind her to get to the store, the last was 9:00 p.m. to remind her to take her pills again.

They seemed to work last night. She slept. Or passed out. Wasn't sure.

But she didn't have any dreams, did she? No nightmares?

The worst fucking hangover of her life, maybe, but at least no nightmares.

Sitting up made the room swoon, or maybe she swooned. She waited whichever one it was out, though she had to piss like mad. Standing was like pressing up through wet cement, and being upright almost wasn't worth the effort. Moving was nauseating. Was she gonna fucking puke?

Somehow, she made it to the toilet, where she held her oil-slick face in her hands as she sat there much longer than necessary. She needed a shower. A good shower and some coffee, then she could probably get through the day. Maybe.

Perhaps the nightmares weren't the worst option here. If this was how the pills would make her feel the day after, mornings wouldn't be tolerable. And what was that smell?

Oh, it was her. Yeah, needed a good shower. She'd been getting by with what H called French baths—a little soap and water rubdown at the sink—since…since…well, for a couple of days.

What kind of life is this?

The siren song of the cold tiles called her to the floor. She let them soothe her hot, sticky, weak body until she felt refreshed enough she could remove the colorful wraps from the hair braids H and Max had put in on Father's Day. One by one, she dropped them to the floor. The hair bands on her wrist joined them, exposing rings of grime and ink smudges from the notes she'd written.

What a fucking loser. How could Cooper see anything in her? Anyone see anything in her?

Using the sink for leverage, she stood, took out the earrings, and then removed the anklets. That was a lot of work. Should have removed the anklets while still on the floor. She leaned against the sink, praying her head would hurt just a little less. After giving up on prayer once again, she accidentally saw her face in the mirror. Good God! No wonder Genevieve always seemed so worried when she saw Dee. Looking rough was an understatement. More like haggard. She'd probably been scaring children on the street. Why didn't she scare Cooper away yesterday? Was it yesterday? When had she seen him? Why hadn't he tried to connect with her again?

Fuck! Tears!

The shower washed them away. She sat on the edge of the tub and scrubbed every inch of her body so hard, it almost hurt. But how luxurious it felt to work the shampoo into the roots of her thick hair and feel the water dripping down as she rinsed it out. The cooling water warned her she was running out of time. She applied a leave-in conditioner to her tangled locks, then, wrapped in a towel, she sat on the closed toilet and combed out the knots.

Wet, the split ends reached her waist. The wild curls would shrink it to mid-back as it dried.

Did her hair come from her father? Didn't Josie say she looked like him? No, she said she sounded like him. No. What did Josie say?

She twisted the split ends together. Mom was always a brunette with reddish tints—very smooth and manageable. H's was dark brown when it wasn't the color of the week. Hers was also curly, but a tighter curl than Dee's. Kaz called it a "Jew-fro," saying her hair was like his Jewish mother's. Dee's curls were loose, big, and she was blond—not the platinum blond of her youth. It grew darker when she became an adult, but it was still blond. Certainly, nowhere close to Mom's cinnamon brown, though granted that color was salon-created nowadays.

She padded out to the kitchen in her bathrobe. Man! Her place was a mess. The couch torn apart. Bed linens like tornado debris. Take-out containers all over the place. Too many empty wine bottles...She'd have to clean this weekend.

Her cell rang from the tangle of sheets on the floor. A stop sign appeared on the screen.

"Hi, Mom." Dee answered and returned to the kitchen.

"Hi, sweetheart. How are you this morning?"

"Fine. Why wouldn't I be?" Because she was anything but fine. Her head hurt so badly she was surprised she didn't find any lumps on it when washing her hair. Stomach so gross she suspected an oily hairball had somehow been lodged in there. And frankly, her whole body felt twitchy. But Mom didn't need to know.

"You, well, you tried the medication last night?"

"Yes."

"And?"

"And I slept."

"No, um, you know..."

"No nightmares. No hallucinations." Or wait. She poured fresh water into the coffee machine. She did dream something. Heard something.

I'll take care of it.

That was it. Did she dream it? No. She heard someone say it. Right before she fell asleep.

Impossible. She couldn't quite remember falling asleep, but every fucking light was on in the apartment and, while Mom prattled in her ears, she discovered the deadbolts were locked, and she'd even pulled the dryer out enough, so it had blocked the back door from opening all the way. When the hell did she do that? Whatever. That meant she dreamed the person said it.

"...thank you. I feel so much better hearing your voice," Mom seemed to be finishing a paragraph. "Promise me you'll let me know if things change, and, and, and you know, if you feel, um, different somehow."

"I will, Mom."

I'll take care of it she wrote on the whiteboard above the puzzle piece and below the willow tree. *I'll take care of it.*

That wasn't a dream. She'd heard the words, if not last night, then at some point in her life. They were a memory.

An alarm went off. Shit! It was 8:55, and she was still in her bathrobe.

Genevieve

Well, Dee Dee looked the best since Genevieve had started working at the store. She wore jeans that actually fit her and a sweet, flowered blouse. Granted, the cruddy flip-flops took away from the look, but it was a start. The braids and wraps had been taken out of her hair, the pink barely noticeable, and the curls, while still a wild mane, weren't exactly messy. Though the woman had plenty of split ends. She should get a trim.

Regardless, Genevieve had a little hope that Brynn and her friends wouldn't worry that she'd completely gone bohemian when they saw Dee later that day.

Now, if she could just stop worrying about Brynn. She'd only sent the invitation to her email as a test. She hadn't expected her sister to show up at a class, away from her husband, the first day she was back from her honeymoon.

That just didn't sit right with Genevieve.

"So, like, the place looks amazing, Genevieve." Dee wandered through the front of the store. "I know you did most of the work up here. You seriously did a great job setting it all up. It's fun to walk through. There's a pleasant balance of styles and color, yet things are placed where they look like they belong."

"Thank you, Dee Dee!" Genevieve knew she was probably glowing, but she didn't bother trying to pretend it didn't feel good to hear such compliments. How long had it been since anyone appreciated her? Well, maybe Brynn did. Perhaps.

Besides, Dee Dee had been a little more off than usual to Genevieve all week. Or so it seemed. But who knows? The woman certainly had her mysterious ways.

"What's left to do?" Dee asked the question as she walked away.

"I think just to set up for tonight." Genevieve followed her. "Unless there's more in the garage?"

"Oh, yeah. I kind of forgot about the garage. Maybe." Dee continued walking, not bothering to turn around to speak to Genevieve directly. Was she being rude? Her tone of voice didn't suggest it. Genevieve stayed on her heels. She had yet to enter the mysterious garage and had no idea what was inside.

"Max!" Dee shouted as if she was unbelievably happy to see her friend come in the back door.

Maxine held up a hand and ran to the restroom.

"Oh no!" Clearly, Maxine was still sick. How long was this going to go on?

Or...could she be pregnant? It seemed as if she felt better every day as time went on.

Max came out of the restroom a few minutes later and immediately collapsed in a chair at the class table.

"Have you been to a doctor?" Dee sat across from her as Genevieve went to the sink in the back. She found a cloth, ran it under cold water, and wrung it out.

Maxine shook her head.

Genevieve approached the table, folded the wet cloth, and placed it on Max's forehead. "That should make you feel better."

"Thank you, Genevieve. But, I'm not sick."

"No. You're pregnant, aren't you?" Genevieve stepped back and smiled at her.

"Holy fuck!" Dee shrieked. "Max?"

Maxine looked into Dee Dee's eyes. Genevieve realized she shouldn't have said anything.

"This doesn't leave the shop," Max whispered.

"Seriously?" Dee ran around the table, sat next to Maxine, and gripped her by the shoulders. "So...how is it possible?"

"Well, um, Dee Dee..." Genevieve pressed her hand against the lump in her throat. How was she to explain where babies come from?

Maxine burst out laughing. She leaned against Dee and just howled.

"I don't get it." Dee looked at Genevieve.

"Dee knows all about the birds and the bees, Genevieve." Maxine stood.

"Is that what you thought?" Dee laughed as she stood.

Maxine pulled Dee into a hug, looked at Genevieve, and waved her over to be part of the hug, too.

This! Genevieve felt so welcome, like a part of something bigger than her. These women could possibly be friends! They hugged her.

When Max pulled away, she wiped the tears from her face. Were they joy or—

"Is everything all right? I don't mean to pry..." Genevieve looked between Dee and Max.

Max wiped her face with her hands. "It's all quite messy. I'd been going through fertility treatments for years. Then quit. Then my marriage got a little shaky..." she closed her eyes and shook her head. "I just have a lot to think about. Anyway..." she breathed long and deep through her nose. "I want to work. Let's finish setting up so we can have a good, long break this afternoon before the class starts tonight."

Genevieve wasn't going to stay mute, unlike she had with her sister. If these women were truly going to be friends, surely that meant she could speak her mind. Maybe one day that would become a habit.

"I know this is none of my business, so...so feel free to ignore it, but..." Genevieve reached out to touch Maxine, then paused with her hand in mid-air.

Maxine took it. "Go on."

"The worst decision I ever made was marrying my husband just because I was pregnant."

Behind Max, Dee flinched as if Genevieve had hit her. Had Genevieve overstepped the bounds of familiarity? "The second-worst decision I ever made…" She just couldn't stop herself, though that thing in her neck seemed like it was about to choke her. "…was to stay married to him as long as I did."

Dee spun around and walked past them. Genevieve could hear her moving the metal tools at her lampworking station.

"Don't get me wrong." Genevieve squeezed Maxine's hand. "I

have a couple of kids I love a lot. He provided a good life for us all. But there was no love between us. And I feel like I just spent the last eighteen years living someone else's life. I'm just now able to live *my* life, and I'm still figuring out what that looks like. I'm so appreciative of the two of you for bringing me on here—"

A loud crash from Dee's corner interrupted her. Genevieve looked back and saw Dee sweeping the broken pieces of a bottle into a dustpan. "You really are helping me figure things out. But, anyway, this is about you. Do what's best for you, now, not for what you think things might be like someday."

Dee

"I brought the goods, peeps!" Hayleigh set a large board covered with a swirling display of charcuterie, fruits, crackers, and dips on a foldout table in the back room.

"This is awesome." Dee reached for a piece of salami, but H slapped her hand away.

"You can't eat anything until one of the class members eats something first."

"You suck."

"Meanwhile, you look great. Did you sleep last night?" H kissed her cheek.

"I did."

"Yay! And that shirt looks adorable on you."

"I look like I'm wearing my mother's clothing."

"And it becomes you. C'mon." She tugged Dee toward the back door. "There's more shit in my car. Hold the door."

Dee did as told, while her sister brought in wine and an

assortment of paper plates and plastic cups. When did H think to do this?

"No side effects?" H asked as she set it all up on a folding table.

"From?"

"The meds."

"Oh, well, felt like shit this morning. Worst hangover of my life. Still have a headache."

"Hey, Gen!" H handed Dee a corkscrew. "Dee, will you open these bottles and finish setting up while I chat with Gen a sec?"

Again, Dee did as told, though completely perplexed as to how H was comfortable enough to call Genevieve *Gen*. Dee wasn't sure she'd ever be able to do that. *Gen* sounded like something you called someone you were close to—or held in disdain.

That was probably Cooper's fault.

For lunch today, she had walked over to the cafe where they'd had breakfast. It was stupid, like something a sad-ass teenager would do—hoping and fearing he'd show up. Would it be so bad if they were together? After what Genevieve said this morning, it's not like she'd even freaking care.

"You good with that, Dee?" H asked.

"I dunno. What were you saying?"

"We're not going to film the whole thing, but I will take action bits. Gen's gonna get her sister and friends to sign off on waivers for us to use on the website..."

Gen's sister is coming. That's interesting. She wondered if Gen mothered her, too.

"Then, when we get back from Jupiter, I figure we'll sell wax statues of the creatures we found there."

Dee giggled. "Sorry. I kind of buzzed out on you, yeah."

"That's OK. It's nothing you really need to know."

"Can we have wine yet?"

"Can you drink on the meds you're on?"

"What?"

"Did you drink last night?"

"Of course!"

"Maybe that's why you had such a hangover."

"Shit! Fuck! Piss! Damn!" Dee stomped away from the food and wine.

"That's some language!" a woman laughed. Dee turned to find a sporty-looking woman about her age.

"That's Dee Dee Bremen." Genevieve held her arm toward Dee as if she were presenting a prize on a game show. "Dee, this is my sister, Brynn."

"Nice to meet you, Dee." Brynn approached the wine. "I'm surprised Gen didn't put out a swear jar. When we were growing up, she used to make me give her a dime every time I said a 'bad' word."

"What'd she do with all the money?" H asked as if she were really interested.

"Gave it to charity."

"Huh. Just think, Dee." H handed her a plastic cup of water, which she didn't really want. "There could have been a couple schools built in your name in a third-world country by now if we'd thought of that."

Dee smirked. So this is how the evening was going to go, eh? Crappy jokes. When was Max gonna get here? She needed a little balance.

H poured cups of wine for Genevieve, Brynn, and herself, and was already Brynn's best friend.

"Dee," Genevieve called. "Would it be OK if I come in late tomorrow? I have a doctor's appointment."

"Yeah." Fucking meds. She really wanted a cup of wine. She fished her phone from her back pocket to consult Dr. Google. "We should check with Max when she gets here, but I think we're almost done. And didn't she say we could all take the weekend to rest up before the soft opening next week? Whatever the hell that is."

"NO YOU CAN'T!" Hayleigh's eyes were so wide, Dee

wouldn't have been surprised if they fell out and rolled across the store. "The soft opening starts this *Saturday*. July *third*. You *will* be open. In fact, your front door will be wide open. And you'll have stuff out on the sidewalk to entice people to come in."

"Oh no!" Genevieve sounded disappointed. "I can't be here. My son has a birthday party at my home."

"I can hang with you and Max on Saturday, Dee." H assured her.

"Shit." Dee hit her calendar. "I don't have any of this on my phone." She tried to enter the details as best she could. "It will be hot as hell."

"You'll sweat through it. This whole freaking town will be open with sidewalk sales. Then Sunday will be a repeat after the parade."

"There's a parade on Sunday?"

"Yes!"

"I can come in on Sunday," Genevieve piped up.

Dee tried to type everything in on her phone as H added more details.

"Mom will probably come by on Sunday." H said it like it was no big deal.

"Oh hell! Really?" She clicked out of her calendar. "Why?"

"My kids will be in the parade. I'll be there with them. She won't miss it."

"You have kids?" Genevieve held her hand over her throat. She did that a lot.

"I teach color guard for the high school's marching band. They'll be in the parade. I need to be there to coach. And Mom always supports my kids."

Dee couldn't do Mom on Sunday morning if she were anywhere near as sick as this morning. "Maybe I'll need a doctor on Sunday. Genevieve, will you lick my face?"

"Excuse me?" Genevieve choked on her wine.

"In case you're contagious."

Genevieve's laugh couldn't be more fake. "No. Nothing like

that."

"What's up?" Brynn sat at the class table, looking at herself in her phone. "Are you all right?"

"I'm fine." Genevieve loaded crackers and fruit onto a plate. Did that mean Dee could start eating, too? "I have this weird feeling that comes and goes in my throat. Feels like something's stuck there sometimes, but I swallow fine." Genevieve handed the plate to her sister.

"*Globus Hystericus*!" Brynn held her cup up as if she were giving a toast before sipping.

"What?" Genevieve asked at the same time H said, "Bless you."

What the fuck was going on? Evan's number lit up her screen. She silenced the sound of the call. She'd talk to him tomorrow.

"Mom used to complain about something being stuck in her throat." Brynn sipped. "I remember being with her at the doctor's office when he explained it. It's a stress thing. A phantom thing. It'll go away when you learn to relax."

Whoa! So that's how you talked to "Gen," huh? Brynn laughed and invited Genevieve to sit next to her. But Genevieve's face suggested she'd rather slap the fuck out of her kid sister. *Maybe this evening would be a little fun after all.*

"Oh, hello!" Genevieve's voice was too fake and too happy.

Four other women came in. They all kissed each other's cheeks without meaning it, and immediately ooed and ahhed over the food and wine. Genevieve's friends.

But not really. Christ. It was painfully obvious to Dee that they were just women Genevieve knew well. Dee would bet her last dollar Genevieve didn't truly like any of them. Did she have any friends?

Meanwhile, her phone felt heavy in her hand. Why was she holding it? To text Max?

She scrolled to find her name, but *Cooper* caught her eye. Without quite understanding it, somehow not able to control her fingers, she tapped his name.

I miss you.

Maxine

Why does every diner in Jersey set their thermostats to zero in the summer? Max huddled in her booth, shivering. She swore she could feel a breeze from the cranking AC. The dining rooms were always cold, and the restrooms! They were like walking into an arctic cave. She hoped she wouldn't have to pee until she left the diner.

"Hey, kid!" Kaz kissed her cheek as he swept by. She immediately felt lighter, more comfortable, as he took his place in the booth across from her. Kaz always had that effect on her.

There was something about him, his presence. She never quite saw the aura in him, or whatever it was that she saw in almost everyone else. He was always Kaz, authentic and true with wise dark eyes, deep smile lines, and an ever-increasing presence of white in his dark curly hair. She was always relaxed and...and...at home with him. With him and Lauren. He brightened her mood; Lauren made her feel like she belonged near her. Just being in their presence. *It was never anything they did. They were family! They were so loving and accepting...how could Dane...*

"Sweetheart?" Kaz's hand gripped hers over the table as tears welled in her eyes.

"Do you two need a minute?" A waitress set paper placemats and sets of flatware wrapped in napkins on the table.

"I do." Max realized the woman had the wrong impression of what was going on at the table. She unwrapped the flatware and used the napkin to dab her eyes and wipe her nose.

"I'll bring some more, honey."

"What's going on?" Kaz unwrapped his own utensils. "And I guess this means when you invited me for dessert, it wasn't because you're helping me cheat on this diet Lauren has me on?"

"Ha!" Max cleared her throat. "Wait. You bike twenty miles a week—"

"Thirty."

"You bike thirty miles a week and play basketball with men half your age, and—"

"And Lauren thinks I eat too much sugar."

"She and Mama must be on the same diet."

"They are." He nodded. "So, I appreciate the chance for pie. But why?"

"Well, I invited you only to dessert because we don't have time for dinner. I need to get to the store soon. We're holding our first class. I told Dee I'd be late, but I didn't see her write that down, so I don't know if she'll remember."

"Is she OK? Lauren's having a breakdown about the medication."

"Seems like she's doing fine, but honestly, I'm having a breakdown about the medication, too."

"So, is this about Dee?"

Max shook her head. "I need some fatherly advice."

"You got it, kid."

"And I may need a divorce attorney."

His face didn't change expression. "Which one first?"

The waitress returned with more napkins and two glasses of water. They each ordered a slice of pie—peanut butter for Max and cherry for Kaz—then as soon as the waitress turned around, Max started. Dane's betrayal when they were newly engaged came out easily enough. So easily, she told him about following him to the hotel, and by then the pies had arrived.

"Can you believe that?" She pointed the end of her fork at him as something else dawned on her. "He couldn't have just found out about the boy the day he left to meet that woman in the heels. He *had* to have known before then. He must have been communicating with her before that day." She stabbed her pie so hard, her fork made that horrible screech sound on her plate. "He never said a word to me!"

"Max, kid, sweetheart." Again, Kaz leaned over the table and placed a hand on hers. "I'm so sorry. I am stunned by this. I never would have pegged the man to be so secretive."

"Why didn't you say 'dishonest'?" Because there was a difference. And Max had been upset by his dishonesty.

"Semantics, I guess. He lied by omission, which, in my mind that makes him secretive."

Max waited him out as he studied his pie. Dee had been secretive about booty call, yet Max didn't accuse her of being dishonest. Was the difference only that Dane had hurt Max with his secrets and Dee hadn't? But she would have hurt Genevieve. Maybe. Genevieve didn't seem to like her husband much.

But why was she even thinking about Dee right now? This is about her and Dane!

"I'm not saying he did nothing wrong." Kaz finally looked at her. "He did plenty wrong. And he certainly hurt you. You have every right to be angry with him."

"So what do I do now?"

"Is that a father question or attorney?"

"Both?"

"Do you still love him?"

"Does that make a difference?"

Kaz nodded. "If you still love him, as a father, I'd suggest you go to him and explain why you're hurt, and what he needs to do to make amends. I'd also suggest that you two get some couples therapy because clearly there's been a disconnect in your relationship for a very long time."

"What do you mean?"

"I mean, probably since your wedding day, maybe even before that—"

"So, it's my fault he cheated on me when we were engaged?" The anger Max felt didn't seem justified. Was it hormones? Or was Kaz, deep down, another jerk-faced male?

"Where did that come from?" Kaz grinned. "Max! It's me, you're talking to. I'm always on your side, no matter what, remember?"

"I, I do. I'm sorry. I'm just..." Tears came again. She pressed another napkin against her face. "I'm so confused."

"And hurt." Kaz sipped his coffee. "It's OK. I didn't take it personally."

"Good." She wiped her nose. Her peanut butter pie sat half-eaten. She should finish it. It was very good. And she was eating for two. "But you said we've been disconnected since before we got married. What does that mean?"

"It means..." Kaz rested his elbows on the table and templed his fingers, clearly thinking before he spoke. He was probably afraid of another irrational outburst. "The old folks in your life suspected back then, and still do, frankly, that you were attracted to Dane because he's the opposite of your father."

"I truly loved the man."

"I'm sure you did. But you've also looked past his shortcomings—"

"Everyone has shortcomings. I'd still be single if I was waiting for Mr. Perfectly Right."

"Indeed. But there's a difference between looking past and dealing with." He resumed eating his pie. "You've been doing all the emotional labor for both of you. He needs to figure out how to do his own emotional work. That's why I suggested therapy. But only if you still love him. If you don't love him, then you need to get a divorce and move on." Kaz picked up the last bit of crust with his fingers and popped it into his mouth.

"What if I'm pregnant?"

His chewing slowed. Eventually, he visibly swallowed.

"My answer remains the same regarding Dane." He wiped his mouth with his napkin. "And just so you know, if you're pregnant, Lauren will be so over the moon—"

"Please don't tell her yet." This time, she reached over to touch his hand. "It's very very early. Anything can happen."

"So," he smirked. "You want me to keep a secret?"

Friday, July 2

Dee

*C**lick.* A thin stream of light flared, then widened as it crossed the floor. It spread to the corner of her bed.

She was frozen in place, fear like an ice pick in her chest. *MOM!* The word was a scream-thought; her voice did not work. *Mom!* She tried again.

Wait! She *could* move. She's not there, wherever she thought she was. She's…here.

Where's here?

Is she alone?

The room was dark. Not pitch black, but charcoal gray. There was no line of light. The door was shut. Who shut it?

She shut it...last night. Right? No one's on the other side of it.

But someone was there…or here.

"God dammit!" she sat up in her bed. Jesus fucking Christ! She fell over. Which way was up again? Slowly, once more, she sat upright. This was *her* bed in *her* fucking apartment above *her* fucking store. Where the hell did she think she was?

Wait! Who was talking?

She closed her eyes against the spinning room. At least the headache wasn't as bad as the day before. But what the hell was going on?

She just woke up, right? And there was a voice, or voices, right?

She heard them as she was waking.

No.

That was last night. She heard them right before she crashed. There were people in her room. Or at least a person. *Someone was here.* They weren't supposed to be here, but they were.

Was that real?

Was she dreaming before she went to sleep?

Is that possible?

What was the dream about?

It was dark. That line of light! That happened, right? Last night? Or was that from some other time? Was that from an older dream? That image had been coming into her brain at the weirdest times when she was awake. Or was she awake?

What happened last night?

She remembered swallowing the pills downstairs while they were cleaning up. Genevieve made her take up a bunch of the leftover food. Then…the alarm on her phone reminded her to check the locks on all the doors downstairs. Did she?

She did. She had to put the food down on the steps to do it. That's right. The doors were locked. Then, upstairs...

What happened? Was someone up here?

No.

Maybe.

She was still in her jeans from the night before. That same ugly flowered shirt Mom had bought.

She wanted to open the curtains, but that meant stepping off the bed. Besides, the light would make it hard to recall whatever the fuck she was trying to recall.

Someone...who was it? Who was in her room?

She was facing this fucker. Whoever it was.

Even if it was just in her head.

What the hell happened last night?

She lay back on the bed.

OK, so she checked the locks on the store doors, then upstairs she set the food down...where? On the...somewhere. She was so tired, it didn't seem important where she put it. She just wanted to go to bed. She did. Did she shut the bedroom door?

There was a blank in her memory. She had the food in her hand, and then she was on her bed. Sitting. No laying.

The voices.

A voice. A male voice.

He was here. Called her Dee Dee. Whispered it.

Ice crystals seemed to dribble from her skull down through her body. Dee startled upright, caught herself from falling over. The room swayed with such violence that she wouldn't doubt that an earthquake had happened.

Somehow, she knew she'd had a full-blown panic attack right before falling asleep. Why? Was someone really here?

How the fuck was it possible to freak out *and* fall asleep?

Those fucking meds.

Now what?

Who was in her room? Were they still here, in her apartment?

Were they ever here? Were they real?

Who were they?

In the back of her mind, a niggling thought came in that she'd had another psychotic break, but she ignored it.

She sat up again, slowly. The room swayed less. Equally slowly, she reached behind the nightstand and unplugged the brass hookah lamp. It was heavy as hell. She could bash the shit out of someone's head with it. As long as she could stand up. Wielding it like a weapon high above her, ready to strike at anyone she happened upon, she stepped as far away as possible from her bed. Slow down. Can't fuck anyone up when battling vertigo. She waited until she felt she had her balance steady before pulling open the curtains. Sunlight slammed in like a hot iron against her face.

Knowing she might fall over at any second, she inched into a crouch position, still holding the lamp, and looked under the bed.

Nothing. Still a shit ton of dirty laundry all over the floor. She should probably do some wash soon. She couldn't remember washing anything since moving in. And it was hard to find a clean pair of underwear the day before. But whatever. One thing at a time.

Who's the demon in the kitchen?

If there is one.

Like a doped-up sloth, she stood, then waited until the dizziness abated enough to walk, one slow step at a time. She inched to her bedroom door, opened it as quietly as possible, just wide enough for one eye to look through.

No one.

Two eyes saw no one.

She crept into the kitchen, her arm starting to feel the strain from holding the lamp high above her head. It'd be a shame to destroy it by banging it into someone's face, but sometimes a girl's gotta do what a girl's gotta do. Besides, she was alone. No one was there. The door at the top of the stairs was locked, including the deadbolt, which meant it had been locked from the inside. The door going out to the back steps was the same.

After a quick check behind the shower curtain and in her closet, she finally set the lamp down.

She was alone.

She'd dreamed the man saying her name. Was that a dream of her father calling her?

Or the hallucinations starting again?

It was almost eleven in the morning. Aisling was probably with a client, but maybe she could squeeze Dee in? She texted the request and put on coffee.

Head wasn't nearly as bad as yesterday. Maybe H had a point: no drinking with the medication. That just made life unbelievably unfair.

Aisling confirmed she had an opening at four.

Great. She'd shower. Throw in a load of wash. Eat. Finish whatever needed to be finished in the store. Then Aisling.

Evan called again while she was in the shower. Left another voice mail: "Please, Dee, call me."

Fuck him. His behavior at Aunt Josie's still left a bad taste in her mouth, even after she'd brushed her teeth. She wasn't sure she was in a headspace to talk to him yet.

As she passed through her bedroom, she picked up every wayward, dark-colored piece of clothing she could find. She tossed them in the washer and noticed there were still more clothes in the hamper. How was that possible? Did she have anything that was clean? She dumped the hamper to cull the darks and...Yes! Her key fob!

She could go grocery shopping again. She could go anywhere again. Oh! She could get Josie's gift out of her car. The box. The box that she'd suspected Evan went through before he handed it to her! That's right! What was in it?

A few minutes later, with the washer running, while nibbling on leftover cheese and charcuterie, Dee lifted the lid on Josie's box.

Photographs. Dozens of photographs. Old ones

There were people she recognized: a much younger Mom, Gram, and Granddad. A few of Francie, Alma, and some others she assumed were relatives. She appeared in many: a little blond girl with wild, curly hair.

And there was a man, who, she was fairly certain, was her father.

Blond wavy hair. Super-skinny physique. A lopsided smile that lit up the tiny square of paper.

He was a presence in the photos.

She felt him again in her apartment. The presence crushed her chest. Whirled her stomach. Filled her body with such...such...grief...static built up in her ears. She slammed the lid back onto the box, tearing the red cardboard edge.

Breathe in, two, three. Breathe out, two, three, four, five.

Breathe in—

Shit! That's the alarm to go to work.

She'd have to leave the photos. Which was good. Maybe.

Though terrified, she ached to open the box again.

She just needed to be better prepared to see whatever was in there.

Maybe Aisling could help. She scribbled a note on a paper towel: *ask Aisling about pics!* Left it on the coffee table, hoped she'd see it later and remember what it meant, worried she wouldn't be brave enough to do it.

Genevieve

Genevieve managed to start her car but couldn't manage to set the gear in reverse. She could only sit while the air conditioner's blast went from hot to cold.

Brynn was right. She rested her forehead against the steering wheel, wishing the Earth would swallow her. There was nothing wrong with her. That lump in her throat was just...just stress. Apparently, she hadn't been managing as well as she'd thought.

"But I'm a mom!" she'd told Dr. Patel. "Stress is an occupational hazard for us. What am I supposed to do?"

"This is not your children's fault, Genevieve." He'd looked up from the computer where he'd presumably typed *patient is so stressed, she's imagining illnesses.* "Let me rephrase things. The lump feeling is a result of stress that is being unacknowledged instead of managed."

"I manage my life just fine!" If he only knew how well she managed. Maybe she needed a second opinion. "I have everything under control, organized, and running as efficiently as possible."

His smile was so kind, Genevieve calmed down. "Sometimes when we manage things very well, we swallow our feelings so they don't get in the way," he said. "After a while, our systems become too full of them. They want to burst through. That lump you feel is your unexpressed emotions."

Clearly, the man was out of his league! Talking to her like a therapist would. But she didn't tell him that; instead, she manufactured a fake smile and asked what she should do.

"Try mindfulness," Dr. Patel had suggested. "Perhaps get help connecting with your feelings and learn to stop holding everything inside."

But the lump felt as big as an orange while he spoke to her, and clearly she was upset. She wasn't holding anything back. She acknowledged to herself that she was angry with that doctor for wasting her time, while maintaining her polite smile.

She slumped against the steering wheel and sobbed. But he was right. This is how she lived, in constant repression of every emotion she'd ever felt since...since...since she was a little girl changing Brynn's diapers because Mother needed her sleep, and it wasn't fair for Brynn to suffer. Genevieve had understood from a very young age that someone needed to be in control.

Control meant keeping emotions out of the equation.

Otherwise, she'd risk becoming an ego-centric, narcissistic, self-martyring, and miserable old woman...just like her mother.

Yet, somehow, she wound up with an imaginary condition *just like her mother!*

How was that possible?

She sat up and pulled the sun visor down to use the mirror. After wiping away the tears and cleaning up her mascara, she looked as put-together as always. Presentable! Oh God! She looked presentable!

This wasn't what she'd ever wanted. This was supposed to be

the safe route. To keep her from repeating the pattern she grew up in, to protect her children.

Genevieve finally realized what she had run out of: the energy to be some other person. The "presentable" one.

But if she wasn't that person, who was she?

Who did she want to be?

She wanted to be the creative, the artist, the person she surprised herself by slipping into in front of her sister and her friends the night before.

She and Dee Dee had pulled out the supplies for the class: small boxes of vintage costume jewelry, lengths of ribbon and fiber, and plain black picture frames. Such a simple project: place pieces of the jewelry and ribbon on the frame in a pleasing way, then glue them on. But Genevieve knew the women would be blown away by how…well, how delicious it would feel to see something beautiful they created when they were done.

Dee Dee started the class, gave the briefest of instructions, and they were off. Genevieve found herself anxiously hovering over the women, scared they'd make a mistake.

"Genevieve." Maxine handed her a frame shortly after she arrived. "You should make one, too."

"Oh?" But she was working! She worried that meant they didn't trust her.

"Yes. We'll use it as an example for future classes."

"Great idea, Max!" Hayleigh had been videoing Brynn. "We'll put it on the website. You should place it by the register with a sign about classes, too. That way, when people check out, they'll see it and ask about it."

So Genevieve sat next to her sister and clawed through the jewels.

"Gen!" Her friend Andrea was siphoning down her second cup of wine. "I haven't seen you in forever. This is so exciting that you're working here! Like a real *artiste*!"

"Yes, well, I um..." She needed to find a reason to tell people. No one needed to know it was because she'd grown to hate her family and wanted to get out of the house.

"Gen realized it was time she did something for herself." Brynn came to her rescue. "You know, the kids are grown, they don't need much from her anymore."

"But this is when you and Chris could really live it up!" Her "friend" Chelsea nudged her with an elbow. "I would be off flying around the world with him if I were you."

"Well..." Of course, Chelsea would go with Chris anywhere. She'd always had a crush on him. Maybe Genevieve should tell her he's available. "I have always wanted to do my own thing. Now's my chance to do it."

That's when it happened. Genevieve got lost in a fluid time-space where colors and textures became an extension of her; she understood them in a way that required no words. She had laughed with ease at the small talk and banter; she never once considered what anyone thought or whether she was doing the right or wrong thing. She'd just been...present.

Mindful, even.

How interesting!

Had she noticed the lump last night?

She didn't think so.

As Genevieve had predicted, at the end of the evening, all the women were just staggered by what they'd accomplished. They were genuinely excited as they posed for Hayleigh to take a photo.

"Hayleigh!" Andrea looked at the picture on the phone. "We have to connect! How can I follow you?"

"Me too!" Chelsea reached for her phone. "Where is that boutique you told me about? Where you got that jacket?"

That was a stunning realization, too: Hayleigh shopped in a boutique? She didn't wear leftovers?

"Hana's." Hayleigh twirled around to give them all a full view of her outfit. "I do their marketing, so I'm always among the first to see what they're selling."

"Lucky you!" Chelsea glowed.

And Genevieve had to admit Hayleigh did have a presence that night, as always. She wore a black jacket with ruffled tails over a Pride T-shirt and a denim skirt. Completing the look were white tights and patent-leather pink oxford shoes. Such a clownlike look to Genevieve...did she really get that at Hana's? They were a very high-end and fashionable store. Granted, Genevieve hadn't been in since before the accident; maybe that was acceptable attire now?

The way her friends and even Brynn were so eager to be seen in selfies with Hayleigh suggested it was acceptable.

Oh. Everything was so clear to Genevieve now: how comfortable in her own skin Hayleigh was, Dee was, Maxine was, and Genevieve wasn't—unless she was creating.

They were genuine, and Genevieve was...managing.

Dee's instructions for the class had been so brief, too brief, Genevieve had originally thought, but really, in hindsight, there wasn't much to teach: this is the glue, these are the things you'll glue on the frame. Dee and Max offered guidance, but only when needed, when things didn't "look right," as her friends said when they asked for help, and not, as Genevieve had done out of worry that the others might make a mistake or wind up not liking what they created.

In other words, she had wanted to manage the situation out of fear that they would be disappointed, while struggling to maintain a light voice and smile.

Oh, so, yes, maybe she did swallow her emotions.

Her phone dinged with a text: Andrea.

> *Gen! I know the answer is no*
> *because you don't ever come.*
> *But we're having people over*
> *to watch the fireworks*

> *Saturday night. You should
> come!*

Genevieve had no idea how to respond. She hadn't seen fireworks in real life since Chris had left the military. There was something about him wanting to be in solidarity with his buddies who were triggered by fireworks, which she'd understood and supported, but she missed them.

Could she go? Remy's party would end around dinner time because he and his friends were going out to see fireworks that evening. Olivia was going to her own party. She'd be alone, but would it be proper to go? Would it look bad to go without Chris?

That lump grew to the size of a grapefruit.

> *You bet! What can I bring?*

Dee

"Sorry, Mom! Didn't mean to worry you. I should have called." Dee wanted more coffee, but the color of her pee suggested coffee was the only liquid in her body. She poured a glass of water from the tap.

"Don't apologize. I know I'm probably nagging. But, well..."

"Well, I'm fine. The meds worked."

"And, and no signs of..."

Dee losing her freaking mind again? Maybe. "Definitely not."

"That's such a relief."

"Yeah. Well, I gotta go. I have a call with Aisling. She wanted me to check in with her."

"Good! I'm so glad she's on it."

Actually, she had enough time to drink the water and finish

texting plans with Cooper for tomorrow night. She had no idea if seeing him was a good or a right thing to do. But it felt good. And fifty percent was better than nothing.

She finished off the charcuterie, pairing it with stale saltine crackers she'd found in her cupboard. She needed to get a grip on being an adult again. At least do a decent grocery shop and clean the place. It was an embarrassing mess.

She reached for a paper towel on the coffee table and saw her words. Yeah. Note wasn't needed. That box was still sitting on the kitchen table, its presence made it hard to enter the kitchen to forage for food and water. But, it was just a presence. Not a scary one. Not a sad one.

Just a presence. Like maybe she could handle it.

The phone alarm went off. She had five minutes before Aisling's call.

She'd see if she could handle it after the call.

She set up the coffee table with a half dozen wine corks, Exacto knives with various blade sizes, and black Sharpie markers. She'd make a series of miniature Tiki gods out of the corks while she chatted with her shrink. Maybe they'd protect her from whatever she needed protection from.

The Zoom call started. Dee snuggled the phone into the plant and picked up a cork. With a fine-tipped black Sharpie, she drew an open mouth, the lips close together in the center, wide apart on the sides.

"How are you, Dee Dee?" Why did Aisling always sound so freaking happy?

"I'm not sure. Let's get right to it. The meds are making me sleep. But I swear to fuck I am experiencing something from them."

"What does 'experiencing' mean?"

"Well, like, I think I hear people talking, or maybe I see things."

"When you're asleep?"

"No, right before I fall asleep, and then right when I wake up.

Or maybe right after I wake up. I'm not sure."

"Well, it is very normal for people—all people, not just those with executive dysfunction or brain damage—to experience phenomena called hypnopompic and hypnagogic hallucinations."

"Hypno-what?"

"Hypnopompic hallucinations are hallucinations that happen when you're waking up, and hypnogogic happen when you are falling asleep. Again, they're normal. They frequently happen to people. We don't really understand wh—"

"Wait a fucking minute!" Dee flipped the pen to the table. Normal? Frequently happen? She pulled her hair back into a band. "You're telling me this is fucking normal? These things have been scaring the hell out of me for no reason?"

"I don't know if that's what's going on with you for sure. I'm just saying they might possibly explain something. Usually, when people experience those hallucinations, they know they are hallucinating. They don't interact with whatever they see or hear in any way. Is that what you experienced when you were a teen?"

"God no. There were people after me, like trying to stop me from talking and moving, and I fought back." She shoved the tip of an Exacto knife into the Tiki god's mouth to chunk out tiny teeth.

"What about now? Do you know what you're seeing isn't real?"

"No. Not until I wake up, and then I'm still not sure." She'll give him a gap-toothed grin. "I literally have to search every inch of my apartment to make sure no one is here."

"Interesting."

"And I think it's the same scene I see or maybe hear." More teeth. "Or maybe there are a couple different scenes, or whatever they're called, that I have on repeat. Aisling..."

"Yes?"

Lots of teeth in this badass. "Is it possible...Sometimes I wonder if maybe these are memories coming to me, not dreams. Is that possible? Could I be remembering stuff from before the brain damage?"

"Anything's possible, Dee Dee. The mind is quite mysterious. Have you asked your mother about—?"

"For fuck's sake! Seriously? She *cannot* be asked anything about this shit." She drew a line around the carved mouth with a thicker Sharpie to make the lips fuller. "The thing is, in one of the...the things, incidents, whatever, I heard somebody say something. And I knew they didn't know I could hear them. Thinking back on it, that feels more like a memory."

"Well, there was something I thought rather odd on the reports from your doctors."

"And you're just now telling me?"

"I haven't had a reason to bring it up before now. But, when I pulled up your history to review it again before giving you the prescription, there was something that stood out to me last time that stood out to me again."

"What is it?"

"You suffered damage to the frontal lobes of your brain. That's where executive function is kind of housed—the attentional problems, organizational difficulties, impulse control, planning, and all that. So, it makes sense that you have such difficulties after experiencing physical trauma to *that* part of your brain. But it doesn't explain your amnesia. The frontal lobes really don't have much to do with memories. I suspected, when I first met you, that perhaps there was some kind of *emotional* trauma locked away in your brain, too."

"Not sure I understand." Angled crevices around the mouth gave the Tiki God more character. Using the Sharpie was the right call to make. After chunking the cork out, the Sharpie created an outline of the features. Cool.

"Sometimes, in a traumatic event," Aisling was talking, "the hippocampus, which is at the *back* of the brain, goes wonky. That's not the technical term, by the way."

"I don't care what it's called. I just want to understand what's happening to me. So, you're saying it's possible the explosion was so traumatic…Wait!" *Explosion? Was there an explosion? Or was it just a fire? Where did that word come from?*

"Dee?"

"Sorry. I'm trying to make connections. This hippo thing?"

"The hippocampus manages memory storage, recognizing past and present, making sense of emotional events. When it doesn't function properly, an assortment of things can happen. You could have memories that are entirely different from what actually happened, for example. Or you could have no memories. Again, the point is, it's at the *back* of the brain, not the front, where the physical trauma happened to you."

Dee put the knife down and closed her eyes. "So, the thing that happened that I don't remember but caused damage to the *front* of my brain is why I lose things, have ADD, can't get organized, and all those executive functions, as you call them, right?"

"Right."

"But that's not the part of my brain that would block out memories from a traumatic event."

"Correct."

She rotated the Tiki god, picked up the Sharpie again, and began drawing what the back of him should look like. The blob on the whiteboard was trying to send her a psychic message. She could feel it and wished it would express itself more clearly. "So, is it possible for memories that were blocked out to come back later in life?"

"Yes."

"Why would that happen?"

"You mean, what would trigger it?"

"Yes. Like, would medications do it?"

"Not usually sleeping medications if that's what you're thinking. In rare cases, some antipsychotics can intensify things. But flashbacks can be triggered from just about anything."

"Flashbacks?"

"Buried memories can come back in flashbacks. It's not uncommon for people with PTSD—"

"Do I have PTSD?"

"Well, you came to me with several inches of files, Dee. No one ever diagnosed you with it. But I'm now wondering if that was wrong. Perhaps, the nightmares *are* PTSD related, not just a by-product of a damaged brain unable to handle stress."

Chunk out more cork into zig-zagged hair. "Do you think the accident was traumatic enough to block the memory and cause PTSD?"

"I don't know the circumstances surrounding it. And, really, it would be irresponsible for me to tell you that's what's happening because we just don't know."

"Do you think photographs would help me remember things I'd forgotten?"

"Possibly."

The Zoom call ended. She had a full Tiki God done. Hopefully, one would be powerful enough to support her with the photographs.

Another glass of water. Hell! She sat at the tiny dinette and looked at the box top. She had to do this sober. She'd have to meet her father stone, cold sober—or have that massive headache in the morning.

This better fucking be worth it.

Her father. Wonder if she had ever known him, whether she would have called him Dad? Kaz remained Kaz even after he adopted her because she'd thought the name "Kaz" was so cool, which it is, and habits are hard to break. Never occurred to her to call him Dad, or Daddy, or anything.

She lifted the lid and set it aside.

And there he was. Her father on glossy paper, sitting in a chair on the sunporch where Brett's gorgeous table was now. One of the elephant tusks reared up behind him as he appeared to play a guitar. Was he a musician?

And here, in a suit, next to Gram in a gorgeous dress. The back read *Wade's wedding.* No date. Wade? The name rang a bell. She had a relative named Wade.

There were several photos of Gram and Granddad. Gram looked so beautiful…Oh, there's one of her in her studio! Dee's vision blurred with tears as she scrabbled through the photographs, looking for more of her. Wait! This wasn't about Gram, it was about…what? What was she looking for?

A building on Granddad's property, or something that wasn't there now. Something that might have burned down.

Wow! A wedding photo. Mom and…Mom's first wedding! Taken with someone's personal camera, not a professional pic. A candid shot, but definitely Mom in a gorgeous fucking dress! She must have designed it. Who made it? Had she? So sleek, body skimming silk. So sophisticated, with that long sash trailing off to the side. And he looked quite handsome, her father. Wavy blond hair, laughing blue eyes. So freaking thin.

God, he looked familiar! She never thought she'd recognize her father on the street, but even if Mom wasn't in this pic, she'd know it was him.

Weird. Yeah, guess this meant Josie was right, and she looked like him. Her face felt wet. What the fuck? Was she crying over this?

She dropped the photograph and pulled out another from their wedding, this time with Evan in a tux. Was he the best man? Definitely one of the groomsmen! Weird. They must have been close. So Mom must have been close to Evan, too, right? But she wasn't now.

So why was Kaz was in Evan's contacts. How does that make sense?

Maxine

"I can't thank you enough for squeezing me in." Max, wearing nothing but a scratchy paper gown and some socks, couldn't help but swing her legs as she sat at the end of the exam table. So nervous. So scared, yet so...so desperately eager for some kind of good, encouraging news.

"With your history, it's important we check you out early and monitor everything." Dr. Paicurich washed her hands in the little sink. "I'd squeeze you in no matter what."

With her history.

What about Dane's history? It's so painless for him, yet he's the one clamoring for her to understand what he's going through.

He had no idea what she was going through. And if he did? Would that make a difference? Would he be able to empathize with her? A sob erupted.

"Oh no!" Dr. Paicurich slid a stool over to sit by Maxine and handed her a tissue. "Listen, I can't promise anything, you know that. But I'm here for you. We'll do our—"

"It's not that." Max wiped her eyes and nose. "Is this hormones? I cry at the drop of the hat."

"It might be. But this is also a very emotional time for you, so it could just be your body acknowledging that. I hope Dane's being extra supportive of you."

That made it all worse. Max crumpled. Such a sad weight on her. Like grief. And maybe it was. Maybe she was already grieving her marriage, or the marriage she thought she had.

Dr. Paicurich waited out the tears, continually passing her more tissues. Eventually, she stood up to kick a small waste bin over for Max to throw them away.

Once she cried herself out, Max took a deep breath, straightened her spine. "Wow, that was really...cathartic!" Yes, her in-breath was so full. She had emptied her body of something with that cry. "I guess I needed that."

"Is there something else going on?"

Once more, the story came out easily. So easy that Max was beginning to think she was at a safe enough place, emotionally, that she could have a conversation with Dane.

"I see." Dr. Paicurich, who usually appeared to Max as a series of numbers on a blackboard—correct mathematical formulas presented in an orderly manner—now came across as she was: a doctor in a white coat, unbuttoned over a pink, silky blouse. Her long dark hair was pulled back into a loose bun at the back of her head. She was the picture of calmness, balanced with efficiency. "I hate to say this, but let's run some STD tests on you."

"What?" Why would she even think that was necessary?

"I'm not saying you can't trust your husband. I consider it a better-safe-than-sorry approach. If there was one secret, then perhaps there are others. Do you want to risk that?"

No. Maxine didn't want to risk anything.

Max needed a minute. She sat in the waiting room to collect herself. The gentle spa-like music, the beautiful fresh flowers in the vase on the coffee table, the comfortable armchair...all were needed now. Not just a pleasant place to help a woman relax before her appointment, it was a refuge of sorts for her now *after* the appointment; a sanctuary where she could sit and connect with whatever was going on inside her.

Her breasts had been prodded. The pee she'd passed into a cup would be studied. A syringe extracted blood for an assortment of tests. Her pelvic area had been examined inside and out. An ultrasound probe had been placed in her vagina to search for signs of life, as if her insides were an alien territory.

Very little of her body had *not* been manipulated by another human being. Under different circumstances, she could say she'd been violated. But under these, under the gentle direction of Dr. Paicurich, she'd been given proof that she could, indeed, be a mother. Even more: she'd gone through it all alone, which meant she could, indeed, be a mother all by herself, too.

The proof was in her hands: a printout of an actual baby…kind of. Maxine had expected to see a blob on the ultrasound, but there was this thing inside her that clearly had a very large head in comparison with its tiny body. When measured, it was almost two inches long, which Dr. Paicurich had said was perfect for a baby about ten weeks along.

She was a mother, all by herself, with a perfect little baby growing inside her.

How did Dane fit into this?

How did she want him to fit into it?

Kaz's question still remained unanswered: did she love him?

Dee

She held a photo of her parents and another couple: her father, Mom, Aunt Louise, and some man.

Mom and Aunt Louise looked very young. On the back was a scribble: *Gatlin and Lauren with Wade and Louise.* No date.

There was that Wade name, again. Gatlin was her father. He was technically Gatlin Stoker, III, because Granddad was Junior. How did she know that?

Was Wade his brother?

She found her phone still in the plant from the Zoom call, texted Brett.

Yo! Was Wade ur dad?

Must be him. He looked like her father. Were they twins? Very close in age and looks, if not actual twins. Must be strong genes in that family. Both looked like Granddad, too. Of course, it was her uncle! Could Aunt Louise find more than one man to be with her? Besides, she was the in-law. That *had* to be Brett's dad.

Why you wanna know?

Brett confirmed it, really.

Never mind.

OK. There were too many pictures for the tiny table. She needed a bigger space if she was going to organize them in any way, which is what she realized she needed to do. She should organize them somehow. Maybe see bits and pieces of the land before and after her accident.

She swiped what she'd pulled out into a pile, stowed them back in the box, and re-secured the lid.

Where the hell could she do this?

"Jesus!" Her place was a fucking pigsty. No floor space anywhere.

In the bedroom, she smoothed the covers to make a flat-ish surface on her bed. She removed the lid from the box, turned it over to tuck it underneath. A photo was stuck to the underside of the lid, the edge in a side crease.

She was in this one, with Mom and her father. No! That's not possible. Must be her uncle. They really looked similar.

They were all dressed to the nines, standing by Granddad's lake, no buildings in sight, but Gram's willow tree off to the side. What was the occasion? *Dee, age 4* was on the back.

Dee wore a light pink dress that puffed out in layers of tulle from her waist. Her uncle stood behind her and Mom, looking down to where Dee was pointing at something in the water. Her mother squatted beside her—in a long gown—with a hand on her back, probably in a death-grip so Dee wouldn't slide in. Had she overprotected her from the start?

Don't go there! One thing at a time.

God, how her uncle resembled her father. *Were* they twins? Were she and Mom close to him?

She rummaged through the box looking for more shots of Wade. And of a building that no longer existed. And of…Pictures shifted around on her bed, some slipped off the side.

Static built in her ears.

Stop! Breathe in, two, three. Breathe out, two, three, four, five. Her ears cleared. OK. Do this methodically. Figure out how to organize these things. Maybe build a timeline. Then see what was missing from different parts.

When did her uncle die? Why didn't she know that? She probably did at one point.

Whatever. Build a timeline of photos. One thing at a time.

Would have been much easier if someone had written dates on all the backs. As it was, only a few had them. The rest gave clues in hair and clothing styles. The ones where she or Brett were in them helped the most; clearly, they grew in size.

But then the pics with her stopped when she must have been about five. That's when the fire happened.

Or maybe explosion. Why did that seem like the right word?

She covered her bed with rows and rows of photographs. Standing at the foot of it, nothing stood out as far as what was different, except her father was missing after she came into the world.

Was anything else missing?

Brett's dad. Except for those two photos.

What else?

How would she know?

She stared at the picture of her in the pink tulle. Her uncle Wade looked familiar to her, too. The way her father did. She must have known him back then. Of course, she knew him. He…Static started. Inhale, two, three. Exhale…She needed a break from this.

Stepping back, she rolled her ankle on a wayward flipflop. Shit. Maybe she should straighten things up, do some laundry. That'd clear her head. Besides, she'd need clean underwear when she met up with Cooper tomorrow.

Maybe she'd need clean underwear.

Hopefully, she'd need clean underwear.

She found she'd already done a load of wash. Hooray! It was her lucky day. She threw it in the dryer, added another to the washer, and, passing back through the kitchen for another glass of water, she realized she didn't have a headache. It must have been dehydration more than anything else. There was even more hope for life to get better.

After setting an alarm on her phone to check on the laundry later, she returned to the bedroom and stared at the photos.

The earliest pic was of her parents and Brett's parents.

Why wasn't her uncle in many others? Brett and Louise showed up in various photos throughout the years, before and after Dee and Mom disappeared from them. There was even a shot of Brett graduating high school with his arm around Gram and Aunt Louise standing on the other side of him. If he was eighteen in that shot, she was...sixteen. That summer would have been the one when he taught her how to ride an ATV.

Why weren't there more photos of Wade?

Was he the one who had taken all the other photos?

Or did Evan remove the photos of him?

Is that what he was doing with the box before he gave it to Dee? If so, why?

Ooooo. Did Brett's dad cause the explosion? If it was an explosion, which is what Dee was pretty certain had happened. An explosion caused the fire, right? The fire that made a beam fall on her head.

But something else happened in that fire. It was on the edge of her memory. She felt it as strongly as she felt her father's presence. Which, she just realized, had crept into the room with her as she looked at the photographs. Why was he hanging around?

Maybe she should have a drink with him and find out. Shit! She can't drink on the meds. Maybe just one glass of wine…

Genevieve

"I've spent the afternoon Googling for advice." Genevieve pulled a tray of cookies out of the oven. "I think we made the right choice not to tell them over dinner."

"You made the right choice." Chris sat on a barstool at the kitchen island, looking over the divorce paperwork.

"You didn't seem to have any ideas." She rested the tray on a couple of cork trivets.

"I wasn't challenging you, Gen."

"Sorry." She leaned her hands against the counter. "Genuinely."

He tapped the ends of the papers to line them up before making eye contact with her.

"I'm nervous." She realized she'd never felt vulnerable around him like she did now.

"What are you scared of?"

He was so rough around the edges. Even in the tux at Brynn's wedding, he looked like he was about to tear it off at any minute. Now, in his company-logoed polo shirt, that stupid tattoo flowing down his arm, his brown hair going in too many directions from being crushed with a baseball cap, then swept back with his fingers—there was a wildness about him that she didn't find comforting. It set her on edge, she realized, the way Dee Dee did. They were both like feral creatures, unintentionally challenging her to come to the wild side.

Is that where she wanted to go?

No. She just wanted to feel free.

"Gen? It's clear in the paperwork, you get the house, great alimony, support, whatever. You can take your time to get a lawyer to look it over. But, seriously, there's nothing for you to be afraid of."

"There's Olivia." That's really what she was scared of. "I don't want to disappoint her."

"If you ask me, Livvy needs more disappointment in her life." He shoved the papers in the backpack he used for an attaché. "She's not at all resilient."

He sounded like the life coach she listened to while exercising. Could Chris really be that wise?

"I suppose that's my fault." Of course, it was. She was the one who raised their children.

"It's both our faults. But it doesn't matter. What's done is done." He pulled a beer from the refrigerator. "It's time to move on."

Wine would be good right about now.

"So, again, how do we say this?" Genevieve poured.

"I only know English."

Stupid jokes, just like Dee Dee. So interesting how much those two had in common. "OK, funny man, is that what we do?" She turned around, held her glass in his direction. He held his beer bottle toward her. "We just say, 'kids we're getting a divorce'?"

"You're WHAT?" Olivia seemed to fall from the ceiling. She and Remy must have smelled the cookies because they were both in the kitchen before Genevieve was ready for them.

"Oh, kids! I made cookies!" Genevieve couldn't stop staring at Olivia's face. Never had she seen her child look so...so...hurt. She wanted to run over to her, wrap her in her arms, and assure her everything would be all right. But there was such an intense anger flaring in her sad eyes that Genevieve feared her at the same time.

"What did you just say?" Olivia growled the words as Remy pulled a plate from the cupboard for cookies.

"She said," Chris resumed sitting at the island like it was a normal day in paradise, "that we're getting a divorce." He tipped his beer to his mouth and sipped.

"What did you do?" Olivia pointed her finger at her mother.

"Olivia—" Genevieve started.

"You have to ruin everything!" She stomped toward the mudroom, as if she were going to the garage. Chris reached out and grabbed her arm, too forcefully in Genevieve's opinion. But Livvy didn't complain. She stopped walking and stood with her back to her parents.

Chris kept his grip on her arm, stood, and somehow gently, yet forcefully, scooted Olivia over to the stool next to him at the island. "Rem, could you get your sister a couple cookies?"

"Sure, Dad." Remy stood to retrieve another plate.

"Want some milk, Liv?" Chris asked.

She didn't answer.

"Rem—" Chris stated.

"Got it, Dad."

There was a natural connection between Remy and Chris. Obviously, they spoke more than Genevieve had ever given Chris the benefit of doing. Did he also have a relationship with Olivia? Did anyone have a relationship with Olivia?

Once everyone was supplied with cookies, even Chris, though

the thought of beer and chocolate-chip cookies was nauseating to Genevieve, who found her Cabernet was perfect with them, Chris met her eyes and nodded. Oh, so he was going to play bouncer while she gave the bad news? Just when she thought she might like him, just a little, he disappointed, once more.

"Well, children."

"Don't fucking call me a child." Olivia squinted her eyes, as if aiming death-rays into her mother's heart.

Genevieve couldn't resist grinning. She wasn't going to take her daughter's bait, which she appreciated she realized was exactly what Livvy was doing—trying to bait her into being the bad guy.

"You and Remy will always be my children." Genevieve sipped her wine. "I mean the term with love, not disrespect or condescension."

"Whatever." Livvy nibbled a cookie.

"Your father and I made a decision to get an amicable divorce."

"OK." Remy finished his plate of cookies. Perpetually unflappable, easy-going. Genevieve hoped his *laissez-faire* attitude was genuine, not something he hid behind.

"And that's that?" Livvy locked eyes with Genevieve. "You two get to make a decision like that without discussing with us first?"

How interesting that Livvy never challenged her father. Did she think Genevieve was the weak one?

Well, Genevieve would have let her leave the house, would have given her daughter the space to work through her feelings. And then, Livvy would come home later and wait for her mother to make everything all right.

"Your father and I divorcing has nothing to do with you, Livvy. Your input simply wasn't needed."

Olivia's eyes opened wide, she pulled her head back. Genevieve knew if her daughter could breathe fire, she'd char her mother. "Seriously! This is how I get treated?"

"Your mother is right." Chris wiped his mouth with the back of his hand. Why couldn't he use a napkin?

"You're turning on me, too?" She finally looked at her dad.

"No one's turning on you, honey." Chris squeezed her hand. "A divorce is what happens when a couple no longer wants to be married. It has nothing to do with anyone else."

"What did she do to you?" Livvy leaned toward him.

"Nothing, ha!" How could Chris laugh at a time like this? "We just don't want to be married to each other anymore. It goes both ways."

"But...but...what about me? Where will I live?"

"Here, in this house." He pulled her into a sideways hug. "At least for a month or so now. Then you'll go to college."

"But—"

"You'll come home for the holidays. Your mother always puts on a great Thanksgiving feast—"

"Will you be here?"

Christ looked over Livvy's head at Gen, met her eyes.

"If he wants to," Genevieve answered for him. Though if she were to be honest with herself, which, granted, she was still new at being, she wasn't sure if she really wanted to make a Thanksgiving feast for this crew.

Saturday, July 3

Dee

C *lick.* A thin stream of light flared then widened as it crossed the floor and reached the corner of her bed.

Mom?

She's not here.

"Dee Dee," his voice was a whisper. "Shhh, baby."

"MOM!"

She was awake. Fuck! She wanted to confront that bastard.

What the hell was that noise?

Oh, her phone. On the coffee table.

Apparently, she'd fallen asleep on the living room floor again. It was Hayleigh calling.

"H! Why so early?" And shit, she forgot to plug in her phone. It was almost dead.

"I'm at Jhansi's. Want anything?"

"Um..." She clicked the phone to speaker so she could look at her clock. Damn. she was supposed to be in the store soon. "The normal. Thanks. See you soon."

She fell into the wall as soon as she stood up. Fucking medication. Sleep was appreciated, but damn, could she just wake up and not have vertigo for half an hour?

She only had time for a French bath. At least there were clean underwear and jeans in the dryer. But, ugh! She was gonna have to wear another one of those horrific, flowered blouses Mom and H had picked out. Where's her other flip-flop?

Why is it that doing two loads of laundry, well, one and a half, didn't make her apartment look any less messy?

Oh yeah…the photographs were still on her bed. That's why she'd slept on the floor. Maybe she could call Brett later. Ask about his father. No marker was in her bedroom for her to write that on her arm. And she needed to get moving.

She pulled on a pair of Dr. Martens boots over mismatched socks, finger-combed her hair, slid on a slash of black eyeliner, and brushed on mascara. *Poof!* Ready for work.

Of course, Max was already in the shop. Outside of it, actually, and fucking gorgeous as she set up displays on the sidewalk. Watching her, a dawning realization became clear in the fog of Dee's mind: she was going to have to talk to customers, fucking show them stuff in the store. Sell! For God's sake! She had no idea how to do that!

"Look at you!" H was way too happy, as usual. "That blouse looks amazing on you." She handed Dee her first cup of coffee.

"Fuck the blouse." Dee ripped the lid off the to-go cup. "What do I do if someone comes in?"

"Say, 'hello,' ask them if they're looking for something specific. Most of the time, they'll say, 'no,' so you let them wander unless you get the vibe they won't mind small talk. If they say 'yes,' find out what it is and then show them the closest thing you have to it."

"How do you know this?"

"How many dress shops did I work in through high school and college?"

"We are all set up outside." Max accepted her to-go cup from Hayleigh. "Dee, you look, well, almost normal. You're sleeping?"

"Under medication." Oh hell, someone walked into the store. "How are you?"

"Best morning, yet."

"What an adorable bag!" Hayleigh shrieked as she accosted the customer.

"She's gonna make me crazier than normal today." Dee slugged back as much coffee as she could chug.

"She's gonna get us on the map in this town today."

"Dee Dee!" Why couldn't H speak in an inside voice? "Max! This lovely gentleman is interested in this chess game. Why don't you tell him how you made it?"

Shit. She really *was* going to have to have conversations with people. Why hadn't she thought of that before? She hated talking to people.

"Hello!" Thank God Max was there. "Dee Dee made the pieces out of recycled beer bottles, that's why they're green and amber in color." Oh! She could have said that. "I made the board. The squares are leather pieces I reclaimed from a 1967 Chevy truck seat."

"It's amazing!" the man was impressed. This could be easy.

"Excuse me." Holy shit! There were like a dozen people in the store! OK, maybe just four or five. "Are you the one who did the glass?" A guy who seemed too young to sport the heavy beard on his face was touching her arm.

"Yes." She hoped she pulled away with grace.

"Can you make anything from glass bottles?"

"Yes. Sometimes. Maybe. Depends on the bottle."

"If I had a red bottle, do you think you could do something with it?" His eyes looked so hopeful, she wanted to.

"Maybe." Red glass was rare. That could actually be fun. "What are you looking for?"

"I don't know, really. My wife and I just bought our first house." Maybe he was old enough for that beard. "We'd saved a bottle from our first date and used it as a vase in our old apartment. It broke in the move. My wife tried to glue it back together, but..." He shrugged.

How pathetic. Probably romantic, but seriously? "Bring it in. I'll see what I can do. Maybe I could make some beads for a wind chime?"

"Could you do beads for jewelry?"

"Probably."

"Great! We'll be in tomorrow."

OK. So that was kind of easy.

By the time H flipped the *open* sign on the door to *closed,* they realized they'd sold enough that if they felt energetic the next day, they could bring some of the products stored in the garage up front.

"Maybe Monday," Max suggested. "I have nothing going on in my life. I can come in Monday."

"Cool. So we'll move things around then." Dee looked at her phone. It was six o'clock. She headed to the back of the store for the leftover wine while H did something called pull a report. "We have time for a celebratory drink. Who's in?"

"Water for me, please!" Max hollered.

Right. She grabbed a bottle of water.

"You can't do alcohol on the meds, Dee," H had the audacity to say as soon as she was back in the front.

"I'm not taking them tonight, H. I'm facing my demons without them." And hopefully sleeping the night with Cooper.

"What..." H tapped a few more times on the computer. "...does that mean?"

"So, that conspiracy theory…" Dee sipped. Truly, *this* was the juice of life. "OK, the meds knock me out cold. I don't have nightmares when I'm on them. But I do have these things that might be hallucinations right before I crash, and then when I wake up."

"Stop taking the damn things." H looked so scared, Dee wanted to hug her. But the counter separated them.

"They could be normal hallucinations people have when they

fall asleep."

"I've never had a freaking hallucination before I fell asleep. You, Max?"

Maxine shook her head.

"Well, not everyone. Aisling explained it to me. Can't remember what they're called, but they're nothing dangerous. However, I said 'might be' hallucinations. I really think they're memories."

"From what?" Max's eyebrows pinched together.

"Not sure. But I think it has something to do with the accident that knocked my brain offline." She tapped her forehead. "There is more to that story than anyone told me."

"The conspiracy has more threads?" H finally looked relaxed as she sipped her wine.

"The threads were about Cooper."

"What?"

"Were you talking about the whiteboard image?"

"No. What's a Cooper?"

"Nothing. Never mind that. But listen, Aunt Josie gave me a box of photographs, and I'm pretty sure Evan removed some before he gave them to me. I think he took out photographs of my uncle, Brett's dad. Meanwhile, Granddad has such a close eye on Brett, he's living in his house."

"Your grandfather is living in Brett's house?"

"No. Granddad made Brett move into his house."

"I need help putting the pieces together, Dee." Max sipped her water. "I don't think I have all the conspiracy parts."

Dee gave herself a beat to try to get her own brain to make sense of it all—the suspected missing photographs, the snippets she remembered from speaking to her aunts at the funeral, Brett's drunken gibberish, Evan and Kaz talking, and Brett under Granddad's watchful eye, as if to make sure he didn't speak with Dee unsupervised. "There's a lot of little things that are adding up to make me wonder if Brett's dad had something to do with causing the fire."

"Oh!" H held her cup up as if in a cheer. "That would explain why Mom hates those people down there."

"Then there's one mystery solved." Dee drained her wine. "Meanwhile, I honestly believe the nightmares are part memories, so I really want to get to the bottom of them. Each time I have one, I get more information, more imagery, voices, or whatever."

"And…" H was looking at Max, not Dee.

"And what?"

Finally, her sister met her eyes. "And you're, you know, strong enough to handle whatever comes to you?"

"Yeah, definitely." Maybe. But it didn't matter if she was strong enough. She needed to be done with this shit forever. She also had to make that terrified look on H's face go away. "I'm wondering if my aunts, my father's sisters, think the fire was my fault, somehow. They seemed to want to pin something on me. But Brett's mom was kind of hinting that she knew what really happened. And I think Brett knows the truth, too. And that maybe it was his father, and he's all torn up about it. That makes the most sense. And if that's what comes out of me facing these demons, then how horrible is that? I can handle it." She waved her hand in the air as if she believed it.

H seemed to buy her confidence. "Cool. So, I guess I'm outta here. What are you two doing tonight?"

"I'm seeing fireworks with Dane tonight." Max looked like she'd rather be drinking wine.

"So things are better with you two?" In solidarity with her, Dee chose not to refill her cup. Besides, she had a bit of a drive to meet up with Cooper.

"I'm not sure. But it's not just the two of us. Jamaal is joining us."

"Who?"

"That's his son's name."

"Dane has a son?!" Hayleigh slammed her empty cup on the

counter.

"Long story, H, but yes. A baby mama from years ago showed up with a seven-year-old."

"Wowsa! Damn! How are you handling that?"

"Not well."

"Did you tell him you're pregnant?" Dee was rather proud of herself for thinking to clean up. She gathered the empty cups and bottle to take to the back.

"You're freaking pregnant?!" Hayleigh almost yelled. "When the hell is anyone going to tell me anything around here?"

While Max caught her up, Dee threw everything away and made sure the back door was locked.

"Jeesh. It sucks you have to deal with that." H hugged Max. "Let me know if I can help somehow."

"Thank you, Hayleigh. Just, please, don't mention to anyone that I'm pregnant. It's so early. Anything can happen."

"Does Mom know?"

"No. Not yet."

"OK. Well, when you tell her, don't tell her you told me first."

Max laughed. "Have fun in the parade tomorrow." How does Max remember everything like that?

"Yes!" Dee hugged her sister. "I hope your kids do great."

"They will. And remember, Mom will probably come in the store after the parade. You know she wouldn't be down here and not visit."

"Sleep in tomorrow." Max told Dee. "I'll come in early and handle your mom."

Maxine

"I'm so glad you're willing to do this." Dane held the car door open for Maxine to get in. Why did it feel like she was about to be imprisoned? Like there was no escape? They were to pick the kid up from the hotel, then watch fireworks at the river. If worse came to worst, she'd walk to a train station, get back to the Jersey side, and have Dee pick her up. Or Mama or H, since Dee didn't mention anything about finding her key fob. Still...she was going to be stuck in the car alone with Dane for a little while.

When did that happen?

When did he become the enemy?

Ever since she realized he'd kept some of his worst opinions and feelings to himself.

"Max?" Dane's hand was on the small of her back. That touch used to feel so comforting, something that encouraged her to lean into him, collapse against his chest, breathe him in. She shook him off. Tonight, it was the touch of a stranger.

"Sorry, Dane." She slid into the car and grabbed the door handle. "I'm not infirm, you know. You never used to get my car doors. Don't need to make up for lost time now." She pulled it shut.

He paused for a minute, then walked around to the driver's side and got in.

"Tell me what to say, Max." He pressed the ignition button and reached toward her. His hand hovered above hers, as if he knew she needed to give him permission.

"I don't want you to say anything because I asked for it, Dane." She clasped her hands together in her lap.

"How do I fix this?"

Was it fixable? She still had no idea why she'd agreed to this, other than she hadn't spent the fourth away from her husband since they'd been together. This is what they did every year. They fought the traffic to sit by the Delaware River and watch the fireworks over

Penn's Landing. And for some reason, it felt unbearable not to do it this year. So, she'd agreed to his texted request. But now the evening was more than watching fireworks with her man. They were picking up his son so he could see the fireworks with them. It was now a family affair.

A family affair.

"What do you want from me?" Dane put the car in gear and headed out of their driveway. "Please."

She wanted him to tell her he was sorry for having sex with another woman when they were in a relationship. She wanted him to assure her that nothing like it had ever happened again, that it was one stupid time when he was young and didn't know better. She wanted him to tell her he knew better now.

But he'd already said all that. And it wasn't enough.

"I want you to be completely honest with me about everything." That was the starting point, after all. "About how you're feeling. About what you're thinking. About what you want."

"I'm still working on the first one. I'm thinking that it's unfair to everyone. It's unfair to you, to Jamaal, and to me. And I want you to be cool with me having a relationship with my son."

"Cool?"

"Yes. I don't want you to hate him or be angry with him."

"Why would I blame the child for what his father did?" Again, did he think that lowly of her? She twisted in the car seat to look at him. He continued staring out the front window.

"I had to wrestle with that." Dane quickly caught her eyes, then returned his focus to the road. "I was kind of blaming him, I guess, at first. That's why it's been so hard to spend time with him. I was kind of, I don't know, being…well, my mother said I was being passive-aggressive with him."

"You told your parents?"

"Yeah." He nodded. "I needed some kind of guidance, Max. I seriously have no idea what I'm doing."

"Be honest with me here, Dane. Completely honest."

He stopped at a light. She gripped his chin to force him to look into her eyes. "Is that why you asked me to join you tonight? To help you figure out how to have a relationship with your son?"

He wet his lips, then blew out a sigh. "I don't know what I'm doing, Max. Not with him, not with you. But, yeah, it'd be great to have you help me have a relationship with him. But I really, more than anything, want you to help me have a relationship with you again. I don't want to lose you over this, Max."

The car behind them honked. She let go of him, leaned away. His silhouette seemed to fill with swirling dots of faded colors as he pressed on the gas.

"Pull into that shopping center."

"What?"

"Pull over so we can talk."

Dane turned into the lot, took a spot facing the road. "We're going to be late—"

"I don't care." She needed more facts before she met her husband's son. "When does he go back to...to wherever?"

"Baltimore. They go back tomorrow. But Shawna—"

He wasn't looking at her. He was just a man in profile now. "What about her?"

Dane visibly swallowed. "She, uh, she said she doesn't want anything."

Play it cool, girl, came Mama's voice as flames of anger lit up Maxine. "Then why did she come now, out of the blue, surprising you like this? Interrupting our lives?"

"It wasn't out of the blue." He braved a quick glance her way. "She, um, back in March, she reached out to me."

March? He'd known since March. Before she told him she was done with the fertility treatments.

"Jamaal made a family tree for school and started asking questions. She'd married a man when he was a year or so old, and he'd considered that man his father. But when they divorced, last fall, the man didn't ask for any custody…" Dane filled in the rest with a shrug.

"So, the kid's really emotionally messed up. What a great mom she is." How is it that shitty moms always seem to get pregnant with ease? Max flattened her palm against her belly, promising her very wanted child she'd do better.

"She's doing the best she can, but yes, Jamaal is quite upset with his mother."

So Max had something in common with Jamaal.

"It never occurred to her that her son would feel cheated out of knowing his real dad."

And Shawna and Dane had something in common: it didn't occur to either that their actions might hurt somebody else. That keeping a secret wouldn't fester.

"What are you thinking, Max?"

"I'm thinking the wrong people get hurt when secrets are exposed." She unclicked her seatbelt. "I can't be with you tonight. I'll call Mama to have her pick me up at this store."

"Max—"

She shut the door and walked away.

Dee

Two showers in one week. She was almost acting like an adult. Though it would be great if she could find that other fucking flip-flop.

She triple- and quadruple-checked all the locks on the building, then got in her car. Cooper was hanging with some vets who wanted nothing to do with booming fireworks. She plugged the address he gave her into her phone and headed to a bar near an executive airport in the middle of nowhere.

And *boom*. There he was. As soon as she entered the place, she zeroed in on him, stared for a few minutes. He was at the bar, in one of his blue Griffin Wings polo shirts and jeans. His dark, wavy hair brushed back from his face, his dimples even deeper as he laughed with some dude in a vest covered with patches and pins.

Of course, he was laughing. He was so easy to talk to. He was so easy to laugh with. And he was so…oh, good God. She was pretty sure this was what love must feel like. She was in love with him.

How the hell was she going to handle this?

Maybe she should leave.

Shit! He saw her. He waved her over and patted the stool next to him. She couldn't leave now. And really, she was already halfway across the floor.

After a brief kiss on the lips, he tapped the man he'd been speaking to on the chest.

"Meet Gunnar," he shouted over the band. "We were…" The music was too loud. Dee couldn't understand anything. She found herself nodding and smiling as the man said something to her. He must have realized she couldn't hear her and chucked Cooper on the shoulder, gave him the peace sign, and disappeared into the crowd.

Somehow, the bartender heard an order for a glass of wine and placed one in front of her.

Cooper pressed his face into the side of her head. "Sorry, it's so loud!"

"I love it!" she yelled back. She was so close to him that she could feel him breathe. Standing so near opened a floodgate of sensations she didn't quite understand. Good sensations. Sensations that made it hard for her legs to support her.

Christ, if he was going to make her go weak, that can't be good, can it?

"Food?" he shouted.

"Not yet!" Because even though she felt weak, and she hated being weak, it was too delicious leaning into him, letting him take the power out of her.

With a loud, crashing drumroll, the song ended. The crowd roared. The frontman said something into a staticky speaker. She couldn't understand, but apparently the crowd did. They roared again.

"What's going on?" She leaned back to yell into his ear.

"The band is going to turn the volume down. They just need a few minutes." His hand was on her cheek. "God, it's good to see you again."

She was falling into some kind of abyss where all she could see was him, feel was him. "It's good to be seen," came out because, oh good God, static built in her ears. What the fuck was going on? She stepped back. Breathe in, two, three.

Genevieve. Genevieve was what was going on. How were they going to do this? What were they even doing?

"We told the kids last night." He brushed his hand over her hair.

"Told the kids what?"

"That we're getting a divorce."

"Holy hell!" She clutched a fistful of his shirt. That could make whatever they were doing easier. "So, like, that's a real thing that's going to happen?"

"No more mess for me to clean up." He kissed her, a second longer than briefly. "There is nothing stopping us now."

"But, like, what do we do? I mean, I just announce to Genevieve that—"

"Let's worry about that tomorrow." The band started another song at a lower level. This one was clearly a love song. "Let's dance."

She let him tug her onto the dance floor, and soon enough, they were pressed tightly against each other, swaying to the beat of the music. Pressed so close together, one of his legs was between hers, making waves of bliss roll up through her belly, into her chest. A humming electricity coursed through her. Surely, she would be lifted off her feet with him. She melted into him, nestled her head into the crook of his neck.

If she could just stay here forever. If they could just stay here forever in this space of blurred boundaries. With no separation between them. No discernible line of distinction. So warm. So alive. Her entire body felt alive, all her cells energized, yet so relaxed. She sank into that abyss, which was really just sinking into herself or maybe into the two of them combined.

Click. A thin stream of light flared and widened as it crossed the floor.

What the hell? She shook her head. People were dancing on the other side of the light.

"What's up?" Cooper's voice was soft in her ear.

No. People were dancing here, in this crowded bar. That low-level panic wormed its way into her chest. She was dancing. But why did she see that light again? It was from a door opening, she knew that. How did she know that?

What was she doing?

"Dee?" Cooper tried to pull back to look at her. She clung tight to him. "Are you all right?"

Who was dancing? Where was she in the dark?

"Dee?"

What was she doing?

"What?" Cooper was with her now. She could let the memory happen, right? If she was going to crash somehow, remember it all, because it was definitely a memory, the line of light, the door opening into where she was in the darkness. Jesus Christ! Fear gripped her. What the hell was going on?

"Dee?"

"What are we doing?"

"Dancing."

"No!" That's not what she meant. She needed to know he would be there when she crashed. Because it was happening. Everything was coming clearer.

"We're just dancing."

That's right. That fucking Bowie song. But people weren't dancing.

Cooper kissed her earlobe. His lips traveled down her neck with a sense of urgency. How the fuck could he be kissing her like that right now? It was hard to breathe. She needed to know he'd still be there...that he'd...that he'd what?

"You wanna keep dancing?" His words cut her breath off.

No. No the dancing was in a song. Bowie's fucking song that she hated.

Her father loved that song.

Who told her that?

That song was playing.

"Are you OK?" His face was serious.

It wasn't playing now. When was it playing?

"How do I know that?"

"How do you know if you're OK?"

She stepped back and tried to wiggle out of his arms.

"I think my mom told me that once..."

"Dee?"

"Wait..." It was almost there. Whatever happened, it was almost there. Sheer panic ripped through her. She realized she was shaking her head at Cooper. He tried to pull her back into him.

"Stop!" She slapped his arms away.

"Dee, I..." He wouldn't hurt her. She knew that. Why did she think he was going to?

"I need..." That ringing started in her ears. She needed saving. Somebody needed to save her. Get her out of this darkness. Only it wasn't dark. She could see Cooper right in front of her. Where was

Brett? Brett always saved her.

"Dee?" Cooper again, standing with his hands up, like she was pointing a gun at him. The music stopped. It wasn't a Bowie song at all. It was...her ears roared.

"I need to go."

So many fucking people between her and the door. She needed to get away from them all. Get outside. Get somewhere alone where she could let the memories come and—

"Dee!" Cooper shouted. They were outside the bar.

"Look," Dee spun around. "I don't know what the fuck's going on. But I need to go home."

"Can I—"

"No. I'll call you."

Genevieve

Genevieve turned into her development.

Happiness. This is what happiness feels like.

She'd had a great day—Remy's birthday party went off without a hitch. She and Chris even got along during it, and when he went off to do his thing with the veterans, she felt no guilt, no obligation.

And she saw fireworks, in person, for the first time in years.

They were so beautiful!

And no one seemed to judge her when she explained she was alone because she and Chris had separated. Andrea was actually a supportive friend.

Yes! Genevieve had a very good day. She didn't want it to end, but it was almost eleven o'clock, and she had to work the next day. Work! She had a job! She had a job where they appreciated her.

Where she enjoyed what she did.

Well, she expected to enjoy what she did. She really hadn't done much but unpack and organize.

Regardless, life was taking a turn for the better.

Oh, but Livvy's car was in the drive.

Didn't expect her to be home. Livvy was supposed to be at Jessica's house for a party.

As she entered the garage, every fear she'd ever had regarding her children when they became teenagers filled her head. Would Livvy be cutting? Would she be drunk? Shooting up? Would Genevieve find her having sex with a much much older man?

She opened the door to the mudroom. Was that...she sniffed...burnt cheese?

In the kitchen, Livvy stood with her hands on her hips, staring at a ruined sheet pan piled with tortilla chips and charred cheese sitting on the granite countertop.

Genevieve cleared her throat.

Livvy cast a glance behind her. "I don't get it." She pointed at the pan. "Why didn't the stupid alarm go off before the whole thing was ruined?"

"The smoke detector?" Genevieve approached the smoldering mess. "I dunno. But I'm sure we have more chips and—"

"I finished off the cheese."

"Oh..." Genevieve opened the pantry. There was some of that processed stuff in a big cube. "Are there more chips?"

"Yeah." Livvy sat on a barstool at the island.

"Well, why don't I make some queso?" Yes, there was also a can of peppers.

"Fine."

Genevieve placed the peppers and processed cheese on the counter and opened the fridge for milk. "So, do you still hate me?" She couldn't believe she was so brave.

"Yeah."

If what Lauren had said was right, that Livvy would probably be a monster until she was twenty-four, Genevieve had another six years. Maybe that was the real reason they started letting women attend college. "But not so much that you won't let me make something for you to eat."

"I can't even make fucking nachos, Mom. You totally sucked at preparing me for the real world. You deserve what you get from me."

Strangely, there was some truth in what Livvy said.

Genevieve shoved the ingredients across the counter in front of her adult daughter.

"This should be easy." She pulled out a wine glass and paused. "I like to have a glass of wine while I cook. Would you like one?"

Livvy's jaw hung slack.

"I'll go ahead and get some for both of us, in case you change your mind." There was a bottle of Pinot Grigio in the wine fridge. It should be light enough for immature taste buds. She poured two glasses and set one in front of Livvy. "So, get the large cutting knife and a board. The boards are kept in that slender cabinet there." She pointed as she sat on a stool across from Livvy.

Olivia found the right knife and pulled out a large cutting board.

"OK then." Genevieve found it hard not to grin. "First, you'll need to cut up that processed cheese into cubes." It wasn't the most nutritious thing in the world, but if Livvy could make queso, she'd probably never starve. And if she learned to appreciate decent wine and how to drink it responsibly, well, maybe she'd never be one of those college girls who binge drank and passed out in fraternity houses.

Dee

Just the occasional vocal direction from the GPS app kept Dee company, telling her where to turn and when until she was on familiar turf. Cooper didn't deserve to be left like that. She felt bad about that, but she also knew she couldn't be with him, couldn't be with anyone, until she figured this out.

This thing, whatever it was, was ready to come through. And when it did, she was sure, she'd be…better in some way. Healed?

It'd been so comfortable with him, so comfortable just now, it loosened up whatever it was in her head that kept the bad shit blocked.

Oh, maybe she should have stayed.

No. What if she had a breakdown? It got so hard figuring out what was real. Figuring out that...that...

That what?

That there was music, Bowie, that damn *John, We're Only Dancing* song playing. Her father had it on. That's what...that's what someone said. "Daddy is listening to music."

Mom was laughing.

Holy fuck! Her mother was laughing on the other side of the light. That sliver of light that kept coming to her led to music and laughter. Her mother for sure…but who else? It couldn't have been her father. Why did she think that?

Her chest ached, like a dirty shovel had rammed through it. She had to stop the car. Had to pull over to the side of the road. Clutching the steering wheel, she wheezed, tried to breathe, tried to get that fucking ache to ease up.

What was Mom laughing at?

Dee was so scared. She was fucking terrified while her mother, that smothering, over-protective, controlling woman, was out there laughing?

Gasping, choking, coughing...she tried to breathe.

That couldn't be right. Mom wouldn't do that…she didn't know. What didn't she know?

And Mom couldn't have been with her father, laughing.

Oh God! Was Mom sleeping with Brett's Dad?

Finally, her breath came in clearer. She had to call Brett. He had the answer. She would make him tell her whether or not he wanted to. He had to. She put the Clash on her phone, turned the volume up as far as it would go, and went home.

"So, there's this guy," she told Brett. A tall vodka-tonic with no lime because she didn't have any, clenched in her fist. She sat in the middle of her bed, cross-legged, with the photographs spread around her. "We weren't a thing, you know? Until he said he wanted to be a thing. And I, I wanted to be a thing, too. So, like, we met for drinks tonight, we were dancing in this dive bar, and I realized…"

"Realized?" Brett's voice was quiet. Like he didn't want anyone to hear him. Was Granddad close?

"Just, I was so relaxed with him. Safe. And…" She squeezed into a tighter ball, sipped her vodka. "So, um, lately, I've been getting these, these things. I thought they were hallucinations, but my shrink helped me realize that, actually, they might be memories."

"Dee Dee…"

"Nothing is clear, but like bits and pieces…like when I'm super relaxed, about to fall asleep or wake up. Or like when I'm feeling some kind of emotion, others want to come in so bad that my brain seems to let down its guard." *Holy hell! That made so much sense. Aisling would be so interested.*

"And?"

And what? Oh! "And tonight, I just left Cooper on the dance floor because a memory or something was coming to me. Brett! I hate this! Something is almost within reach of me remembering it."

"You sure you want to remember?"

"I think I just fucked up the one relationship that would actually be, like, real or something. We were dancing. And this, this thing kind of took over my brain. It happens when it gets really dark at night, too, and I can't control what my brain might think, and I get really scared. So I have to create or whatever. But…but, I think it's a memory coming through, not just my imagination. And I think maybe it has to do with the fire, the accident. But I don't know why or what it is."

It was very quiet for a long while, then eventually Brett cleared his throat. "I know what it is, Dee Dee."

"I knew it." She stared at her chipped toenail polish. Probably a good thing she couldn't find her other flip-flop.

"I know why you get so scared."

Christ! How could she forget what they were talking about?

"Why?"

"What stage you at?"

She looked at her glass. "Not even close to one, yet."

"Take a shot."

"That bad?"

"Worse."

Fuck. She climbed out of her photo-covered bed, lunged over piles of dirty clothes and…just shit. *What the hell was all over the floor?*

In the kitchen, her Tito's vodka bottle was pretty far gone in the freezer. There was more vodka in the pantry, a higher-end bottle she was saving for a special occasion. She hoped the Tito's would be enough to get her through the evening. She'd prefer to keep the special occasion bottle for something, well, special.

"Bottoms up." She shivered against the burn going down from her shot. "Not sure this is a good idea."

"It's never a good idea, but it does make things easier."

There was nowhere to sit. Even that awful wingback chair was piled with a little of everything. Clothes, trash, all those stupid supply catalogs that kept coming in the mail even though she bought everything online, when Mom wasn't buying.

"Dee Dee?"

"Huh?" she settled into a chair at the dinette.

"Do you know why I'm at Grandad's?"

"He said he was keeping an eye on you."

"Yeah, well…"

"Why does he have to?"

"He didn't tell you?"

"No. Just said you had some demons to slay."

"Huh." Sounded like Brett took a sip of something. "You should have made him tell you."

"Tell me what?"

"Why they're all afraid of me talking to you. They think I'll tell you what happened. Tell you why we're, why you and me, are so fucked up."

Her leg bounced up and down, and a thumb drummed the tabletop. She should be creating something. That's what was missing from this call. She clicked the phone onto speaker, tucked it under a bra strap, and headed toward the supplies under the whiteboard. "Do you know why?"

"Yeah…Fuck, yeah."

Dee opened a drawer, pulled out a packet of sandpaper. She'd sand the gloss off the table, begin prepping it for whatever she'd do with it next. That was like a metaphor for how she felt right then. This call was going to strip off her outer shell, expose whatever was underneath. Her life was going to change somehow. Could she handle that?

Hell, it's not like she was really handling her life now.

"Tell me about the demons, Brett."

Some kind of sound broke through the other end of the line. "Brett?"

"I'm so sorry, Dee Dee!" He was crying.

"Listen!" The shot hit. Sand! She needed to sand that gloss off the table, stay focused. "I'm not, I'm not trying to hurt you. I just need—"

"Don't be sorry. I deserve it." He was breaking down. "It's all my fault."

"What is your fault?" She sanded, back and forth. "What—"

"So, I need to know, Dee Dee. I need to know that you, you can move on."

"Move on from what?" But she knew as she sanded back and forth, Brett was about to tell her about whatever was in the darkness, whatever was happening when that stupid song was playing. Static built up in her ears. Keep sanding. Breathe.

"I need to know, after I tell you, that it was worthwhile for you to know. That it will, it will give you peace. Even if you can't forgive me."

The static continued. She sanded back and forth. He had saved her. No one told her that. She just knew that. Did she make it up? She paused to blow the sanded dust away, but her breath wasn't strong enough. Why wouldn't she forgive him? Did he hurt her? Did he—

"Did you kill my father?" A tear landed on the sanded wood. A dark spot in the dry, pale yellow.

"Oh God, No! Dee! I didn't!" His voice was thick. "But…I…I made it happen."

Keep breathing. Keep breathing. Focus. Back and forth. Back and forth with the sandpaper. Static whooshed in her ears. The table blurred. *Click.* A thin stream of light flared and widened as it crossed the floor. The rest of the room was so dark. So dark. "Who…were you in the bedroom with me?" She wasn't alone. Someone had opened the door, came into…into…"I was in a dark room. In bed. Someone came in. Was that you?"

Brett's sobs shot through the phone. "No. Dee Dee. I'm so sorry!

It wasn't me."

The whooshing became a roar; her eyes clouded over. She couldn't pass out! Though she could barely breathe. She scooted her chair back, dropped her head between her knees. Her voice faltered. "Who was it?"

"My father."

The light…she watched it grow wider as it came to her bed, crossed the corner. Then it was dark again; he blocked it. "Dee Dee. Shhh, baby."

Jesus. She dropped to the floor, almost wanting to pass out now. Reached for the vodka bottle, drank.

Fuck! She struggled to sit upright, leaned her forehead against the chair. He told her to be a good girl. That they were going outside for a little bit. But it was night. She wheezed. Breathe! Inhale, one, two, one. "Fuck! Brett! Talk!" Another swig. "What did he do to me?"

"He was there 'cause he saw us."

Be a good girl Dee Dee. His voice, his voice. She heard it. She tried to shake it out of her head. He wanted her to be quiet. He put his hand over her mouth as he carried her out of her room. Mom and Dad were in the other room. Mom was laughing. Music, Bowie was playing. Dad? How was that…

Brett's voice came in. "He knew we'd been playing with the dolls."

"What?"

He picked her up. He was so big. She was so small, so powerless, so weak. She hated feeling so weak.

Brett kept talking. She heard his voice, coming to her from someplace farther away than Georgia. Images came to her. He told her about the dock house that was over the lake. How his father, Uncle Wade, had been dealing in black market artifacts. They'd found some Egyptian figurines they thought looked like funny dolls and had been playing with them on the dock. They sent some swimming and threw them in the water.

She wasn't sure if she was conscious. She could hear the laughing. They were playing Bowie and laughing.

"And he took you from your room. I saw him. I looked out my door. He carried you, with his hand over your mouth. You…you were kicking." Brett cried.

His hand was so big. It hurt her. She wriggled against him, but the more she wriggled, the harder he held her.

"He took you out to the dock house. I snuck out and followed…Dee Dee! I'm so sorry!"

Under the tiny dinette, Dee curled up in a ball. "Keep talking, please." But the images came in clearer. Brett didn't need to tell her. She saw the dock house. She saw Uncle Wade pacing in the lantern light.

He was so mad. Or maybe scared. "They're coming, Dee Dee! Where are they?" he kept asking her. She had no idea what he meant, just stood there, in her nightie, confused. "Please, Dee Dee! The ushabtis! You and Brett were playing with them!"

"No." She shook her head at him. Uncle Wade was confused. "We played with some dolls."

"Dolls?" He stopped, stared hard at her. "Where are they?"

That's when she realized they'd been playing where they weren't supposed to. They weren't allowed in the dock house by themselves. They weren't allowed by the lake by themselves. But they went. They often found all kinds of things to play with there. Once there were shiny rocks, Dee now knew were precious gems— probably stolen precious gems. The dark side of the art and antiquities business.

But back then, she couldn't tell Uncle Wade about them being there. She couldn't say anything.

"I'm a dead man, Dee Dee. They're coming for them. Where are they?"

Uncle Wade looked so scared. She explained the dolls went

swimming.

He rounded on her, screamed at her. "In the lake?"

She fell back, crying. She'd never seen him so angry! His eyes were so big in the lantern light. Was he going to hit her?

"Shhh. It's OK. Uncle Wade didn't mean to make you cry." He ran around the dock house, putting things in his pockets. But she was still scared. Still crying, huddled on the floor. He got a gun! He had a gun and was talking to himself. "I'm a dead man. I'm a dead man."

She cried harder. What was wrong with Uncle Wade?

He picked her up, sat on something with her on his lap, and rocked back and forth. "I'm sorry, baby. Shhh. I know you didn't know any better." He kept rocking. "Please stop crying." But she couldn't, she was too scared. Uncle Wade wiped her face with her nightgown. "Listen baby, you have to go now. They're coming. You go on up to the house, and you promise me you'll never tell anyone about this. OK?"

She shook her head, clung to him. She couldn't go back to the house. It was dark outside. She was barefoot. She cried harder.

"Shh." His hand was over her mouth again. Footsteps thumped up the dock. "They're coming for me. You gotta hide." He tried to pull her off. She clung harder.

A man burst into the house.

A loud popping sound came from Uncle Wade's gun.

"My daddy shot yours." Brett's voice was so low, it was like he was talking in her head. "He killed him."

"My…how is that possible?" Was this conversation real? Was she dreaming?

But she remembered this now. Her father had blood coming out of his head. His pretty curly blond hair was all ruined. She ran to him. She wanted to clean it all up.

But Granddad barked at Brett to get her.

"Granddad?" She wasn't sure if she said it out loud, but Brett answered.

"I brought him and your Daddy to the dock house."

"My father—that's not possible."

"Your father didn't die before you were born, Dee." Brett was sobbing. "He died because my father killed him. And he killed him, because I told him to go out to the dock house. He killed him because I showed you the shit Daddy was smuggling."

Dee had to drink more. She wasn't able to process this. She really wanted to black out. She wished this conversation had never started. How could they all keep such a secret from her?

But Brett kept talking.

"Everyone was kinda stunned and didn't move for a second." He sounded as if he were panting. "But then my father, I guess he realized what he'd done, he…he put the gun to his own head and…" he lost control. Bawled through the other end of the phone.

He didn't need to tell her anymore. Dee remembered it, clearly. The horror of Uncle Wade falling down, knocking the lantern over.

A fire started.

Then an explosion.

Maxine

Oh, Max! The place is...just...just..." Lauren spun in a circle, her hands on her cheeks. "This is...it's...Well, Wilde once said, 'The work of art is to dominate the spectator.' You are certainly dominating me! I'm speechless. It's just superb!"

"Lauren!" Max tried not to laugh. "Are you crying?"

Lauren nodded. Wiped her eyes. "I'm just so proud of my girls!"

"*Your* girls?" Genevieve stood in the front window, hanging a bird feeder made from a Rare Bird gin bottle.

"Max's mother and I have known each other since the girls were little." Lauren shuffled through her purse for a tissue. "We've been thick as thieves ever since." She blew her nose as she wandered through the store talking to Genevieve. Everyone was Lauren's friend—instant lambs in the fold. "Our girls bonded. We bonded. When Kaz and I started dating, I told him he had to meet with Kathleen's approval before—aaack! *That clock is gorgeous!*" Lauren pointed to the blue Wedgewood china plate clock.

"And it's for you, Lauren." Maxine opened the step ladder they kept folded in the framing station and climbed up. "See?" She pulled the clock off the wall and handed it down. "Dee left a note on it for you."

"I love it!" Lauren ran her hand over the white bas-relief images. "That was sweet of her. See Genevieve?" She twisted around to show Genevieve the note. "That's why you cherry-pick what to get upset about with your daughter. Focus more on what you love, and you'll get more of that from them."

Mama and Lauren, always talking about focusing. Maxine climbed down, thinking about the number of times Mama had told her to just focus on what she wanted—as if she always knew what she wanted.

"Does that work with every teenage girl?" Genevieve's face looked so hopeful, it was obvious she wanted to buy into whatever Lauren was selling.

"Absolutely!"

"All daughters?"

"Every one of them."

"We have a box for that in the back." Max took the clock from Lauren. Sounded like Genevieve and her daughter were having trouble. It was startling how very few girls got along with their mothers. What if she had a girl? Could she have the patience of Lauren and Mama with her daughter? Could she handle a little girl as wild and willful as Dee was? A teen as sneaky as both she and Dee were—lying about what they were doing and with whom? And what would she do when her adult daughter marries a man she didn't love?

But would she be any better with a boy?

"Sweetheart?" Lauren was by her side. "Is Dee OK? Why isn't she here?"

"She's fine. She'll be in later." She pulled out a box. "She opened yesterday. So, I came in early today. Here." She held out the box. "I think this is a good size for your clock."

Lauren's brow had that look it does when she tries to frown, but Botox doesn't allow enough movement. "What about you?" She took the boxed clock, but still had that weird look pointed toward Maxine. "Kaz mentioned you were having problems with Dane. I don't want to pry, but, you know, I worry about my girls. Are you all right?"

Max was pregnant. Something she had wanted terribly. That was more than all right...so far. The store was off to a fabulous start. That was another all-right thing. But the steadfast-and-true marriage she thought she had was growing weaker by the minute. Ugh! She was crying again.

Lauren pulled her into a tight hug and let Maxine cry into her shoulder. "Whatever it is, we'll get through it. I promise."

Max pulled away and wiped her face with her hands. If she was going to cry this much while pregnant, she was going to have to start carrying tissues with her.

"So..." Lauren stared hard into her eyes.

"So, I'm pregnant."

Lauren morphed into one of those three-D animation characters—her face bright, eyes shiny, hope emanating from her. "I think I heard you say something you didn't really."

"You heard me right." Max grinned through her tears. "I'm pregnant."

Once again, Max was crushed in a hug. "Oh my God! This is so wonderful! So amazing! How far along are you? Do you know if it's a boy or a girl? When can we go shopping?"

Max smiled into Lauren's shoulder. "About ten weeks. I don't know yet. And no shopping until..." She pulled back from the hug. "Until it feels safe to do so."

"I understand." Lauren nodded. "But you do realize Kathleen and I will be starting a Pinterest just for—"

"Do whatever you want." Max took her hands. "Just, um, I haven't told Dane yet."

"No?"

"No. I told Mama she couldn't tell you until I told him, but...I don't know. I needed to tell you."

"I'm so glad you did! Who else knows?"

"Well, Dee, of course. Hayleigh, Kaz—"

"You told Kaz before me?"

"It was part of the Dane conversation."

"Well, I guess I can forgive you. But him! He didn't tell me *that!*"

"I begged him not to. It's so early."

"I guess I should appreciate that he keeps his word, but, anyone else?"

"Genevieve knows."

"I'm after Genevieve?"

"Well, she kind of guessed when I had morning sickness in the store."

"Ah, then you're forgiven."

"Lauren, you will be another grandmother for this little one, I promise you. Just you and Mama."

"And Dane's mother."

"Well, yes, I guess."

Dee

That wasn't an alarm. That was someone calling.

Dee opened her eyes, didn't quite know where she was. A hard floor pressed against her cheek. Her body curved around chair legs.

What the fuck?

Her phone silenced. She rolled over, as best she could in the cramped space, and blinked at the underside of her dinette table.

Had she slept down here?

The empty Tito's vodka bottle lay on its side next to her. No sign of a glass.

Must have passed out.

A voicemail notification sounded on her phone. She should probably see who it was.

It was so hard to roll back over. Maybe it could wait.

But this wasn't comfortable.

Like an injured and exhausted football player knowing if he could just go one more yard, they'd win the championship, she managed to get the mammoth weight of her body to roll back to her side and propped on one elbow while she reached for her phone.

Evan.

What the actual fuck? That wasn't worth the effort. Fucking shit tried to keep her in the dark.

The dark. Right, she was down there 'cause this was where she...Brett's call came back to her in Technicolor, or maybe it was Dolby sound. Whatever, she realized she was down there, under the dinette, because that's where she faced her demons last night. That was a good phrase, Granddad. Thank you.

She had almost all the puzzle pieces put together. Her father hadn't died before she was born. She'd spent five good years with the man. Uncle Wade had wigged out thinking he couldn't provide the black-market artifacts he'd promised someone, mistook her father running into the dock house for one of the goons looking for them, and shot him. When he'd realized what he'd done, he shot himself.

The fire, the explosion, was because the lantern caught something on fire when it was knocked over, and one thing led to another. "No one knows for sure," Brett had said. But there'd been several gas and oil cans in there for the boat and gardening equipment. The authorities believed one had spilled, started a big enough blaze to make others explode.

A beam had fallen on her, knocked her into the water. Brett had saved her. So she'd remembered that correctly. He was just seven years old and had jumped into a dark lake at night to save her. Granddad, too, apparently, but Brett was the one who'd found her.

"I'll take care of it." The memory was sharp. That was the part Brett wasn't sure about. But that's because he wasn't there. Dee knew that now. Before she'd woken up in the hospital, she'd heard voices.

"I'll take care of it," Granddad had said. "No one will ever need to know the truth about this." He was talking about what had happened to Deirdre.

So the question now was: why was that necessary?

On all fours, she crawled out from under the table, rested, kneeling against a chair, as she caught her breath, and let the pounding headache abate a little.

Hangovers just sucked. She really should drink less.

Her phone rang again.

For fuck's sake. She'd left it on the floor. Like she had the energy and ability to get back down there that easily?

Once more, it quieted before she got to it. This time it was Hope, but no voicemail.

Fuck them both. Evan had gone through the photographs. Probably had taken out all of Brett's father and her Dad because he was part of the secret-keeping.

She just had one final piece, and the puzzle would be complete. Why hadn't anyone ever told her?

Brett had gotten so upset last night. Just weeping. All he wanted, and he wanted it desperately, was to make sure she could forgive him. Of course, she could. He was just a kid. Why would anyone be angry with him? He was so upset; she didn't want to push why he had never said anything until now.

She'd made sure he was as OK as he could be, and then finished off the vodka. She just wanted to black out, not think about anything anymore. At least for a little while.

"Let the thinking begin."

Oh, but that hurt her head.

There was some orange juice in the refrigerator. It was past its best-by date, but it didn't look green or smell bad. She drank from the carton. Sucked the whole thing down. The trash was too full, so she threw the carton into the kitchen sink.

Shit. She still needed to clean.

When she felt better.

She stumbled over to the whiteboard, wrote CALL GRANDDAD in black over the fire image, then hit the shower. She sat on the tub floor until all the hot water ran out.

Mom had called while she was in the shower.

Dee hoped she was worried sick. Maybe she'd get an ulcer if Dee didn't return the call. She deserved it. Why had she kept Dee's father from her? Five years!

God, she was fucking hungry.

There was no leftover charcuterie. The box of stale crackers was empty on the counter. Mrs. D's ice cream was gone, too. Wasn't sure she had the strength to go to Jhansi's, yet...peanut butter it was. By the spoon, while she waited for the coffee to brew.

She needed to check on Brett.

The whiteboard told her to call her grandfather. So she did that.

"Hello, Deirdre." His southern baritone seemed to hint that it was aware of more evil in the world than it should know about. He'd always sounded that way to her; she just never put words to it before. But yeah, he sounded like he knew a terrible sadness always lurked nearby.

Or maybe she just wanted him to be that human.

She sat in her chair on her tiny porch, coffee cup on the wine crate set on its end, staring at the glaring white steps that she still needed to do something about.

There was so much she'd been ignoring. She needed to pull her shit together.

Maybe now she could.

"So, um, Granddad..." How to begin this conversation? "Have you seen Brett this morning?" Or maybe afternoon. Dee really wasn't sure.

"He's down working with a new horse. Doing a damn good job breaking him."

"Good. Good. Um, how was he?"

Granddad took his time answering. "About normal, I suppose. Maybe a little quieter. Why?"

"Well, we um, late last night, we had a long talk."

God, but the man took the phrase *think before you speak* way too seriously. After a glacial ice floe sailed from Greenland to the equator, he finally replied. "What about?"

Dee sipped her coffee. Christ, this was hard. "About what...what happened to us."

"I'm sorry, Dierdre."

Tears choked her.

"If there was anything God ever gave me the power to change..." His voice was as quiet as rain in the distance. "...I'd go back in time and make it impossible for what happened to have happened."

She still couldn't talk.

"But I gave up on God a long time ago." He said a little louder. "So, how are you? You gonna be all right?"

"I'm working on it." Finally, words! "Um, I, I just want to know, why, um, why didn't anyone tell me? Why did they keep my father a secret from me?"

"I made a deal with your mother. I didn't want Mimi to know the extent of it. She just thinks, thought, her sons were out at the dock house, and an explosion happened that killed them both. That you heard it and ran out to see what was going on, and somehow got hurt. That was bad enough for her. I didn't want her to hurt any more than that. If I'd told her what her own son had...Well, your mother agreed to keep that secret from Mimi, as long as no one here told you about it. "

"So, Brett..." Brett had been keeping a secret from the two

females who loved him most, and who he loved most, since he was just a little kid.

He'd been blaming himself for all those years. Blaming himself for…for something that was actually her fault. She should have run when Uncle Wade told her to go. Her father would still be alive if she'd just gone back to the house and let Uncle Wade deal with his buyer.

Genevieve

What was she going to do tomorrow? Genevieve replaced the punk rocker garden gnome she'd just sold with a lamp made out of a red-sequined thigh-high boot in the front window. It's funny how quickly this strange store had become the place where she longed to be all the time.

Yet they were closed tomorrow. She'd have to spend the day at home, possibly with Olivia. She wasn't sure if the queso lesson had meant anything to Livvy. The girl made it, silently following orders, then took her wine glass and food into the den, without looking back at Genevieve or inviting her to follow. Genevieve longed to ask her if she'd had fun earlier. It was odd that Livvy was home so early on a Saturday night. She hoped she wasn't having friend problems. And if she was, she hoped she'd reach out to Genevieve for advice.

"God! Sorry I'm so late." Dee came through the door that led up to her apartment. Her feral hair was held back from her face with a plastic headband and splayed out like a lion's mane. "Max just texted you needed me?"

"Ye-es." Good God! She was a wreck! A red-and-black flannel shirt, mis-buttoned by one over black leggings, paired with black combat boots. It had to be about ninety-five degrees outside. And Genevieve couldn't decide whether she needed makeup to cover the bags under her eyes, whether her eyeliner from last night was smeared there, or maybe it was a bit of both. Once again, Genevieve couldn't help but compare Dee Dee to what she assumed a heroin addict would look like.

"What's going on?" she blinked at Genevieve.

"Well, Hayleigh called to say she'd ordered some refreshments for us to have on hand, but she was still involved with her kids. So Max ran out to pick up the food. We've had a steady stream of people in and out and…"

Dee's head bobbed as she wandered away from her. Thankfully, no one was in, but oh no. Now there was a couple.

"Can I help you?" Genevieve smiled at them, praying Dee would stay in the back.

"I think we need her." The gentleman pointed toward Dee. "Excuse me?"

She turned toward them.

"I was in yesterday." He held up a paper bag. "This is the bottle I told you about."

Dee Dee did that slow blinking thing at him. Oh, why wasn't Genevieve here yesterday? She could help her remember.

"Right." The bobbing turned to definite nodding. "Let's take it to the back, to the glass station."

Genevieve followed. She stayed in the doorway so she could still keep an eye on the front area. Dee's phone rang. *Did she really just pull it out of her bra? She did!* She put it back without answering it.

"Have a seat." Dee pointed to the class table. "Let's see what you have here." She sat opposite them, took the bag, and gently dumped out the contents. Clearly, it had been a red bottle at one time, but now it was in several parts.

"I used SuperGlue," the woman said. "I know it's silly, but it has sentimental value."

Dee's phone rang again. Once more, she pulled it from her bra and looked at the screen. This time, when it silenced, she didn't put it back where she found it, thank God. Instead she stood. She looked around, then approached the back table where she used the torches. She set the phone down and...Genevieve couldn't figure out what she was doing. Dee pulled out a few large metal tools, eventually chose a heavy hammer, bounced it a few times in her hand, as if practicing pounding. Then, in one fast movement, she swung the hammer behind her, wound her arm over her head, and slammed it down on the phone, shattering the screen. She swept it into a trash can and returned to the class table.

Genevieve couldn't speak. The couple didn't seem to be able to, either.

"So, you're thinking beads?" Dee asked.

The couple looked at each other, mouths open, eyes wide. The man shrugged his shoulders and turned toward Dee. "I…thought…maybe it would be cool to have some kind of jewelry from it for my wife."

Dee held a piece of the bottle up to the light. "I can do that. Thinking anything in particular? Plain round beads? Heart shape, since it's red and all? Maybe a mixture?"

"You can really do that?" the woman asked.

"Of course." Dee stood again, this time to retrieve some paper and a few colored pencils. "It's not an instant thing. I'll have to melt the glass to form the beaded shapes. Then they'll need to slowly cool. We call it annealing. That's what takes the longest time. If we rush the cooling, the glass's internal structure weakens, and the beads will break more easily. I guess you could say if they got stressed, they'd shatter. And then there won't be anything to do with them but sweep them into a trash can." She nodded to the can where she'd just dumped her cell.

Oh no. The store phone was ringing. But it seemed like Dee was doing OK. Genevieve answered.

"It's really important I speak to Dee." Lauren was on the other end.

"She's with some customers, let me see." Genevieve took the receiver with her to the back room. "Dee Dee, it's your mom. Says it's important."

Dee didn't look up from whatever she was sketching. "Oh, I'm not speaking to her right now."

"I'm sorry, Lauren." Genevieve stared at Dee. "Dee can't come to the phone right now, can I—"

"No!" Dee's head shot up. She glared at Genevieve. "That's not right. I could come to the phone, but I won't. I'm not speaking to her."

Genevieve realized it was her turn to blink at Dee. "What, what do you want me to tell her?"

"Whatever you want. Tell her to go fuck herself for all I care."

"Dee!" How could she speak like that?

"Use a euphemism, Genevieve. Again, I really don't care." Dee spun the paper around to show the couple. "So, what about something like this?"

"Oh, Lauren." Genevieve walked back toward the front of the store, one hand holding the phone receiver to her ear, the other pressing that lump in her throat. "She's, um..."

"It's OK, Genevieve. I heard her."

"I'm so sorry."

"There's nothing for you to apologize for. I'll, um, I'll connect with her later tonight."

Genevieve didn't know what to do with herself. She wanted to storm into the back and ream Dee out, but when she got there, she realized she was still working with the clients.

"So, if you come in at the end of the week, it should be ready." Dee scribbled on the paper.

"Great, thank you!" The man stood first, then his wife, who

paused and seemed to want to say something.

"And I'm sorry." Dee stood too. "Didn't mean for you to witness some family drama."

"That's OK." The woman grinned, then the couple left the store, as if it really was OK that what just happened, happened.

"Dee!" Genevieve started as soon as they left, but then more people came in, and then Max returned with the refreshments. Dee ate most of them and seemed to mellow as time went by. Genevieve realized that if she was going to work successfully in the store, which she really wanted to, she was going to have to keep Dee supplied with food.

"Well." Max turned the closed sign over on the door. "Another successful day, I would think. So...I'll see you both on Tuesday? Unless you want to take Tuesday off, Genevieve?"

"I don't even want to take tomorrow off." Genevieve pulled her purse out from behind the sales counter.

Max laughed, hugged Dee. "I'm going to talk to Dane." Genevieve heard her whisper.

"Cool. Then, um, can you come by later? I think I need help figuring something out."

"Yes, girlfriend, that's exactly how you look!" Max grinned. "I don't know what time—"

"Doesn't matter. You know where I'll be."

"You can lock that door, Dee," Genevieve said after Max went out the front. Was she to hug Dee goodbye, too? "I'm going out the back."

"Cool." Dee slipped the lock in place, then seemed to follow Genevieve to the rear of the store. Surely the woman would apologize for her irrational behavior earlier. And surely, Genevieve would forgive her. They'd move on, just like with the swearing episode.

But Dee stopped at her glass working table and shuffled through papers. Seemed to be looking at the images she'd drawn.

Dee

"Will you really be able to make beads for that couple?" Genevieve still wasn't out the back door yet.

Dee pinned the sketches to a bulletin board near her workstation. "It should turn out pretty cool. I'll make a y-necklace, a few round beads, done rosary-style for the chain, then a heart dropping from the bottom.

"Sounds lovely!"

God how she wanted to hate Genevieve right now.

"Is there anything I can do for you Dee Dee?"

Great! She had to make it even harder. "No. But thank you for asking." Dee gently put the broken bottle pieces on a tray, heard Genevieve open the back door. "Actually, that's wrong."

"Yes?" Genevieve was right next to her.

Dee slid the tray onto a shelf by the bulletin board. She had to do this. Now. Secrets just sucked.

"I need you to listen to me. Take a confession. Are you ready?" She turned around to lean against her worktable.

"Sure, absolutely." Genevieve's hand pressed against her throat. Her eyes suggested she was terrified Dee would turn her torch on her.

"Your face isn't saying 'absolutely.' You know, you should never play poker."

"You're not the first person to tell me that." Genevieve covered her mouth with her hand, then moved it back to her throat. "Are you…are you firing me?"

"Good Christ!" Where the hell did that come from? "No! This has nothing to do with the store!"

Genevieve's body seemed to melt a little. "Oh, thank goodness. You have no idea how much I appreciate being here."

And that just made things even worse, again.

"Fuck. Well, here goes…" The headband irritated the back of her ears. She pulled it off. "So, um, I can't remember what all you know about what's going on with my brain or anything."

"I'm not sure what I know about you."

"Well, when I was very young, there was an accident that banged up my head. The attention problems, forgetfulness, whatever are from that accident. I have no memory of it. Was told about it afterward. I was a little kid, not quite six, and kind of woke up in a hospital. I couldn't talk because I couldn't remember how. They had to re-teach me everything I'd ever learned up to that point."

"How tragic!"

"So, um, anyway—" why did she start there? How does she get from there to—

"I can't imagine what your mother went through! She's so attached to you."

That shit? That's where she's going? "Right, well, yeah. So, like I've spent my life with weird little fears and issues. Every now and then, if I get super stressed, my brain kind of shuts down, and I can't think. I'll have panic attacks. And I'm plagued with nightmares."

Maybe that should be a was? Would she still be plagued?

"That sounds just awful! Dee Dee, I'm so sorry." Genevieve took a step toward her. Can't let that happen. Dee held up her hand to stop her from getting too close.

"I don't want to go down that rabbit hole, right now. Remember this is a confession."

"I don't understand." Genevieve did that stupid thing where she stood with her feet close together and her hands clasped in front of her. Like a fucking school kid hoping the teacher would tell her she was a good girl. Dee needed to get this done and over with.

"So, like, there was more to the story than anyone ever told me. I've spent years—almost thirty at this point—not knowing the truth about the first years of my life. Not knowing my uncle murdered my father."

"Oh my God!" Genevieve's face paled. "I, I'm so sorry! I don't know what to do or say here."

"You don't have to do or say anything. Surprisingly, I'm handling that news OK, right now. Which is fucking weird, I know. Maybe in a month I'll freak out or something, but right now, I'm kind of numb." *Yes, that was the word. Numb about that. Pissed off at the rest of the fucking world. But numb about that.*

Genevieve sucked on her lips and tilted her head. Dee wondered if her knees were locked and if she was about to keel over.

"I'm just telling you all that because it was all kept from me. And maybe, if I'd known, my life would have been different. More sane or something. But I wasn't given that option. So now, I dunno. I just don't wanna keep any secrets."

"You have a secret you want to tell me?"

Dee nodded. "So, like over a year ago, Kaz, my dad, stepdad, said a client of his wanted a mural." Nothing seemed to register on Genevieve's face. "I met the man at his office to talk about it. He wanted a griffin, based on his tattoo."

Genevieve raised her eyebrows. Maybe she was starting to get a hint.

"We had chemistry, you know. Like he made me laugh. I made him laugh. I drew up some designs and made an appointment to meet with him late on a Friday afternoon. Late last May. He was alone in his office."

"Oh my God. Don't tell me he raped you!" Genevieve finally collapsed onto a stool.

"No!" What the fuck? Is that what she thinks her husband was capable of? "He was actually asleep at his desk. I woke him up. He apologized, said he hadn't been sleeping well."

"Late May? Was this around Memorial Day?" Genevieve turned her eyes to the floor.

"Yes."

"Chris hates that holiday. Always has trouble sleeping around it, the Fourth, and, well, anyway." She continued staring at the floor. Dee wished she could read her mind.

"So, I told him about how I'm a pro at bad sleep and all. We traded barbs about how we both stay awake sometimes just to keep the ghosts away. I showed him my drawings for his wall. He really liked them and commissioned me."

Genevieve remained quiet.

"I did the mural, mostly in the evenings because that's when his business was slower. Some nights, he stayed late and watched me create. We'd eat pizza afterward. Then one night, a client had gifted him with a bottle of bourbon." Dee began pacing, pulled her hair up into a wad, and wished she had a band on her wrist to keep it back there.

"You had bourbon." Genevieve prompted her, though she continued to stare at the floor.

"We, um, well, um, things kind of got intimate in his office."

Genevieve nodded, but still didn't look at her.

"I knew he was married at the time, but also that he had started the process to get a divorce—that's why he was in Kaz's office when he saw my mural. He didn't want a relationship at the time. I didn't want a relationship because I totally suck at them. But we both agreed the sex was good, so we kind of had an agreement—Max called him my booty call."

"When are you going to say his name?" Genevieve finally made eye contact with her.

"I call him Cooper. That's how he introduced himself to me.

That's how Kaz referred to him."

Genevieve went mute again.

"And, and you call him Chris." Dee stopped walking.

"That's his first name."

"Yeah...um..." She hadn't thought this all the way through...what was she to say now?

"And he never spoke to you about his wife?" Why was there no expression on Genevieve's face?

"He called her Gen, which I thought was short for Jennifer."

"I see."

"And I never knew your last name."

Genevieve nodded.

"I didn't make any connections until he came in with, with—"

"My, *our* daughter. That explains why you were a little off that day." Genevieve nodded.

"Possibly. Sometimes I'm a little off for no reason."

Thank Christ, she smirked. "And that explains why he looked terrified."

"If it means anything to you," Dee walked closer to her. "When I realized who he was married to, I cut him off. Cold turkey."

"That does mean something to me. I'm not sure what." Genevieve stood up. "But, why are you telling me now?"

"Because every fucking person who claims they love me has been keeping my past a secret from me. And... and...maybe there was a reason. But it only fucked things up for me even more. I don't know what was really going on behind the walls in your house, but maybe knowing the truth makes things better for you?"

"It doesn't." Genevieve headed out the back door.

Maxine

Where was Dane? His car wasn't in the garage when Maxine pulled in her side. Where would he go on a Sunday night?

Probably somewhere with Jamaal. But wasn't he going back to Baltimore tonight with his mother?

She entered the house and instantly sought her favorite spot: the corner of an L-shaped sofa on the sunporch, where she watched the quiet backyard. A green expanse with one lone tree near the back right corner. She'd often envisioned a playset in the middle of the yard, a sandbox with a child-sized picnic table under the tree. That scene didn't come to her today. Nothing did. The yard remained a plain, healthy lawn. That was one of the things Dane prided himself on: a lush lawn. He was out there frequently with fertilizers, weed killers, pesticides.

She wouldn't want him doing that with a little one rolling around in the grass, though.

How long was she going to wait for him? A little too late, she realized she should have given him a warning that she was coming over. But he never went anywhere on a Sunday night.

Who was her husband?

"Hey!" his voice made her jump.

"Oh, hi." Where had he been? And 'hey' again? *Hey?*

"I didn't know you were going to be here." He sat on the sofa, not too close.

"I just realized I probably should have checked to see if it would be all right."

"It's still your house, Max. You don't have to check to see if it would be all right to be here."

She shifted to better study his unreadable face. Soon, the sun would be behind too many trees and houses, she'd barely be able to see him. "That was the wrong choice of words. I know I have the right. I guess, I should have called to be sure you'd be home. I assumed you'd be here. You seldom go anywhere on a Sunday night."

"Yeah. I just played a round of golf with my dad."

He knew how to play golf? He didn't even own any golf clubs.

"Been a long while since I did that." Dane seemed to read her mind. "But, I don't know. After spending a week with Jamaal, I wanted to spend some time with my old man."

"Getting pointers?" Was his dad a good father? Max had never really gotten to know her in-laws that much. They barely seemed interested in anything about her. In fact, his mother had rather pointedly made it clear that Maxine was beneath her husband. Of course, she didn't use actual words to say it, so when Max tried to talk to Dane about it afterward, he brushed it off on her being insecure around his rather domineering mother.

That was unkind of him to say, and it had pissed her off—yet another argument that just kind of faded after Max challenged him on it. She'd always felt she won it, though, because he never insisted she spend time with his mother again.

"Not really." Dane leaned over to tap her knee. "I don't know what to do here, Max. I really don't."

"What do you want?"

"Our old life back."

"That's not quite possible anymore."

"I know." He scooted closer. "So, we bought this big house with the idea that one day we'd fill it up with kids, remember that?"

Max nodded. "And now you have one. What kind of arrangements have you made with his mother?"

"Well, she's actually changing jobs. She landed a position with a fintech company in Philly."

"How convenient."

"Yeah." He totally missed the sarcasm in her voice. "So, she's going to have an attorney write up some papers to define custody."

Define custody?

"Then she'll send them to me, and I'll have an attorney look them over. I guess I'll ask Kaz. He does family law, right?"

"I guess that's convenient for you, too."

"I'm not sure if I'm picking up a negative tone in your voice, Max."

"Sorry, Dane. This is kind of hard for me." Didn't he get that, yet? "I'm hungry. Do you have any food?"

"There's leftover pizza in the fridge." He followed her into the kitchen. "But why don't we go out?"

"I don't want to go out." She removed the box from the fridge— he was already living like a bachelor: hadn't even put the leftovers in a storage container. There was half a pepperoni pie. She'd have heartburn, but it was from Vito's, so it'd be worth it. "This will do." She slid a few slices on a piece of aluminum foil to heat up in the toaster oven. He could fend for himself.

"Want some wine?" He removed two glasses from a cabinet.

Yes. "No. Just water for me, thanks."

God! Why was his face so unreadable? And why was she so angry? Surely, he could hear the noise as she breathed through her nostrils. When is he going to ask her how she's doing?

"Mom said Jamaal looks just like me when I was that age."

Is he all about Jamaal now? "Did she meet him or see his photo?"

"Met him. I took him over Friday afternoon. Didn't I tell you yesterday? That's when she said I was passive-aggressive with him?"

She could only nod.

"They seemed to hit it off better than he and I did."

She found a plate for her pizza and slammed the toaster oven door shut, unintentionally, maybe. "Dane, I really don't want to talk about Jamaal." She did intentionally take his normal place at the kitchen table.

At first, he didn't seem to know what to do with himself. He looked left, then right, as if expecting another table set to appear so he could take his rightful spot. But then he placed the glass of water in front of her and sat with his wine in a different chair.

"I guess you want to talk about us." He stared at her pizza.

"Only tangentially." She chewed, watching his face. It remained Dane, no swirling colors, no steely beams. Just Dane. And he looked tired.

"Only tangentially? There's that tone again."

"My tone?"

"I get it. You don't like that I have a kid with another woman."

"Correction: I don't like that you cheated on me, never told me about it, that you thought so lowly of me that you suspected me of using some of the people I love most in this world, and that you have known about this kid longer than the day you told me about him."

Dane sipped his wine. "Is that all?"

"Don't you think it's enough?"

"What am I supposed to do about it all, Max? That's what I want to know. I keep asking you what I'm supposed to do or say. But you don't tell me. Whatever it is, I want to give it to you so we can move on." He leaned forward, put his hand on hers. "Baby, I love you. I don't want to lose you over a stupid mistake I made eight years ago."

"That's the thing, Dane. You wouldn't be losing me over just that stupid mistake. Did you not hear the rest of what I said?"

"So, all I can do is apologize, which I have, haven't I?"

Max shook her head.

"Really?" He tilted his head, as if he couldn't quite believe what was happening.

"Really. 'I'm sorry' hasn't crossed your lips." She pulled her hand away, resumed eating that delicious pizza. "Try it now."

"Maxine, I'm sorry I, I messed up numerous times. I'm sorry about Jamaal. I'm sorry I doubted your intentions."

She waited a heartbeat. "And?"

"Was there more?" He may have meant the question in total

sincerity, but it only made her doubt his motivation for any of the apologies.

"There was the part about you knowing about Jamaal for a long time without telling me anything."

He sipped his wine again. Hesitating? He wasn't sorry for that?

"Max, I just wanted to line up my ducks, to know for sure what they wanted from me—"

She no longer wanted the second piece of pizza. She washed her last bite down, shoved the plate over to him. "That's not what I wanted to hear."

"It's the truth."

"And it sucks."

"Max—"

"Dane." She stood up, pushed her chair back, and leaned her hands on the table so she could put her face close to his. He wasn't escaping these words. "That just told me I can't trust you to be honest with me about anything until you're ready to be honest. So, here's how that feels. I've been keeping something from you for almost a week now."

"What is it?" His eyes remained locked on hers.

"I'm pregnant."

The bastard actually winced.

"How...what?"

Max turned away from him for a few heartbeats, reminded herself to play it cool. Facing him again, she explained the pregnancy tests at Mama's, and Dr. Paicurich confirming everything.

Dane's eye flashed. "How could you not tell me? Why wasn't I in the room with you and the doctor?"

"Seriously?"

"Don't you even want me to be a part of your life anymore?"

"Has everything always been about you, Dane?" Had she always coddled him, the way his mother did? Taken care of his needs so much that it was just normal and natural in his world that he didn't have to, nor did he have to take care of anyone else's?

"There's that tone again!"

"My tone?" Her voice was shrill in her own ears. There was no playing it cool, not with her hormones as wild as they've been lately. "My tone has nothing to do with this conversation." From somewhere, her cell phone dinged.

"I can't talk to you if you're going to sound so, so—"

"So what? So out of control? Too bad, Dane, because I'm barely able to hold myself together right now." Her cell began ringing. She'd left her purse in the mudroom, on the washer. Dane followed her in to get it.

Hayleigh? She answered. "Is everything all right?"

"No. Not really. Dee's not taking Mom's calls. Would you meet me at the store to let me into her apartment? It's kind of important."

"Absolutely. You know, she said she wanted me to come by, anyway. I'll be there in about ten minutes."

"You're leaving?" Dane's hand was on her arm.

"Dee needs me." She shook free.

"What about me?"

"Isn't it time you figure that out for yourself?"

Dee

What was that? Sounded like someone coming up the stairs. Quiet again. Maybe not. It was getting dark outside. She should probably turn on a light or something.

Dee reached for the hookah lamp. It wasn't there.

Right. It was somewhere out in the living room.

"Dee?"

"Max?" Of course. She'd asked her to come by. Couldn't remember why.

It wasn't only Maxine, but Hayleigh, too. Both came through her bedroom door. Hayleigh hit the switch on the wall, smacking her in the face with brightness.

"Christ! Is that necessary?" She shielded her eyes with a hand.

"Um, looks like it."

"I don't need a fucking lecture, H."

"Who's lecturing? I brought food."

Oh. Food could be good.

When Dee lowered her arm, she saw H and Max at the foot of her bed, staring at her. Clearly concerned about something. The photograph of her parents, Aunt Louise, and Brett's dad was in the center of her bed, facing toward her huddled form at the top, in front of the headboard, her feet tucked up tight close to her rear. The one picture of her by the lake with Mom and the man she now knew for certain was her father was in one hand, pressed against her chest, the other photographs were scattered on the floor somewhere.

"Can we help you in any way?" Max's face contorted into a frown.

"I'm OK, Max. Just, to use Dane's word, I'm processing stuff."

"What are you processing?" H used a foot to shove some dirty clothes out of the way on the floor, got closer, and put out a hand. "C'mon. You can't eat eggplant parm in bed."

She was right. The sauce could stain the sheets. Dee kept a grip on the photo as she let her kid sister help her out of bed.

H led her to the kitchen. She wore a top hat and a purple corset-looking bodice with a denim skirt. Rainbows spread across the back pockets over her ass. Her feet were clad in white bobby socks, and her trademark oxford shoes were white leather.

"What the hell are you wearing?"

"Isn't this hat fantastic?" H placed the container of eggplant parm on the table. She removed the hat and showed Dee and Max the inside. "Touch it! The lining is white velvet! Who would have thought to line a hat with white velvet?"

Dee ignored the velvet. Instead, she briefly wound one of H's curls around her finger. The hair was brown again, with pink tips in the kitchen light. God, how she loved her kid sister. "Someone who knew you would one day be born." She sat at the dinette.

H began opening and shutting drawers until she found three forks. "Well, you have to answer: what are you processing?"

Dee set the photo aside, safe from any potential drips, and pulled up the cardboard lid from the eggplant. "Demons."

"Um…how's that going?" Max sat across from her. H dropped some forks on the table, then popped up on a counter to sit.

The eggplant was awesome. Just the right amount of cheese. Dee closed her eyes and savored the flavor. "Life is pretty fucking cool if you can appreciate it." She opened her eyes in time to catch H and Max exchange worried glances. "In other words, this eggplant is amazing."

They didn't seem to know what to say. Apparently, they were waiting for her to continue.

"The demons, it turns out, was just one demon. My uncle." Another bite of the divine. Happy tendrils followed the food down her torso. She appeared to be the one carrying the conversation, so she continued. "As it turns out, that whole conspiracy thing, wasn't a conspiracy after all."

"No?" H jumped off the counter, opened the refrigerator.

"I'm out of wine." Dee wiped her face. "Water will have to do." There was still that insanely expensive vodka, but that had to be kept for something important.

"What about the conspiracy?" Max asked while H got water for them all from the tap.

"My family, at the request of my mother, withheld two important facts from me. One is that my uncle killed my father, then shot himself."

"What the...?" H seemed frozen.

Another bite of...it wouldn't be called nectar. That would be liquid, right? What did the gods eat? Ambrosia. Yes, this eggplant parmigiana was ambrosia.

"You said that as if it's no big deal." Max leaned back in her chair.

"Oh, I know it's a big deal. That's what I'm processing. Partly." Water cleansed the palate beautifully. The next bite was just as good as the first. "That's why I was staring at the picture on my bed. Like, when I recognized my dad in a photograph a couple days ago, I felt a connection to him. I felt like I knew him. I keep waiting to feel something from my uncle in that photo. But he just looks familiar."

"Maybe that's a good thing?" Max picked up a fork and took a bite. "Oh my God! This is amazing! Where did you get it, H?"

"Georgio's." H headed toward Dee's bedroom. "They're a new client." She came out and searched through Dee's art supplies until she found scissors. In the kitchen, she looked at the photo before showing it to Dee. "Is this the shit?" She pointed to Brett's dad.

Dee nodded, then watched her wise, old-soul sister in action. Wanting to tell her to stop but knowing whatever she was doing was the right thing, she remained quiet.

H carefully cut the photo in two, letting the half with Dee's parents fall to the table. "Got a lighter?" She started going through the drawers again, found one before Dee could answer her. Over the sink full of dirty dishes, she held the other half of the picture while she set it on fire. Before her fingers burned, she dropped it. She ran the water to rinse the ashes off the dishes and shit, and turned on the disposal to let it run for a few seconds.

"So, what happens now, Dee?" H forked out a chunk of eggplant.

"Life goes on, I guess." Dee swirled her fork in the pasta. "Wow! This marinara is damn good, too." She wiped her face with a paper towel. "Isn't that the thing about death? Life goes on whether or not you want it to."

"You do want it to, right?" H carved out another bite but didn't put it in her mouth.

"Of course." Would they ever stop thinking about that? She had been a fucked up, overmedicated teenager. Besides, she now owed somebody something. She had to pay for being responsible for her father's death. "Remember, I said there were two things Mom kept from me. That was just one."

"What's the other?" H continued to eat.

"My dad didn't die before I was born. That murder-suicide thing I just told you about happened in front my me."

The kitchen was so silent, Dee's head felt as if it was squeezing in on itself.

"That's not possible." H's mouth hung open in an O.

"Yes, it is. Brett told me, and Granddad confirmed it."

H let out a whistle.

"But why?" Max picked up the photo of Dee with her parents. "Is this…?"

"Yeah. That's my father, with me and Mom."

Again, silence while Hayleigh and Max stared at the photo.

The squeezing continued, and her breath came in short. "And it all happened because of me." She could only gasp. Dropped the fork, held her head in her hand. "How do I move past that?"

Someone's hand was on her back. Yeah. That's all they could do. That's all anyone could do. Because there was no undoing the horrible thing she did. She could have run away from her uncle. He'd told her to go...She could have run into the house...but she was too afraid to be barefoot in the grass at night. She was so fucking weak.

"Dee, that can't be right." H stroked the back of her head. "How old were you?"

"Five."

"You were a child." Max's hand was on her arm. "How—"

"My uncle told me to leave. He told me to get out of the dock house. But I wouldn't go." She looked up at Max, shook off H's hand. "It's too much for me to talk about right now. I can't…I'll talk to Aisling on Tuesday."

"Is there, like, an emergency number or something for her?" H patted her jacket pockets, pulled out a cell phone.

"It's not an emergency. And I seriously want to think on this for myself for a few minutes." Dee stood and went out to the living room.

At the whiteboard, she erased the fire, the puzzle piece, and the other clues.

"And don't fucking tell Mom anything about this."

"Um, Dee." Max was beside her again.

"I'm so pissed at her! Why didn't she tell me the truth?" She threw the eraser against the whiteboard. It bounced off and fell onto a wadded-up sheet on the floor.

"Dee, I don't know why she'd do that. But it's Mom! I'm sure she thought she was protecting you somehow." Was H really on her side?

"I deserved to know the truth!" She didn't mean to shout, but the words just flew out of her body. "My father didn't die until I was five years old. I had a relationship with the man."

"What good would it have done if you knew that? You don't remember him." Yes! She was on Mom's side!

And damnit! She didn't have an answer. What good if she knew?

Max and H did that god-damned thing where they looked at each other instead of her when they didn't understand her. They just didn't get it. And neither did she, really. But she really wanted to be alone to figure it out. "So, like, why did you guys both come, anyway?"

They exchanged another look.

"For fuck's sake! What?"

"So, um, Mom's been trying to call you." H took off her hat again, petted the inside.

"I'm not talking to her. I can't yet." Dee wondered if any eggplant parm was left. She headed back toward the kitchen.

"Well, um, the thing is..." Hayleigh stepped into her path.

"You both better fucking swear secrecy to me. Let *me* be the one to talk to Mom about all this. Don't give her time to mount a defensive."

"That's not the thing, Dee. It's your great aunt, Josie. She, um..."

This time, when H and Max looked at each other, Dee knew what they were thinking.

"Fuck. She died." That's why Evan was trying to get a hold of her. Shit! She should have answered the fucking phone at least once! "When?"

"I don't know. But the funeral is tomorrow."

Dee patted her bra, her pocketless leggings. Where is her phone? She stumbled over a boot in the chaos that was once a living room. "Where the hell...Oh, shit!" She turned toward Max and H. "I kind of killed my phone." At the whiteboard, she picked up a marker and hovered in the newly erased area. "When's the funeral and where?"

But then that buzzing entered her ears. Suddenly, so loud, her knees gave out. She collapsed to the floor. Gasp! Why's it so hard to breathe?!

Kneeling, rocking on the floor, the tears erupted. Josie! Gram! Daddy! They all kept leaving her. Max was here, though. H was here. One of them shoved a paper towel in her face. Eventually, she wiped her nose and almost caught her breath.

H was standing at the board, writing something.

"Want us to stay with you tonight?" Max held Dee against her.

That would be nice, but...where?

"Maybe you can stay at my place," Hayleigh suggested.

Dee sat up, blew her nose on the paper towel. No. She wasn't that fucking weak. Inhale, two, three. Exhale, two, three, four, five.

"Um, no. I..." Damn! That felt good. "That cry actually felt good. Wow! I had a feeling, and let it happen. Aisling will be so happy to hear it."

Max squeezed her in another hug. "I'll crash on your sofa. It can't be worse than the one I've been sleeping on at Mama's."

Dee's breath felt so clear, so free, so…nourishing. She finally got why some people said crying was cathartic. "Seriously, you don't have to. I have so much to do." She waved her arm through the space in front of her.

"You sure, Dee?" H plopped down on the floor with them.

"Yeah. Just gonna do some laundry. And, and, and…obviously, clean this place up."

"I don't want to leave you." H leaned too close to her face.

"I know this is selfish as shit." Max's eyes were wet. "But, I can't lose you, Dee."

"Jesus Christ! Trust me. I'm not going anywhere. I'm finally taking fucking control of...of something. Maybe my mind." Dee pulled them both into a hug, but she wanted to be alone. She wanted to prove to herself that she would be OK being alone. She had the fucking weight on her. She knew what the black blob was: guilt. It was her fault her father died. She had to figure out how to make amends, if that was at all possible. "I promise. I'll be OK."

Genevieve

Looked like Remy was playing basketball with someone in front of the garage. From a couple of doors down, Genevieve could see two people making a bobbing back-and-forth motion with a ball under the houselights. When she turned into the drive, she lit them up:

Remy and Chris.

Oh. The evening might get interesting.

They moved aside to let her drive past and into her side of the garage. Thank the gods Olivia's car was nowhere to be seen.

She parked, turned off the ignition, and hit the garage door button to close the door behind her. No need for either of them to come in and speak to her. Remy, of course, would be fine. But Chris...how long had he been cheating on her?

Inside, she headed straight to her office and opened her laptop. She'd been using the Excel spreadsheet for several years now to track everyone's whereabouts. Instead of overriding each week, she'd copy and paste the weeks one after the other, making changes as life went on. When she clicked the file open, in effect, she had details on every minute of every family member's life laid out in neat rectangular cells.

In Chris' column, she scrolled back to Memorial Day weekend the year before. Yes, that was the year Remy switched from soccer to rugby. Genevieve could recall googling orthopedists to put on speed dial, alongside the pediatric neurologists she had discovered during the soccer years as a "just in case."

Remy had a traveling soccer championship that Monday. Chris never showed up. He'd spent the weekend working "working." He was never around on Memorial Day, another holiday they couldn't spend with friends, so she hadn't been surprised. She just didn't realize he'd been sleeping at the office. Though she really did believe he had. That seemed in character. He never talked to her about emotional things. He said he didn't "do" the patriotic holidays; she never asked why.

Yet, he told a strange woman. Is that what chemistry will do for a couple? Did chemistry make people expose themselves to each other?

A shift appeared in the cells after that weekend. She'd used slanted lines to fill in when he came home much later than expected.

Must have been the pizza nights when he watched Dee Dee create. Genevieve was a little jealous. She would have loved to have that experience, to watch a whole mural come to life under Dee's hands.

Ha! Shouldn't she be jealous of Dee?

Instead, she was only mildly angry. But with whom?

Not with Dee.

Certainly, with Chris, but also…with herself.

Here was more proof she hadn't been managing as well as she thought. Remy was the only one in that house who seemed content with his life—the other three were pretty miserable. Chris had gone to see an attorney to file for a divorce over a year before she'd asked him for one. Why had he not gone through with it?

On the spreadsheet, she saw that Chris had started seeing a trainer in mid-June last year—on Monday and Wednesday mornings. He'd been unable to drive Remy to rugby camp those days.

Yet now that she thought about it, she had handled all the household finances and had never seen a bill for a trainer. It was possible that the company paid for it. Sometimes he used a company card for things, but would a trainer fall under a business expense? Or was he meeting up with Dee those mornings? She said she had problems sleeping. Maybe she'd just be going to bed at that hour?

Genevieve wasn't going to go there.

She had the car accident at the end of June. Everyone's schedule shifted then because she couldn't drive. And he'd moved into the guest room...permanently. She understood that now. His clothes were still in the closet and dresser in the master bedroom, and he showered in that bath—who wouldn't, though? She'd done an amazing job making a sanctuary in there. That was one of the benefits of keeping the house. She wouldn't have to replicate that. It was hard enough finding those Italian tiles once.

"Hey, Gen." Chris was at the door of the office, sweating. "This is kind of awkward." He took a few steps inside her office.

"Is this about Dee?"

His head twitched. "What?"

"What's awkward, Chris?"

"Remy asked me to buy him condoms."

"Seriously?" Genevieve knew her son had several girlfriends, but...

"He said he was too embarrassed to buy them." Chris shut the office door and sat his sweaty self in the leather chair on the opposite side of her desk. It was there more for decoration than use, but still...he was sweating! "I told him that if he were old enough to use a condom, he had to be man enough to buy them."

If only they had used a condom back in the day! But now, she did love her Olivia and Remy. She just didn't like them sometimes, well, with Livvy, it was most of the time.

"But, I was afraid he'd have sex without them, so I told him to buy them on Amazon. Just thought I'd let you know."

"In case they came, and I assumed they were for you?" There was no lump in her throat. How freeing that felt.

"Well..."

Good Lord! His underarm hair peeped out of his shirt sleeve when he rubbed the back of his neck. Like a nest of black caterpillars. Could he be any more disgusting?

"Dee Dee told me about you two." Genevieve relaxed into her sumptuous, gloved-leather executive chair. How powerful it felt sitting in that chair, behind that enormous desk. Was a ridiculous idea when the designer had suggested it, but now she felt lofty, powerful. In control.

Chris seemed to relax, too. "Wow. Well, I'd hoped the two of us would tell you together—"

"She's in a tough place right now."

"What do you mean?" Was that genuine concern on his face?

"I mean...No. You'll have to talk that over with her. You and I have some unfinished business."

"Gen, I swear to you. I was discreet."

She appreciated that, but, still. "You've been sleeping with her for over a year?"

"If you'd never have had the accident, we'd be divorced by now."

"So, this is my fault?" But that explained things.

"Christ!" He threw his hands in the air. "Did it ever occur to you that the world was not in a constant battle with you?"

"What?" Yes, he was saying this was all her fault.

"Everything that happens, Gen, you somehow see as an attack on you. Well, guess what? Sometimes a man meets a woman and falls in love with her, and it has *nothing* to do with you."

"You're in love with her?"

"Yes!" He bounced out of the chair, paced a half circle, and returned to sit in it. He loved Dee. She was such a mess. A wild mess. The total opposite of herself.

Well, that did rather make sense.

"Gen, yeah, at the beginning, I was just kind of hooking up with her. I really thought I was getting a divorce, and I guess I was...I don't know. Rebelling or something. But then you had the accident. I didn't want to make things worse for everyone, so I put a hold on the divorce, but by then..." He rested his elbows on his knees, looked at the floor for a couple of ticks of the clock, then met her eyes. "By then, I was in love with her."

"So, you were biding your time until I was better?" Well, that was gentlemanly of him. But then Olivia would have hated him more than her if she knew. No. Olivia would manage to blame his cheating on Genevieve.

"I swear to you, there has never been another woman."

She hadn't even considered that until now. "And I'm to believe that you became a cheater just a year ago?"

"Why do you think I'm on so many sports teams, Gen? The basketball league, pickleball team, flag football, the golf league—"

"You're in a golf league?"

"Twelve weeks a year—"

"On Tuesday afternoons?"

"Yes."

Genevieve nodded. It was labeled *Chris networking at the club* on her spreadsheet. "And that relates to you not cheating how?"

"I channeled all that energy into competing."

"Interesting."

"We were down to every other weekend, Gen. And you never seemed to, well, I never seemed to be doing whatever it was you would have wanted."

She had no idea what she would have wanted, but he seemed too athletic in bed for her tastes.

"You don't have to say anymore." Genevieve felt her neck. No lump. "Funny thing. I'd recently said to Brynn that if you had a lover on the side, I would appreciate that."

"Do you still feel that way?"

"I'm not sure."

Dee

Fuck. The more she tried to clean, the worse things seemed to get. It was just so hard to focus. Josie was dead. Had she said goodbye? That made two people, three counting her father, who she was close to, who died, and she never said goodbye.

What was she doing with the couch cushion in her hands? Oh, it should be on the couch, stupid!

She really needed her phone. She needed some music blasting. But it was a Sunday evening. All the stores where she could get a replacement were closed. Besides, she'd lost her key fob, again. And her purse. Where the hell was her purse? Had she left it at the bar with Cooper?

Sitting on the couch, she stared at her whiteboard. So many things to do. But she should probably call Brett. Tell him she was OK. Was it too late?

Shit! Why the fuck did she do that to her phone?

Mom! Fucking Mom!

She stormed to the whiteboard, erased the willow tree, the shoes. Cooper with strings was there.

Did she fuck that up, too?

Had he been trying to call her? She had to get a new phone first thing in the morning. Before going to Josie's funeral—she could say goodbye there, right?

Christ! She was crying, and of course, no tissues in sight. She used her T-shirt to wipe her face.

By midnight, according to the clock on the microwave, she'd managed to get all three cushions on the sofa, the linens that she'd used on the floor in the wash, which is how she finally found that other flipflop. But still no key fob, no purse.

She had also gathered the empty vodka and wine bottles. She should rinse them out and take them downstairs. People had bought a lot of the things she'd made from bottles, right? She should salvage these.

Downstairs, in the back room, she set the bottles on a shelf with others. So many clear ones and shades of yellow and green. The occasional blue. If only someone had created pink bottles for rosé wine, maybe then she'd have the right pink for the bougainvillea. She had mastered the shape of the flower, just wasn't satisfied with the color. Though one of the green bottles would make a great, vining stem...She held it up to the light, set it on her worktable. After scoring it with a razor, she placed the bottle in a paper bag, banged it against the table.

Oh, but wait! She should make those beads for that necklace first. She stared at the sketch. Yeah. She could do that tonight. Should do that tonight, in fact, to be sure it was done by whenever she said it would be done by.

Should have written the deadline on the sketch.

Soon, with hair secured in a few ties, wearing a filthy Queens of the Stone Age concert T-shirt, and feet stuffed into Dr. Martens, not because she couldn't find her flipflops again (because she remembered to put them beside each other by the door) but because she was always safety minded, thank you very much, Mom, you fucking control freak, you don't need to tell her to be careful!

Dee soaked the broken red bottle in a shallow bowl of acetone. The glue loosened, so she could pull it off. She rinsed the glass clean in the sink. Rolled it in paper towels to absorb any moisture.

Whssshhhhh...the oxygen and propane torch lit.

Yeah, she adjusted her safety goggles. 'Cause this is what she did. Fire had nothing on her. She controlled that bitch. She was the master, maven, whatever the fuck you called females in control.

Dominatrix maybe? Nah, the clothes looked uncomfortable.

Whatever, fire yielded to her. *She* controlled it. *She* commanded. *She* dominated.

Like a fucking goddess, she created with fire.

When she was little, just rediscovering language, re-learning what the world was about, she'd been terrified of fire. Mom couldn't put candles on her birthday cake until she was about ten.

Just look at her now. Because this is what she did. Fear was overrated. There was no need to let it paralyze you, let it defeat you, let it open the way for harm to come to you. She wasn't weak. She controlled the situation, and fear bowed down to *her!*

By dawn, her kilns were once more filled. The beads for the necklace were in there. Gram's bougainvillea flowers were complete, in a slightly off shade of pink, on small, arching branches. How she'd stabilize the shoes was yet to be figured out, but that would happen later.

Right now, she'd sleep. Without the help of a prescription or alcohol. Whoever wanted to visit her could visit. She was a fucking warrior.

Monday, July 5

Maxine

Ever since Lauren said that magical word—Pinterest—Maxine couldn't stop thinking about creating a baby board on that platform. She wouldn't let herself actually do it; she couldn't create a whole board devoted to her unborn child—no sense jinxing things if things really could be jinxed. But she'd already searched on it enough times that now whenever she opened the app, her screen was full of everything baby.

So many gorgeous decor ideas! She'd love to do her own furniture, but probably wouldn't have the time. Besides, Mama and Lauren would have to get involved. She couldn't leave them out.

She'd already clicked through nine signs of being pregnant with a boy—and discovered she had all nine—then ten signs of being pregnant with a girl—and had all ten. She had the growth charts of a prenatal child memorized. And, should she ever get crazy cravings, found a resource telling her what vitamin or nutrient she really needed.

She loved every minute of it.

Every minute except for what she was doing right there, right then. Sitting in Mama's kitchen, drinking green tea, alone, while Mama slept in. Even if Mama hadn't stayed up watching that silly comedy last night, though, the whole scene would still feel off to Max. This wasn't where she was supposed to be.

She was supposed to be at home, with Dane, in their kitchen. Right around this time, he'd be filling his coffee cup, the one he took upstairs to his office.

Did she still love him? Could it be she was just so angry with him for being an ass lately—he wasn't normally, was he?

He'd always felt so safe, so stable…so unlike her father.

Was Kaz right? Did she never really love him but instead love the idea that, since he was the opposite of her father, he'd never leave her, abandon her like that?

Granted, he never left her. But, another woman? Keeping secrets from his wife? That was such a Daddy thing.

She put her cup in the dishwasher, grabbed her purse and keys, and scribbled a note for Mama. On her way to the store, she called her father, not really expecting him to pick up so early in the morning. It was almost ten o'clock, after all.

"Well, hello, Maxie!" his voice boomed through her car. "What are you up to on this rainy morning?"

"Calling you!" She laughed. "But I wasn't sure you'd be up so early."

"Of course, I am. Been smoking ribs all night long. I'll go to bed soon. Why you calling so early? You all right?"

"Why did you leave Mama and me?"

"Lord, Maxie! Where's that coming from?"

"I'm having some problems with Dane right now, and—"

"Did he hurt you? I'll kick his ass!"

"Aren't you old enough to collect Social Security?"

"Doesn't mean I can't kick his ass." He was probably right.

"Anyway, it's nothing like that. We're just, he's just not acting like the man I always thought he was, and…I don't know. I guess I just wanted to know, what makes a man—and Daddy, I don't mean this disrespectfully, because you know I'm talking the truth here—what makes a man just…just not think about his family?"

"I wouldn't know, Max. I never stopped thinking about you and your mama."

He's giving her lines? Really? "Then why did you leave us?"

"Well, when you came along, I realized what I'd always suspected was the truth. I'm not cut out to be a father. I was miserable. Made your mama miserable, too. Just seemed like you'd both be better off without me. So I hit the road with my trumpet."

"Why'd you come back?"

"Because I kept thinking about you. If your mama had taken me back, maybe I'd have stayed...nah. I'd probably still come and go like I did. I was a wanderer, Max. It's in my blood."

"So, what made you..." caught herself before saying *settle down.* Her father was anything but settled. "Stay in one place? Stay in Philly for so long?" He'd been there since she got married, over six years now.

"I think I'd just had enough. I hit a point where I'd been on the road long enough, nothing seemed new anymore. It just didn't call me like it used to. So, I opened BBQandBlues. And hell, Max, I came to Philly to be near you because I was thinking about you." Was he playing her? She could never really tell when the man was sincere.

"What'd Dane do?"

She gave him an abridged version, decided to keep her pregnancy to herself.

"Wait a minute. Things got tough, and he stayed home?"

"Yes."

"And you left?"

"Yes...Oh..." She slowed as she approached the store from the front and parked at the curb on Main Street. "Daddy, I think I need to go."

"I'm here anytime for you."

Hell. She'd acted just like him. She owed Dane an apology. But he also owed one to her. Or did he give it already? It was one of those rare times when she understood Dee's confusion. There had been so many emotional exchanges between Max and Dane that she couldn't remember what he'd said.

But she was here, now, at her store. Originally, she was going to move stuff from the garage to the store. But it was raining. She'd have to wait it out. Might be good to spend a few hours painting something or altering something. Just doing something that didn't require her to think, maybe sneak up and check on Dee.

Dee

Fuck! Shit! Damn!

Why couldn't she find anything?

If the microwave was right, and really she wasn't entirely sure, after all, who programmed the freaking thing? But, if it was right, then she was running out of time. There was no way she was going to get a phone before the funeral started now. Where the hell was her fob?

Off with the couch cushions again. Nothing in the crevices.

She dumped all the mail piled up on the wingback to the floor. Nope. Not in there.

"What are you looking for?"

"Aaack! Jesus fucking Christ!" Cooper was suddenly in the doorway to the mudroom.

"Sorry. I, um, I knocked. I guess you didn't hear me."

"I'm really seeing you, right?" Was she losing her fucking mind again?

"You're really seeing me." He stepped toward her, stopped when he made it to the living area. "Wow."

Her eyes seemed to take in chaos as if seeing it the for the first time, as he was.

"I..." What the hell had she been doing? Her head itched. Ears buzzed. Fuck. Inhale, Dee! Infuckinghale! But she couldn't. Her nose was clogged. She could only get short breaths through her mouth.

Suddenly, Cooper was holding her. She sobbed into his chest.

"It's OK." His hand ran over the back of her head. "Whatever it is, it will be OK."

"It's not OK. It can't be OK. My place is a disaster. I can't find my purse. I lost my key fob again. And I don't have any coffee." How the fuck was anything ever going to be OK again? But eventually, she could breathe again. She stepped back, wiped her face on her sleeve.

"And, and, like, my aunt...Aunt Josie. She died."

"I'm so sorry."

Dee pointed to the whiteboard. "I can't...like...function. I kind of killed my phone—"

"Good! I was hoping you lost it and not that you were cutting me out of your life."

"I really should, you know." She went past him into the mudroom. A basket with clean, unfolded dark clothes was still there. "Or you should cut me out."

"Why?" Cooper was behind her.

"I'm a fucking mess, Coop." She pulled out a black T-shirt. That would do. She took the Queens of the Stone Age shirt off and tugged on the clean one.

"You know that's wrong side out, right?" He pulled at the neckline.

"Oh." God, she was so fucking tired. "I thought it was just plain black." She tugged it off, looked at the front: empty. The back had a tequila bottle on it. She put it on. "If I can find an appropriate top, would you take me to the funeral? I need..." Jesus! Would the tears ever stop? Enough with the feelings already. "I need to," sniff, "say goodbye."

"Of course. Go get dressed."

She wasn't wearing one of those fucking flowered shirts Mom had bought her. Should burn them over the sink. She found a super-loose-knit black sweater she'd have to wear with a tank top. There was one on the floor that looked like it had only been worn once or twice. Soon, wearing that with her black boots and baggy jeans, she was in Cooper's car, driving in a light rain.

"I don't have an umbrella." He looked in the rear-view mirror before cutting over a lane. "We may get soaked."

"I don't need to stay for the full service." Why was she so driven to be there, anyway? She could always visit the grave alone later...but he'd agreed to take her.

"That's good. I don't think we're gonna get there in time for the beginning. So," he sped up, "now you're my hostage. What the hell's going on? Why did you leave like that on Saturday?"

She gave him the full rundown. Let it all out. If he wants to be with a fucking nut case, why hold anything back?

The rain had picked up by the time she finished, and they arrived near the gravesite.

"Damn, Dee!" Cooper put his car in park, turned sideways to look at her. "I'm sorry. I know that doesn't help you in any way. But, really. I'm sorry you had to deal with that."

"What's done is done. My calmness about it is scaring me, though. I keep thinking, kind of worrying, I might explode. I might—what the hell is she doing here?" Her mother was at the fucking grave site. Who the hell did she think she was? This was not her turf!

Dee stormed out of the car, not feeling the rain as she approached the service. Seething, she stood at the edge of the crowd where she could barely hear the reverend or whatever. She wanted to calm down enough to honor Josie. What the hell were you supposed to do at funerals anyway?

Cooper came over, tried to hold a jacket over her. What a fucking gentleman! Eventually, the crowd shifted, and people walked under umbrellas back to their cars. She inched toward the grave, maybe she could throw a handful of dirt in and say goodbye.

"Dee?"

"Don't talk to me, Mom." Dee stomped past her. Cooper tried to stay with her and keep the jacket over her.

"Sweetheart, are you all right?"

Near the casket, Dee stopped, closed her eyes. Aunt Josie always appreciated her spunk, her liveliness. If Mom kept at it, she'd say goodbye to her great aunt in a style she'd enjoy.

Aunt Josie…she guessed this was goodbye. Opening her eyes, she realized throwing a fistful of dirt in the grave wasn't going to happen. The dirt was muddy, and the casket was still above ground. What the fuck? What was she to do?

"Deirdre, please. I don't know what I did." Her mother's voice was so insistent, Dee had to turn around.

"What?"

"Obviously, you're upset with me. What did I do?"

That's right. Her mother didn't know that Dee knew. The rain came down harder. Dee realized it because the people behind her mother were harder to see as they sped toward cars. Mom stood still, under her umbrella, beckoning Dee to come toward her. Surely, she wanted to shield her precious child from the rain.

Dee shook her head, stepped out from under Cooper's jacket, and opened her arms wide. Let the heavens pour down everything they had.

"Nope. You don't get to define my world anymore, Mom."

"Get under this umbrella!" Mom glanced behind her. "Kaz is coming with another one from the car. Please let's talk. What is going on?"

"I don't want your fucking umbrella!" The words came out in a yell. Her throat felt clogged. She must be crying again, but whatever. Her face was soaked with rain. Who'd notice? "I know everything!"

"What?"

"I know everything. And he helped you." She pointed behind her mother, where Kaz was approaching with an umbrella. "He agreed to do whatever you wanted. Everyone did. Just keep Dee Dee in the dark. Right? Do whatever you can so Dee doesn't know what happened to her."

"You spoke to Brett?" Mom caught on.

"Your worst nightmare, right, Mom? Welcome to my fucking world!" Her chest struggled to get air in. She thought she might be about to lose control. Took a step backward.

"Dee Dee, I—"

"Why? Why didn't you tell me?"

"You'd gone through so much." Mom was crying now. "I couldn't stand the thought of you experiencing any more pain."

"*You* couldn't..." Dee wanted to smash her mother's face in. "This was all about *you*?" She spun around, ran a few paces to get away from her. Cooper kept up.

"Dee! Deirdre!" Kaz yelled.

She stopped. They were right behind her.

"It's us. It's your mother. It's me. I know all this is tough to take in, but you know we've never done anything but try to give you the best life possible. You cannot treat your mother—"

His hand gripped her arm.

She ripped away from him, stumbled a few steps out of his reach, out from Cooper's protection. "I can treat her whatever way I fucking want to, Kaz! Don't you get it? Don't you get what she did to me?"

The words hurt her throat.

"ME!" She slammed a hand against her soaked shirt, gripped tight to the loose knit. "Look what I did with fire! I was terrified of it, remember Mom?" She just couldn't stop yelling. The rain had soaked through everything. She felt it streaming down her spine into her jeans. "Fucking *terrified*. I couldn't even have lit candles on a birthday cake! But when I found out it was because I was in a fire, what did I do?"

They stared at her. Mom, Kaz, Cooper. There were others in the background under umbrellas, probably staring, too. She didn't care.

"I fucking took *control*. I commanded it! I overcame it and turned my fear into my *power*!" The words came out with such force, she bent over. Straightening, she saw Kaz and Mom peering into each other's faces. "Look at ME!" They stared at her with fear or something on their faces.

"What do I do? I remake things. I take their fucking flaws and turn them into *art*. Don't you realize what I could have done with myself?" She pointed at Cooper. "Do you know how hard it is to be with him?"

"Dee, I don't—" Mom made the mistake of taking a step toward her.

Dee stomped backward. "How many years were you going to let me be single? Unable to...to actually fucking love someone? Get close to someone? Huh?"

Just rain splattering, pouring, the only noise.

"Just to protect *your* feelings?" She pointed to her mother. "Because *you* couldn't stand something? So *you* wouldn't be hurt? So *you* wouldn't have to suffer by telling *me* the truth?"

"Dee, sweetheart! That's not right." Mom tried to approach her again.

"Well, guess what, Mom! I fucking suffered. Do you know what it's like to have man after man push you away, telling you you're a fucking lunatic?"

Mom covered her mouth with her hand.

"Do you know what it's like to...to abandon someone, knowingly abandon someone you love because a weird-ass fucking memory is driving you away from them?"

Tears dribbled out of Mom's eyes.

"That fucking *hurts*." The sobs overcame her. "And you did that."

Dee turned and ran. She couldn't be around her. Couldn't be around Kaz. How many fucking shrinks did they work with when she was growing up? How could they all collude with her? How could Mom be so selfish? Always wanting her girls to stay at home with her.

Dee got it now.

She used to think her mother was just attached, just overprotective, truly didn't want her girls to get hurt.

But no.

She was just fucking selfish.

Where the hell was she? Dee stomped onto a path and continued running down it. Where the hell was her car?

Genevieve

Genevieve thought she saw Olivia pass behind her as she entered her bedroom.

"You went shopping?" Livvy asked.

"I did." Genevieve dropped the rain-dampened bags on the floor. Probably wasn't the wisest move to go shopping in such a downpour, but she had to get out of the house. "I thought I'd get some work clothes."

"You went to Hana's?" Livvy held a bag by its handles far away from her body, as if it were too hot to handle.

"Yep. The young lady who does our marketing suggested it. Her name's Hayleigh. She's a sister to that Dee woman you met." And who her father was sleeping with. Ha! Chris thought it was awkward having a conversation with Remy about condoms. Wait until he explains Dee to Livvy. "I went to a few other place, too. Want to see what I bought?"

Livvy was probably waiting for Genevieve to show her what she'd bought for her. And she *had* picked up a few things for her daughter. She just wasn't rewarding her nasty behavior and was going to hold off on giving them to her until there was some kind of peace.

"No." Livvy flicked her hair behind her face. "I was just heading out."

"OK. Well, I'm making meatloaf and mashed potatoes for dinner. I'm sure there will be leftovers if you're not back in time to eat when the rest of us do."

She waited for Livvy to storm out before reviewing her beautiful purchases. Hana's really did have some unique and rather artistic clothing. Though that top hat with the velvet lining! Who would wear such a thing?

She'd just slithered into a long tunic screen-printed with a street scene from London, highlighted by a few strategically placed rhinestones.

"You're telling me you don't care if I eat dinner?" Olivia stormed back into her room.

"I'm telling you I'm making meatloaf and mashed potatoes. In fact," Genevieve glanced at the clock beside her bed, "I'll probably get started soon. Whether or not you're home to eat dinner when it's ready is on you. I'm not the one going anywhere. I've been making meals for you for eighteen years. By now, you should know that dinner is on the table by six-thirty, and that those who aren't here at that hour, will either have to fend for themselves or eat leftovers."

"What are you wearing?" Livvy's eyes narrowed at her.

"A tunic, which I will probably pair with black leggings." Genevieve smoothed out the front and looked at herself in the mirror. She absolutely loved it! Yes! This is how she wanted to dress.

"I'm not sure I like it." Olivia folded her arms across her chest.

"Good thing I didn't buy it for you, then."

"Who are you?"

"Your moth—Genevieve Eileen Gardner Cooper. Currently, that is."

"Is this what happened to you when you got a job? You just turned into some...some..."

"Independent-thinking woman?" Genevieve twisted to see her backside. That had become a scary thing since the incident with the palazzo jeans. But the tunic was still perfect. "I would hope that would make me a role model for you, finally."

Olivia left. Genevieve slipped out of her white capris and tugged on a pair of black leggings. Yes, indeed! Perfect.

She wore the outfit downstairs. In the kitchen, she draped an apron over her head and began gathering what she'd need to make dinner. Livvy was outside, standing at the edge of the covered patio, gesticulating as she spoke into her phone. Eventually, Liv threw her phone on the end of a chaise lounge and sat down. Genevieve opened the slider. "Liv! Come in, please. I need your help."

"What do you want?"

"Since you seem to be home this afternoon after all, and you realized yesterday that I'd done a crappy job at preparing you to be an adult, why don't you make the meatloaf today?"

"Are you kidding me?"

"Nope." Genevieve waved her hand over the ingredients lined up on the island. "I made it easy for you. Everything you need is here."

Olivia slowly approached the island. "What if I say no?"

"Why would you?"

"Why are you punishing me?"

"I'm not punishing you, Liv. I'm acknowledging you were right.

I've done a crappy job preparing you to be on your own. You're leaving for college in a couple of months. Your dorm has a full kitchen. Wouldn't it be nice to know how to make a few of your favorite things? Maybe even impress your suite mates?" Or possibly a young man who would appreciate a conversation over dinner more than breasts shoved against him for a selfie?

"Fine. What do I do?"

"First, chop the onion and green pepper."

Livvy found a cutting board and a knife.

"Do you know how I learned to cook?" Genevieve removed her apron and put it on her daughter.

Livvy shook her head.

"When I was very young, I realized I wanted more than the frozen, microwaved meals my mother made. I wanted the food I saw on television."

"I barely remember Grandma, but yeah, I can't imagine her cooking."

"She entertained quite a bit but didn't cook." Genevieve returned to her stool at the island. "She taught me how to make a good martini when I was about nine, and I could put together things like crackers and cheese platters, nuts and fruits, and all that. At ten, she'd drop me off at the market with a credit card and tell me to get everything we'd need for the week. So I bought things like cereal, sandwich fixings, a bunch of frozen meals, and then, of course, everything we'd need to go with cocktails."

"That's really pretty pathetic." Livvy was the slowest food chopper in the world. It was 4:45. If dinner was going to be done by 6:30, she'd need to help, and they'd still be pushing it.

"It is. But, one day at school, I asked the librarian for a book that taught kids how to cook. She didn't have anything, but I think she realized why I was asking—my mother didn't exactly have a stellar reputation. A couple days later, she brought in a book that she said she 'found,' and I could keep. Looking back, I remember it being brand new, so I'm sure she bought it. Anyway, it was an introductory kind of cookbook."

Genevieve found another apron, knife, and cutting board, and began cutting the green pepper. "I studied it, planned a menu, and the next time my mother dropped me off at the market, I bought real food to cook for my brother and sister."

"What about your mom?"

"She ate, too. But I was more concerned with Brynn and Archie. Mom seemed to care less and less about each child she had. She was always willing to give me her credit card, though, so eventually, I bought everything for us—school supplies, medicines, clothes, whatever."

"Wow!" Livvy frowned at Genevieve. "Well, thank you for not being *that* shitty."

Good Lord! The perspective on the kid.

"Anyway, after that, everything became my job. All the cooking, cleaning, putting Band-Aids on scraped knees...whatever. When I was fifteen, I had this financial responsibility class in high school and learned a little about banking. So, one day after school, when I found my mother in a very good mood because her latest fling had bought her a diamond necklace, I suggested we go to the bank so I could get my name on the account to make things easier on her. See, sometimes the electricity or water was shut off because she'd forget to pay the bills. I knew we had money. Her parents had left her a boatload. And my dad paid some kind of alimony."

"When did Grandpa move to California?"

"When Archie was about a year old. He didn't want much of a family life, either." Genevieve scraped the chopped pepper into the bowl of meat. "Though I guess he changed his mind since he has a couple of children with my step-mom, who is four years younger than me. Ha!"

Livvy smirked.

"Anyway, I found out there was more than one account at the

bank. There was the main checking account, and then there was this big savings account that would automatically transfer money into the checking account once a month. That was from my grandparents' trust and dad's alimony and support."

"So, she was like really rich?"

"Yes. Really. She should have had a financial planner or someone to help her invest it. But whatever, it was a lot of money. Too much in her regular savings account to be insured by the bank should it go under."

"What do you mean?" Livvy scraped her onion in with the meat and pepper.

"Pour in the breadcrumbs, egg, ketchup, and all that other stuff." Genevieve pointed to the ramekins lined up with the pre-measured ingredients. "I'll write these directions out, so you'll know how much we used. Anyway, it doesn't matter about the bank. I didn't understand it at the time, either. But what I realized was we had more money than I thought, for one, and for another, my mom spent a shit-ton on really expensive gin."

"Did you just say 'shit-ton'?"

"I think Dee Dee is rubbing off on me." Genevieve giggled.

"Who?"

"My boss. I bet you'll get to know her. Anyway, I was so angry. I mean, I'd been feeding her, Brynn, Arch, and me for five years by that point on the cheapest pasta, instant potatoes, and crappy fatty hamburgers and hot dogs, and she was spending loads on gin. So, I started 'stealing' from her a little. I started buying better food at the market, and each time I checked out, I'd put that debit card into the machine and ask for a bunch of cash back. The amount was always the same that she'd spent that week on gin. I opened my own account with that money, saving it for what, I don't know. But I figured one day Brynn, Archie, or I would need money, and it'd be there."

"She never noticed?"

Genevieve shook her head. "At that point, she couldn't notice details like that. She had some mental health issues that I think were never diagnosed. From what I've read online, she was probably bipolar. But she didn't look at her money in the bank because she always took for granted that it was always there. What she noticed instead was things like there was too much light in the house, so she would smack Uncle Archie into a corner, blaming it on him. Or that Aunt Brynn was "too proud" for getting an A on a test, so she'd hit her with whatever was in her hands until Aunt Brynn retreated into her bedroom. I did everything I could to protect them. I was constantly on the alert for anything that might set her off and either interfere or create some kind of buffer."

Livvy paused in her attempt to mix the meatloaf with a spoon. She stared at Genevieve with a snarl and wide eyes.

"You have to use your hands to squish that all together, Liv."

"That's really gross."

"You'll wash them."

She began mashing the meatloaf ingredients. "So what happened?"

"Well, obviously, I stayed throughout high school. I had no idea back then what kind of resources I had available. I was so busy just trying to get through the day, come home from school, and keep Mom separated from Archie and Brynn until she went to bed. Then, I'd do whatever she was supposed to do. I went to PTA meetings. I forged her name on permission slips for field trips. I tried to make their lives as normal as the lives of the other rich kids around us. When I think about it, I can't help but get angry—some teacher should have noticed I was the one who was always there. But I guess things were different then."

"Sounds like it."

"Anyway, whenever I could, I'd retreat into my art. That's what I blew most of my mom's money on. Fun stuff for us kids. Archie couldn't get enough comic books. Aunt Brynn loved playing tennis.

And I made art. I drew horrifically emotional and scary things. I still have my old sketchbooks in the basement. I pulled them out recently and was too afraid to show them to anyone. I'm not that person anymore. Anyway, Livvy, my point in telling you all this is…" She wiped her hands on the apron and waited until Livvy met her eyes. "I admit I was one of those helicopter parents who never let you do things like make your own dinner. I set up your life so you'd experience disappointment as little as possible. And now, you're right. You need to know how to cook. And you have no idea how to bounce back from disappointment. I apologize for that. I just wanted to be sure you didn't get the life my mother gave me."

Livvy held her gaze for a minute, then returned to punishing the meatloaf, without making a comment.

"I had planned on taking a gap year so that I'd be there for Aunt Brynn during her freshman year of high school. Ninth grade had been one of the worst years of my life."

"Mine, too."

"Right? It is for girls. And before my gap year even started, is when I got pregnant with you. And, well, plans changed. By the time you were born, my mother was diagnosed with lymphoma. The chemo weakened her; she mellowed. She and Brynn actually started getting along." But it was too late for Genevieve to even want to get along with her mother.

"Is this good enough?" Livvy held the bowl for her to see. Genevieve nodded, handed her a loaf pan lined with parchment.

"Put it in here, then we'll spread some more ketchup over the top, and decorate it with a few rings of green pepper."

Livvy shoved the meatloaf into the pan. "This doesn't change the fact that I'm pissed off at you."

"That's on you. I can't do anything about that."

Olivia washed her hands in silence, focused on getting the meatloaf out from under her nails. "So, um, well, thank you. You know, I kind of like cooking."

Genevieve smiled.

"Maybe you can teach me more over the summer?"

"I'd love to."

Dee

A black SUV pulled up beside her as she stomped along a narrow lane in the cemetery. The window slid down.

"Dee!"

"Cooper?" She peered through the rain. "What the hell are you doing here?"

"I brought you!"

Shit! That's right! How could she forget?

Because her mother drove her fucking batty! That's how.

"Get in!"

She threw herself in the passenger seat and hunched over, shivering. Just needed to collect herself. Figure out what she was doing. No, she knew what she was doing. She'd just screamed at Mom and Kaz, and now Cooper was taking her somewhere. Probably home. *It would probably be easier to figure this out if that fucking noise would stop.*

"What is that beeping?" She sat up.

"You're not wearing a seatbelt. It's a safety thing."

"Fucking world obsessed with being safe!" Dee pulled the belt across her, snapped it into place.

A snorting sound erupted from Cooper.

"Are you fucking laughing?"

"Are you fucking upset about seat belts?"

She leaned back into the seat. Ran her hands over her head.

Christ, she was soaked. Stupid choice of a shirt.

"Why are you here, Coop?"

"We just had that conversation. I drove you."

"No, I mean...why did you show up? Why did you stay here?"

"You're hurting, Dee. I wanna help you through this."

What was "this" anyway? The windshield wipers were almost hypnotizing. She let them put her in a daze as they left the cemetery and headed back to her messy apartment. "Is this, like, what we have, what you want?"

"Is what...what do you mean?"

"Are you really that dense?"

"You weren't exactly clear."

Another stretch of hypnotic wipers.

"God, I fuck everything up." That was the only way to explain it.

"Honey, let's start over."

"I can't go back to the beginning. I don't have it in me."

"I mean, start this car ride over. What happened back at the cemetery?"

Swish swish swish swish.

"So, all that shit I told you about Brett's dad killing mine?"

"Yeah?"

Swish swish swish swish.

"Like, I never realized it in actual words...but, as I went into glass arts because that's how I took control of fire. Dominated my fear of it. I guess the accident made me afraid of it."

"Can I hold your hand?"

"You're so fucking weird." But, God. That's just what she needed. Wanted. She never needed people.

"I'll take that as a 'yes.'" He reached over, she unclenched a fist, and placed her hand in his.

"I've been in therapy for what feels like my entire fucking life. Most of it was spent trying to figure out how to sleep, how to relax, how to…how to have feelings, or let myself feel feelings…" He squeezed her hand. "And none of it ever led to a breakthrough where maybe, just maybe, I could have healed and not become the lonely fucking nutcase I am."

"You still lonely with me?"

More fucking tears! Since when was she so soft? She wiped her face with her free hand. "No."

"Any reason why you can't heal now?"

She overcame fire.

But it was her fault her father was killed. He wasn't lost. He was murdered. Because she didn't run. How was she to overcome that? "I'm not sure I deserve to heal."

"What?"

"It's my fault my dad is dead."

"Dee, no."

"My uncle told me to leave. He said to run. I didn't. I stayed there until my…my father—" She called him Daddy. She knew that now.

Swish. Swish. Swish.

"The best way to get over survivor's guilt is to think about what the person who died would want for you." His voice was almost a whisper.

"What?" Had they been in a different conversation?

"Remember when you found *Sweet Caroline* on your phone?"

"I actually do."

"Remember what you did?"

"Why are you testing my memory?"

"You called me an asshat and tackled me. Jumped on my head."

"I hope I hurt you. That song sucks."

He pulled her hand to his mouth and kissed it. Her breath felt comfortable, warm in her chest.

"We wrestled. Wound up rolling on the floor, tussling, laughing."

"Yeah."

"Something clicked in me that moment, Dee. I realized for the first time in, I dunno, forever, that I felt free, safe, comfortable, uninhibited. I realized I was happy and...and that's what Benny meant."

Benny, his buddy who died? She turned sideways in the seat to study him as he drove, still keeping a grip on his hand.

"He was fucking bleeding out. I was freaking out. Screaming at him. I just wanted him to tell me what to do. The fucking medic was taking forever to get to us." He swallowed, grimaced, and sniffed. "All Benny kept saying was for me to live for him. Really live." He released her hand to wipe his face. "I thought I was, you know? I built the business, Griffin Wings, 'cause that's what we were gonna do together after our service. But maybe if I'd paid better attention to all that first aid crap, I'd been able to save him."

"Coop! No! You can't—"

"I know. It's survivor's guilt. Not sure I'll ever get over it. But I am sure I can live with it when I know I'm doing what Benny wanted. Doing what he said. But the business, that's only partly what he meant. I understood it that morning, on the floor with you. He meant *live*. Do what he'd want to do. Laugh. Roll on the floor with a woman you love."

"You love me?"

"You haven't figured that out? And yet you called me dense?"

Phone call, Kaz Bremen his car announced.

"Hell! I gotta deal with them."

Cooper accepted the call. "Hey, Kaz, I have Dee."

"Thank you. She's still not answering—"

"She needs a new phone. Listen, I'm taking her back to her place now."

"Thanks, Coop." They clicked off.

"Does he know about us?" Dee was curious how Kaz would feel about that.

"He's probably making guesses."

Swish. Swish. Swish.

Cooper's words made sense to her—she could see how living the life Benny would have wanted kind of gave him something…gave him peace. What would her father have wanted from her? His mother and his wife only wanted her to get the most joy and love out of life. Granted, in Mom's world, that meant ugly clothes and smothering overprotection.

Cooper turned on the side street next to her building and parked. "So, what happens now?"

"Jesus! I don't know. I mean, I gotta clean, do laundry, get a new phone…"

"Can I help you with any of it?"

"The fact that I'm so messed up, and you still wanna be around me, has me concerned about your mental health."

"Is that another 'yes'?"

"Coop, do you think we can really work? I mean, what if something down the road triggers me, and I kind of lose my shit again and shove you away?"

"What if I need to stay indoors, in the quiet, with the lights off all Memorial Day weekend?"

"What if your kids hate me and blame me for destroying your marriage?"

"What if my kids hate me and try to make your life miserable?

"So are you saying two misfits make a right?"

"I think I am. Do you want help cleaning or what?"

"You have no idea how messy my place is right now."

"I was in there earlier, remember?"

"Not really, but I guess that does make sense."

He turned the car off. She stepped out, jumped a puddle, hit the bottom step of the backstairs, and *bam*.

All went black.

Maxine

Max went to the front of the building, curious about the sirens. It sounded as if an ambulance was right outside. The sound suddenly quieted, and all she saw was Dane's huddled form looking in the glass at the door.

She opened it, but didn't immediately let him come in. "What are you doing here?"

"I came to see you." Dane stood close, hunching against the weather.

"Do you know how many umbrellas are in the laundry room at home?" She stood aside to let him in. "Didn't think of grabbing one?"

He stepped inside and shrugged. "Didn't even know we had any?"

How was that possible? He brought a logoed umbrella home every time he went to a conference, which was twice a year. They had probably a dozen...oh, what did it matter?

She let him in but made him stand in the entry while she ran to the back to grab a hand towel. Through the side window, she could see the tail end of an ambulance. Its flashing lights flickered inside and danced on the workroom's walls. She wanted to go out and see what had happened. Someone in the building across the street must be having an issue, which was really none of her business. Meanwhile, Dane was making a puddle in the entry.

She returned to him and handed him the towel. He accepted it without saying thank you.

"You closed already?" Dane took off his glasses and wiped them dry.

"Closed all day, like all the other businesses on Main Street, on Mondays." She reached out for his towel but changed her mind. Why was she always doing things for him? Why did he let her do things for him?

"I never noticed." He wadded the towel, looked around. Max waited for him to ask what to do with it. She was pretty sure she'd told him she'd never work on Mondays and that...

"So why are you here, then?" He roamed over to the sales counter and dropped his wet towel on it. She should have taken it from him.

"Nothing else to do. Nowhere else to go." She picked up the towel.

"This is home to you now? Already?" He held his arms out. A look of horror on his face. Or maybe it was disgust.

"It's a second home, Dane. Since I…"

"Since you what?"

Since she left him. Daddy was right. She'd left him.

He squeezed his forehead as he walked past, heading toward the back. Was he intentionally not looking at her? In the middle room, he stopped and stared at all the clocks.

"Dee and I made those," she told him.

"Yeah?" The corners of his mouth turned down like he grudgingly approved.

"Wanna see the lamps and lampshades?"

The tension seemed to leave his body; he slouched, but with attitude. "Are you kidding me, Max? Did you have to go there?"

"I went where you went." But no, she didn't need to go there. She had tried to hurt him somehow. "I'm sorry, Dane. You, you caught me off guard, showing up like this. I...why are *you* here?"

"My mother." He wandered toward the framing area, pausing in front of a large armoire.

"Does she need a gift?"

He shook his head, smirked. "The hits keep coming, huh?"

"You opened yourself wide for that one."

"This is nice." He ran his hand over the top of a home bar.

"Dee and I made that out of an old console TV."

"Really?" He found the switch and lit up the glass shelves from below. "This is amazing! When did you do this?"

"Over spring break."

"Can you make one for our house?"

"That almost sounds like you support me here."

"I do, Max." He faced her and put his hands in his jeans pockets. "I...look, I spoke with my mom today."

She sat at the consult table, nodded to the other side. "And what did your mom have to say?"

"She let me know I've been behaving like a selfish ass."

Max's laugh came out as a snort. "What, exactly, did she say?"

"She said, 'Dane, you're behaving like a selfish ass.'"

"Ha!" Max belly laughed. That was almost too much to believe. Pamela Booker idolized her son. He could do no wrong!

"And she said you'd been enabling me."

Oh? "I've been what?" Who did that woman think she was?

"Just like the umbrella thing, Max." Dane clasped his hands on the table, hung his head. "I had no idea where an umbrella was. You take care of those things. You'd hand one to me as I was going out. You'd—"

"You're making me sound like Lauren."

"I'm just saying, Max, we kind of settled into some...some habits. You were basically in charge of how our lives went. I was lazy and let you do it all. As I did less and less, I became kind of incapable of thinking—"

"No." Max stood, shoved her chair back. "Don't you dare blame your actions on *me*. How long have you known about your son?"

He shook his head. "That's not what I mean. What I mean is, you...you made things easy on me. I got lazy and kind of took you for granted. I kind of forgot you...you...well, my mom explained it better than I'm doing."

"I'm not calling her for clarity."

"Well, what I realized is that, man, Max. I messed up."

He's owning this...maybe.

"I messed up when we'd just gotten engaged and never told you about Shawna because I didn't want to lose you. I messed up when I found out about Jamaal and didn't tell you. I messed up by not considering your feelings when I did tell you."

"You're off to a good start."

"What else is there?"

"You thought I was low enough to use Dee's family, and yet you were willing to be with me anyway."

"That was just immaturity. I'd never experienced any other family relationships like that. I still don't quite understand it, but I accept it now."

"And you got all this from one phone call with your mother?"

He nodded. "Can we be us again?"

She really wanted that, but…"You know that 'us' now includes a baby. You haven't even mentioned that."

"Yeah…" He puffed out his cheeks, blew a little air out. "Yeah, I know. I mean, I'm glad, Max. But honestly, after last week with Jamaal, I'm scared, too."

Max nodded, and she realized Kaz was right to warn her. "I think we need couples therapy and, and maybe parenting classes."

"They have those things?"

Tuesday, July 6

Dee

Thank you, Ms. Bremen." The nurse took the iPad back. "Yes, looks like you are all signed out. A wheelchair will be here momentarily, and you can leave."

"Why do I need a wheelchair?"

"It's hospital policy."

"That's a stupid policy. If I can stand on my own two feet—"

"Nurse, do you have a waiver for my daughter?" Kaz was suddenly in the room. "We won't hold the hospital legally liable should she trip and bump her head again."

"I can just make a note of it in her file here, sir."

"Do that." He nodded at Dee and opened his arms wide, a shopping bag dangled from one hand. "You look splendid for a girl with a concussion."

"It's not a concussion. I just learned that for sure. They had no reason to keep here, but they did, against my free will, I'll have you know—"

"I already knew—"

"Because of my previous head trauma history—How the hell did you know that?"

"Well, when Cooper called me and told me what happened, of course, your mother and I rushed over—"

"Never mind." She waved her hand at him. "Why are you here

now?"

"How else did you think you were going to get home?"

She looked around the hospital room. He was right. No phone. And she had no clue what anybody's numbers were to call from the room phone. "Are those clothes for me?"

"From your mother." Kaz handed the bag to her.

"I'm probably going to hate this." She took the bag and disappeared into the restroom. And she was right. Mom sent him with patterned slacks—pale blue with white shells and palm trees, and a goofy, flowy, gauzy, white shirt. She looked like a fucking idiot tourist. But her own clothes were a soggy pile in a plastic bag.

Hopefully, she wouldn't break out in a rash. Though that would punish Mom.

Out of the hospital and buckled into his ridiculously expensive Jag, Dee felt brave enough to manage a full conversation. "So, catch me up chief...what happened?"

"How far back?"

"How did I wind up in the hospital?"

"Your back steps were wet and slippery. You slid, bumped the bean, and the rest is history."

"Damn. I've been meaning to get those taken care of."

"Me too, kid. But your mother called Marco over. He put tread on them this morning."

Well, she couldn't be mad about that, could she? Though, she really wanted to be.

"Anything else?" Kaz's enthusiasm for life must have been a DNA thing. Clearly, H had that same gene.

"No." That's all she wanted to know.

"I have a couple for you then."

Oh God! Please don't ask about Cooper!

"What's going on with you and Cooper?"

"He didn't tell you?"

"He said to ask you."

"Oh, um. I think we're a thing."

Kaz drove quietly a little while. "I think he's probably the only man I might approve of being with you."

She hoped that wasn't a bad sign.

"Next," Kaz reached over and tapped her arm. "Why are you so mad at your mother?"

"I wasn't clear yesterday?" She touched the bruise on her forehead. "That was yesterday, right?"

"It was yesterday. And it seemed you were angry because she kept a secret from you."

"*The* secret."

"Are you telling me you've never kept a secret from your mother?"

A lone laugh coughed out of her. Dee had kept plenty from her. Then there was that whole thing with Cooper. But that was different. "Of course, but *her* secret is different."

"How?"

"Seriously? You people didn't listen to a word I said yesterday?"

"We heard. Just didn't quite understand."

"Maybe, just maybe, my life would have been different, better, if I'd known."

"Possibly. Or it may have been worse."

"How can you say that with a straight face?"

"You think your life would have been better if you actually remembered watching your father get killed?"

"I think…" What did she think?

"Your mother had been warned by an assortment of professionals who assured her you'd be tormented by unresolved grief, by survivor's guilt, by a host of other psychological woes if you ever remembered what happened to you."

"Even if I didn't remember, why not tell me the truth later?"

"Kid, think about the practicality of it."

"I don't understand."

"When should you have been told?"

"When…well. I don't know. At some point—"

"Should it have been part of the explanation when you woke up from a coma and couldn't even remember how to speak? Should we have said something on your twelfth birthday, since in some cultures that's when young ladies are considered mature women?"

"Kaz—"

"Or maybe on your eighteenth birthday, we could have said 'here's the insurance policy, by the way, this is what you witnessed when you were five.'"

"Holy fucking cow! So I had a psychotic break, almost had two of them now, all because it was never a good time to tell me what the fuck happened to me?"

"Well, yeah. Sounds kind of shitty when you put it that way. But do know the decision was made out of love, kid."

"You people suck."

"I interpret that opinion as a sign of affection." He turned onto her side street.

"Jesus fuck! Why is she here?" Dee pointed to her mother's car blocking hers in the driveway.

"She's your mother. You just got out of the hospital. Can you at least say 'hi' before you kick her out?"

"Do I have to?"

He pointed to the backstairs. "Walk that way."

Genevieve

Still no Dee. They'd been open for almost two hours, and Dee hadn't shown up. Didn't look like Max was communicating with her, either. Maybe she was out getting a new phone?

She could have sworn she'd seen Chris's SUV parked on the side street when she arrived, but she'd only caught a glimpse before a customer interrupted her at the front door. It was gone now.

How were things going to work out? Was Dee avoiding Genevieve? Did Dee expect her to quit working in the store? Why hadn't Genevieve thought about that possibility before investing in her new wardrobe?

"I just can't believe these numbers!" Max looked over some pages she'd printed out. "Hayleigh just emailed. Clearly, we're doing really well. But you know what?" Her face just glowed when she looked at Genevieve. Pregnancy became her!

"What?"

"We're going to have to make more items. I hope your creative wheels are churning."

"I'm looking forward to it!" In fact, she'd been brave enough to give Olivia the jewelry box that morning, and Livvy actually liked it. Said she would take it to her dorm and asked what else she'd made. How wonderful things were turning out. If, of course, she still had a job. Didn't seem like Dee told Max about things.

"Hayleigh mentioned that we might also think about bringing in work from other artists," Max returned her focus to the papers. "I'll have to discuss that with Dee. She's closer to that community than I am."

"Oh? Where is Dee, by the way?" Genevieve hoped she sounded casual, curious.

"Oh, Genevieve." Maxine put the papers down. "I can't believe I didn't tell you. I was so wrapped up in my own life yesterday. I'm sorry. I should have called you."

"Why? Did something happen?" Granted, Genevieve wouldn't be surprised. Dee was further from off center on Sunday than she'd ever seen her. Maybe she really did have a drug problem. Did she overdose?

"She fell yesterday. Slipped in the rain and hit her head."

"What?" Genevieve was just a horrible person. And yes, maybe Chris was right. A judgmental, horrible person. Dee doesn't show up at work, and she immediately went to drugs?

"She is." Max smiled. "The hospital kept her overnight to be sure. She's supposed to get out at some point today. I'll bet she'll be in the store tomorrow."

"Does Chris know?"

"Who?"

"My husband." Genevieve took a deep breath. Maxine's face froze in a rather fearful expression. "You see, Dee and my soon-to-be-ex-husband are, um, involved."

"Oh, my God! How did you find out?"

"So you knew, too?" Who else knew?

Max nodded. "Dee told me the day he came into the store with your daughter."

Ah. That's why she suddenly had to go see Max. "Right. Well…" Genevieve turned on her heels, not really sure what to say or do with herself.

"Genevieve, this is totally not my business, but...are you OK with, with whatever is going on with the two of them?"

Genevieve strolled to the front of the store. The display she'd created in the window had such a happy, whimsical feel to it, she wanted to be near it. Feel the joy, the fun of it, the pride in knowing she'd built it. She ran her hand over the new knit sleeveless dress she wore, down the oversized black-and-white houndstooth pattern. A dress that might have been called presentable but was also unique and funky. She faced Maxine with a lumpless throat.

"Yes, and no. The affair wasn't anything Dee entered into maliciously. And he'd started divorce proceedings already, so I can't blame *her* for any of it. And if I'm honest with myself," Genevieve inhaled deeply, "I don't really blame him. Our marriage had been over for a very long time, which is both of our faults. But

I want to blame him for something. Does that make sense?"

Maxine nodded. "It's always easier when there's a clear villain."

"Yes. So, I'm struggling with that." She turned around and trailed her hand over an assortment of bangle bracelets with charms made from beach glass. "The thing is, this job means more to me than just a job. I can't let whatever is happening with Chris and Dee and me to get in the way of me finally being the woman I want to be."

"I get it. And it doesn't have to."

Dee

Marco did a great job putting black tread on her steps. So good, Dee was pissed at the man. There was no way she could fall down again and avoid seeing her mother in her obscenely messy home. She trudged up the stairs, somewhat tempted to go into the store. Maybe Max and Genevieve were still there. Their cars weren't on the side street where she could see them, but they may be further down, out of sight. And really, Dee had no idea what kind of car Genevieve drove. Probably a Mercedes, like her freaking mother.

Was Genevieve still working for them?

What the hell had she been thinking, telling her? Though she'd have to know at some point.

At the top of the landing, she looked farther up the side street. Max's car was parked a couple of blocks down. She could go downstairs and see her. But if she didn't go in her apartment, Mom might just show up on the store floor, and that could be worse. There'd be more things for Dee to throw at the woman.

The backdoor was unlocked.

Her mudroom was tidy and orderly. Weird. The washer and dryer were even running.

Oh, no. Mom didn't clean her apartment, did she?

If she did, she did a damn good job. Dee's living room looked as good as it did the first day they'd all helped her unpack.

"Hello, sweetheart!" Mom called from the kitchen. Dee's skeleton jumped out of her skin. "I just made some coffee. Would you like a cup?"

God, it would be so much easier to face this woman if Mom would scream and yell and act irrational...the way Dee did. That's what made sense to her. She nodded. "Coffee would be great." And maybe she should open that expensive bottle of vodka and add a shot. Maybe Genevieve had a point. Maybe that would make this little heart-to-heart so much easier.

Dazed, shocked that her mother had cleaned—nah. Surely she'd gotten her housekeeper to do it—Dee continued her slow trek through her apartment until she saw the whiteboard.

"Really?" She pointed to the new quote Mom had written on her whiteboard: *To lose one parent...may be regarded as a misfortune. To lose both looks like carelessness.*

"Wilde did *not* say that." Dee accepted her coffee cup.

"He did. Lady Bracknell in *The Importance of Being Earnest.*"

Yeah. She was opening that bottle of vodka.

"What are you doing?" Mom's cup was frozen in front of her mouth.

"Making the day tolerable. Want some?" Dee held up the bottle.

"It's not quite noon."

"I see. You can't have vodka at this hour unless it's served with a celery stick in tomato juice."

"Dee, can you please try not to be unkind."

"That's why I'm pouring vodka in my coffee."

"It does sound good." Mom approached the kitchen. Dee topped off her cup. "But will the alcohol be OK with any meds they gave you at the hospital?"

"Yes, because I refused to swallow them." Dee cheered her with her cup. Mom cheered back. They both drank.

Don't be unkind. Don't be unkind. "I, I guess I should say thank you for cleaning my apartment."

"This is really good." Mom nodded over her cup. "But I didn't clean anything. I just got here a few minutes ago."

"Who did?"

"Probably that man you were with at the cemetery. He was just coming down the steps as I pulled up."

"Cooper?"

"Is that his name? Kaz had his contact, but said I'd have to ask you about him because he didn't know why he was with you yesterday."

Mom sat on the sofa, the lumpy sofa that she was generously replacing with a pink suede one because...because that's what she did. It would probably be comfortable as hell, have some kind of stain-retardant stuff on it, and come with a warranty that would last a bajillion years. And when Dee would thank her for it, she would say the only thanks she needed was for her girls to be happy.

Jesus fucking Christ!

"So, um." She joined her mother on the sofa, sitting close to her. "Actually, he's the guy who broke Kaz's nose."

"From the basketball team?"

Dee nodded before taking another sip. If the eggplant parm was ambrosia, coffee with vodka was nectar. Not that she'd indulge in it too often.

"How do you know him?"

"Know who?"

"Cooper? Is that this name? The gentleman who broke Kaz's nose."

Only Mom would call a guy a gentleman after he broke her husband's nose. "Well, he's, like, he's been my booty call for the past year or so."

"Good God!" Mom sipped.

"But I think I'm in love with him."

"Oh, how nice!" Her voice lifted into her happy tone. "And he must have feelings for you to get you to the cemetery and make sure you had a nice home to come to."

"Yeah, well, he's married."

"Good God!" Mom sipped again. "Really?"

"Yeah. But he's getting a divorce. That was in the works before he met me."

"Oh, well, that's nice, too, I guess."

"Genevieve is his wife."

"Good God, Deirdre!" Mom gulped.

"Wilde would be warning you about the dangers of consistency right now, Mom."

"I think even Wilde would be dumbfounded over this."

Dee set her cup on the coffee table. The photograph of her with her parents at the lake was placed in the center of it. She picked it up, tilted it so Mom could see.

"Do you…I think…It's my fault he's dead, isn't it?"

"What?" Mom ripped the picture out of her hand. "Why on earth would you even think that?"

"I didn't run."

"What do you mean?"

"Brett's dad told me to run away. He wanted me to go back to the house. But I didn't. I was barefoot. I—"

"Didn't want to be in the grass barefoot."

"I, yeah. What?"

"I don't know. You used to be afraid of the natural world." Mom looked at the photo. "Here, I was trying to show you the fish in the lake, show you how pretty their iridescent colors were in the sunshine. You were terrified."

"You were trying to get me to look at them?" She'd assumed

Mom was holding her back, but she was actually doing the opposite.

"Your father would be so proud of how fearless you are now."

She leaned into Mom, let Mom put her arm around her shoulder, and snuggled in. What'd Coop say about survivor's guilt? "Why?"

"You're fearless. You pursue what you're passionate about. Your art makes the world a more beautiful place."

So that was what she would do to honor him.

"Tell me about him."

Mom's perfectly manicured finger ran over the picture. "When you look in the mirror, you see him. When you create, you embody him."

"He was an artist?"

"A musician. Played with the philharmonic in Philly, but he dabbled with other people, creating new versions of old tunes. Isn't that interesting? He loved to take old songs and remake them into something new and unique."

"Yeah. That's interesting. But tell me about *him*. What was he like?"

"He had a wicked wit, like you, quick with punch lines. Fearless. Lived uninhibited. Loved with passion." Mom wiped a tear away. "All so very much like you."

She'd known him all along.

Wow!

You read the whole friggin' thing? This baby is long, so please know your time and interest are immensely appreciated! So appreciated, that I don't want to write the next line, but having no pride is an occupational hazard of being a writer. If you enjoyed this book, please consider rating it or leaving a review on Amazon or wherever you purchased it. That helps other readers know find books they'd like to read.

Again, thank you for reading this! I hope the women in this book inspire you to reconnect and strengthen the bonds with the people in your life. We all could use a little unconditional acceptance.

Cheers to us all!

Acknowledgements

This book is a testament to the power of female friendships, which is why I dedicated it to my hens: my favorite women, my ride-and-die friends. We joke that we'd always be there for each other to help bury a body, if need be, but the sentiment is no laughing matter. I know I am blessed to have people I can trust to accept me as I am, warts and all. And, yes, the feeling is mutual. In alphabetical order by last name, they are: Michelle, Jen, Miriam, Lori, Jen, Sophia, Lois, Olga, Joyce, Kim, Sandy, Dana, and Stephanie.

Thank you Joel Bresler for always believing in me and encouraging me. I appreciate that almost as much as I appreciate your humor.

Thank you to Kristin Osborne. You gave me the name for what Dee is dealing with: affect phobia.

And to my amazing kids: The original Hayley for being so uniquely you and inspiring the Hayleigh on the page. And thank you for the fabulous book cover design. Your skills and talents are amazing! Please, learn to believe that! And to Taylor. You didn't blatantly show up on the page, but you are always an inspiration to me. Probably the smartest person I know and one of the most creative. I love how you set the example of valuing your creativity.

And thank you to the hubs, Glenn, you tolerate this brain a lot. Do know it's appreciated. I'd probably never get a word written if it weren't for you.

About the Author

Lisa Shiroff is also known as the Queen of the Rewrite, the role she fills when midwifing other people's books into existence as a ghostwriter, developmental editor, or author coach. Outside of that, she writes the kinds of stories she likes to read: Stories about quirky, messy, lovable disasters who somehow find their way to happy endings. Stories filled with the kind of women you'd want as neighbors, or at the very least as drinking buddies.

Other books by Lisa include:

Revenge Café, a tropical mystery with a little humor and heat.
Show up Dead, a sweet mystery from the City of Brotherly Love
Hitting the Sauce, a funny suspense with a little romance set in Atlantic city.

Keep up with Lisa by signing up for her newsletter at: www.lisashiroff.com

www.ingramcontent.com/pod-product-compliance
Lightning Source LLC
Chambersburg PA
CBHW030058310726
48970CB00004B/1055